"I dare you to read a 'Kurland' story and not enjoy it!"—*Heartland Critiques*

**Praise for the novels of *USA Today*
bestselling author Lynn Kurland**

Dreams of Stardust

"Kurland weaves another fabulous read with just the right amounts of laughter, romance, and fantasy."

—*Affaire de Coeur*

"Kurland crafts some of the most ingenious time-travel romances readers can find. Cleverly merging past and present, she spins a dreamlike web that so completely captivates readers . . . Wonderfully clever and completely enchanting."

—*Romantic Times Book Club*

"*Dreams of Stardust*, by Lynn Kurland, who is truly a masterful storyteller, will enchant you with its spellbinding plot, fascinating characters, and sizzling sensuality. If you thought you were not a fan of time travel, this mesmerizing novel will not only change your mind, but also delight you in the process!" —RomanceJunkies.com

"One of our most beloved time-travel authors and deservedly so. Each new book is cause for celebration!"

—FreshFictionReviews.com

"A terrific time-travel romance."

—*ParaNormal Romance Reviews*

A Garden in the Rain

"Kurland laces her exquisitely romantic, utterly bewitching blend of contemporary romance and time travel with a delectable touch of tart wit, leaving readers savoring every word of this superbly written romance." —*Booklist*

"Kurland is clearly one of romance's finest writers—she consistently delivers the kind of stories readers dream about. Don't miss this one." —*The Oakland Press*

(continued on next page . . .)

MUCH ADO IN THE MOONLIGHT

LYNN KURLAND

JOVE BOOKS, NEW YORK

THE BERKLEY PUBLISHING GROUP
Published by the Penguin Group
Penguin Group (USA) Inc.
375 Hudson Street, New York, New York 10014, USA
Penguin Group (Canada), 90 Eglinton Avenue East, Suite 700, Toronto, Ontario M4P 2Y3, Canada
(a division of Pearson Penguin Canada Inc.)
Penguin Books Ltd., 80 Strand, London WC2R 0RL, England
Penguin Group Ireland, 25 St. Stephen's Green, Dublin 2, Ireland (a division of Penguin Books Ltd.)
Penguin Group (Australia), 250 Camberwell Road, Camberwell, Victoria 3124, Australia
(a division of Pearson Australia Group Pty. Ltd.)
Penguin Books India Pvt. Ltd., 11 Community Centre, Panchsheel Park, New Delhi—110 017, India
Penguin Group (NZ), Cnr. Airborne and Rosedale Roads, Albany, Auckland 1310, New Zealand
(a division of Pearson New Zealand Ltd.)
Penguin Books (South Africa) (Pty.) Ltd., 24 Sturdee Avenue, Rosebank, Johannesburg 2196, South
Africa

Penguin Books Ltd., Registered Offices: 80 Strand, London WC2R 0RL, England

MUCH ADO IN THE MOONLIGHT

A Jove Book / published by arrangement with the author.

PRINTING HISTORY
Jove mass-market edition / May 2006

Copyright © 2006 by Lynn Curland.
Cover design by George Long.
Cover illustration by Grisbach/Martucci.
Handlettering by Ron Zinn.

ISBN: 0-515-14127-5

JOVE®
Jove Books are published by The Berkley Publishing Group,
a division of Penguin Group (USA) Inc.,
375 Hudson Street, New York, New York 10014.
JOVE is a registered trademark of Penguin Group (USA) Inc.
The "J" design is a trademark belonging to Penguin Group (USA) Inc.

PRINTED IN THE UNITED STATES OF AMERICA

10 9 8 7 6 5 4 3 2 1

To the ladies
on my board . . .

Acknowledgments

In addition to my fabulous family who makes life heaven on earth, I would like to thank the following:

Gail Fortune, for giving me my start in this business and for her unwavering faith in my stories;

Anne Sowards, for her wonderful ideas, her eagle eye, and for being willing to take on this complicated cast of characters;

Leslie Gelbman, for continuing to provide me a place to publish my stories;

Judy G., intrepid camper extraordinaire, for helping me figure out East from West;

And last on this page but foremost in my thoughts on this book, my readers, with an especial thank you to all those who have made my website and my email inbox wonderful places to be. I always think about all of you wonderful souls who shell out your hard-earned money for my books (multiple copies, in numerous cases, to replace those you've loaned out!). Without you, my books would have no home. A thousand thank-yous!

Cast of Characters

CONNOR MACDOUGAL, *laird of Thorpewold Castle*

VICTORIA MCKINNON
    Thomas McKinnon, *her brother*
    Iolanthe McKinnon, *Thomas's wife*
    Jennifer McKinnon, *Victoria's sister*
    John McKinnon, *Victoria's father*
    Helen McKinnon, *Victoria's mother*
    Mary MacLeod, *Victoria's grandmother*

THE BOAR'S HEAD TRIO
    Ambrose MacLeod
    Hugh McKinnon
    Fulbert de Piaget

MRS. PRUITT, *the innkeeper at the Boar's Head Inn*

THE ACTORS
    Michael Fellini
    Cressida Blankenship
    Fred, *the stage manager*

JAMES MACLEOD

Prologue

THORPEWOLD, ENGLAND
SPRING 2005

Twilight fell softly on Thorpewold Castle. Its rugged splendor was home to a scene that could have been played out in any number of medieval keeps across the isle.

The laird issued his commands firmly, but justly, and with great concern for his kinsmen. Kinsmen were attentive to their laird's commands. Peasants went diligently about their work, content with their lot in life and anxious to serve their considerate lord. The air was full of noise from the blacksmith's hammer and the conversings of livestock. Men commented mildly on the spring chill and the rain that seemed to fall most inconveniently when they were headed out to train.

All in all, 'twas a day much like any other, one that could be lived out on either side of Hadrian's Wall by men possessing goodly minds and strong arms.

Only this wasn't medieval Scotland.

And the souls inside the keep weren't precisely mortal.

Ambrose MacLeod knew that and more as he stood just inside the barbican gate and watched the goings on. He propped his foot up on an upturned rock and made himself more comfortable against the wall. Aye, he was familiar enough with what it took to be laird, having been one once himself, and of a powerful and unruly lot. He studied the newly made laird of Thorpewold keep with a practiced eye to judge just how effective the man might be at managing a keep this size and a motley collection of lads to go with it. And based on what he was seeing, Ambrose suspected that *effective* just might be too tame a word for the kind of dominion Connor MacDougal was going to exercise.

The MacDougal stood in the midst of the bailey, organizing his forces with an imperiousness any monarch, past or present, would have admired.

"You, there," he said, pointing at a hapless Scot with knobby knees, "join up with the first watch. We'll man the walls at all hours."

"But," the man said, bobbing his head respectfully, "we've no walls to man, my laird."

Connor thrust a finger back toward the only wall that hadn't crumbled under the ravages of time. "There's a wall over there. Go man it!"

The man scurried off, his plaid flapping about his skinny legs.

"And you, there," the MacDougal said, singling out another man, "see to the gates. And you, the livestock. Ho, Robert, come see to the stables. Don't want my horseflesh being mistreated."

Ambrose eyed the lone horse in the bailey, a very old, quite useless bit of flesh that wouldn't have made a decent mount for a horseless Highlander on his most desperate day, and wondered why Connor bothered.

Then again, the man had waited almost seven centuries to call the keep his own, so perhaps he had a right to be protective of what was now his.

"My laird," said a man, venturing close with his knitted

cap clutched in both hands, "what of the tower? The tower young Thomas McKinnon finished—"

Connor interrupted him with a curse. "We'll pretend it isn't here."

"But, will he not be coming back to use it?"

"Not if he knows what's good for him," Connor snarled. "Now, get you gone and don't trouble me further with foolish questions. See to the chickens."

"But, my laird," the man said, on the verge of massaging his cap into felt, "we don't have chickens. We have chicken."

Connor frowned. "Chicken?"

"One chicken, my laird."

"Then go and tend it, you imbecile!"

"But, my laird, 'tis nearly dark. The chicken is roosting."

"Wake it up, *then* tend it!" Connor exclaimed.

The man nodded gamely, bowed low, then hastened off to see to his business.

A chicken soon squawked in the distance.

Ambrose laughed. The saints preserve all these poor fools with Connor MacDougal setting their course for them. Well, at least they had a decent keep in which to endure their tortures.

Ambrose looked over the keep with satisfaction. Aye, 'twas a decent place, at that. The far tower had been rendered useful by Thomas McKinnon during the previous summer. Thomas's stay at Thorpewold keep was an interesting tale, true, but not one that Ambrose could take time to reminisce over at present, past noting that Thomas had lived in the castle for a bit, then returned to America with his bride. He had left his castle uninhabited, but he certainly hadn't intended that it remain so.

Indeed, there was a mortal who stood to come and take up residence of a sort in less than a fortnight. Ambrose smiled to himself. What would Connor MacDougal say when he found out he was having a houseguest?

Ambrose didn't dare speculate.

Nor did he dare linger much longer. The MacDougal

had already thrown him a pointed glare. Not that Ambrose had any fear of it. He and Connor had engaged in skirmishes in the past and he had always acquitted himself well. Unfortunately, today was not the day for such delights. Who knew but that in the heat of battle, when he might be inspired to spew forth curses, taunts, and other insults appropriate to the moment, that something regarding the details of Connor's upcoming visitor might inadvertently slip out and ruin the surprise?

Nay, far better to leave the MacDougal to his settling, and be about his own business elsewhere.

So Ambrose had himself a last chuckle at the men scrambling to see to Connor's commands, then turned and walked down the path from the castle to the road. The sun was setting and he took the time to enjoy the colors of the evening. He ambled along until he reached a snug Tudor inn sitting nestled against a small hill, pleasantly far away from the bustle of the local village.

Ambrose admired the sturdy dwelling with heavy beamed frame and well-wrought leaded windows. He nodded in satisfaction at the cozy location and the ample room for visitors. He also paused to admire the lovely garden, full of the first flowers of spring and rife with the promise of a robust bit of blooming later on in the summer.

Unfortunately, admiring was all he could do, given that his nose had ceased to function several years earlier.

Several hundred years earlier, actually.

But losing the ability to smell with a mortal nose was more than a fair trade for all he had gained in his very busy afterlife. Who would have suspected that being a ghost would have been so rewarding?

Aye, and demanding as well, but there was nothing to be done about that. Who else could possibly see to what was needful but he himself? He strode through the garden, his plaid swinging about his knees and his great sword slapping against his thigh as it had for over four hundred years. Some things never changed, he supposed. A Highland lad was braw and clever, no matter the century and no matter his condition.

He had almost reached the entrance to the inn when the front door burst open and an older woman of goodly character and steely determination leaped out, feather duster in one hand and a look of purpose in her eye.

"There'll be no noxious flies in *my* entryway," she said with a final thrust of her duster. "Be off with ye, ye wee fiends!"

Then she paused, feather duster still at the ready, and looked about purposefully.

As if she looked for something other than flies.

Ambrose did the only thing he could: He flattened himself behind the door and waited until Mrs. Pruitt, the innkeeper hired to see to things in the owner's absence, made a quick search of her garden, then reluctantly retreated back inside her domain.

He heaved a sigh of relief and quickly contemplated his next action. He could, of course, use the front door. He did that often. Indeed, the inn was, for all intents and purposes, under his direction; he was certainly free to enter and leave it when and where he chose. But tonight he would take a different path—

And hope to heaven that Mrs. Pruitt would be so weary from her daily tasks that she would leave the kitchen empty for the night.

He tapped his foot for what he hoped was long enough for any and all innkeepers inside to have put themselves to bed, then tiptoed around to the back of the house and peered into the kitchen window. All was dark inside. He sighed in relief, then walked through the door, lit candles with a flick of his wrist, and stoked up the shiny black stove with another negligent movement of his hand.

He drew up a chair to the stove with a sigh, reached out and plucked forth a cup of ale from thin air, then sat back and prepared for an evening spent contemplating the happy events that would no doubt transpire when his granddaughter, several generations removed, arrived from America later in the month. She was feisty, to be sure, and headstrong, but since he found those traits to be quite acceptable in himself, he couldn't see why he should begrudge her the same in her own person.

The back door opened and shut with a bang. A man stood on the rug, stomping his feet and blowing on his hands. "Cold out, still," he groused. "One would think that by the end of March we might have a had bit of relief from the chill."

Ambrose pursed his lips. "You've lived in England for four hundred years, Fulbert, and I daresay you've complained about the weather for at least that long. Why do you continue to expect it to be warmer than it wants to be?"

Fulbert de Piaget threw himself into a chair and conjured up his own cup of hot ale. "Hope springs eternal," he grumbled. "Or some other such rot."

"Hope may spring eternal," Ambrose conceded, "but spring comes when it wants. Be grateful you grew to manhood in this soft, southern country. In the Highlands, March is still hard with ice and chill."

"Which is no doubt why you Scots are of such foul and ill-seated humors," Fulbert said.

Ambrose had scarce opened his mouth to instruct Fulbert on the finer points of Scottish character before the back door opened and his own kinsman, Hugh McKinnon, peered in hesitantly.

"Is she about?"

Fulbert pursed his lips. "Who?"

"Mrs. Pruitt," Hugh said, his teeth chattering. "Who else?"

"Haven't seen her," Fulbert said shortly. "She's likely off tidying up her aspect to better impress her sweetheart here."

"The saints be praised," Hugh said as he entered the kitchen, shut the door behind him, and took up his place by the fire. "I wish you'd just get on with it, Ambrose," he said. "Have yer meetin' with the poor woman and be done."

"Aye," Fulbert said, turning a jaundiced eye on Ambrose. "You promised the good Mrs. Pruitt a parley and you've yet to keep that promise."

"I will speak with her when I have the time," Ambrose said, through gritted teeth.

Fulbert grunted. "Be about finding that time as soon as may be. The woman's beginnin' to ruin my sleep with all her gear beepin' and squealin' at all hours."

"She'll tire of hunting us," Ambrose said confidently.

"Perhaps," Fulbert conceded, "but she'll never tire of hunting *you.*"

"I have to agree," Hugh said with an uneasy nod. "She certainly has the gear for a goodly bit of paranormal investigating. It seems that every fortnight that big brown UPS lorry brings her something new to use."

"Well, we've no need to worry about that tonight," Ambrose said. "I'm quite sure Mrs. Pruitt has gone to bed—"

The door behind them, the door that separated the kitchen from the dining chamber, squeaked.

"Eeek!" Hugh said, then vanished.

Fulbert tossed back his ale and vanished, as well, without further comment.

Ambrose extinguished all but a single candle, but didn't have time to vanish before the door made another squeak. He looked over his shoulder, hoping against hope that his ears, and those of his companions, had been mistaken. But, nay, that was no errant noise.

The door was eased open another finger's breadth and a foul instrument of investigation was pushed through the crack. Ambrose recognized it for what it was: a ghostly Geiger counter. The beast made little clicks, lights ran up and down its sides, and its two little metal arms jumped, as if in anticipation of discoveries to come.

Ambrose cursed silently. Was there no peace to be found any longer in this world?

The counter began a bit of sniffing just inside the chamber, held by a hand that was surely more suited to seeing to guests and preparing fine repasts than tormenting poor, hapless shades. Unfortunately that hand, and the woman it was attached to, had to concern itself with things that surely didn't concern it.

Namely him.

The door was flung open suddenly and into the kitchen leaped Mrs. Pruitt, dressed in head-to-toe black.

Ambrose jumped in spite of himself. He hastened over to stand by the back door where perhaps Mrs. Pruitt wouldn't sense his presence.

"I know ye're in 'ere," Mrs. Pruitt said, waving her implement of torment about. She used her flashlight as well, to good effect. "Show yerselves, damn ye!"

Ambrose hopped up onto a handy work table. Mrs. Pruitt and her torch investigated every corner of the kitchen, finally coming to a purposeful rest before the door. Her counter was clicking and the lights were blinking in a fashion that was quite alarming. Ambrose stared at it in horror as it came even closer. The little arms waved frantically.

Apparently too frantically, for the entire contraption soon gave one last, great noise, then fell suddenly, and blessedly, silent.

Mrs. Pruitt slammed the thing down on the table a time or two, peered at it, then pursed her lips.

"Must 'ave been a bit o' sour wind from under the door," she grumbled.

Ambrose breathed a sigh of relief.

"Coward," came a voice from beside him.

Ambrose squawked in spite of himself, then turned to glare at Fulbert, who had appeared next to him on the table. "Can you blame me?" he whispered in irritation.

"You gave the woman your word. I heard you fix the bargain with her yourself."

"Damn me, but I never said when!"

Mrs. Pruitt tossed her contraption into the rubbish bin, turned, and stalked from the kitchen with a curse. Ambrose watched her go with a great sigh of relief.

"I'll tell her you intend to woo her," Fulbert said with an

unwholesome look in his eye, "and then we'll see how things progress . . ."

Ambrose wondered if wringing Fulbert's neck would give him any peace. Then again, the man was his sister's husband—and if that wasn't enough to convince a man that there were just some things in the world, and out of it, that were simply beyond a man's comprehension, he didn't know what would be. He likely couldn't just up and do damage to the man without there being hell to pay at some point in the future.

"I'll show myself to her in my own good time," Ambrose said firmly. "Until then, we should concern ourselves with our next task." He leaped athletically down from the work table and took up his place again by the fire.

"Matchmaking," Fulbert said with a snort, coming over to draw up his own chair. "I'm beginnin' to think it isn't a dignified occupation for a man of my stature."

"Then find something else to do," Ambrose said pointedly.

"I would, but you'd never manage any of these marriages without my aid and then where would I be?"

"Well—"

"Unraveling your disasters, that's where I'd be," Fulbert continued in a superior tone, retrieving his mug from its invisible storage place. "Now, who is it this time? The name escapes me . . ."

"You know very well who is coming."

Fulbert took a deep pull of his ale. "I've been trying to forget." He looked at Ambrose over the rim of his cup. "Go ahead. Spew out the name."

"Victoria McKinnon, and do not dare disparage her."

"Disparage her?" Fulbert echoed weakly. "I wouldn't dare! But, by the saints, must we be involved with *that* particular McKinnon wench? I remember Mistress Victoria from young Gideon's wedding to that granddaughter of yours, that Megan MacLeod McKinnon." He shivered. "As if Megan wasn't bad enough, wedding me nevvy and ruinin' him for decent labor, now we've another of your descendants to be tormented by—"

"Don't you talk about me wee granddaughter thusly!" a voice bellowed suddenly. Hugh McKinnon appeared, his face red, his sword grasped in his hand, the business end pointed toward Fulbert's chest.

"I won't say more about Megan," Fulbert grumbled, "but that Victoria—"

"Do not malign her, either!" Hugh thundered. "She's a spirited gel—"

"Hugh, she's a bleedin' garrison captain!" Fulbert exclaimed.

Hugh squirmed uncomfortably for a moment or two, then scrunched his face up in his most determined expression. "She's . . . er . . . *focused.*"

Fulbert leaped to his feet, sending his chair toppling backward. He drew his sword with a flourish. "And *I* say she's impossible! Spending her life trying to keep those flighty actors and dancers in proper form . . ." He snorted. "Foolishness. Damn me if I couldn't wish for just one wench who's for a bit of bloodshed—"

"I'll give ye all the bloodshed ye want, ye pompous Brit!" Hugh vowed, giving Fulbert a healthy shove.

Fulbert took a firmer grip on his sword. "Whey-faced skirt-wearer."

"Whey-faced," Hugh echoed. "*Whey-faced!*"

They raised their swords as if they intended to do damage with them. Ambrose cursed. He was all for a bit of proper exercise when circumstances warranted, but now was not the time and the kitchen was not the place.

"Take it outside," he bellowed.

Hugh hesitated in midswing; Fulbert paused before he cleaved Hugh's skull in twain. They looked at each other, shrugged, then tromped out the door with word or two of pleasant conversation between them.

Soon there came the sound of a mighty battle from the back garden. Ambrose wanted to believe that would be the end of it, but he knew better. He began to count silently. He expected that he wouldn't reach a score before the kitchen door would burst open—it did at ten-and-six—and a be-curlered, hastily garbed Mrs. Pruitt would come racing through the kitchen with her video camera at the ready—which she did, clutching her pink robe to her breast and nearly putting out an eye as she dashed across the wooden floor. She rushed out the back door.

Ambrose sighed as the sounds outside changed in tone. Bloodshed? Aye, there might be a bit, and not just Mrs. Pruitt tripping over garden implements.

Curses and screeches mingled outside. Ambrose tipped back in his chair, waiting for what was to come. The curses ceased abruptly and the screeching became the low murmuring of a woman who was reviewing her videotape and finding it completely lacking the kind of paranormal activity she had intended it to capture. Ambrose was unsurprised several minutes later when Mrs. Pruitt marched through the kitchen and cursed her equipment thoroughly as she continued on her way into the dining chamber.

Hugh and Fulbert came in not far behind her, with swords sheathed, and heads shaking.

"Parley with her," Fulbert said to Ambrose.

Hugh nodded nervously in agreement.

Ambrose sighed. "I will. Soon. After this next bit of business is finished. I should have been preparing for that long before now, but the winter was quite pleasant in the Highlands—"

"It always is," Hugh agreed wistfully.

"And I lingered when I should have labored. Now, I've much to do and little time in which to do it." Ambrose took a long pull from his mug. "Fortunately, we know all we need to about the lad up the way."

"Do we?" Fulbert mused. "I'm the first to choose interesting rumor over tedious fact, but I must ask meself how much of what we know about him is true."

Hugh gaped at him. "What's there to know?" he managed. "Connor MacDougal is unpleasant, impolite, and dangerous." He looked at Ambrose. "*I* wonder why it is we're sending such a sweet, delicate gel as my Victoria into that lion's den."

"Sweet?" Fulbert choked. "Delicate? Have ye gone mad—"

"Be that as it may," Ambrose interrupted firmly, " 'tis the match we're determined to make. I daresay in the end, there will be several things we've misjudged about the pair. Well," he added, "I daresay *I* will not be surprised, but others will no doubt be so. In the end, all will be well. Now, for the present, we'll rely on rumor to guide us with regard to the laird up the way and I'll be about a bit of digging into what our dear Victoria is combining. We'll rendezvous here in a fortnight and make our plans."

"That is ample time," Fulbert agreed.

Ambrose frowned at him. "Ample time for you to remain hereabouts with Hugh and make no trouble."

Fulbert opened his mouth to argue, which forced Ambrose to produce one of his fiercer scowls. Fulbert contented himself with muttering into his cup. Hugh looked ready to protest as well, but Ambrose cowed him with a similar look. Hugh folded his arms over his chest and stared into the fire with a scowl of his own.

Satisfied that his companions would remain where they had been instructed to, Ambrose bid them a firm goodnight, dispensed with his chair and cup, then turned and walked out of the kitchen. He made his way through the dining chamber, through the entryway, and up to his own bedchamber, the one that always remained empty even when the rest of the inn was full and more guests wanted to stay. No one ever seemed to want to spend the night there in that bit of sixteenth-century splendor, though he couldn't understand why not.

Well, whatever the reason, it gave him a place to rest and he suspected he would do well to be well-rested for what was to come. There was still much to do, many details to ferret out, and many plans to be laid which would need to go undetected by the man and woman in question.

There were games afoot, and he could scarce wait to be about the playing of them.

Chapter 1

Something foul was afoot and Victoria MacLeod Mc-Kinnon didn't like the smell of it.

It wasn't dinner; she was fairly certain of that. She sat at the beautifully distressed farm table in her brother's equally beautiful house in Maine and enjoyed a supper of wonderful, if not overly healthy, delights designed to tempt the most discriminating palate. Victoria looked up from her dinner steaming on the table and admired Thomas's dining room, overlooking as it did the Atlantic ocean in all its tumultuous glory. The smell of salt air seeping in through the kitchen skylight mingling with dinner should have left her refreshed and contented at the same time. The peaceful, tastefully decorated interiors should have soothed her. The thought of an entire weekend with nothing more to do than relax in such choice surroundings should have left her with her only regret being that she could not stay longer.

She sniffed.

There it was again. Something that said there was something quite rotten in Denmark.

As it were.

Victoria looked at the Brussels sprout on the end of her fork and suppressed the urge to shove it down her brother's throat.

"I fail to see what is so funny," she said, waving that particularly plump sprout threateningly at him.

Thomas, the cook, decorator, and benefactor extraordinaire, only shook his head, seemingly unable to stop smiling. "I just can't help myself."

Victoria pursed her lips. "You *offered* me your castle, if you remember," she said pointedly. "You *gave* me money to pay for putting on my next play there. You *are* covering every expense associated with this production and not even demanding any part of the receipts in return. Why is it when we discuss any of it, you seem to suddenly be overcome by uncontrollable fits of giggles?"

"Your brother has spent too much time at high altitude," her father said from where he sat next to her. "He's damaged the appropriate humor sensor centers of his brain."

"Oh, John, it isn't that," Victoria's mother said with a laugh. "Thomas is just happy. He's going to have a baby."

"No, Mom," Thomas said, reaching for his wife's hand, "Iolanthe's going to have a baby. I'm just the giddy father-to-be."

Victoria submerged her sprout into as much cheese sauce as was available on her plate and ate it before she thought better of it. *Giddy* hardly described her brother and his bride, but *demented* described her own mental state at the time of the phone call she'd received inviting her up into her brother's love nest. What had she been thinking, to say yes?

It was familial guilt, pure and simple. Her mother had invited; Victoria had capitulated. She'd been lured up to Maine on the pretext of having a little rest and relaxation before diving headfirst into her next production. *A restful weekend away from the rat race* was what her mother had termed it. Victoria had been suspicious, but she hadn't seen her parents in a month and her brother in longer than that, so she'd given in and reluctantly accepted the invitation.

Unfortunately, a weekend spent in Thomas's dream house, being forced to watch him be deliriously happy with his equally joyful and barely pregnant wife was, in her opinion, neither restful nor relaxing. She needed to be back in the city, where she could be the captain of her own ship, the mistress of her own fate, the cook at her own fire.

She hated Brussels sprouts, if anyone was interested.

They were Thomas's doing; she knew that. He was on a health kick. Gone were the days when her brother divided his time among the various pursuits of making buckets of money, scaling dangerous mountains, and eating things full of saturated fat. In the place of that wild man was *Homo sapiens domesticus*, complete with apron and list of foods appropriate to fix a wife who was in the throes of violent morning sickness. How Brussels sprouts were supposed to help that, Victoria didn't know. It was no doubt the least of the indignities Iolanthe MacLeod suffered in being married to Thomas McKinnon.

Though Iolanthe didn't look unhappy. Victoria studied her sister-in-law from across the table and saw only a glowing but rather green beauty who seemed quite content to find herself shackled to a man who had once picked his nose onstage. Never mind that he'd been nine years old at the time. Victoria had written him off as an actor and never looked back.

Obviously, Iolanthe didn't have the benefit of history to alert her to Thomas's failings.

No, it was clear that the poor woman was suffering under the delusion that being married to Thomas McKinnon was a good thing. In fact, it was worse than that. Thomas and Iolanthe periodically shared glances that spoke of a truly deep and abiding love—as if they had overcome some great trial to be together.

Victoria snorted. The only trial they'd suffered was that Iolanthe had been unlucky enough to run into Thomas at his castle, where she had apparently taken complete and permanent leave of her senses and married him.

Leaving Victoria with the unhappy pleasure of watching them coo at each other like a pair of bilious pigeons.

Victoria turned away from the nauseating lovebirds and looked at her parents. Things were no less loving there, but considerably less mushy. Her mother looked serene. She was looking serenely at Iolanthe, who was holding her nose and waving away Thomas and the vegetables he was trying to foist off on her. Victoria hazarded a glance at her father. He was looking suspiciously at what was left of Thomas's vegetables.

Victoria loved her father.

Not that she didn't love her mother. She did. Helen MacLeod McKinnon was a lovely woman, supportive, enthusiastic, able to sit through very long dress rehearsals without shifting uncomfortably. But despite those virtues, Helen also possessed an abundance of what she termed "MacLeod magic." Victoria called it like it was: woo-woo business. As far as she was concerned, those MacLeods could keep their second sight and knack for always being in the middle of odd happenings; Victoria would take her father's solid, staid dependability over the unexpected any day.

"So tell me again what your plan is," her father asked. "Point by point."

Victoria gladly abandoned the rest of her sprouts to her father's searching fork. "Lights and sound left two weeks ago. The costumes are being packed tomorrow. I'll be back in Manhattan on Monday to make sure they get shipped off properly with the rest of the remaining gear. The actors are all quitting their restaurant jobs to get on the plane a week from Monday."

"Restaurant jobs?" Thomas echoed. He choked, but apparently saved himself by means of a long drink of water.

Victoria briefly mourned a missed opportunity for just desserts, then decided it was for the best. Thomas was, after all, funding her. No sense in wishing too hard for his demise right away.

"Passports in order?" her father asked. "Actors with up-to-date shots?"

Helen laughed. "They're humans, dear, not pets."

"So you keep telling me," John said, "but I remain unconvinced." He shot Victoria a look. "Now, you understand that England is a strange place." He paused and nodded in a knowing manner. "You know. *Strange.*"

"Dad, it's not Mars," Victoria said. "I'll survive."

"It'll be good for her, Dad," Thomas added cheerfully. "A little fresh air, the idyllic English countryside, a castle just waiting to be used as the backdrop for her latest show. By the way, Vic, what is it you're doing?"

"*Hamlet*, you idiot," Victoria said shortly. "I've told you as much a dozen times."

There went that grin again. Victoria would have flung something at him, but her plate was empty and her father had finished any vegetables that might have made good missiles. She settled for a glare, but that did nothing to remove Thomas's smirk.

It was that smirk that bothered her. It was a snarky look, full of mischief, full of things he knew that she didn't. It was a look that, in the past, had always meant trouble where she was concerned.

"*Hamlet,*" he chortled. "How lovely. And you open, when?"

She rolled her eyes. "Four weeks from tonight. You know that, too. You have tickets for that opening show, and seats on a plane a few days before to get you there. Remember?"

"A month's time?" her father asked doubtfully. "That's a mighty tight schedule, missy."

"I'll manage."

"I'm not worried about you; I'm worried about those flighty actors you have. Especially that Felonious guy."

"Fellini," Victoria corrected. "Michael Fellini. Don't worry about him; he's a professional."

"He's arrogant," her father said.

"He's gorgeous," her mother countered.

He's perfect, Victoria added silently, but her opinion was another matter entirely, and one she had no intention of discussing with anyone at the table.

"The cast will be fine," she said out loud. "I've been rehearsing them into the ground for two months. Besides, they're on their best behavior. It's the opportunity of a lifetime for most of them. When else will they get to do Shakespeare in a real castle?"

"Mmmm," John said skeptically. "Hope you have good understudies. Did Thomas give you enough money for understudies?"

"Thomas gave me more than enough," Victoria assured him.

And that was true. Her brother had been outrageously generous, footing the bill for accommodations, food, transportation, and salaries for the whole of a month-long run of *Hamlet* on yonder blessed isle. She still wasn't sure why, but she'd determined immediately upon hearing the offer that she wasn't going to look a gift horse in the mouth.

Well, she might cast sidelong, suspicious glances at it, but she wasn't going to do a full-on inspection.

Not in his presence, while he was awake, that is.

Of course, his money hadn't covered Michael Fellini's complete fee, but she'd managed to make that up out of her own savings. Again, another story for another time and one she would never discuss with her parents or her brother.

But she could ruminate about it plenty in private, which she was going to do as soon as she could escape the table.

There was no time like the present. She smiled at her folks.

"I'm a little tired from all this relaxation. I think I'll head upstairs. Iolanthe, thank you for dinner."

"And me?" Thomas asked politely. "No 'thank you' for me?"

"I thanked you by not jabbing a fork between your eyes."

Thomas only laughed.

Victoria took her plate to the sink, then fled upstairs before she said anything she would regret to her still-chuckling brother.

She shut herself in her room and tried to walk out her frustrations. She needed to be off and doing, not sitting and waiting for her vacation to be over so she could be off and doing.

She paced from one end of the room to the other, going over her mental lists, checking off the items she had already accomplished and considering the things still outstanding. It was no small feat to move an entire production to another country. In fact, if she ever second-guessed herself, she might have suspected she was out of her mind. But since she never engaged in that kind of self-doubt, she was unfazed. She knew she could pull this off and do it well.

Her opinion of her skills had not come without price. Whatever good things she could say about herself, she had earned. She was a director of substantial theater, rubbing shoulders with the very gifted, preparing and presenting to the world a quality of art that was equal to anything seen on Broadway.

Never mind that her company performed a very, *very* long way from Broadway. Never mind that her stage was in a loft above a New Age teashop. Never mind that her prop room was in the cellar next to where vats of things cunningly labeled "herbs" were kept, which left her costumes always smelling faintly like health food store. People could come to the theater, then relax with some chamomile during intermission. It was a great set-up and she was grateful for it.

And now England, with an honest-to-goodness castle to use as her backdrop. Did it get any better than that?

Well, it might, if Michael Fellini would be as interested in her as a woman as he was in her as a director.

But given that there was nothing she could do about that until she had him alone in backwoods England, she turned her thoughts to what she could control. She looked around for something useful to do. Unfortunately, her bags were packed, her bed was made, and the eight-hundred-page treatise on Elizabethan politics she'd brought with her was over and done with. She should have bought that pithy little tome on farthingale construction with her. One could never know too much about the time period.

She sighed. What she needed was a good romance. A good love story was nothing more than research where she was concerned. She had to direct romantic plays from time to time; she might as well know something about how they were supposed to go.

It was a certainty she had nothing of the sort from her own life to draw on.

She sincerely hoped that would change very soon.

"I have," she said to the empty room, "spent too long in this house."

She plopped herself down on the window seat and pushed open the window. It was still bitterly cold, but maybe the chill would distract her from her restlessness. She closed her eyes and listened to the sound of the waves rolling in against the shore. It was no wonder Thomas loved his house so much. Even she might be tempted to trade in the traffic noise of Manhattan for this kind of peace.

Then she frowned. There was something more weaving through the wind than just the sound of the ocean. It sounded like music.

Bagpipe music.

Victoria pressed her ear against the screen and strained to listen more closely. Yes, there was no doubt about it. That was definitely bagpipe music. Had Thomas been importing some of Iolanthe's cousins in from Scotland to serenade him? Did Iolanthe have cousins? There was a cloud of mystery surrounding Thomas's wife that she certainly hadn't been able to penetrate. Thomas had promised to tell her all the year before, but he'd seemingly thought better of it . . .

A soft knock sounded, making Victoria jump in spite of

herself. Too much imagined bagpiping had obviously started to get to her.

"Come in," she said, sitting up straight and mentally girding on her armor for battle on the off chance it was Thomas, come to chuckle one more time.

But it wasn't Thomas who poked his head inside the door; it was Iolanthe.

"Oh," Victoria said, surprised. "Well. Come in."

Iolanthe came inside the chamber, a little uncomfortably to Victoria's eye.

"I didn't mean to disturb ye," she said hesitantly.

"You didn't," Victoria said honestly. "I could use the distraction from my idle thoughts."

Iolanthe came across the room and perched on the seat. "Victoria," she said slowly, "I know we haven't had much time to get to know one another and mayhap this is an untoward offer . . . but if ye find yourself in need of aid whilst you're in England, I would be pleased to give it to you."

Victoria blinked. "Aid?" she echoed. "Why would I need it?"

Iolanthe shrugged. "Who's to say? There have been times in my own poor life when I could have used the company of a sister." She smiled. "The offer stands, if it suits ye."

And with that, she stood, bid Victoria good-night, and left the room.

Victoria stared at the closed door. Aid? What kind of aid? Why did she have the feeling it wasn't your run-of-the-mill, there's-the-first-aid-box-for-Band-Aids kind of aid?

She sat there with bagpipe music wafting in the window, and shivered.

She really had to get out of Thomas's house before she lost her mind. If she could have, she would have grabbed her suitcase and bolted from the house right then. But that might have tipped any number of family members off to just how weird she was beginning to think this whole gig in England was, and that she couldn't have.

No, she would get herself ready for bed, get in, pull up the covers, and force herself to sleep.

Then she would get up and run like hell the next day, instead of waiting for Monday, and get herself back to the world she knew and understood, where people looked up to her and didn't dare question her, where she could arrange things exactly the way she liked and watch them be carried off in the same manner. Yes, the theater was the place for her. The script was already written and there was no mystery as to the manner in which the ending was reached.

A particularly poignant bit of music swept through the window and came close to bringing tears to her eyes. Fortunately, she was made of sterner stuff than that, and had no trouble slamming the window shut, hauling together the curtains, and stomping over to the bathroom.

Bagpipe music.

It was enough to make her wonder if Thomas's house wasn't haunted. Iolanthe was certainly otherworldly enough to have acquired a few ghostly companions along the way.

With a snort, she shut the bathroom door, dug out her toothbrush, and applied herself to the very pedestrian task of brushing her teeth.

It seemed the most sensible thing to do.

S_{he} was sure she had just closed her eyes the moment before she heard Thomas banging on her door, saying something completely unintelligible. Victoria rubbed her eyes and fumbled for the clock. She couldn't make out the numbers, but she had the feeling they weren't in double digits.

Thomas opened the door and tossed a phone at her. "It's for you."

Victoria fumbled for the phone, then took a moment to figure out which end to talk into before she managed to get the other end to her ear. And then she wished she hadn't.

There were shrieks in the background.

"It's Saturday morning," she said grimly. "This better be good."

"It is."

It was Fred, her stage manager. Victoria sighed and dragged a hand through her hair. "What's wrong?"

"You won't believe this," he began.

Victoria could hear the shrieks fading in the background. That, at least, had to be an improvement. "Believe what?" she asked unwillingly.

"That was Gerard," he finished.

"Why was he screaming?"

"He says the prop room is haunted."

She was fully awake now. "But it's a prop room."

"So I told him."

"Prop rooms aren't haunted."

"I told him that, too."

Victoria counted to ten. When that didn't work, she tried counting laid-back-looking sheep. In reality, all she wanted to do was count the ways she could have made Gerard suffer if she'd just been in a different century where thumbscrews and the rack were considered appropriate basement *accoutrements*. She needed him cataloging tights and doublets, not indulging in hallucinations. She ungritted her teeth. "Where is the coward now?"

"Nursing his nerves with a double-tall double-mocha latte down the street."

Victoria pursed her lips. Gerard wasn't important; he was indispensable. If he wasn't there to manage the costumes, she was sunk. She sighed. "Will he come back? Does he think," and she could hardly say the words, "that just the room is haunted? Or is it that just the costumes themselves are . . . um . . ."

"Possessed?"

"Something like that."

"He was screaming too loudly for me to tell."

"Then go ask him. Tell him I'll pay him extra if he gets on that plane and plies his needle for the summer at Thorpewold Castle. Tell him we're positive it's the room and not the clothes. Tell him England doesn't have any ghosts. Tell him anything to get him on the plane."

"Will do, boss."

"I don't suppose he packed up everything before he saw what he thinks he saw, did he?"

"Nope."

She paused. "What are you doing today?"

"I'm on my way home. Marge has tuna casserole on for lunch."

Victoria squinted at the clock. "It's too early for lunch."

"I need time to recover for rump roast tonight. It'll leave us enough for leftovers tomorrow as my last meal in the States."

Victoria smiled in spite of herself. "Is she afraid you'll starve this summer?"

"She hasn't heard good things about English cooking."

Victoria had eaten at Marge's supper table more than once and suspected Fred would survive British fare well enough. "All right," she said with a sigh, "I'll catch a flight home this morning and do the packing myself."

"Boxes and tape await you. The moving boys will be here Monday morning to cart the stuff to the cargo flight."

"And the rest of the gear? Lights? Sound?"

"It arrived in England two days ago. It'll be delivered on Monday to the locations your brother set up."

"All right," she said, surrendering. "I'll see you next week at Thorpewold. Have a good flight. And make good notes of what you find at the castle. I don't know that I trust my brother's descriptions."

"Will do," Fred said, and hung up.

Victoria flopped back in bed and allowed herself three minutes of enjoyment before she heaved herself out of bed and made preparations to get back to the city.

$S he$ made it to the theater by midafternoon, a miracle in itself. She'd looked in the coffee shop up the street and hadn't seen Gerard there mainlining mocha lattes, so it was a safe bet Fred had straightened him out. She didn't dare hope Gerard had returned to finish the packing. She sighed, then walked into Tempest in a Teapot and greeted the owner, Moonbat Murphy.

Moon's smile was strained.

Victoria paused at the counter. "What's wrong? You haven't been seeing spooks in the basement, too, have you?"

Moon wouldn't meet her eyes. "No, Vic." Then she busied herself scooping tea out of recycled glass containers and putting it into hemp sachets.

Victoria considered. Was Moon upset because Victoria wasn't going to be doing shows upstairs over the summer? Was she worried about the potential fallout for her business? Was she upset over a bad batch of chickweed?

Victoria discounted most of those reasons. The stage upstairs had been rented to some yoga outfit for the summer and Victoria had already paid rent on the prop room through the end of the year, plus she had already reserved the upstairs for her fall season. They'd been doing the same drill for five years now. If Moon had been unhappy with that, surely she would have lit a little incense and gathered her courage for a direct complaint.

Victoria almost paused to ask more pointed questions, then decided it was probably more than she wanted to know at the moment, so she shrugged to herself, then made her way through the shop, back through the kitchen, and down the stairs to the cellar.

Then she came to a halt in front of the prop room door.

Taped there was a note. Victoria took it and unfolded it. Handmade paper, apparently. But somehow, that just didn't improve the message.

Vic,
Sorry, but we can't do your theater upstairs anymore.
The guy who's renting the stage this summer offered

*to buy Tempest in a Teapot and open a yoga studio
upstairs forever. Just Say Yes to the right price, right?
I knew you'd understand.*

Moon

*P.S. Can you get your stuff out by Monday? Mr. Yoga
says your costumes throw off his chi.*

Victoria looked at the note. No, she gaped at the note. No
wonder the Bat hadn't wanted to look her in the eye. Victoria could hardly believe it. Moon was no doubt planning a
very long stay on a tropical island, where she could drink
green tea and practice Downward-Facing Dog in peace.

Victoria wanted to wrap her and her newly acquired fistfuls of cash in her damned yoga mat and drop her in the
Hudson.

Well, maybe it was for the best. Maybe the show would
be such a hit in England, she would be asked to stay and set
up shop there. Shakespeare had made it in London; why
couldn't she? She'd think about that later, when she'd finished packing.

If she thought about it now, she might be tempted to do
someone bodily harm.

She shoved the note into her bag, then took her key and
opened up the prop room. She looked around for a minute,
then indulged in a few less-than-ladylike comments about
costume designers in general and Gerard in particular.
There was nothing in the room in front of her besides
Hamlet costumes and props, all of which she would have
to pack herself, damn it, anyway. Where were the manly
men when she needed them?

She rolled up her sleeves and looked on the bright side
as she got to work. At least there wasn't really all that
much to pack. Most of her theater gear was in storage. It
could have been a lot worse. She could have been looking
for members of her crew willing to come down on their
last weekend of freedom to help her pack. She could just
imagine the complaints—

The costumes rustled.

Victoria looked up from where she knelt in front of a box, packing shoes. She frowned. Wind? Too much gusty sighing on her part? She stared at the medieval-looking clothing hanging on the rack above her. Well, nothing was moving now. She snorted to herself. Too much talk of ghosts. Either that or sleep deprivation was catching up with her. She turned back to her work.

One metal hanger clanked against another. Victoria looked up sharply. She wondered, a little desperately, where the breeze was coming from.

But there was no breeze.

And she could see now that one of the capes was definitely moving.

All by itself.

Victoria dug the heels of her hands into her eyes and rubbed vigorously. When she could see again, she looked at the spot where the clothing had been moving.

Only now she could she what had been moving it.

A man stood there, dressed in what she could only identify as medieval Highland gear. His hair was a flaming red not unlike her own. He had a very large sword hanging down by his side. He was wearing a crisp white shirt and had a heavy plaid blanket of sorts pleated around his waist, with one end thrown over his shoulder. It was fastened with an enormous silver brooch that sparkled with emeralds and rubies.

He was fondling a purple velvet cape and making noises of appreciation. He stood on tiptoe to reach the caps on the rack. He lovingly caressed one with a long, luscious feather on it. Victoria felt her jaw go slack. She pinched herself.

"Ow," she said involuntarily.

The man whipped around to look at her, squeaking in surprise.

Victoria couldn't seem to retrieve her jaw. She could only manage garbled sounds of surprise and disbelief.

The man shifted nervously.

Victoria clamped down on her raging imagination with an iron fist and forced herself to speak. "Are you a ghost?" she demanded.

The man gulped, then took off his own cap and clutched it nervously between his hands. "Hugh McKinnon," he said. He made her a low bow, then promptly vanished.

Victoria felt herself start to go numb. It began at the top of her head and traveled downward. She realized in horror that she was going to faint. She didn't have time to faint; she had to finalize production arrangements. She had to get the last of her stuff out of her apartment for the summer. She had to make sure Michael Fellini had everything he needed and would enjoy that first-class flight she had booked for him. She had to empty out the prop room that she no longer had rights to—but that was okay because she now knew for a fact that it was haunted. Let Mr. Yoga Man put that in his feng shui and smoke it.

She felt herself keeling over. At least she was close to the ground and it wouldn't hurt so badly when she landed.

She looked up at the ceiling as consciousness began to fade. She was greeted again by the sight of one Hugh McKinnon, dressed in his Highland gear, leaning over her and watching her with consternation on his face.

She sincerely hoped that this wasn't some kind of cosmic foreshadowing. Her dad had warned her there were otherworldly things going on both at the castle and the inn Megan owned down the road from that castle. No wonder Thomas had laughed out loud every time he heard her mention doing *Hamlet*.

She wondered if, for the first time in her life, she might have leaped where she should have looked.

Too late now . . .

Chapter 2

Connor MacDougal stood on the parapet of Thorpe-wold Castle and stared out over the bleak landscape before him. It wasn't in his nature to be overly sentimental, but in times like these, when the tourist season was coming on and there were hauntings and otherworldly things going on at all hours, he found himself longing for the quiet of his hall in the Highlands.

Of course, in his day there had always been a bit of bloodshed with neighboring clans to enliven what might have otherwise been a dull spring afternoon. And, true, there had invariably been the excitement of a properly executed cattle raid to hold his interest for a day or so. But for the most part, he had enjoyed the sound of wind and rain and the odd curse from his men echoing in the silence of the hills.

Somehow, the bloodcurdling screams that echoed from time to time in his present keep didn't satisfy him in like manner.

But a shade did what he had to and took what pleasure he could. Thorpewold was not Connor's preferred location, but he had no desire to return to his hall in the Highlands, so it would serve him well enough. Besides, he'd waited a bloody long time to call the stones beneath his feet his. He hadn't paid for it with his blood, nor had he paid for it with his gold, but he had paid for it with his very will to have it, and have it he would.

And hold it he would, as well.

At least now he no longer had houseguests. He'd managed to rid himself of Thomas McKinnon and several other annoying shades with one deft move during the fall.

He paused.

Very well, so Thomas McKinnon had wed himself a MacLeod wench and departed for safer ground without any of Connor's aid. Connor was certain he would have driven the man away on his own, given time. It was enough that Thomas was gone. If he never had to set eyes on another McKinnon, it would be too soon. They were trouble, that family, and though he had no fear of trouble, he also couldn't deny that a little peace, such as it might be in a hall full of chattering tourists, would be a welcome thing.

And peace from Thomas McKinnon and anyone else of his ilk could not be prized too highly.

He turned and walked along the wall, surveying the goings-on in the inner bailey. There was nothing remarkable there. Men milled about, doing what men did on a pleasant morning when there were swords to be used and enemies to use them on. He looked at them and nodded to himself. Aye, those men would all call him laird in the end. He would make certain of that.

Now if he could just find himself a decent garrison captain, he might have an enjoyable and smoothly running afterlife.

"My laird?"

Connor turned and looked at his first aspirant, Angus Campbell, a shade of goodly skill, but not one overendowed with wit. But when looking for a captain, one had to begin somewhere.

"Aye?" Connor asked, vowing to begin the day with a bit of patience.

"I've tidings, my laird." Angus swallowed with difficulty, as if he could barely contain his fear.

Were the tidings so terrifying, then? Connor frowned. "Well?"

Angus shifted nervously. "There are souls intending to assault the keep."

"Tourists?"

"Nay, my laird, I think not."

"You think not," Connor repeated slowly. "Perhaps you should think less and use your eyes more. If they are not tourists, what could they possibly be?"

"Other sorts."

"Other sorts?" Connor echoed. "What kind of other sorts?"

Angus began to tremble. "Well, you see, my laird, it is thus that I understand it . . ." He paused dramatically, in spite of, or perhaps because of, his shaking. "There are preparations for guests at the inn." He paused again. "The Boar's Head Inn, my laird. The one down the way there."

"They are always preparing for guests at the inn. That one down the way—aye, I knew which one, you imbecile!"

Angus cowered. "But gear has been sent on ahead of what looks to be a full assault of *many* guests upon the inn, my laird. The shed is full to the brim and old Farris's barn down the way has been filled as well. I watched a large lorry move in items of strange and ominous portents."

"How do you know those items belong to the guests at the inn?" Connor asked in a measured tone.

Angus blinked. "I eavesdropped, my laird."

Well, that was something useful, at least. "What else did you hear? And pray that 'tis something I will find to my liking," Connor said with a growl.

"I heard the name McKinnon mentioned, my laird," Angus said, his teeth chattering.

"Impossible!"

Angus trembled violently. " 'Tis so, my laird."

"I thought I'd rid myself of that bloody family!" Connor bellowed. He turned his most ferocious scowl on the man before him. "I've no liking for these particular tidings. You're dismissed. Send up the next candidate for captain."

Angus bowed, scraped, and backed up. Apparently his sense of direction was as lacking as his good sense, for he fell off the parapet.

There was soon a quite audible "Ach, that hurt," floating up from below.

"Impossible," Connor muttered. "He must have heard it awrong."

"Actually, my dear fellow, I daresay his ears were functioning quite well."

Connor spun around to find another shade boldly occupying the same parapet. "Get off my roof, you frilly bugger," he said.

"You know," Roderick St. Claire drawled, "it had so much more, oh, I don't know, *élan*, I suppose, when Duncan MacLeod used to say the same thing to me."

Connor scowled as he drew his sword. "Perhaps my delivery is not as good, but I daresay my sword is just as sharp."

Roderick only smiled pleasantly. He fussed with his lace-bedecked shirtfront and brushed a speck of nonexistent dirt from his trouser leg. "I say you put your sword back where it was and we call a truce. You might need me on this caper."

"Caper?" Connor echoed. "I've no intentions of being involved in a caper!" By the saints, he most certainly did not—and especially not with the frilly, long-winded, irritating Victorian fool before him!

He paused, unwillingly. It was possible, he conceded, that Roderick might know something useful. If so, wisdom dictated that he not do damage to the man before he spat out his tidings. Connor resheathed his sword with a curse, vowing to himself to use it without hesitation if the situation warranted it.

"Very well," Connor said gruffly. "What do you know?"

Roderick examined the volumes of lace dripping from his wrists. "I understand there is a rather large group of mortals intending to descend on our poor home. Angus did rather feebly describe what I have seen for myself to be great activity in the village."

"It means nothing," Connor said, suffering a brief but unsettling moment of unease.

"Doesn't it?" Roderick mused. "Well, I suppose we'll see when they arrive at the keep. Ah, look you there. Here comes someone now."

Connor looked down the way and up the road to find a lone man walking toward the castle.

"Bloody hell," he said, scratching his head. Then he remembered himself and his position. "Not to worry. 'Tis but a tourist."

"Let's go see, shall we?" Roderick suggested. "We'll collect the new candidate for your captainship whilst we're about it. Oh, look at all the men lining up for the pleasure."

Connor looked to where Roderick was pointing. Well, men were certainly scurrying about, but it was hard to tell if they were trying to get in line, or out of it.

He gave Roderick a shove off the parapet, just on principle, then made his way in a more dignified fashion down the stairs to the floor of the bailey. Roderick was cursing him fluently as he dusted himself off, but Connor ignored him. He had more important things to see to.

Mainly, the man coming inside the gates, gaping like a slack-jawed fool who had never been farther from his cooking fire than his village green.

"Well, this one looks to be impressed by our idyllic little pile of stones, doesn't he?" Roderick remarked.

Connor grunted, then took up a position in the middle of the bailey. He folded his arms over his chest and watched as the man took a lengthy tour of the castle, still wearing that look of amazement.

Not a tourist, Connor noted without hesitation. No sketchpad, no *National Trust Handbook* with sights to be seen marked in red, no video camera ready to capture

Thorpewold at its best. Who, then, was this simpleton who couldn't seem to shut his mouth as he stared at everything around him?

The man looked nothing like Thomas McKinnon, so Connor thought he might be safe on that score. To be sure, no McKinnon Connor had ever known would have been caught sitting down on a rock and staring off into space as if all his wits had suddenly vacated his poor head.

Then the man leaped up and began to pace.

Connor glanced at the men gathered in the bailey. To a soul, they looked as baffled as he felt. They stood in huddles well away from the madman as he walked, stopped, counted, then walked some more. He made little writings in a notebook he produced from a pocket on his shirt.

Connor watched with growing alarm as the man continued to perpetrate his unfathomable activity. What did it all mean? Striding here and there, scribbling, muttering, holding his hands up as if he framed bits of the castle between his fingers? Indeed, he even managed a chortle or two, as if his discoveries were so delightful, he couldn't stop himself from letting everyone within earshot know of them. By all the saints above, what was this man about?

Connor wondered.

He didn't care to wonder overmuch, actually. He wanted peace and quiet, not a mortal cluttering up the inner bailey and distracting his men with his antics.

The man finally ceased his strange and unfathomable behavior. He gathered up the sheaves of paper he'd scribbled on and made his way out the front gates. Connor looked after him, then slowly turned back to the bailey.

A single sheaf lay there, discarded.

Connor felt doom descend.

He strode over to it and looked down. It galled him to the very depths of his soul to admit it, but he could not make out the scrawls scribbled there. He should have learned to read. He'd had the opportunity, a year or so ago. Many men in the keep had submitted to lessons from another of their kind trying to master the skill, but Connor had kept himself aloof, feeling it too far beneath him to engage in such foolishness.

Now, he wondered if he might have been the foolish one.

He looked unwillingly at Roderick, who stood next to him, waiting patiently.

"Well, damn you," Connor snapped, "what are you waiting for?"

"An invitation?"

"You'll have a skewering—"

"I can't read if I can't breathe," Roderick said pleasantly. He leaned over and peered at the paper. "It says, '*Hamlet,* produced by V. McKinnon.'"

Connor only heard *McKinnon.*

He roared.

"Oh, do be quiet," Roderick complained. "You don't know that it's one of *those* McKinnons."

Connor unclenched his jaw. Roderick had it aright. There was no sense in aggravating himself without cause. "What means the rest?" he said, gesturing impatiently toward the ground.

"*Hamlet* is a play by William Shakespeare. Do you know him?"

"I've no stomach for jongleurs," Connor said shortly.

Roderick smiled dryly. "You might find this play quite to your liking. There is a great amount of death involved, some revenge, and a good haunting or two."

Connor refused to be distracted by those enticing thoughts. "I'm certain I would find it deadly dull," he muttered. "Now, what is this Vee McKinnon business? What does that mean?"

Roderick shrugged. "Produced means 'put on by,' so I daresay this McKinnon fellow intends to mount a stage play here in our own humble home."

"Never," Connor vowed. "Not while I have means to stop it."

"If you can survive Thomas remodeling the corner tower last year," Roderick began, "you could certainly survive—"

"I will not have another McKinnon in my hall," Connor

said curtly. "Not even if he isn't kin of Thomas McKinnon's. I will make the life of this new one a misery. Indeed, I will make him sorely regret his intentions before he even sets foot inside the gates. Or perhaps I will wait until he comes inside the gates, then not allow him to leave, giving me ample time to torment him as I will."

He paused and contemplated the possibilities, finding that just thinking on them made him feel warm and contented inside.

"Lads, to me!" he called cheerfully. "Murder! Mayhem!"

All the men looked up. Some of them came quickly; others dawdled, as if they hoped to avoid some bit of unpleasant labor. Connor's good humors departed abruptly.

"Damn ye all to hell," he snarled, "must I best ye all in the lists yet again to prove my worth?"

They gathered around him, not as eagerly or as quickly as he would have liked, but they gathered. He made a note of those whose feet seemed to drag the most, then turned his mind to the matters immediately at hand.

"A McKinnon lad is coming here to put on a play," he announced.

Many scratched their heads; others looked at him blankly.

"We're going to be under siege," Connor clarified, irritated. By the saints, he needed to import more intelligent guardsmen. "Do not show yourselves until I give you leave. I'll explain as we go."

The men gave him various nods of assent and shuffled off. Connor called for the men who had been the least enthusiastic about answering his call. They looked a bit green as they clustered together in front of him.

"The lists," he said, nodding to the place that at various and sundry times had served as a garden. "One by one. You may watch until your turn comes. Then perhaps you will not be so slow next time I bid you come."

He strode over with his afternoon's entertainment trailing feebly behind him. He supposed he might have felt a little sorry for them, for they would certainly receive the brunt of his irritation with one Vee McKinnon.

Damn the man, whoever he was.

Evening had fallen and was fast turning into night before Connor finished instructing his recalcitrant guardsmen in their duties and could take himself off to do a bit of investigating. He made his way purposefully to the Boar's Head Inn. It wasn't a bad place, as far as inns went. If Connor had cared, he might have been pleased by the look of the place, its fine construction, and the lovely garden laid out to delight both the eye and the nose.

But Connor did not care for such things. He wanted to know what he could expect and given that there wasn't a soul in his keep who could match him in wit, it was obviously up to him to do all the scouting as well as all the thinking.

He shunned the front door and went around to the kitchen. It was simply a fact of life; more interesting conversations happened near the stove than in the entryway.

He had just rounded the corner of the building when he saw none other than Hugh McKinnon descending upon the place in a tearing hurry, clutching a cap bedecked with feathers to his head with one hand and struggling to carry an armful of gear with the other. He was swathed, head to toe, in a luxurious velvet cape of indeterminate color.

Connor stared at him in horrified fascination.

He certainly hadn't had much experience with that sort of thing, but it looked to him as if Hugh had decided to become, in his undeath, a perpetrator of frolics. Connor knew he shouldn't have been surprised.

Hugh was, after all, a McKinnon.

Connor waited until Hugh had gone inside, then walked to the kitchen door and peered in the window.

Aye, the customary lads were there: Ambrose MacLeod, Hugh McKinnon, and Fulbert de Piaget. Connor knew them all, had bested them all at one time or another, and disliked them all quite thoroughly. Matchmaking busybodies. Could they not find a more serious work to do than meddling in the affairs of poor, hapless mortals who likely could have found love on their own?

Connor put his ear to the door. When that failed to provide him with the access he desired, he put his ear *through* the door. That was better, but still unsatisfactory. Connor leaned his whole face into the kitchen, where he could both see and hear. The lads before him were far too involved in their own conversation to pay him any heed. He waited patiently, ready to hear things that would prepare him for what was to come.

"Hugh," Ambrose said in a garbled voice, "what are you wearing?"

Fulbert made accompanying sounds of horror. Connor had to agree, but he refrained from comment.

Hugh doffed a purple velvet cap and made the other two a low bow. "Theater gear." He drew his sword with a flourish, but it became caught in his cape, flipped into the air with a bit of aid from its hapless wielder, then dove point-down against the floor, where it collapsed into itself. "'Tis meant to do that, that sword," he said quickly. "You know, it isn't as if those players can go about stabbing each other truly, can they now—"

"And how would you know any of that?" Ambrose asked suspiciously.

"Well, I had a day or two of leisure and though I was first for France, I soon felt the pull of the apple."

"The apple?" Fulbert echoed.

"The Big Apple," Hugh said, staring off into the distance with a dreamy expression on his face. "Broadway. Central Park. Those loudly braying cabbies in their swift-moving yellow automobiles . . ."

Connor wondered if Hugh had lost his mind. Apples? Cabbies?

"Do you mean to tell me that you actually ventured into New York City?" Ambrose demanded.

Hugh stuck his chin out. "I thought it best to do a bit of investigating before the troupe arrives." He dragged up a chair of his own and struggled to get himself, his cape, his sword, and sundry other props including wigs, rather authentic looking Elizabethan scientific instruments, and a lute, into his seat. He failed. His gear clattered in a heap about him.

Ambrose hissed him to silence. "Will you wake the entire household?"

Hugh scowled. "I came prepared. I see nothing in your hands to further our plan."

Ambrose tapped his head meaningfully. "It all resides in here, my good man. I've spent hours ferreting out secrets, learning important details, discovering—"

"The play being done?" Hugh asked archly.

Connor almost blurted out the name, but stopped himself just in time. It wouldn't do to let on to his eavesdropping self.

"*Hamlet,*" Fulbert supplied.

"And how do *you* know that?" Ambrose demanded.

"I eavesdropped."

Connor shrugged to himself. He wasn't above it; he couldn't fault Fulbert for the same thing.

"Where?" Ambrose asked. "Where did you go to eavesdrop?"

"In London," Fulbert said. "Went to make certain that young Megan MacLeod McKinnon—"

"De Piaget," Hugh added.

Fulbert cursed at him, then continued. "I took meself to London to see that that McKinnon gel who wed with me nevvy wasn't keepin' him from doing a proper day's labor. For as ye know, me nevvy Gideon de Piaget is the powerful and quite capable head of a vast international conglomerate."

"And I take it you left my sweet granddaughter Megan— several generations removed, of course—untroubled?" Ambrose demanded.

Fulbert shrugged. "Untroubled enough, I suppose. She only screeched once, but that wasn't *my* fault."

Connor reached a hand inside the door to stroke his chin

thoughtfully. Unrepentantly causing mortal screeching? Perhaps he had judged Fulbert too harshly. 'Twas possible he might have overlooked a lad with his own sentiments on the living—

Hugh glared at Fulbert. "She screeched? You forced such a sound from Thomas's sweet sister?"

"Only once."

"Did you show yourself to her?" Ambrose asked sharply.

Fulbert scowled. "She's seen me 'afore and knows me well. But as I was sayin', she was about some new beauty treatment and when I saw her with her face all a'slathered with green goo, well, can ye blame me for a screech of my own?"

Connor frowned. 'Twas one thing to wrest a scream from a mortal; 'twas another thing entirely to give vent to one oneself. Perhaps he *hadn't* judged Fulbert too quickly. Obviously, those de Piaget lads possessed the weak spines he'd always suspected they did.

"Anyhow," Fulbert continued, "I heard her sayin' that *Hamlet* was the play being done up the way this summer and that gear had already been sent ahead in preparation."

Connor almost made an exclamation of triumph before he could stop himself. He *knew* it! 'Twas one of Thomas McKinnon's relations come to put on the play.

His elation, but not surprise, at being correct was immediately extinguished by the realization that he had been correct. One of Thomas's kin was coming to put on a play.

Connor pulled his head back outside with a curse. Damnation, but would he never rid himself of that blasted family? Everywhere he turned, there was another one cropping up like a poisonous mushroom. Obviously, this would require a newer, more unpleasant strategy. He would have his peace and quiet that summer, no matter the cost. He turned to walk away . . .

Only then realizing that he was not alone. That damned innkeeper, Mrs. Pruitt, stood there, dressed all in black, loaded down with all sorts of modern gear that beeped and blinked and, truth be told, startled him so badly that a manly shout of surprise was wrenched from him against his will.

Mrs. Pruitt whipped herself around to look up at him. Her mouth dropped open and a look of astonishment descended upon her features.

Connor scowled. Had she never heard a lad bellow before? Aye, well, so that might have been considered a scream, but who was this woman to judge?

Then again, perhaps she wasn't judging. Her eyes rolled back in her head and she slumped to the ground, senseless.

Connor briefly considered ascertaining the extent of her injuries, but two things stopped him: He did not care; and Ambrose and his mates were coming out the door. Connor hastened away before they saw him.

So, he had not been mistaken in what was to come. It appeased him only slightly, for he had yet the matter of that McKinnon lad to deal with. Not that such troubled him. He would greet the man with his sword bared, leaving him with no choice but to flee.

He had not paid for the stones beneath his feet with his blood like another specter he'd once known, or with his gold, as Thomas McKinnon claimed to have, but he had damned well paid for it with his will to hold it.

And hold it he would.

And pity the next McKinnon who thought otherwise.

Chapter 3

"Vikki, we're here."

Victoria struggled to wake. She knew she had a good reason to open her eyes, but she'd been lost in the most delicious dream and wanted to savor it a bit longer. Shakespeare had been involved somehow. She thought Michael Fellini had been starring in the production. She was almost positive there had been a Tony award and rave reviews in the background.

She was certain it hadn't included ghosts, ghosts in prop rooms, or prop rooms that she no longer had access to.

She opened her eyes. It took her several minutes to reconcile herself to the fact that she was sitting on a train and the train was no longer moving. Her sister Megan was struggling to get out of her own seat. Victoria frowned. Megan was only five months pregnant with her first child but one would have thought she was on the verge of delivery. Why was she waddling like a duck already?

It was probably better not to ask. Megan had picked her up at the airport, chauffeured her to the train station, joined her on the train, and kept her purse from getting ripped off while she slept. Now a car was picking them up at the station and taking them to the inn. Megan could waddle all she wanted in return for all those favors.

She got into the back of the car with her sister and stared out the window, feeling as if she were in some sort of French Impressionist painting of the English countryside. The whole experience was surreal. Gone was the smell, the busyness, the comforting closeness of skyscrapers and other buildings stacked up next to each other. In their places were rolling hills, a quaint village, and a road that led out of town to heaven only knew where.

"The inn's not far," Megan assured her. "I'm sure supper will be waiting. If you can stay awake for it."

"I probably should," Victoria said with a yawn. "If nothing else, I should make sure everything's ready."

"Don't worry about that," Megan said. "Mrs. Pruitt runs the place like a boot camp. Everything will be in order."

Victoria looked at her sister and had to shake her head, though she didn't do it too vigorously; jet lag wasn't all that bad from New York to London and beyond, but she hadn't had all that much sleep in the previous seventy-two hours, so she wasn't exactly fully functional.

But in spite of her impaired mental state, she did manage to look at her sister and marvel at the change. At twenty-nine, Megan was three years younger than Victoria and had been struggling to find her place for years. She'd worked at all kinds of jobs; gone to and moved past college; tried her hand at all the family businesses, including Victoria's theater troupe and their mother's clothing company. Nothing had fit. Then Thomas had sent her to England to check out the castle he'd bought himself, sort of as a last-ditch effort to give Megan something to do.

Instead of failing yet again, Megan had wound up owning a little country inn and marrying some titled Brit who was so filthy rich that even Thomas genuflected when they met.

That had been a serious deviation from the script, but since it was Megan's life and not hers, Victoria hadn't said anything about it. Of course, she wouldn't have the tolerance for that kind of detour herself, but to each her own.

She found herself distracted by the countryside as they wound their way through it and then up a small road to what was indeed a quaint, Tudor-style inn. They pulled to a graceful, dignified stop.

"Like it?" Megan asked.

"It's wonderful," Victoria said honestly.

"You were here before, you know," Megan pointed out. "For my wedding."

Victoria yawned. "Megan, I flew in the morning of your wedding, went straight to the church to put on my bridesmaid dress, watched you get married, vaguely remember lunch at a very dark pub in the village, then I got back on a plane to close a very satisfying run of *Romeo and Juliet*."

Megan laughed. "I suppose you never made it this far, did you? It's probably just as well."

The chauffeur opened Megan's door for her. Megan leaned over and whispered, "It's haunted," before she leaped gracefully from the car as if she hadn't spent the first five months of her pregnancy eating and puking for two.

Victoria sat there for several moments with her jaw hanging down before she realized that if she didn't do something soon, she was going to drool on her shirt. She shut her mouth, clambered out of the car on shaky legs, and looked at the inn in front of her.

Haunted?

Perhaps all that smog in London had gone to Megan's head and withered her brain. Then again, hadn't their dad warned her there were otherworldly things going on here? She'd assumed he'd been kidding . . .

She hoisted her bag farther up on her shoulder and made her way uneasily through the front door. And then she came to a sudden standstill.

She stood in the entryway of a place that looked as if it had been lifted straight from a movie set. The furniture and paintings were perfectly period. The carpet was less so, but who was she to quibble? The innkeeper, doubtless the intrepid Mrs. Pruitt, was holding her feather duster over her shoulder like a bayonet and commanding a hapless teenager to be about settling Lady Blythwood as quick as might be.

Victoria realized with a start that Megan was Lady Blythwood. If all the people who had fired Megan over the years could have had an earful of that . . .

"That's my sister, Victoria," Megan was saying. She retrieved Victoria from the doorway and pulled her over to the reception desk. "Vikki, this is Mrs. Pruitt. She'll be keeping your actors in line for you while they're staying here."

Mrs. Pruitt put her free hand over her ample bosom. "I'll do what I can for the cause, Miss. We can't have a proper play without proper rest for the players now, can we? Not that ye'll need worry about that," she said, lowering her voice conspiratorially. "We have lights out on time here at the inn."

Victoria leaned in closer, in spite of herself. "We do?"

Mrs. Pruitt nodded knowingly. "I need peace and quiet for me investigations."

Victoria immediately had a vision of an Inland Revenue audit that would make the IRS look like a bunch of third-grade math students. "Investigations?" she asked warily.

"Don't ye know?"

Victoria blinked. "Know what?"

Mrs. Pruitt looked her over, then straightened suddenly. "Nothing," she said in a businesslike tone. "Nothing to trouble yourself over, Miss. Your room is up the stairs. Last one on the right. The nicest—after Lady Blythwood's, of course. I've a map where I've placed the rest of your troupe, if you'd care to study it. I daresay you could use a bit of supper first, though, then a good rest tonight."

Victoria found herself with a key in her hand and Megan's hand on her back, pushing her toward the stairs before she could slow things down long enough to ask just what kind of investigations Mrs. Pruitt was talking about. She would have stopped on the stairs, but Megan was now pulling her.

"Later," Megan said. "Go take a shower. I'll meet you downstairs in an hour for dinner and we'll talk then."

"Why didn't we talk on the train?" Victoria asked, hoping she would make it to the shower before she fell asleep.

"You were drooling. And snoring. Not conducive to conversations of full disclosure."

Victoria managed to stop in front of her room. She looked at her sister. "Full disclosure? What have I gotten myself into?"

"Something it's too late to get out of. The roller coaster has already left the station," Megan said with an unwholesomely amused smile. "All you can do now is hang on for the ride."

Victoria clutched her key. "I'm going to blame Thomas for this."

"It worked for me."

And with that Megan sailed, in a wobbly sort of way, into her room, leaving Victoria standing out in the hallway, wondering what she was supposed to do now.

Key. Lock. Dinner.

"Oh," she said, non-plussed. "Thank you."

She was standing in the shower before she realized that the voice hadn't been her sister's.

Victoria discovered she had fallen asleep on the way back from the shower only because she woke up in the dark, starving and disoriented. Then again, she'd been disoriented for most of the day, so maybe that was nothing new. But the hunger she might be able to fix.

She felt around for the lamp. After she'd managed to get that on, she sat up and dragged her fingers through hair that was no doubt matted on one side and riotously curly on the other. Well, there was surely no one left awake to see. She dressed in dirty jeans and walked to the door. She paused.

She *had* heard a voice, hadn't she?

She left her room before she could think about it too

seriously. Obviously, she was having a hypoglycemic hallucination brought on by airline food and exacerbated by no sleep. She would be more rational after raiding the fridge and returning immediately to bed.

She made her way down the stairs, thanks to the nightlight on the reception desk tucked back under the staircase. She walked across the entryway and began trying doors. Sitting room, library, parlor; she examined each in turn. They were wonderful, looking as if they'd been plucked from the past and set down in the present with tender care. She closed the door on the parlor and continued her search for sustenance.

It took only one more door before she found the dining room. She walked through it, with its tables already laid for breakfast, then pushed her way into the kitchen.

Megan sat in a chair, toasting her toes against an Aga stove. Three older gentlemen sat with her, nursing something in rustic mugs. Interesting, but not exactly what she was looking for. Megan looked over her shoulder.

"Hey, Vikki," she said warmly. "Nice nap?"

"I'll tell you about it after I don't want to gnaw your arm off. Where's the fridge?"

"Over there," Megan said, pointing to the far end of the kitchen. "Help yourself."

"I thought I would," Victoria said. She made quick mental notes about Megan's companions on her way by. She wouldn't have normally, but the men were wearing authentic-looking period costumes: kilts, rustic-looking shirts, caps tilted jauntily atop heads. Well, at least two of them were in Scottish dress. The third was dressed in something made for Elizabethan nobility, though perhaps not as bedecked with baubles and lace as she might have expected for full-blown court attire.

She shook her head wryly. Would there ever come a time when people didn't throw themselves in front of her in hopes of becoming part of her next play?

She turned her back on the wannabes, opened the fridge, and began looking inside for something edible. She poached some cheese and bread, then looked around for something to go with it.

"Fruit on the table," Megan said.

Victoria frowned at her sister. She sounded as if she were on the verge of laughing. Why? She surreptitiously felt her hair. Was it that traumatized by her unexpected nap? Megan's hair was just as curly as hers, and presently looked just as napped on. Victoria pursed her lips as she stomped back across the kitchen and put her things down on the table. She reached for an apple.

Then she froze, her hand outstretched. She looked at the men sitting with Megan. Again, it wouldn't have been the first time would-be actors had dressed up and put themselves in her path, hoping for an audition. These three certainly looked the part. But it wasn't that. It was that she recognized one of them.

Hugh McKinnon.

The same Hugh McKinnon who had stroked the purple cape and feathered cap in her prop room.

She sat down. Hard. Fortunately, there seemed to have been a bench put there for just such an exigency.

"What's wrong?" Megan asked innocently.

Far too innocently.

Victoria chose to let that pass. Instead, she pointed at the red-haired costume fondler.

"I've seen him," she managed.

The man dressed in Elizabethan finery snorted. "I told ye, Ambrose, that Hugh would befoul the plans before we even started!"

"I befouled nothing," Hugh McKinnon said. He smiled at Victoria. "Good e'en to ye, granddaughter."

"Granddaughter," Victoria repeated, but somehow she couldn't manage to attach any sound to the word. She swallowed, but that didn't work all that well, either.

"Several generations removed," the other two men said in unison.

"Aye, weel, that as well," Hugh said, ducking his head modestly.

Victoria looked at Megan, who seemed quite at ease where she was and with whom she was sitting. She looked at her own hand to find it was shaking, so she curled her fingers into a fist and hugged herself.

"He disappeared," Victoria managed, nodding toward Hugh. "He was in my prop room, groping costumes, then he vanished."

"Hugh!" the other Scottish gentleman exclaimed. He stood, turned, and made Victoria a low bow. "My apologies for the disturbance. I am Ambrose MacLeod, your grandfather. Please feel free to call upon me anytime. I'm always about."

"He doesn't sleep much," Hugh offered. "A bit of a restless spirit, you might call him."

The third man gave a mighty snort, then stood and cast his mug into the stove's belly.

It disappeared without a trace.

"I'm Fulbert de Piaget," he said dourly. "I'm Megan's great-uncle by marriage. Don't suppose that makes us relatives, but since I'm always a key player in these escapades, you can call on me as well. But I *do* care for me afternoon rests, so don't be about disturbing me then."

And with that, he turned and walked out the back kitchen door.

Out *through* the back kitchen door.

Victoria was very glad she was sitting down.

Ambrose made her a low bow as well, then left in much the same way.

Hugh made no move to go. He smiled widely, revealing a rather gap-toothed bit of dental business. "Well, gels, now 'tis just us McKinnons here—"

Hugh . . .

Hugh scowled and remained seated.

HUGH!

He muttered something under his breath, then rose and made a low bow. "I will return. When Ambrose is napping," he added in a stage whisper.

He tossed his cup into the fire, then walked out the

kitchen door in the same manner as the others had in exiting the inn's kitchen.

Victoria sat at the table with dinner she wasn't sure she was going to be able to eat spread out in front of her and stared at the place where three men had just recently sat, all looking as corporeal and alive as Megan.

Now there was only Megan, still sitting there in front of the fire. "I think I should be going to bed," she said, stretching. "I've got to get back to London tomorrow morning—"

"Don't you dare," Victoria commanded. "You can sleep on the train. Right now, I want you to turn around and spill the beans."

"Beans?"

Victoria blew out her breath in frustration. "The ghosts, Megan!"

Megan laughed as she turned her chair around and drew it up to the table. "I warned you that the inn was haunted."

"Yes, but I didn't believe . . ." Victoria paused. She couldn't say she didn't believe her, because now she'd had ample proof to the contrary. "I'm not hallucinating all this, am I?"

"What do you think?"

"I think I saw Hugh McKinnon in the basement of Tempest in a Teapot a week ago. But I didn't know ghosts were—" she had to take a deep breath before she could finish, "—international travelers."

"Most probably aren't," Megan conceded.

Victoria looked at Megan and felt a sudden new respect for her. Her sister, the ghost-buster. "Did you discover these three on your own?"

"It was sort of a mutual encounter," Megan admitted. "Though if you were to ask Ambrose, he would tell you that he planned the whole thing."

"What whole thing?"

"My meeting Gideon here."

Victoria blinked. "They arranged your marriage?"

"Well, I wouldn't go that far—"

"They're *matchmakers*?" Victoria asked incredulously.

"They would certainly like to think so. After all, we are

kin. I think they feel somewhat obligated to see us settled well."

"Well, that stretches even the formidable reaches of my whopping imagination." She pursed her lips. "Really, Megan. It was just coincidence that you met Gideon here. A happy coincidence," she added quickly, "but just chance. Not fate. Not matchmaking ghosts."

"Think what you like," Megan said airily.

"And Thomas?" Victoria demanded. "Do you actually believe they had anything to do with his marriage? I admit I haven't had much time to get to know Iolanthe, but surely she was just bamboozled by his pretty blue eyes—without any other kinds of otherworldly convincing going on."

But even as she said it, she wondered.

Thomas had just happened upon news of Thorpewold going up for sale. He'd bought it, sight unseen. He'd rearranged his life on a whim to take possession of it. Oddly enough, he'd somehow managed to meet his wife while working on it.

Oddly enough.

Victoria got up suddenly, rummaged around for a knife, then sat back down to make short work of dinner.

"You know, I'm getting tired," Megan began.

"Tough."

"You'll be all right by yourself."

"It isn't that I need company," Victoria said, trying her damndest to convince herself that it was true. "It's just that I want *your* company."

"Liar."

"We haven't had a chance to catch up," Victoria continued, feeling rather desperate all of a sudden. "And we won't have another chance anytime soon, what with you going home tomorrow and me being involved with the play for the summer . . ."

Megan laughed. "All right. I'll protect you for a while, but then I'm going to bed."

"I'll be fine. Especially once the sun comes up," she added under her breath.

"They're ghosts, silly, not vampires."

"Whatever. So, tell me about your disembodied friends—"

"Our grandfathers," Megan corrected. "Plus Fulbert. He's Gideon's uncle."

"Sure," Victoria nodded. "Now, are our grandfathers just sort of inn ghosts or do they roam around?"

"Do you mean, are you going to have paranormal peace and quiet in the castle up the way, or are things going to get really interesting?"

"I don't want a bunch of ghosts scaring away paying customers," Victoria said grimly.

"Why are you asking me about all this?" Megan asked. "It isn't as if I can do anything about it. Besides, you might just be hallucinating."

Victoria paused and considered. "I might be. But you're here, too."

"It might be a really powerful hallucination."

"Matchmaking ghosts do seem pretty far-fetched."

"Stranger things have happened."

Victoria chewed thoughtfully on a rather tasty cheese sandwich, managed to get most of it down, then pushed her plate back. She looked at her sister.

"If they're matchmaking ghosts, who are they match-making for these days? You're happily married. Thomas is, beyond all reason, happily married to that dear, baffled Iolanthe. Is our little sister set to arrive soon and be their next victim?"

"Jenner's helping Mom with next spring's line," Megan said placidly. "I guess that just leaves you."

Victoria laughed uneasily and without humor. "I hardly need to have a match made for me."

Though three rather fierce looking ghosts might just be the thing Michael Fellini needed to inspire him to take a good hard look at her and see the woman behind the script.

"Come on, sis," Megan said. "You've had a long day and so have I. Things will look better in the morning. Of course, I won't be here in the morning to see if things are looking better. You can call me in London if things get really dodgy."

Victoria washed and put away her plate and knife, then looked around the kitchen one more time before she followed Megan back into the dining room. She *could* be delirious, but that would certainly be a shocking deviation from her usual policy of taking big gulps of reality in very large doses.

But as she followed Megan back upstairs, she couldn't help but wonder if indeed there might be a match to be made for her. After all, it was entirely possible that those jet-setting ghosts had seen Michael and decided he just might be the one for her.

Had it been coincidence that she had been invited to that faculty tea at Juilliard where Michael had just happened to be there without a date? Hadn't she hit it off with Michael in an unexplained way? Hadn't he thought the idea of Tempest in a Teapot to be the most original thing he'd heard in years? Hadn't he suggested that they meet for a cappuccino and a currant scone with agave frosting at Tempest in a Teapot very soon?

She paused. All right, so there was that protracted period of time—almost a year—when Michael hadn't seemed to be able to find her phone number, but he was a very busy man.

Was it mere luck that when Thomas had made her the offer of his castle, she had called to offer Michael the part and had him accept almost immediately? She suspected not. In fact, he'd mentioned that it was uncanny that she should offer him such a plum role when he just happened to have his spring free of classes.

Uncanny.

She nodded to herself. Surely all that could be attributed to matchmaking ghosts up to more serious things than Three Stooges–style antics.

She said good night to her sister and went immediately into her room, then headed for the bathroom. She brushed her teeth, already working time into her schedule the next day for scouting out cozy locales for what she was sure would be long conversations with Michael about Shakespearean metaphors. Once Michael arrived, she would be over her jet lag and ready to make her own match.

Of course, if she really got stuck, she might enlist a grandfather or two, but she would save those big guns for later.

She paused, then shook her head slowly. That she was even contemplating the like said much about her mental state. She was not accustomed to having things around her take on lives of their own. Ghosts had not been in her plans.

Well, at least, not *off* stage.

She slapped her toothbrush down on the counter. She could handle the ghosts as long as they remained safely in the inn's kitchen. If worse came to worst, she would make them sign a contract agreeing to stay out of sight and out of her love life.

She went to bed before she could deliberate any longer on the merits of Fate versus Ghostly Interference. She wasn't sure she believed in either. If there was luck to be had, or love to be won, it would be had and won by her own efforts.

Of that she was certain.

Chapter 4

"**M**y laird, my laird, my laird!"

Connor sat on a rock in the middle of his bailey where the smithy had been several centuries earlier, sharpening his sword. He looked up at the current candidate for the lofty position of captain of his guard and sighed lightly. When would come the day that provided him with a man worthy of such an honor?

Not today, apparently.

At least Robby Fergusson possessed a smidgen more wit than Angus Campbell. Unfortunately, he also possessed traits that were better suited to a sheepdog than a guardsman.

"My laird," Robby said, bouncing up and down excitedly in front of Connor. "I've tidings!"

"Then stand still and deliver them," Connor exclaimed. "By the saints, man, you're giving me a queasy stomach watching you skip about!"

Robby planted his feet firmly against the dirt, looked at them a time or two as if he had to make certain they would remain where he placed them, then delivered his tidings triumphantly.

"There's someone on the road, coming toward the castle."

Connor considered. It could be a stranger, he supposed, but it also could be the lad who had capered about so incomprehensibly several days ago.

Or it could be Vee McKinnon.

Connor looked at his sword, gleaming despite the overcast day, and smiled. Then he looked up at Robby.

"Indeed," Connor said pleasantly. "Who do you think it could be?"

Robby blinked. "Well, my laird, I've no idea."

"Man or woman?"

"I don't know that, either."

"Friend or enemy?"

"Um . . ."

"Mortal or not?"

"Ah . . ."

Connor swung his sword. Robby might have lacked wit, but he didn't lack agility. He managed to duck before he lost his head, then he took one look at Connor's frown, and fled.

"Next!" Connor bellowed.

No one seemed anxious to volunteer.

Connor rolled his eyes and went to stand in the middle of the bailey. Some men sauntered over to see what he was about. Others limped over as quickly as their feeble legs would carry them. Connor smiled to himself in satisfaction. Those were the ones he'd tormented in the lists earlier in the week, and there they were, still feeling the aftereffects. He really should make time in his undeath to run through the garrison more regularly. There was nothing like a little humiliation to really bring recalcitrant guardsmen to heel.

"Hide yourselves until I give you word," Connor said jovially. "Someone comes. I am hoping for a foe worthy of my skills for a change."

"A man can dream," one of the men said wistfully.

Connor nodded. "Aye, but dreaming may be all I do this day. Is there one to stand against me in truth?"

Most of the men shook their heads, as if they simply could not contemplate such a thing. A few looked as if they thought they might be equal to the task.

Connor made a mental list of those misguided souls for use another time.

"Is it perhaps the madman from the other day?" a man asked nervously.

Connor grinned.

Several of the men fell back, their hands at their throats.

"If he is, he'll regret his cheek," Connor said, with relish. "If the lad is some other, then I'll give him a tale to tell. But I want no aid. Not until I have souls about me with spine enough to do a proper bit of haunting." He looked at them mockingly. "You spent far too much time dancing to the tune of Iolanthe MacLeod."

"But, my laird," one daring soul interrupted, "she was mistress of the keep until just a short time ago . . ."

Connor looked at him. It wasn't a particularly unpleasant look, he knew that, but it was intended to promise things the man wouldn't want to experience if he continued to babble on.

The man shut his mouth abruptly and slunk behind several wiser, more silent souls.

"Perhaps she did have a claim to this place," Connor said, "but she left it behind and now 'tis mine. Unfortunately, before she left, she made women of you all. When you've learned to act like men again, then you can combine mischief alongside me. Until then, the haunting is mine."

The men slunk away, their consciences obviously shaming them into silence.

He turned only to find that ridiculously dressed woman, Roderick St. Claire, standing next to him, a look of amusement on his face. Connor scowled and put his hand to his sword. Roderick held up his hands in surrender.

"Do not stab me," he said, still smiling. "I'm just admiring your technique. I wish I had your commanding presence."

"No doubt you do."

Roderick walked with him toward the front gates. "Who do you think this is? V. McKinnon?"

"I can only hope," Connor said with a yawn. "I'm in sore need of decent sport."

"You mean to do this new McKinnon lad a serious injury, do you?"

" 'Tis a fair repayment for Thomas's irritation," Connor said.

"I suppose," Roderick said slowly. "But he's gone now and the keep is yours. Why torment any of his hapless relations?"

"I wish none of them to have the idea that they would be welcome here," Connor growled. "Damnable place that it is, 'twould be far worse with pesky, interfering McKinnon mortals loitering about."

"Hmmm," Roderick said thoughtfully, "I suppose. But it is entirely possible that this new McKinnon relative might be to your liking."

Connor found that not even worthy of discussion. Of course, this new lad wouldn't be acceptable. He was a McKinnon. Connor suspected that he wouldn't even care for a MacDougal.

Connor turned away from the gate. What he needed was the proper location for a good scare. He paused in the bailey and looked about him. There were many places that vied for his attention, but in the end he decided upon the great hall. It was full of old, rotting furniture and several overturned stones. All quite useful in truly making a mortal uncomfortable as he endeavored to flee for safer ground.

"My laird," one of the garrison lads said breathlessly, running up to Connor. "The mortal comes!"

Connor rubbed his hands together expectantly. "I will await him in the hall. Keep the other lads *out* of the hall and out of sight. I prefer the screams of terror to be thanks to me alone."

The man nodded nervously, then bolted for parts unknown.

Connor looked at Roderick. "Have you stomach for this deed?"

"I'm honored to be included in the scheme."

Connor looked at him to see if he jested or not, but could tell nothing from Roderick's expression. Indeed, it was hard to tell anything at all about him. Roderick was completely out of Connor's experience. He'd known no one in his time who would have permitted himself to be bedecked in the frilly bits that Roderick seemed to enjoy so greatly. But despite his obsession with lace, Roderick did occasionally manage to poke the stray, senseless guardsmen with his sword, and where sword skill seemed to fail him, he could produce words that cut as easily.

But now was not the time for cruel words; now was the time for a well-earned bit of revenge and that was Connor's specialty.

He strode forward, entered the great hall, and looked about in satisfaction. A goodly bit of light there, ample to reveal him in all his glory when the time came.

He frowned up at the sky, sky he could see thanks to the lack of roof. He snorted in disgust. Thomas McKinnon had promised to put a top on the bloody great hall, but damn him if he hadn't been so distracted by wooing a certain wench that he'd apparently forgotten all about it.

Yet another reason to be irritated with that entire family.

And yet another reason to hope that the lad coming up the way was indeed of the McKinnon clan.

Connor paced restlessly about, studying the nooks and crannies of the hall, trying to decide where the best spot might lie. Indeed, he placed himself in several locations and leaped out experimentally.

He decided finally upon the dais at the back of the hall where Thorpewold's original lord had no doubt sat on many occasions to dine on fine victuals. Connor went to stand on that raised bit of floor with his back to the hall door—or what had at one time been the hall door. He would remain invisible until the proper moment, then turn around and leap with his fiercest battle cry. He bounced on the balls of his feet a time or two, preparing for what he was certain would be one of the more rewarding moments of his afterlife.

Would the lad coming up the way scream in terror and faint? Would he dash his head against a rock and bleed to death slowly? Would he turn and flee, his womanly screams floating pleasingly in the air behind him? The possibilities were tremendously appealing to contemplate.

"I think I hear footsteps approaching," Roderick said from where he sat on a rock that marked the place where the high table had once stood.

Connor flexed his fingers in anticipation.

"I see a shadow," Roderick whispered.

Connor stretched his arms over his head a time or two, preparing to draw the mighty sword strapped to his back. There was, he had to admit modestly, nothing quite like the sight of him, standing at a handful of inches over six feet, clutching his sword, also a bit over six feet, and both of them with death on their minds.

He'd witnessed his share of men soiling their plaids and fainting before he could hack off their heads. He'd never cared overmuch for that reaction, truth be told. What sport was there in a clean swipe of the blade without a bit of screaming involved beforehand? So unsatisfying.

He put his hands behind his head and grasped the sword hilt. He took a deep breath, closed his eyes briefly to still his racing heart, then drew his sword . . .

Or he would have, if Roderick's gasp hadn't distracted him so thoroughly.

"Damn you," Connor said with a growl. "You interrupted the drawing of my sword!"

Roderick seemed incapable of speech. He was staring in astonishment at something behind Connor.

Connor mulled that over for a bit. Perhaps the McKinnon lad was large and fierce, possessing more daring than Connor had dared hope. It was possible that there might be a battle where mettle and courage might truly be put to the test. It had been so long since Connor had actually had to exert himself to preserve his honor and his life, he half wondered if he might have forgotten some of the particulars associated with a good brawl.

Or perhaps Roderick gaped for another reason, another more disagreeable reason. Was the McKinnon lad so feeble that he inspired that reaction in whomever saw him? Was he a mealy-mouthed, milquetoasted girl of a man who couldn't withstand the faintest bit of adversity before becoming senseless?

Connor decided he preferred the former. Let the McKinnon be strong of arm and willing to fight to the death. It would make the screams so much more rewarding.

Connor drew his sword with relish, then spun around, ready to bellow his war cry and make himself visible to the accompaniment of McKinnonly shrieks of terror.

Only the body standing there wasn't a lad.

He was a lass.

And a beautiful one at that.

Connor was so surprised, he hardly knew what to think. His sword, however, seemed to suffer from no such indecisiveness. It continued in its downward arc, pulling Connor with it. He stepped forward to correct his balance, only to realize that he had forgotten about the raised dais. He stepped off the edge, hard, and stumbled. His sword continued forward. Connor found himself with no choice but to follow it.

His sword landed on the dirt with a thud.

Connor went down to his knees.

He opened his mouth to complain about the indignity of it all, then made the enormous mistake of staring at the woman again.

And he realized, with a start, that he couldn't frighten this ethereal creature if his life depended upon it.

Damn it anyway.

It wasn't that he didn't want to. He would have given his right arm to have popped off his own head, tucked it under his arm for a good throaty scream or two, or used it to adorn the tip of his sword and then wave it about to induce a suitable swoon. Even a gasp of surprise or a hand set to fluttering about the throat would have been satisfactory, and that he could have induced with just a frown.

But he couldn't.

He remained on his knees where he'd fallen and gaped at the apparition who had come into his great hall as confidently as if she owned the place.

By the saints, she was a beauty.

And he was notoriously picky about his beauties.

He stared at her in wonder. He had expected a McKinnon lad; he had gotten an angel. Obviously, there had been a terrible mistake. This wench was surely no McKinnon. He was quite sure there had never been a McKinnon spawned who was this fair.

Her hair was a riot of curls, falling down her back in a cascade that rivaled the falls near his home. It was the color of flame, but darker, as if evening firelight had been captured and given to her for her use alone. Her face was flawless, her skin porcelain, her features straight from his most memorable dream.

He knelt there, not twenty paces from her, completely invisible to her, and wondered why it had taken eight hundred years into his afterlife for him to find a woman who rendered him speechless.

Astonishing.

The woman moved confidently about the great hall, leaving him unable to do anything but stare after her in admiration. He would have leaned on his sword, but it was too tall and already unusably flat on the ground, so he contented himself with sitting back on his heels, where he wouldn't find himself flat on the ground.

Who was this wench?

By the saints, a single moment, a heartbeat snatched from eternity had changed him forever. He could hardly believe the change in himself, but when he tested his resolve, it remained steady and firm.

He was tempted to show himself to her, but quickly decided that he wouldn't. Not yet.

Lest she find him lacking . . .

"Victoria! Victoria McKinnon!"

The woman turned. "What?"

Connor felt himself start to list to the left. It was only his quick hands that saved him from keeling over completely.

Victoria McKinnon?

McKinnon?

The man who had been in the keep several days earlier, the capering one, came into the great hall and stopped. He smiled.

"What do you think?" he asked. "Your brother didn't exaggerate, did he?"

"I think I might actually have to call Thomas and be nice to him," Victoria McKinnon said. "It's amazing . . ."

Connor could scarce believe his ears. Thomas? Her brother? Nay, 'twas not possible! A woman this beautiful, sprung from that line? It could not be so!

But what else was he to believe? How many men named Thomas McKinnon claimed to own Thorpewold Castle? How many women named Victoria McKinnon had brothers named Thomas? He shook his head in stunned and quite unpleasant consternation. Vee McKinnon was obviously a shortened name for Victoria McKinnon.

Thomas McKinnon's sister.

"Well," Roderick drawled from behind him, "now you know who she is, aren't you going to do her in?"

Connor pushed himself upright, grasped his sword, then turned slightly and flung the blade into Roderick's chest with all his strength. The shade fell backward with a gurgle.

"You've got to come now," the man said to Victoria.

"But I'm not finished," she protested.

"Be finished."

To her credit, Victoria McKinnon gave her keeper a look that would have made many a man back up a pace and shut his mouth. But apparently the man who capered about when others weren't looking was made of sterner stuff than one might think.

"There's a situation down at the inn," the man said.

Victoria McKinnon rolled her eyes, grumbled, then tromped off with the man out of the great hall.

Connor heaved himself to his feet and followed the pair unsteadily to the door of the ruined keep. He put his hand on the crumbling rock and watched as the kin of his enemy walked away, none the wiser about the terrorizing she had just avoided.

"My laird?"

"Aye?" Connor wheezed.

"My laird, what will you have us do?"

Connor watched Victoria McKinnon walk down the path and through the barbican. He found he couldn't move, couldn't speak, and couldn't look away.

"My laird?"

Connor marshalled his steely self-control and turned to face the men suddenly gathered behind him. "I'm working out a proper haunting," he managed.

Many there scratched their heads.

Connor frowned fiercely, apparently fiercely enough that his men found it intimidating, for they backed away respectfully.

"This haunting will take a bit of time to do properly."

Roderick gurgled loudly from the back of the hall.

The men dispersed, leaving Connor alone with his thoughts.

Well, his thoughts and Roderick's complaints.

Connor walked out into the bailey and stared off down the path to the road.

A McKinnon wench.

He should have known.

He got hold of himself and his ridiculous thoughts. He'd been dazzled by her beauty, but now he knew better. She would be easy to frighten into never again returning to the keep. Indeed, ideas on how to terrify her were already clamoring to present themselves to him. All he had to do was sit back and choose the one which would be the most effective.

Aye, he would frighten her and rid his hall of her. He would do it and have not one regret—no matter her beauty, or how the mere sight of her caused something inside him to sigh . . . in relief, or terror; he could not say.

He turned and strode back into the great hall. He wrenched his sword from Roderick's chest, with the appropriate comment on the fop's frailties, then resheathed his sword with a mighty thrust and set his heart aright inside him.

Aye, he would do her in and be glad of it.

In spite of her beauty and because of her parentage.

Chapter 5

V ictoria walked swiftly down the little road that led away from the castle. This wasn't what she wanted to be doing. What she wanted to be doing was standing in that great hall again with the sun streaming down inside and that feeling of medievalness washing over her. "This had better be good," she warned Fred.

"It is."

"Don't tell me: more ghosts."

"No, Michael Fellini, irritated by his accommodations."

"Oh," Victoria said breathlessly. She said it breathlessly because she had now increased her walking to a flat-out sprint. The last thing she wanted was to have the star of her show in a snit because he didn't care for the wallpaper.

By the time she reached the front door of the inn, she was gasping for breath. She was going to have to get more exercise, or join a gym, or something. Apparently the occasional sprint for the subway just wasn't doing it for her.

"Fellini's whining loudly," Fred noted. "Can't you hear it?"

Victoria decided that more breath-catching could happen later. Right now she had to stop hell before it broke completely loose.

She threw open the door to the inn and strode inside in her best director fashion. Then she came to a teetering halt, confronted by things she hadn't seen coming.

Well, some of it she should have seen coming. Michael stood there wearing his most formidable give-me-what-I-want-or-I'll-call-my-agent expression. Cressida Blankenship, her star actress, stood there, a single tear trailing artistically down her cheek as she contemplated the key to what was no doubt an equally inadequate room. Mrs. Pruitt was scowling fiercely at the both of them.

But what she hadn't expected was to find the geriatric jet-setter who stood to one side, surrounded by piles of designer luggage and carrying over her arm a clear plastic knitting bag full of funky colors and several pairs of knitting needles in materials ranging from steel to rosewood. Victoria recognized the needles—and the woman toting them—only because that woman was her grandmother.

"Granny!" Victoria said weakly, "what are you doing here?"

"She's waiting in line for me to get my room changed," Michael said loudly.

Victoria found her gaze helplessly drawn to him as if he'd been a vampire mesmerizing her with a presence that could not be ignored. She felt a little breathless.

Of course, that could have come from her recent bout of sprinting, but then again, maybe not.

Michael Fellini was, put simply, perfection. His dark hair was just a little on the long side, swept rakishly across his forehead in perfection rarely achieved outside of the salon. His face was perfectly chiseled, his eyes a deep, chocolate brown, his mouth sensual and mobile. And that was only the beginning; the rest of him was just as divine.

He was an inch or two under six feet and slender, but somehow that worked to produce a wiry, powerful frame that just begged to be set on stage and admired for lengthy periods of time. He could, by turns, appear kingly, peasantly, crazy, and commanding.

And that was just what she'd seen at the afternoon tea.

She had the feeling she might just see the range of his emotions if something didn't happen soon. But it was difficult to concentrate fully on Michael because Cressida had begun to make such a loud, weepy fuss over her room and Mrs. Pruitt had become disgusted enough to begin doing her best to shout her down. Granny simply stood there, smiling in sympathy.

Victoria took a deep breath to prepare to straighten everything out when she was distracted by a scream that cut through all the noise like a knife. Mrs. Pruitt, Cressida, and even Michael fell silent.

The screaming continued.

"Gerard," Fred said wearily from behind her.

Victoria had no trouble imagining just what—or who— had wrung such a noise from him. She swept the collection of troublemakers before her with a single warning glance.

"No more fighting. Cressida, take my room," she said shortly. "Mrs. Pruitt, give Michael whatever he wants. Granny, I'm sure Mrs. Pruitt has a very nice room—maybe Megan's—that you can have. I'll be right back."

And with that, she turned and ran back through the front door, through the garden, and around to the back of the house where a shed lingered on the edge of Mrs. Pruitt's vegetable patch.

She wasn't at all surprised by what she saw.

Gerard was clutching the door frame and screaming his bloody head off. Victoria was tempted to plug her ears, but before she could do it, the squeals of terror reached a pinnacle of shrillness, then suddenly ceased. Gerard slumped to the ground, senseless.

Victoria strode forward, stepped over the body, and looked into the shed.

Hugh McKinnon stood there, fondling finery.

He smiled sheepishly, doffed his cap and made her a low bow, then disappeared.

"What do you think he saw?" Fred asked from behind her.

"A hallucination," Victoria said firmly.

"Hmmm," Fred said doubtfully.

She sighed and turned to look down at her unconscious prop manager. "I don't suppose we can just leave him here and hope for the best."

"I'll wake him up." Fred leaned over and slapped Gerard smartly across the face.

"Fred," Victoria started to exclaim, but she forwent any more lecture because at that moment Gerard sat up—silently. It was such an improvement, she couldn't help but smile. "Gerard, how are you?"

Gerard looked around himself wildly, then leaped to his feet. "It's haunted," he said hoarsely. "The costumes, the inn, the whole damned island!"

"Gerard," Victoria said, not having to try overly hard to put a little shock in her tone, "you're imagining things. Why don't you go have a little rest and then we'll talk . . ."

He shrieked once more, then turned and ran away.

Victoria tried to grab him, but she wound up clutching air. She looked at Fred and the horror was real this time.

"What are we going to do?" she asked.

He shrugged. "Hope nothing tears?"

Victoria was half tempted to track down Hugh McKinnon and ask him if he knew how to ply a needle, given that it was his fault she was in this fix, but she had the feeling he wouldn't make a very good prop manager. For one thing, he would likely spend all his time stroking the costumes and no time making sure that they were ready to wear.

She gritted her teeth. "I'll deal with this later."

"I won't be volunteering later."

"I didn't imagine you would be." She trudged back through the garden to the front door. "Please let this be the extent of the disasters," she muttered as she went back inside the inn.

Well, the entryway was empty—a big plus—except for Mrs. Pruitt, who was standing at attention by her reception desk.

"His Majesty wants his bags brought up," she said in a voice that clearly implied she was not going to be the one doing it.

Victoria looked behind her only to find that Fred had conveniently managed to lose himself between the garden and the front door. She sighed and picked up one of Michael's suitcases. Or tried, rather. What was he toting in there, thousand-page tomes on every aspect of Shakespeare he might possibly need in an emergency?

It took quite a while to get the one suitcase up the stairs. She struggled to haul it down the hallway, realizing too late that the path wasn't clear. She went sprawling, narrowly avoiding being crushed by Michael's gear, only to further realize that it was her stuff she had tripped over.

She crawled to her feet, swore, then channeled her irritation into dragging Michael's suitcase to the end of the hall. She knocked. It took a very long time for the door to open, but when it did she found herself rendered speechless—and not just by Michael and his intensely attractive self.

The room looked as if it belonged behind ropes. It was something straight out of an Elizabethan movie set, only this stuff was authentic. No wonder Mrs. Pruitt guarded the key so ferociously. Victoria suspected the room should have been guarded by National Trust employees with stun guns.

"Michael . . ." she began.

He grabbed his suitcase, dragged it inside, and shut the door in her face.

Victoria stared at the door for a minute or two before she shut her mouth. Well, jet lag could make even the most rational, polite soul turn a little feisty. Michael was obviously suffering from a difficult case of it.

Surely.

She gathered up her stuff that was strewn all over the floor, shoved it into the handy suitcase that had been tossed into the hall as well, then propped the whole mess up against one wall. She would sort it all out later. For now, she had to find her granny, find her granny a room, and figure out what to do with her granny who was currently hundreds of miles away from where she should have been.

She thumped down the stairs and came to a teetering halt in the entryway. Raucous laughter came from the sitting room on her left. Her grandmother was definitely one of the revelers. It was with no small bit of trepidation that Victoria approached and threw open the door.

She was somehow unsurprised by the sight that greeted her. There, sitting around the coffee table and chatting as if they'd known each other for years, were Ambrose, Fulbert, Hugh, and, of course, her grandmother. Hugh was looking a little out of breath—probably from his quick dash back from the costume shed. Victoria frowned at him briefly before turning back to her grandmother.

"Granny—"

"Vikki," her granny said, rising and coming to envelope Victoria in a hug and a cloud of Wind Song. "You look tired, dear. Come and sit with us. We're just catching up."

"Catching up?" Victoria wheezed. "Do you know these three?"

"We just met," Mary MacLeod Davidson said, "but you know how it is with family. It doesn't take long to feel as if you've known each other for years."

Really, could the day deliver any more surprises? Victoria felt her control begin to slip through her fingers at an alarming rate.

"Granny, what are you doing here?"

"I'm here to save the day, love. Your mother was worried about you and since I'd had a spat with my Stitch 'n Wench knitting group—you know that Fiona McDonald and how she just can't wean herself from man-made fibers—I decided that maybe a bit of traveling was just the thing. I don't know if there's room enough for me here, though."

"Our good Mrs. Pruitt will sort it all out," Ambrose said reassuringly. He stood. "But perhaps for now, you might wish for a walk up to the castle?"

"Why, Laird MacLeod," Mary said with a flirtatious smile, "what a wonderful idea."

"Granny," Victoria said weakly, "you're related to him!"

"*Several* generations removed, my dear." Mary patted her hair and smiled. "A handsome Highland lad is always a pleasure to engage, no matter the degrees of separation." Mary smiled at Ambrose. "We'll join you in a moment."

Ambrose, Hugh, and Fulbert all made low bows, gave vent to a handful of appropriate leave-taking sentiments, then tromped out of the sitting room as the crow flew.

That would be through the wall, not the door.

Victoria looked at her granny. "I need a drink."

"But you don't drink, love. Come on. I'm anxious to see this castle of yours."

Well, in this, at least, Victoria found that she had no trouble mustering up enthusiasm. She followed her grandmother from the sitting room through the usual exit of the door.

"Tell me what's been going on," Mary said, drawing Victoria's hand through the crook of her arm as they left the inn and wandered through the garden. "What was all that screaming about?"

"Gerard saw a ghost."

Mary laughed. "Here? How unusual."

"Granny, it isn't funny," Victoria said, but she had to laugh a little herself. "I had to pay him extra to get him to England in the first place because he saw Hugh McKinnon groping my costumes in the prop room under Tempest in a Teapot. The same thing just happened in the garden shed here."

"Never mind, dear. I'll keep your costumes in line."

Victoria wanted to protest; she knew she should protest, but she couldn't. Mary MacLeod Davidson was possibly the most delightful woman on earth and while Victoria didn't have any trouble refusing an invitation to spend time with her brother—her recent trip to Maine aside—she never passed up an opportunity to spend time with her grandmother.

Besides, her granny had once upon a time sewn marvelous costumes for her and her siblings as they were growing up and flexing the muscles of their imaginations. Victoria suspected that those costumes had been the beginning of her desire to do what she did.

"All right," Victoria conceded, "but only if you'll limit yourself to a supervisory role. Maybe Mrs. Pruitt can round up some seamstresses for us."

"I'm sure she'll help," Mary said. "She's a lovely woman, if not a little preoccupied with the paranormal."

Victoria didn't bother asking how her grandmother had found that out so quickly. Secrets did not last long around her. "Can you blame her?"

Mary looked briefly over her shoulder. "Given our escorts, I suppose not. Who knows what we'll find at the castle?"

Victoria was unsurprised to see her grandfathers and sundry strolling along behind them. She looked back at her grandmother. "I was there earlier and I didn't see anything unusual."

Then again, she hadn't been at the castle but five minutes, so perhaps that wasn't a true test.

The whole situation was unsettling. It wasn't like her not to be in full command of her surroundings and everything happening in those surroundings.

Then again, she wasn't usually dealing with ghosts.

Non-Shakespearean ones, that was.

Well, at least the hauntings were limited to old men loitering the inn's kitchen. Heaven help her if the infection spread to the castle.

How would you like to put on your next play in my castle next spring? And by the way, what play are you doing?

Hamlet.

Perfect.

Her conversation with her brother last December came back to her like a bad smell. Hamlet had a ghost in it, didn't it? Was that why Thomas had been so thrilled?

She felt her eyes narrow. Thomas knew something. She

wasn't precisely sure how much he knew, but she knew he knew something. She would get him for this, purse strings or no purse strings.

"I'm going to kill Thomas," Victoria announced.

"How nice," Mary said. "Oh, look, there's the main road. Which way do we go from here?"

Victoria opened her mouth to say, then found that her input was not necessary.

"This way, dear lady," Ambrose said, striding up to Mary's side and giving her a gallant smile. "Allow me to escort you."

"And me, as well," Hugh said enthusiastically, popping up on Victoria's left. " 'Tis a dangerous world these days. Two lovely wenches such as yerselves shouldn't be out without protection."

"Wenches," Mary repeated, beaming at Hugh. "I like that. It makes me feel quite adventuresome."

"Heaven help us," Victoria muttered. Her grandmother was seventy-five but she didn't look a day over fifty and her opinion on what constituted a good adventure was something Victoria didn't want to contemplate. She'd been convinced her granny was satisfied pitting her skills against complicated Fair Isle patterns.

She should have known better.

Grumbling began behind her. That she knew it was Fulbert tromping along behind them and not some other grump of indeterminate age and life situation . . . well, it said a lot about the current state of affairs in her life.

Her granny came to a sudden stop. "Oh, my goodness," she said, her hand over her heart. "Why, Victoria, this is spectacular."

Victoria looked at the castle and couldn't help but smile. "It is amazing, isn't it?"

Mary nodded, then began to walk again, slowly. Victoria walked with her, admiring Thomas's castle afresh. It was a pretty remarkable place, even though half of it had been eaten away by the ravages of time. The walls were crumbling, but it wasn't hard to imagine them being manned in another time by fierce knights eager to do their lord's will. It also wasn't hard to imagine the sound of hammer on anvil, of peasants conversing, of men-at-arms cursing and shouting as they trained.

Victoria frowned. She was imagining those things, wasn't she? She shot Ambrose a look. He was watching her thoughtfully.

"Aye, granddaughter?" he said.

"Do you hear it?" she asked. "That medieval stuff?"

Ambrose listened, then smiled. "I hear many things, lass. Come and let us be about your inspection. I imagine the construction has begun. I can hear the generators from here. I assume you'll run them from one of the tower chambers during the shows."

"Yes," Victoria said, distracted by the sounds layering themselves on top of each other. "I don't think the audience will hear them and there's certainly no other way to get power inside the castle without them. Granny, do you hear those medieval sorts of noises?"

Mary patted her hand. "Inspect your workers, love, then we'll go back to the inn and you can have a nap."

She didn't need a nap; she needed a specter-free castle in which to do her play. She walked into the bailey and looked at the place where the stage would be built. Workers were setting up their gear and the area seemed to be quite free of all paranormal activity.

She couldn't help breathe a faint sigh of relief.

"They've worked hard," Victoria said, gratefully.

"Like as not, they have cause," Fulbert said. "I wouldn't want to stay here longer than I needed to."

"Why not?" she asked.

Ambrose cleared his throat. "Well, there are a few unsavory lads loitering about the keep. *Those* kind of lads," he added knowingly.

Damn. So, her worst fears were going to materialize. "Ghosts?" Victoria asked.

"Aye, but no one of consequence," Ambrose said. "Certainly no one whom I would give a second thought to—"

"Aye, but your head might, as it left your womanly shoulders," a voice growled from behind Victoria. "Draw your sword, MacLeod!"

Victoria whirled around.

That unsettling prop-room numbness started again at the top of her head, but she clamped down on her self-control with all her strength and gave that tingling the old heave-ho. She would *not* faint. There were probably several things one could say about her that might be uncomplimentary, but it could not be said that she had ever swooned. Not once.

Well, that prop room debacle aside, of course.

Oh, and also the first time she'd seen Michael Fellini, but there had been a handy couch nearby and she'd managed to fall gracefully upon it in a lounging posture. That had been less of a swoon and more of a dignified slump.

But this time she wasn't sure she would manage anything so dignified. First off, there was no couch nearby. Secondly, this wasn't a sleek, suave New Yorker wowing her with his good looks and easy charm. This was a Highlander standing not two feet from her, his enormous sword in his hands, and a look of death in his eyes.

"Let's move out of the way, shall we?" Mary said easily, taking Victoria by the arm and tugging.

Victoria backpeddled until she was well out of the way of that very large sword. She came to a stop next to her grandmother, wishing desperately that she'd brought along a chair so she could sit while she grappled with the reality she was facing.

She was used to handsome men on stage, but they were generally not very tall and more of their muscles came from dance than hefting very big swords and swinging them around like thin, lightweight rapiers. She was also used to powerful men whose money she had no trouble trying to solicit for her productions, but their power came from their bank accounts and their ability to control destinies with those bank accounts.

She was not used to men who intimidated by their mere physical presence alone.

She was tall, but that ghost towered over her. He towered over Ambrose, as well. She frowned. That didn't seem quite fair. Who did he think he was, going after her grandfather—the accustomed number of generations removed—with such lack of care for Ambrose's age or the measure of respect that should have been accorded him due to that age?

"That's Connor MacDougal," Fulbert said from beside her. "He was laird of his clan in life. He thinks he's laird of this castle in death—"

"I *am* laird of this keep," Connor MacDougal snarled, "and I'll thank ye to keep yer bloody English nose out of my affairs!"

Fulbert grunted. "He's a miserable wretch, as you can hear, but handy enough with a blade."

"And I'll show you just how handy, once I'm finished with this mewling babe here," Connor promised.

Victoria watched, open-mouthed, as he attempted to do just that.

She took stock of her rapidly unraveling situation. She had ghosts down at the inn. She now had ghosts up at the castle. Apparently, she had a very feisty, very fierce, *very* handsome lairdlike ghost who would probably take every opportunity to make her life hell. He would probably also scare away the paying customers. It was for certain he would terrify her actors if they could see him.

Well, she conceded, he might not terrify the women. If he would just put down that sword and smile, he might actually bring in some business.

"He's quite handsome, isn't he?" Mary whispered.

Victoria managed a nod. *Handsome* really didn't quite cover it. Gorgeous, dangerous, breathtaking, partake-at-your-own-risk; those were better descriptions of the man.

Er, ghost.

Victoria could hardly believe he wasn't real. He had dark hair that hung down to his shoulders and moved with him when he wielded that enormous broadsword. His muscles strained under his shirt and could occasionally be glimpsed doing the same thing under his kilt.

His face, too, was a marvel of creation. Chiseled cheekbones, a patrician nose, a strong, determined jaw. Victoria had no idea what color his eyes were, but she could say that they blazed with an intensity that made her feel a little weak in the knees.

If she'd been prone to that kind of thing, which she wasn't.

He carried on an animated conversation with Ambrose in what she could only assume was Gaelic. He did not smile, but that didn't matter. His sword was enormous, but that didn't matter, either. There was something about him that was so relentlessly commanding, so unforgiving, so ruthless, that she could only stand and gape at him as if she'd never seen a man before.

Which, after seeing this one, she had to suspect might be the case.

A vicious thrust made Ambrose suddenly jump aside and that startled her into jumping as well.

"Vikki, look at your crew," Mary said in a low voice.

Victoria collected what was remaining of her wits and turned to find all her workers staring at her uncomfortably. Well, some were staring at her uncomfortably. Others were counting it as a break and apparently looking for either drinks or somewhere to pee.

"Can they hear this, do you think?" Victoria whispered behind her hand.

"I don't know, but I don't think we want to find out."

Victoria made a snap decision. It was of paramount importance that her crew not pull a Gerard and bolt for the front gates, never to return. Obviously, she would have to take matters into her own hands.

She turned quickly to her workers. "Nothing to see here," she said in her best director's voice. "There is a rehearsal going on outside the gates. Swords and that kind of thing. It's echoing in here."

Those who were not searching for drinks or the bathroom shrugged and turned back to their work.

Victoria turned back to the combatants and clapped her hands together briskly. "All right," she said, "let's be finished here."

Connor MacDougal almost dropped his sword. Unfortunately, he managed to hold onto it long enough to point it at her.

"And who are *you* to tell me what to do?" he demanded fiercely.

"You're frightening my workers."

He jammed his sword into the dirt and strode over to stand toe-to-toe with her. "I haven't begun to frighten them," he growled.

"Who said you could?" she returned.

"*I* am lord of this keep and I will say what goes on inside it!"

She forced herself not to gulp. She was fairly certain that his sword was fake and that his only weapon was verbal intimidation.

Heaven help her if she was wrong.

"You can say all you want," she said, dredging up all the courage she had to hand. "Just don't say it to my crew."

"And if it pleases me to hear them scream?" he asked smoothly.

"I'll alert the paranormal investigators to your presence," she threatened.

"Ha!" he said with a derisive snort. "I've no fear of them."

"I'd rethink that, MacDougal," Ambrose said with a shiver. "The last thing you want is a gaggle of ghosthunters keeping you awake at all hours."

Connor appeared unconvinced and continued to look as if his fondest wish was to do someone in.

Victoria thought quickly. She was accustomed to dealing with men for whom money talked. Could it be all that different with a ghost? All she had to do was determine what his currency was. She suspected he dealt in screams.

"I'll make a deal with you," she said. "If you leave my crew alone, I promise to let you haunt me for the same number of days we're here in your castle."

He paused and considered.

"*After* the play is over," she qualified. "And it will be worth the wait, I assure you."

"Show me."

Victoria let out a bloodcurdling scream. Hugh and Fulbert hit the ground. Half her workers screamed in sympathy. She looked up at Connor and raised one eyebrow.

"Well?"

"I'll give it some thought."

"No, I need a firm commitment."

"I am accustomed to screams from more than one person," he said with a frown. "Not to belittle your skill with a shriek, of course."

Good grief, would the indignities never end? She sighed gustily. "All right, how about we sweeten the deal. Leave my workers and my actors alone and not only will I let you haunt me for an equal amount of time, I'll see if I can't find a place in my play for you."

Hugh and Fulbert protested vociferously. Victoria silenced them with a glare. She turned back to Connor. He was blinking as if he hadn't quite understood her. Maybe he was surprised. Maybe he was insulted. Maybe she'd had so little experience in dealing with disembodied spirits that she was mistaking his reaction for what was really just a bit of ghostly indigestion.

Connor retrieved his sword and sheathed it thoughtfully. "A place in your play? As a player?"

She could hardly believe she was doing it. "Yes," she said heavily. "I'll get back to you on what role."

"I will give it some—"

"No," she said shortly, "I need a commitment and I need it now." She sighed in frustration. "Look, I'm sure that with a face like yours, you're accustomed to getting what you want—"

"A face like mine?" he interrupted. "What meaning is there in that?"

She frowned up at him. "Well, you're very handsome, but that doesn't mean you can always have what you want."

He blinked. "Handsome?"

"Yes, and handsome is as handsome does, so commit to behaving yourself."

"Handsome?" he repeated, blinking some more.

"Commit!" she exclaimed. "Don't scare my crew. Don't terrify the actors."

"Handsome," he mused, stroking his chin.

He turned and walked through the gates.

He vanished.

Victoria turned to look at her granny. "Can you believe him?"

Her grandmother said with a laugh, "I think you distracted him. My, my, Vikki, that was a big scream."

"He had a big sword."

"And he knows how to use it," Ambrose admitted. "He's unpleasant, unfriendly, and unabashedly angry."

"He sounds like trouble," Mary said happily.

"He could be," Ambrose agreed. " 'Tis a pity Victoria doesn't have a part for him in truth. Of course," he said, resheathing his own sword and smoothing down his plaid, "he hasn't my gift for drama. If you need an understudy for any of the roles, my dear Victoria, I hope you'll consider me. For Hamlet's father, perhaps. I think I could do that justice."

"I'm certain you could," Victoria said. "Though I think it might be beneath you. If you have time, you could look at Hamlet's uncle, or Polonius. You know, the more substantial roles."

"I'll make a search for a script."

And with that, he was gone.

Mary looked at her, her eyes twinkling. "You're good."

"Years of practice."

"Are you really going to give them parts in your play?"

"Granny, to keep the peace, I'd almost be tempted to let them *direct* the play."

"That handsome young Highlander is a different sort of problem," Mary said, "but that is the kind of problem a woman could look at happily for quite some time."

Victoria shivered in spite of herself. "Yes, he is."

Mary gave her a quick hug. "I'm going to head for the inn. Be careful."

"Granny, he's a ghost."

"He's a *big* ghost."

"I cannot believe we're having this conversation."

Her grandmother laughed and walked through the barbican gate. Hugh and Fulbert bid Victoria a good day and followed her. Ambrose reappeared and jostled his companions for the preferred spot on Mary's right hand. Victoria watched them go.

Life was weird.

She turned around and looked at the castle. So, it was haunted. She shouldn't have been surprised. She highly doubted Thomas would be surprised by the news. She would kill him at her earliest opportunity. For now, she just had to get through the next four weeks. After all, how much more annoying could ghosts be than venture capitalists? Her actors had survived the latter; they could survive the former.

Then again, venture capitalists didn't pack six-foot broadswords they were wont to draw at the slightest opportunity and use on whomever had displeased them. Who knew if she would be able to keep that damned Connor MacDougal and his very big sword out of the way—despite her appeasement offers?

She didn't want to contemplate the alternatives if she couldn't.

Chapter 6

Michael Fellini stood in the middle of a medieval castle and fought to keep the smile off his face. So it had been a miracle to score the gig at Juilliard. This promised to be a thousand times better—if he could just arrange things to suit himself. At least General McKinnon was gone for the day—probably back to the inn to lie in wait for him. Well, she would just have to be disappointed a little longer. He had business here.

He folded his arms over his chest and took a moment to relish the feeling of being in the director's spot. It wasn't that he didn't like to act. The applause, the accolades, the fawning—it was all highly enjoyable and unquestionably merited. But to act meant to be at the mercy of a director who, for whatever reason, always seemed to think he was in charge.

Michael didn't like others to be in charge.

He wanted to be in charge himself.

The university setting was fine as well, he supposed, if one had the temperament for it. He'd enjoyed possessing the power to ruin careers and destroy egos. In fact, he did as much of that as possible, but unfortunately, there was so little notoriety in it.

He began to pace. Broadway was another option for him, but he knew that even had he landed a plum role there, he would have been a large fish in a rather larger pond. And still taking orders from someone else.

Of course, he could have taken the plunge and gone off on his own, but that would have required taking risks, temporarily lowering his standard of living, and quite possibly losing tables at the best restaurants he'd learned to call his own. No, far better to simply stride right into a ready-made situation.

Such as this present situation.

He looked around. He spread his arms out wide just because he could. Here, yes, *here*, he could be the king of his own castle. Shakespeare had had the Globe; Fellini would have Thorpewold.

He paused and frowned in his most thoughtful manner. Thorpewold . . .

Yes, that would definitely have to go. When he was lord of the manor, he would choose a different name.

Of course, getting the castle away from Victoria's brother was going to be tricky, but Michael wasn't going to worry about it. That's what his barracuda agent was for. He would concentrate on his art.

And the first item of business in working on that art was getting control of his current production. It would be, he thought smugly, a piece of cake. Victoria was too starstruck to do anything but give him what he wanted. And once he took over the production and turned it into the fabulous masterwork he knew it would be, Thomas McKinnon would see that his sister was not only starstruck, she was a lousy director. He would gladly accept Michael's offer to take over the castle and make it into a money-making proposition.

It beat the hell out of listening to drama students butcher soliloquies all day long.

A breath of cold air blew suddenly down his neck.

Michael whirled around in surprise but saw nothing.

Was the bloody place haunted?

He lifted one eyebrow and contemplated that. It could work in his favor, of course.

Then again, it could continue to give him the willies as it was presently doing. He shivered, shook off the feeling of unease, then strode toward the gates, doing his best not to break into a run.

The feeling of being watched subsided once he walked through the gates. Fortunately. He didn't really go in for creepy. Once the castle was his, he would call in the exterminators.

Of course, that would require funds and he was somehow perennially short of those. He walked down the path and considered what might be the best way to start his nest egg. Selling off a few antiques from his room down at the inn? The furniture was too big to lift, of course, but there were several other things that would fit quite nicely into his suitcase.

He paused and looked back at the castle. He couldn't help a smile of triumph. He tossed his script up into the air in a joyous celebration of his own splendidness, then continued down the path to the road.

It was going to be a fabulous summer.

He could just feel it.

Chapter 7

C onnor stood at the end of the path leading up to the inn and wondered if he had lost his mind. There he was, on the verge of going inside and asking a favor of a MacLeod. It was a favor he needed in order to take advantage of an offer made by a McKinnon—a McKinnon, it should be noted, that he had vowed to kill not a day earlier.

He almost turned around and strode back to the castle, but a bellow from within the Boar's Head Inn caught his attention. It was followed by another raised voice. Connor couldn't help but be intrigued. Never one to pass on at least observing a good skirmish, he made his way with alacrity into the entryway.

Aye, there was a bit of a squabble going on, but unfortunately it did not involve swords.

Mrs. Pruitt stood clutching her feather duster like a weapon and glaring at a man who could only be one of Victoria's players. He was full of very large gestures and quite loud complaints. Connor had seen him the day before in the keep, striding about as if he owned the bloody place.

He'd shadowed him for a time until the rabbit had scampered for the gates.

Coward.

It wasn't in his nature to detest another so quickly. He generally gave others as many chances as possible, allowed for the faults that he himself was rarely vexed by, took into consideration that those of weaker stuff might not be equal to the tasks he took on without thought. All in all, it generally took him at least a fortnight to truly begin to loathe another human being.

That mortal standing there complaining about his chamber was obviously going to be the exception.

The man ceased with his shouting at the innkeeper only because he apparently caught sight of himself in the mirror. Connor leaped out of his way as the man came over to peer at himself in the glass, rearrange his hair, then return to take up the battle again with Mrs. Pruitt.

Connor couldn't help a peep in the looking glass as well. After all, it was one of the reasons he had come to the inn, not having a looking glass of his own up at the keep. How else could he determine if Victoria McKinnon's assessment of his face was accurate or not?

He frowned at himself, stroked his chin, then reached up and brushed the hair from his eyes.

"That won't improve things."

Connor turned toward that voice with his sword half drawn. Ambrose, who had just materialized next to him, held up his hands in surrender and smiled.

"I think there is more entertainment here for us than swordplay."

"Think you?" Connor asked archly. But he resheathed his sword and found himself, surprisingly, standing in what could only be termed companionable silence with Ambrose MacLeod.

By the saints, what indignity would befall him next? A pleasant conversation with a McKinnon?

"Michael Fellini," Ambrose said, gesturing to the

sniveling mortal assaulting Mrs. Pruitt with his complaints. "Victoria's star actor."

"So I assumed," Connor said. "He is quite a womanly sort."

"Aye, quite," Ambrose agreed.

As Connor continued to watch Michael Fellini, he was hard pressed to suppress an intense desire to draw his sword and clout the man into insensibility. It would have spared them all a great deal of irritation.

"The room is haunted!" Fellini screeched.

"I told you," Mrs. Pruitt said darkly. " 'Tis not a room we normally let out."

"I can see why!"

Connor looked at Ambrose to find him wearing a faintly amused smile. "Are you responsible for this?" he asked.

"I might be," Ambrose admitted modestly. "It is *my* bed-chamber he speaks of, after all."

"Hmmm," Connor said, faintly impressed. "I approve of your choice of victims."

"I doubt Victoria will."

Fellini's complaints increased in volume until Connor wondered if he would become senseless from lack of air or simply keel over from the memory of his terror the night before.

Unfortunately for that potential bit of enjoyment, Fellini's diatribe was interrupted by the hasty arrival of one Victoria McKinnon. She came flying down the stairs in what Connor could only assume were her nightclothes, her fiery hair streaming along behind her, her face full of concern.

He was somehow quite relieved he was leaning against something.

"She is magnificent, isn't she?" Ambrose murmured.

Connor had to take a deep breath. "She screams quite well. For a McKinnon."

Ambrose chuckled. "I suppose that's true. But look at the way she commands all around her. Now, there's a wench for a man with the courage to tame her."

Connor grunted. That man certainly would not be Michael Fellini. The lout couldn't manage to get himself past a harmless bit of sport from a womanly MacLeod; how would he ever tame that spirited Victoria McKinnon?

"Michael, what's wrong?" Victoria asked breathlessly.

"My room is haunted!" Michael bellowed.

"Haunted?" Victoria echoed. "Why, that seems *sooo* unlikely!"

Connor found himself the recipient of a very pointed glare Victoria managed to slide his way without Fellini paying attention.

"I wouldn't have bothered with the wretch," Connor announced to anyone who would listen.

Victoria shot him another look of warning before she turned back to Fellini. "What makes you think your room was haunted?" she asked.

"Something blew down the back of my neck while I was practicing my lines in front of the mirror," Michael complained. "I'm certain it was a ghost."

"You know, I've heard the inn is drafty," Victoria said soothingly.

"Not *that* drafty."

"I'll look into it," Victoria assured him.

"You'd better," Fellini warned.

And with that, he turned and left both Victoria and Mrs. Pruitt standing in the middle of the entryway. He sailed up the stairs and out of sight.

"I tried to warn him," Mrs. Pruitt said darkly, "but did he listen?" She paused. "Perhaps I should wait outside the chamber tonight. Who knows what I might see?"

She departed with all alacrity to points unknown. Connor opened his mouth to comment on the whole ridiculous affair, but was interrupted by Victoria turning and glaring at him.

By the saints, she had a look about her that rendered him almost speechless.

If he'd been prone to speechlessness, which he most certainly was not.

"What?" he demanded.

Victoria strode over, a vision of fury. "We had a bargain," she spat.

Connor drew himself up. "I haven't broken it." And he hadn't. Not entirely. He forced himself to overlook his own bit of breath-blowing up at the keep the afternoon before.

Victoria turned her wrath on Ambrose. "Was it you?"

Ambrose nodded remorsefully. "Aye, granddaughter, it was."

"How could you?" she exclaimed. "He's the star of the show!"

Ambrose bowed his head. "I beg pardon. I was in my chamber briefly to gather a few items I might need for the duration. I fear I might have brushed past him whilst looking for something atop the dresser. And a body must breathe, mustn't he?"

Victoria started to say something else, then checked herself. She sighed. "Actually, I'm the one who should apologize. He has stolen your room, after all."

"He has," Ambrose agreed cheerfully. "But I know what he means to you and your play, so I will leave him be."

Victoria smiled at him, then turned a frown on Connor. "And you? Why are you here?"

What was he supposed to say? That he'd come to look in the polished glass and see if she had described him aright? He'd never been called handsome before and he wasn't sure he believed it. Damn Michael Fellini for having ruined his opportunity to really learn the truth of it.

"You aren't here to frighten my actors, are you?" she continued. "You promised you wouldn't."

"I vowed no such thing."

She put her hands on her hips. "I promised you an entire month of screaming in return for you leaving my cast and crew alone. You agreed to that. Live up to your promise."

And with that, she turned and stalked away.

"*You* promised *me* a part in your play," he growled, before he thought better of it.

She stopped. Then she turned slowly and looked at him. "So I did."

Connor could hardly believe he'd blurted that bit out, but, by the saints, he couldn't deny that he didn't find the idea somewhat pleasing.

Victoria studied him for a moment or two. "There is a ghost in the play, you know, but you're sort of young for it. You would actually be better as Hamlet, but that's a pretty big part."

Connor shifted uncomfortably. "I likely wouldn't have time for the foolishness of either," he said gruffly.

"I'll leave a copy of the script for you," she said. "Up at the castle, just in case you change your mind. You could start with just the ghost's lines, if you like. We have an actor doing it right now, but he doesn't have an understudy."

"An understudy?"

"Someone who would do the part if something happens to him," Ambrose offered.

"Yes, but don't be responsible for that," she warned Ambrose before she turned and went back up the stairs. She disappeared down the passageway. Connor turned to Ambrose.

"I needed no aid."

"I never said you did," Ambrose said with a pleasant smile.

Connor paused, chewed on his next words, and wondered how he might spit them out without choking on them.

"I've a bargain to make with you," he said quickly.

"Indeed?" Ambrose asked with interest. "What sort of bargain?"

"I won't humiliate you anymore in the lists if you'll aid me with my reading."

Ambrose only lifted one eyebrow a fraction. "Reading? Aye, I could do that. In return for your generosity, of course."

Connor grunted. "I wish no one to know of this."

"As you will," Ambrose said easily. "Midnight, in the kitchen?"

Connor nodded curtly, then made for the front door. He paused, then looked back at Ambrose. He wanted to voice some bit of thanks, but it seemed to have a bit of trouble getting past his throat.

Ambrose only waved him on. "We had best be off to other pursuits. I'm certain you have guardsmen to intimidate."

"And I'm certain you have an innkeeper to avoid," Connor replied.

"Do you know about that?" Ambrose asked, sounding surprised.

"She mutters as she weeds her garden."

Connor left the inn before he had to divulge more. Perhaps Ambrose was to be pitied for more than his parentage, what with Mrs. Pruitt dogging his every step. Of course, that was no reason to go soft on him, but perhaps he could spare a bit of mercy when it came to time in the lists.

He intended to go back to the castle and think on all the ways he would terrify Victoria McKinnon before he did her in—something he should have been doing that morning, and would have been doing if he hadn't been so disrupted in his normal rhythm of murder and mayhem by that comment about his face—but his feet didn't carry him back to his keep.

Instead, he found himself and his feet loitering near the inn, as if his poor form couldn't entertain a useful thought or manage to set a proper course for his day.

Besides, the flowers were pretty.

He drew his sword and examined it to make certain it was still sharp. It was quite tempting to test it upon himself and perhaps cut out those ridiculous thoughts that seemed to have suddenly taken root in his breast. Indeed, he was within a heartbeat of doing so when he was distracted by Victoria McKinnon herself, coming out the kitchen door.

He froze, standing in the midst of a clutch of petunias with his sword upraised.

Fortunately, Victoria continued on her way through the vegetable garden without paying him any heed. Connor resheathed his sword and frowned. Well, the wench was reading—any fool could have seen that—and was likely too distracted to see that he was there. He watched her poring over some sort of something, scribbling now and again, and frowning when it suited her. She felt her way through the vegetables and paused before a garden shed.

Connor tiptoed up behind her and peered into the shed. It was filled to the brim with finery. Connor was vastly tempted to reach in and stroke a sleeve or two. He was equally tempted to reach out and stroke Victoria McKinnon's long, flame-colored hair.

Instead, he clapped a hand to his head so strongly that he yelped.

Victoria whipped around and shrieked.

Briefly, unfortunately.

"A good attempt," Connor said, "but you've given vent to better. Now, if you're interested in how I prefer it, I would rather hear a full-bodied shriek that trails off into either moans or whimpers, rather than that business of a little scream cut short before its time." He clucked his tongue. "Highly unsatisfying."

She pointed her writing instrument at him as if it had been a sword. "You promised."

"*You* are not one of your actors."

She frowned at him, opened her mouth to say something, then shut it with a snap. She frowned. "You're right."

"I generally am."

She cradled her papers against her chest and frowned at him over them. "What do you need?"

"Need? I need nothing."

"Then why are you here? I thought this was Hugh's, um, haunt."

Connor drew himself up. "I do not limit my roamings to the castle. But," he said, cutting her off, "I generally do not haunt the chambers of the inn. But I will, whether you like it or not, be visiting the kitchen as it pleases me."

Aye, there was truth in that. He would probably be loitering in the bloody place all night for countless nights if he was to drive into his poor head some ability to make out letters on parchment.

"I wouldn't dream of limiting your movements," she said, straight-faced.

"Save in Michael Fellini's chamber."

"I need him for the play. Besides," she added with only a slight frown, "he's quite loud when things don't go his way."

"He is powerfully irritating."

"Yeah, well, he was *very* expensive. I have the feeling he's still getting over being tired from his trip here."

Connor was quite certain Michael Fellini was irritating no matter the circumstance, but he thought better of saying so. He folded his arms over his chest and searched for another topic to discuss.

That he wanted to be discoursing with and not decapitating the woman before him was almost unsettling enough to make him turn on his heel and make all haste to another location.

But he didn't.

The saints pity him.

"Your costumes are not unhandsome," he said, gesturing imperiously at them.

She blinked, as if she couldn't fathom what he was saying. "You think so?" she said, stepping aside so he could more easily admire them.

He leaned in closer to peer at them. They were made of far finer stuff than he had ever worn in his day. "Lovely colors," he said politely.

And then he made the mistake of turning just a hair to look at her.

He was far closer to her than he suspected.

By the saints, a man could lose himself in eyes so blue.

"There you are!"

Connor fell over. He didn't mean to, but the shrill voice behind him startled him so badly that he stumbled into the shed and 'twas only his natural grace that kept him from sprawling fully upon his face. He caught himself and turned to find none other than that whining miss, Michael Fellini, standing at the shed door.

"I want to talk to you," Michael said forcefully.

"Well, of course," Victoria said, looking pleasantly surprised. "What about?"

"The play."

Connor angled himself so he could view Victoria's face. Why, the silly wench was looking not only pleasantly surprised but surprisingly flattered! Connor resurrected ideas of doing her in. Surely she had to see past all the show to the man inside, a man who, in Connor's opinion, did not deserve any of the breath Victoria had wasted upon him already.

"Of course," Victoria said, smiling. "The play."

"Yes," Fellini said briskly. "I have some ideas on how it should be directed. I know we haven't begun rehearsals here and of course I wasn't at any of the ones you held in Manhattan, but I have ideas on several things you could be doing differently."

Connor folded his arms over his chest. Now the wench would let him have his due. Connor couldn't imagine that having one of her soldiers come and tell her how to lead the battle was going to sit well with her.

The slightest of frowns came to rest upon her alabaster brow.

Connor blinked.

Alabaster brow? By the saints, already he had been affected by these bloody players and he had yet to see them play!

"Differently?" Victoria echoed, her brow creasing more firmly. "How so?"

Fellini launched into an animated narration, which Connor ignored without hesitation. Instead, he eased past the costumes and came to stand behind Fellini, where he could more readily observe Victoria's reaction.

It also put him, handily, in a place where he might cool the lad off—as it were.

He was just settling in and preparing for a good blow down the back of Fellini's collar when he caught sight of the glare Victoria was sending him.

"Well!" Fellini exclaimed, sounding offended. "You needn't look so, well, *sensitive* about it all. My suggestions are quite well thought-out and accurate."

She blinked. "Oh, I wasn't frowning at you."

Fellini stiffened. "Then at whom?" He looked around uneasily, then turned back to Victoria. "This whole place gives me the creeps. Let's go back to the inn. At least I know there aren't any ghosts there except in my room."

Connor snorted loudly, then clapped his hand over his mouth.

Fellini shivered, then took Victoria by the arm and pulled her away from the shed. "Inside," he said.

Connor watched, wondering what she would do now. Would she cuff him as he so richly deserved for taking such liberties, or would she simper along behind him?

To her credit, she did neither. She somehow managed to remove her arm from his clutches yet walk with him toward the house at the same time. Connor stroked his chin thoughtfully. Far be it from him to heap praise upon a McKinnon's head, but he had to admit it took a wench of notable cleverness to appear to acquiesce when indeed she was not.

He leaned against the door frame of the shed and watched them walk to the kitchen door. Fellini went in first, of course. Victoria turned briefly and held her fist out toward him with her thumb pointing skyward.

She went inside before he could decide if he should be flattered, offended, or merely go in search of that erstwhile desire to do her in.

What, by all the saints, had she intended by that?

He scowled. Yet another reason to frequent the inn that night and demand answers from Ambrose MacLeod.

She had smiled as she'd done it, though. He pushed off from the shed and strolled through the garden, giving thought to all the events of the morning.

He found himself somewhat surprised by the pleasantness of them.

And by how many of those recollections included Victoria McKinnon.

Chapter 8

Victoria sat in the sitting room with her granny, finding the complete silence of the inn to be a little unsettling. After a week of rehearsals, her actors had deserted her *en masse*, decamping for Edinburgh. She had, over the course of the morning, periodically suffered flashes of panic, wondering if they might return safely . . . or return at all.

She needed them to return. She'd gotten a call that morning from the ticket agency Thomas had engaged for her. She'd known he'd done it, she'd heard from Ambrose that he'd been running ads in the paper, but she'd had no idea the extent of his business dealings. She was sold out through the first three weekends, matinees included, and booked heavily most of the rest of the nights.

Was Thomas rounding up patrons from far away villages to fill the seats, or had Ambrose and company been making midnight visits to theater aficionados?

But whatever the reason, and because of the apparent popularity of her little ensemble, she was beginning to worry just the slightest bit about the condition of that ensemble.

"Vikki," Mary said suddenly, putting down her knitting. "I don't know about you, but the morning seems to be dragging a little. How would you like some tea?"

"I'd love some," Victoria said. "I'll go make it."

"I don't mind—"

"I'll never see you again if you go," Victoria said with a faint smile. "You'll find yourself monopolized by the Boar's Head Trio and I'll still be here at midnight, wondering what happened to you."

"And you think you'll make your escape more easily?" her grandmother asked with a twinkle in her eye.

"They are, despite their charm and no offense to you, too old for me. Besides," she said, doing her best to escape the overly soft chair that didn't seem to want to let her go, "I'm immune to ghostly charm."

"Of course, love."

"I am," Victoria muttered under her breath as she walked out of the sitting room. She hadn't seen enough ghosts all week to verify that immunity, but maybe that was a blessing in disguise.

She had the feeling Connor MacDougal could be pretty distracting if he wanted to be.

But she hadn't seen him in a week, either, which was just as well. She had a play to put on and no time for tangents. No time for coddling terrified actors, either. At least Connor was holding to his word. Michael hadn't complained once about walking through cold spots or hearing things go *bump* in the night. Things were going along swimmingly.

She walked through the dining room but heard no squabbling coming from the kitchen. It was a safe bet that either Mrs. Pruitt was napping or her grandfathers and sundry were out haunting someplace more lively.

She marched into the kitchen, then skidded to a halt.

Connor MacDougal sat at the table, surrounded by books. He was holding a piece of chalk in his hand, looking down at the scribbled-on tablet darkly, and swearing like a sailor. Gone was the man who seemed to think the only thing he should be pointing at anyone else was a sword. In his place was, apparently, a scholar.

"I'm sorry," Victoria said. "I didn't know you were in here."

He threw the chalk across the kitchen. It disappeared without a sound.

"Never mind me," he said with another curse or two. " 'Tis all foolishness anyway—"

"Wait," she said before he swept everything off the table, which she suspected by the angle and trajectory of his upraised arm was his intention. "Let me see."

He balked. "Absolutely not."

She rounded the table and pulled out the chair next to him. She sat before he could say, "Don't," and looked before he could say anything else.

"Wow," she said, "what beautiful letters. Very ornate and lovely."

He grunted.

She stared thoughtfully at his tablet, which did, as it happened, contain some rather beautiful printing. Connor seemed to be quite uncomfortable, though. She could only assume by what she was seeing that he was just learning to read.

"I don't imagine you had many books in your hall," she offered. "Or much time for reading them, if you had any."

She looked at him out of the corner of her eye, just to see how he might react to that opening salvo.

That was her first mistake.

She found herself suddenly burning with quite a few things, not the least of which was curiosity. Who was this man who sat next to her and looked as corporeal as she did, but who obviously had been born long ago and had lived in this half-life of existence for centuries? What drove him, besides a great desire to do in any McKinnons he ran across?

How was it his keep was only filled with men and not with every available female for miles?

He shifted uncomfortably. "You're staring at me."

"Oh," she said, blinking. "Sorry. I couldn't help myself."

And she thought that might just be the case. It was an easy thing to sit next to him; an even easier thing to look at his very handsome face.

His eyes, she discovered, were gray.

Gray like the stormy sea near Thomas's house in Maine. She knew all about that gray because a horrible storm had been brewing the day she'd flown back to Manhattan. It had made for an extremely bumpy ride back home.

She wondered what that meant for her now.

"You know," she said, grasping at what seemed to pass for her last vestiges of good sense, "we really haven't been formally introduced."

He looked at her in surprise. "I beg your pardon?"

All right, so she was losing it. Was this what it felt like to lose your mind, this slow easing away from the shore of sanity? Unfortunately, in her case, she seemed to be putting to sea rather rapidly.

"Ah, I'm not sure what I should call you," she said. No sense in not finishing what she'd started. "Though it might be too late to stand on formality, given that you've heard me scream." She paused. "Already."

He stared at her in silence for a few moments, probably wondering what would be the easiest way to get away from a madwoman of her ilk, then he frowned.

"I am accustomed to being called 'my laird,'" he said slowly, "but given that you are not of my clan, I suppose you may call me MacDougal."

"How about Laird MacDougal?"

He nodded, then fiddled with his chalk. "And I daresay Mistress McKinnon would do for you."

She could think of worse things. "I think it would. Now, Laird MacDougal, I'm going to make my granny some tea, then head back to the sitting room." She made the mistake again of looking at him. "You can bring your books and come along, if you like," she said, sounding appallingly breathless, even to her own ears.

Then again, who could blame her? She was sitting next

to a man who simply reeked of medieval lairdliness and had a six-foot broadsword propped up next to him against the table. Maybe she was allowed to be a little short of breath.

"I'll think on it," he said briefly.

But she watched, out of the corner of her eye, as he began to gather up his books and his blade. By the time she had everything on a tea tray, he was ready to go.

"Mrs. Pruitt isn't there, is she?" he asked suspiciously.

"I think she's off cataloging her equipment," Victoria said. "I wouldn't worry."

"You wouldn't, but I do," he said, in a not unfriendly tone.

"I understand," she offered. "I've seen her at her worst, but you can relax. She's not hanging out with us."

She left the kitchen and was acutely and uncomfortably aware of him following her. It made that Michael-Fellini-induced swoon at the faculty tea look like the faint hint of a hot flash.

Heaven help her, she was too young to even know the word perimenopausal.

She managed to get the teapot, cups, saucers, and cookies to the sitting room without dropping or spilling anything. She set them down on the coffee table and breathed a sigh of relief.

"Granny—"

"Oh, Laird MacDougal," Mary said, smiling at him. "How lovely to see you. Oh, I see you've brought things to study. There is never enough time in the day to get your lines down, is there?"

Victoria wondered how it was her grandmother managed to get so chummy so quickly with everyone she met. Victoria was sleeping on a rollaway cot in the same room with her and was quite certain her grandmother wasn't sneaking out during the middle of the night to consort with ghosts. Then again, who knew? Megan's room was the biggest in the inn. It was entirely possible that her granny was tiptoeing by and Victoria wasn't the wiser.

"Nay, there is not enough time," Connor agreed. "And it would aid me greatly if I could read the bloody words to start with. Put indelicately, that is."

"You should have Vikki help you. I'm sure she has her afternoon free and nothing would please her more. Would it, dear?"

Victoria wished her grandmother wasn't too old to have something thrown at her. This was turning out to be another in a long line of fix-ups. Victoria was still trying to get her name and profile removed from several online dating services on which she was listed thanks to her grandmother's ability with the Internet.

"I would happily help," Victoria found herself saying, despite her better judgment—and her sense of self-preservation.

"Then I'm going to have some tea and a nap before Victoria's menagerie returns and ruins my peace. Laird MacDougal, I would like to hear you read your lines when you have them learned. He would make a fine Hamlet, don't you think, Vikki?"

"Sure," Victoria croaked. She looked at Connor, who was standing uncomfortably near the fireplace, his books and other scholarly trappings in his arms. "Shall we get started?"

He paused, then slowly laid his books out on the table. Then he dragged up a stool of his own making and sat down.

There was nothing quite like the sight of a Highland laird perched on a little stool in front of a low table spread with things he intended to learn to read to make a girl wonder if she'd just lost her mind.

So Victoria pulled up a footstool, sat down next to him, and proceeded to do the best she could.

Until the afternoon wore on and he began to swear with regularity.

"I have a thought," she said.

"A nap?" he glowered, nodding toward her grandmother, who was snoozing peacefully in her chair.

"No, let's go over the ghost's part. In the play," she added quickly.

"I cannot read it," he said grimly.

"Maybe not now, but you will eventually. Besides, all actors end up memorizing their parts one way or another. I always did."

He looked at her in surprise. "You've done this business on stage?"

"Yes."

"Then why do you not continue with it? Besides the obvious reason that you found sense."

She smiled. "It's a very long story."

"We have a very long afternoon before us."

She thought about it for a few minutes, but decided it just wasn't a tale fit for his ears. She hadn't even told her family. All they knew was that she'd fallen off a stage, broken her arm, and decided that directing was her calling. She hadn't dared tell them that she'd been doing some stupid trust exercise with her acting class and that the guy who had been supposed to catch her as she ran across the stage with her eyes closed had let her slip by. Accidentally, of course.

She'd landed in the orchestra pit. It was probably a good thing it had been empty; she might have done some serious damage to the cello section otherwise.

That accident had been enough to point her in a different direction. There was really no going back now.

She smiled at Connor. "I like directing."

"Do you?"

"I like being in charge."

He almost smiled.

She almost fanned herself.

"I share that feeling," he said, with something of a purr. He seemed to consider his next words for several moments. "And the actors? What do you think of them?"

She took a deep breath. That was the question, wasn't it? "It is difficult to be an actor," she said finally. "It takes a special sort of person to be willing to get up on a stage and create a character."

"Hmmm," he said.

"I like them, for the most part," she admitted. "As for the rest, I put up with them because of their talent. If I only hired people I liked, I wouldn't have a theater for very long."

"Would you," he began slowly, "truly not prefer to be up on that stage?"

"No," she said firmly. She'd been saying it firmly for years. She didn't want to act. She didn't want to dig deep for emotions night after night on stage, then go home afterward and sleep it off like a drinking binge. She didn't want to wake up every morning with an emotional hangover.

Really. She didn't.

"I much prefer just directing the plays," she said. Firmly.

He looked at her thoughtfully. "Indeed."

"Indeed," she agreed briskly. "But you might like acting in them very much. Let's get with these lines, shall we? You've been watching us rehearse for a few days now. We don't need to go over the storyline, do we?"

"I believe I have that in my head," he said, raising one eyebrow. "Death, death, and more death. A bit of madness. A little romance. More death."

"That about sums it up. Let's start where Hamlet sees the ghost for the first time."

She tried not to remember the first time she'd seen a ghost. Namely the one sitting next to her, dutifully repeating the lines she fed him, then giving them back to her on his own without hesitation.

She was impressed.

And she did not impress easily.

Things went along swimmingly for the space of about an hour, then Connor's mood soured rapidly.

"What?" she asked. "What's wrong?"

"I do not care for how the king was murdered. And I like it even less that his lady wife could not wait until he was cold in his grave before she wed with Hamlet's uncle."

"Hey, I didn't write this stuff," she said, holding up her hands in surrender. "I'm just directing it."

Connor stood up and turned toward the empty hearth. "I've little liking for these lines. Little liking at all."

She was tempted to ask him why, but she suspected that he didn't want to talk about it and, if she pressed him, he would probably either draw his sword or disappear.

So she took the opportunity to look at him while his back was turned. How was it he could look no different than a mortal man would have? He put his hand on the mantel just as any other man in torment would have. He bowed his head and his hair fell over his face in a way that any hairdresser would have killed to copy. She could see his chest rising and falling as he cursed his way through his distress.

Before she thought better of it, she reached out and touched his kilt, just to see if she had lost her mind.

And she felt not his kilt, but his eyes suddenly boring a hole into the side of her head.

"What," he asked crisply, "are you doing?"

She looked up at him. All right, so she had just made a complete ass of herself, which she never did. It didn't help that he was looking down at her as if she were a bug he intended to crush under his worn leather boots. She stood up as if she'd meant to do it all along, then retreated to a comfy chair a safe distance away.

"I was just curious," she said, trying desperately to convince herself that she had every right to be groping his clothes. It certainly seemed to work for Hugh; why couldn't it work for her?

"Were you indeed?" he asked, his voice dangerously soft.

"Can you blame me? You look so real."

"I'm real enough," he muttered. "But yet not."

"Can you touch things from the mortal world, then?" she asked.

"It is not easy. It takes a great amount of strength and drains me quite thoroughly for several hours afterwards. Or days, depending on what I've done."

She looked into his gray eyes and had the oddest feeling

that she'd looked into them before. Yes, she knew she had and that morning, to boot. But this feeling was something far different, some sort of cosmic déjà vu that made her wish for a chair.

Fortunately, she was already seated and there was nowhere to go besides the floor. She cast about desperately for a distraction.

"Who did this . . . um, how did you . . ."

"Die?" he finished briskly.

"Yes," she said, in what sounded to her like a very, very small voice.

"My wife cuckolded me and I was murdered by her lover."

She felt her mouth fall open of its own accord. "But what woman in her right mind . . ."

She decided belatedly that maybe she was headed in a place she really shouldn't go.

"I think I'm sorry I brought this up," she said finally.

"You likely should be." He stared unseeing at the other side of the room. "I have told no one this tale," he began slowly. "At first, I was too full of rage. Then I could not grasp that I was dead and had no chance for living the rest of the life that should have been mine." He met her eyes. "I suppose I should have grieved."

"I think it might be easier to stay angry."

"I daresay."

"I like to forget my troubles in work," she offered. "It keeps me from thinking too much. But, of course, I don't have any great tragedies in my life." And she didn't, unless you could counted being thirty-two, not married, and her only prospect in the last two years being a man whom she suspected was far more interested in her play than in her.

Well, at least she wasn't a ghost.

"Did you love her?" she asked quietly.

Connor looked at her in surprise. "My wife? Of course not. She was fair enough, I suppose, but she was my enemy's daughter. Wedding with her seemed as good a way as any to keep the McKinnons from stealing my cattle."

"She was a McKinnon?" Victoria gurgled. She reached for her tea and downed a swig. Damn. Cold.

Connor was, to her complete astonishment, almost smiling. It was more of a wry quirk of half his mouth, but that made her spew what was left in her mouth out—fortunately not onto him.

"Excitable, aren't you?" he asked.

She mopped up with one of Mrs. Pruitt's linen napkins. "No wonder you don't like us."

"Aye, well, I'm considering making an exception or two. I've still no use for your brother, but your sister Megan is quite a fetching wench and I like her laugh. I think I could become quite fond of your *grandmère* as well." He pulled up a chair out of thin air and sat down comfortably. "I haven't come to a final decision on you."

"How nice," she managed. She dragged her sleeve across her face, giving up any semblance of dignity. "So you married a McKinnon. What happened then?"

"She bore me twins. A lad and a wee lassie."

"Oh," Victoria said. "How lovely—"

"And then a pair of years later, she took up with a French minstrel who had come to try and pluck out a living from whatever foolish Highland chieftain he could," Connor said, his frown returning with vigor. "If she'd had a thought in that empty head of hers, she would have realized he could not keep her as she desired to be kept."

"And the children?"

He looked down at his hands again. "When she fled with the Frenchman, she took my bairns with her. Of course, the fools couldn't find east when they were staring straight into the morning sun and they became hopelessly lost. A fortnight hadn't passed before they sent a messenger back to me, begging for me to come and aid them."

"And did you?"

"Of course I did!" he exclaimed, looking up at her. "What kind of man do you think me to be?"

"Honorable," she said promptly. Maybe a little irritated after seven hundred years of haunting, but that was justifiable.

"For all it served me," he said. "I hadn't ridden half a mile from my home before I was murdered by that French whoreson. But before my life ebbed from me, he let me know that my bairns were dead from the ague. My wife as well."

She shivered.

"But I invited him to come with me to the grave with a sword across his belly."

"Oh," Victoria said, feeling a little faint.

"Breathe," he instructed.

She nodded. She had to put her head between her knees. She half expected that when the sitting room stopped spinning, Connor would no longer be sitting across from her.

But when the stars cleared and she could see again, he was where she had left him, sitting quite comfortably in a wooden chair of his own making.

"I'm sorry," she said weakly. "I'm sorry to have asked, sorry to have suggested the play—"

"Are you?" he interrupted. "Do you think I am unequal to the task?"

"Of course not," she said. "I actually think you would do a very good job. I'm sorry for the memories it dredged up."

He shrugged. "They are never very far below the surface anyway, so you did nothing that a thousand other small things during the day don't do on their own. Who knows that this might be of a purging nature, to settle my humors—"

Victoria opened her mouth to agree that it very well might, when she heard a ruckus in the entryway.

Michael's voice soared above the rest.

It was not a sober voice.

Connor's expression was grim. "I could see to them all, if you liked."

"If I thought I could allow it without most of my actors bolting for the nearest airport, I would take you up on the offer." She sighed and rose. "I'll handle it, but thank you just the same."

He stood as well. "And my thanks for the aid with my lines."

"It was my pleasure."

"Nay, the pleasure was mine."

Victoria was just certain that she was feeling faint from the thought of lost sales and bad press thanks to actors with hangovers. It couldn't have had anything to do with the man standing not three feet from her who made her feel small, fragile, and protected.

Good heavens, she *was* losing her mind.

"I have to go," she managed.

He took a step back, then made her a very low bow. And when he straightened, his gray eyes were full of something that was not at all hostile or irritated.

Then again, her own eyes could have been crossed from too much speculation on the emotions being entertained by the medieval laird of the Clan MacDougal, who was not only out of her league, but out of her century and out of her mortal sphere, as well. Besides, she was infatuated with Michael Fellini.

She was.

She was almost certain of it.

"Gotta go," she said, then she turned and bolted from the sitting room. She ran right into a gaggle of performers, who staggered about the entryway in a most convincing manner. Now, here was a problem she could solve with a loud voice and a few threats.

She wasn't at all sure how she was going to solve the dilemma she'd left in the sitting room.

Chapter 9

*C*onnor stood on the newly completed stage behind the deceased King of Denmark and wondered, very briefly, if he might have set himself to a task for which he was not particularly well suited. Never mind that he had blurted out all his secrets the day before as if he hadn't a thought in his empty head.

Nay, his troubles lay before him. By the saints, could this fool do nothing but stride about and moan in that ghostly fashion? Was this acting?

He thought not.

"Adieu!" the ghostly king bellowed suddenly. "Remember me!"

"By the saints," Connor exclaimed, "I daresay we won't have a bloody chance to forget you, what with all that noise you're making!"

Hamlet's dead father continued bellowing his parting words, accompanying them with the moans a man is wont to make when he has ingested victuals that do not agree with him. Connor rubbed his ears in annoyance as he watched the would-be shade make his exit stage right, finally disappearing behind a handy bit of scenery and giving vent to one final moan that Connor could only assume was intended to convince all and sundry that he was indeed a ghost.

Pitiful.

Connor looked at Victoria to see how she was reacting to this piece of particularly bad acting.

She was standing there with her arms folded over her chest, her expression inscrutable. Connor supposed she was afraid to show her true emotions lest the king of Denmark burst into tears.

He had watched her, surreptitiously of course, herd all her actors to their chambers on Sunday. The tongue-lashing she had given them had led to a cessation of all pub visits by those so chastised. Connor suspected that was her intent.

Connor leaned back against a bit of scenery and watched the rest of the play unfold. Or, rather, he watched Victoria watch the remainder of the play proceed. He'd told her he would call her Mistress McKinnon, but he realized, with a start, that such was not how he thought of her.

Victoria.

He wondered, as he watched her watch the play, how she would have been on stage with that flaming red hair and her face a marvel of creation. She likely would have made that bleating sheep Cressida look much like . . . well, a bleating sheep. Connor wondered how it was Victoria could bear watching Cressida's descent into Ophelia's madness without wanting to slap her briskly a time or two and bid her get on with it. Connor blamed Michael Fellini. He had spent more than enough time instructing Cressida in his particular brand of pitiful acting.

But Victoria merely stood there, impassive, and let the play unfold as it would. And when it was finished, she bid her actors be about their business and prepare for another attempt at the beginning of the following se'nnight.

But only a fool couldn't have seen that she was less than pleased with their efforts.

Most souls scurried past her and bolted for the gates. Fred chatted with her for several minutes and seemed impervious to her measured, even answers. Mary barked out orders to her seamstresses, then came and hopped up onto the stage. She sat on its edge and glanced back at him. She nodded toward the spot next to her. Pleased, Connor walked across the stage and dropped down to sit with her.

"Good morrow to you, lady," he said politely.

"You could call me Granny," she said, with a twinkle in her eye.

"It seems disrespectful, somehow," he said seriously.

"Then call me Mary."

"Lady Mary," Connor countered. " 'Tis all I can do."

"It works for me." She nodded toward Victoria. "She's not pleased."

"Aye, so I gathered."

"We open in less than a week. The cast is still making mistakes."

"I cannot lay those at Victoria's feet," Connor said seriously. "But I can lay them at Fellini's."

Mary nodded thoughtfully. "Yes, that's my feeling, too." She looked at Connor and smiled. "It's too bad you can't give him a little scare."

"Ambrose attempted that and all it served was to make the man soil his trousers," Connor said, feeling his nose turn up of its own accord. "And Ambrose doesn't dare do more, lest the coward turn tail and flee, leaving Victoria without a Hamlet."

"You're certainly friendly of late with the lads down at the inn," Mary said, looking at him assessingly. "Softening toward those dastardly MacLeods?"

"Desperate for a captain for my guard," Connor corrected. "I've managed, in spite of my heavy schedule shadowing Denmark's sniveling king, to weed out several more candidates. I fear I must begin to look farther afield. It reduces me to asking Ambrose for suggestions."

"How awful for you."

"My lady, you've no idea."

Mary laughed. "You are a delightful man. I don't know why Thomas told me to be careful around you."

"Perhaps I threatened to cleave his head in twain once too often," Connor offered.

"Perhaps," she agreed with a smile. "I promise not to tell him how kind you've been. I wouldn't want to ruin your reputation . . . Connor." She smiled at him. "May I call you Connor?"

"Is it possible to stop you?"

"I doubt it," she said with a laugh.

"Then you may," he said, feeling himself begin to smile. It felt quite odd.

Indeed, he wasn't sure the last time he'd done the like.

"Don't show that smile to Vikki," Mary said in a conspiratorial whisper. "At least not until the run is over. She won't be able to concentrate otherwise. Not that she would say anything, of course. She's quite closed-mouthed about you."

"She is?"

"I imagine you had quite a conversation while I snoozed last Sunday in the sitting room."

He looked at her darkly. "Did you eavesdrop?"

"I did my best," she said unrepentantly, "but an old woman apparently needs her rest. I've been trying to pry details out of her for almost a week."

"And?" Connor demanded. Damn that Victoria McKinnon. No doubt she had blathered on like the woman she was—

"She wouldn't give," Mary said. "I tried guilt, even. Nothing. Nada. *Nichts.* I've had to carry on, unsatisfied."

Connor blinked. "She said nothing?"

"Nothing. But if you aren't busy later, I'd like all those details myself."

"Shameless old woman," Connor said easily.

"Of course."

He thought he might have smiled. He suspected it might have had something to do with the fact that Victoria McKinnon could apparently be trusted with his secrets.

Astonishing.

"Perhaps you'll divulge a few of those juicy tidbits later

this afternoon," Mary said. "Let's go on a picnic. We need to get Vikki out of here. There's nothing she can do to improve things and she'll only spend the afternoon worrying if I don't do something to distract her—oh, damn it, anyway."

Connor blinked. "I beg your pardon?"

"Look," Mary said, nodding toward where Victoria stood.

With Michael Fellini.

Connor understood immediately.

"I'll go tell her to buck up," Mary said firmly.

And with that, she hopped off the stage with the energy of a woman half her age and bounded over to where Victoria was being beguiled by that slippery snake.

"Michael, if you'll excuse us," Mary said loudly, putting her hand to her head, "I'm feeling a little faint all of a sudden. I need Vikki to help me back to the inn."

"I'd be more than happy to offer my arm," Fellini said gallantly.

"No, I'm sure you have places to go," Mary said smoothly. "Besides, we're going to have a little picnic and I can't imagine that would interest you—"

"A picnic," Fellini said, sounding as if he'd been invited on an outing by the Queen herself. "I'll carry the basket."

Mary discouraged, she hinted broadly, she even bluntly told him he was not wanted. Connor was unsurprised to see that the man remained unmoved.

Unsurprised, but deeply suspicious.

He would have followed them, but at that moment Ambrose strode into the bailey. He spoke politely to Mary and Victoria, then hopped up onto the stage.

"A bit of training, MacDougal?" he asked.

"I might stir myself for it," Connor said absently. He watched Victoria and her granny leave the bailey. He didn't like leaving them on their own with Fellini, but perhaps they would fare well enough. Mary MacLeod Davidson was fierce and with any hope, she would keep Victoria on task. The wench was far too friendly with Michael Fellini for his taste.

"Hmmm," Ambrose said meaningfully.

Connor looked at him sideways. "Eh?"

Ambrose shrugged. "Idle thoughts."

"Do you have any other kind?"

Ambrose laughed. "Occasionally. But presently, I daresay my thoughts are as they should be. You know, I worry about those two defenseless women being out on their own. Indeed, I think that perhaps I should forgo the pleasures of the sword and accompany them on their outing—"

"I'll go." Connor heard the words come out of his mouth and could not for the life of him think of where they had come from. "I'll go?" he repeated experimentally.

"I don't know," Ambrose said doubtfully. "It isn't as if you have any fond feelings for either of the two. Who's to say that if something untoward happened, you wouldn't leave them to a terrible fate . . ."

Connor drew himself up. "I am quite fond of them both," he said stiffly. "And if nothing else, my honor would demand that I do what was needful."

"Indeed?"

"Indeed," Connor said. "Allow me to take a moment to let my sword speak for me and argue that point."

"As you will," Ambrose agreed.

Connor found the stage to be a rather handy place to fight. There were boxes stacked here and there, and thrones for Hamlet's mother and uncle, and even a handy coffin that had been pushed aside until it was needed. Connor leaped about the stage, bounding off various props with relish. It had been centuries since he had felt so at home, or so much himself. Aye, this was the kind of fighting for him, where a daring lad had all manner of natural outcroppings to use for better leverage.

"Oh, look, there they go," Ambrose said, pointing suddenly at the front gates. "Oh, and there is Fellini, trailing after them, as well." He turned back to Connor. "But we'll leave them to their fate, I suppose. This is more manly labor here . . ."

Connor stopped in mid-lunge, pulled back, then resheathed his sword with a mighty thrust. "Perhaps you see it as such, but I do not. What kind of man is it who leaves women to protect themselves when there is breath left in him to heft a sword in their defense?"

He expected to see Ambrose bristle. Instead, the man hastily covered a cough with his hand.

"Too true," Ambrose said quickly. "I admire you for your convictions. Best be off, then, and see to your charges."

Connor frowned fiercely, but that seemingly did not impress the former laird of the clan MacLeod. Then again, those MacLeods were a feisty lot, so perhaps it took quite a bit for Ambrose to take notice.

And then another thought occurred to him. Did Ambrose *want* him to go watch over Victoria and her grandmother?

Did it matter?

Connor decided that it did not. Truth was truth and the truth of the matter was he was the better warrior. If those two women were to be looked after, 'twas best he be the one to do it.

"Until midnight then, in the kitchen as usual," Ambrose said, resheathing his own sword. "I have a new reader or two."

"Ach, by the saints," Connor groaned, "no more tales of those American bairns. If I must read any more about the adventures of Dick, Jane, and that bloody hound Spot—"

"Nay, these are proper Scottish tales. Bloodshed. Mayhem. Victory and glory for Highlanders."

"Then I will be there," Connor said as he jumped off the stage and strode out the front gates.

He followed the little party to a handy spot in a farmer's field. Victoria and Mary lugged the basket while Fellini strode about artistically, no doubt studying his surroundings for things to use in his portrayal of Hamlet. Connor was hard-pressed not to draw his sword and indulge in a portrayal of an irritated Highland laird.

He didn't, only because he couldn't decide who he

should use his sword on first: Victoria because she was staring at Fellini in fascination, or Fellini, just for general purposes.

So he made himself comfortable in the shade of a nearby grove of trees and watched the goings on with disgust. Mary ate, but did not seem to enjoy her food. And how could she, with all that overacting going on right there before her.

Victoria didn't eat either, but that was because she was too busy gaping at Fellini and hanging on his every word. Connor was tempted to tell her to tuck in properly to her bangers and mash and tell Fellini to go to hell, but 'twas none of his affair, so he kept his suggestions to himself.

Fellini managed to ingest all the rest of their food, yet keep up a steady stream of conversation that left Connor struggling to stay awake. By the saints, the man was irritating in the extreme.

Fellini finally dabbed at his lips with a bit of white cloth, then rose. "Victoria," he said imperiously, "come with me. I have things to discuss with you."

Victoria, not looking nearly as irritated as she should have, rose. "Granny, will you be all right?"

"Of course, darling."

"We won't go far."

"Don't worry about me. I'll keep busy."

Victoria nodded, then followed Fellini off into the distance. Connor stepped from behind the tree he'd recently appropriated as a hiding place, and watched her go. She looked weary. He supposed he understood. After all, how was she to have any energy at all when she had to spend it on those obnoxious actors?

He thought about that for quite a while, then realized with a start that Mary had turned to look at him.

"Connor, come and sit."

He sighed and unbuckled his sword, then came to sit down next to her on the blanket.

"What an unpleasant afternoon," he said bluntly.

"Isn't it?" she mused. "Let's speak of something else before I go do that man an injury." She smiled at him. "Tell me how you are passing your days at present. Is it a complete distraction to have Vikki's company in your hall, or are you managing?"

"It is a distraction from my main purpose of finding a captain for my garrison, but I am managing to conduct searches in spite of it."

"Must you really conduct a search?" she asked. "Surely men line up for the privilege."

"One would suppose that to be the case, wouldn't one?" he asked. "Damn me, if I don't have to prod them into that line with my sword!"

"It hardly bears thinking on."

Connor liked Victoria's grandmother more all the time. Not only did she immediately appreciate the difficulties of commanding a garrison, she possessed the most interesting implements of death he had ever seen.

"What are those delightful bits you have there?" he asked, peering at them closely.

"Knitting needles," Mary said, holding a pair up for his inspection. "These are steel ones."

"Do they bend?" he asked, terribly interested.

"They're not really supposed to."

"And if they were to strike a rib on their way through a man?" he asked. "How would they fare then?"

"I'm not sure," she answered, holding one up. It glinted nicely in the sunlight. "I've never tried to stick one through a man."

"A pity. Then what useful thing do you do with them?"

She held up a beautiful sweater fashioned from the colors of water and forest, heather and thistle.

"Lovely," he admitted frankly. "And quite an interesting use of threads, if I might venture an opinion."

"Fair Isle," she said, stroking the fabric. "I like the colors together. It reminds me of the Scottish countryside, somehow. How it used to be before the English cut down the forests."

"Have you been?" he asked.

"I'm a MacLeod," she said simply. "How could I stay away? But you haven't been back, have you?"

He shook his head. "Not since . . . well, not in many, many years."

"You should go."

"There is nothing for me there."

"But what a pity to deny yourself the pleasure—"

"I cannot bear it," he said shortly.

Mary looked at him long, then smiled gently. "I suppose I can understand. I have lived in places that I've loved and not been able to go back, or really even think about them. The loss is too great."

He grunted in answer. Aye, he had lost much in the Highlands, much more than his own life, and he supposed it might have been because of that that he hadn't returned. In truth, he wasn't certain and had no desire to peer into his own black heart and discover the truth.

So he sat and watched Victoria's grandmother work her magic with needles and yarn and found himself quite mesmerized. She began to instruct him about various techniques and species of yarn. He listened with interest to the manner of creating invisible increases and the technical formula to calculate loft, then he felt himself growing tired. He closed his eyes.

And it was when his eyes seemed the most heavy that Victoria's grandmother began her true assault.

She was more than making up for her nap in the sitting chamber the week before.

He was fairly sure he answered questions—and Mary seemed to have many of them. He was quite certain he divulged his mortal age of thirty-five and his status as the eldest son of three, the other two being worthless leeches who were content to live off their father's wealth and not do an honest day's labor in their lives. He suspected he had told her that he'd been wed at one time and the father of a pair of bairns.

But after that, his eyes grew far too heavy to keep them open and he wasn't quite sure what he told her.

"Laird MacDougal?"

He woke with a snort and sat up, reaching for his sword. "What?" he said, looking around with wide eyes.

"Vikki has been gone for quite some time."

It took him a moment to get his bearings, then he realized what Mary had said. "Has she been gone long?"

"Long enough that I wonder why she isn't back."

"I'll go immediately," he said, getting to his feet. He looked down at her. "Do you have your needles?"

She patted her bag. "Right here. I'll be all right."

"We won't be long, if I have anything to say about it," Connor said grimly.

It took him only minutes to find his quarry on the far side of a little hill. Victoria had her arms folded over her chest and looked a little bored.

Well, that was something, at least.

Connor approached carefully. It was tempting to draw his sword, but he thought of Victoria's warning that her actors might leave her without themselves to decorate her stage if they became too frightened. In Fellini's case, it would not be a great loss, but Fellini's understudy was almost as arrogant as the man himself, so perhaps there was no point in staging a proper haunting now.

"So, how large a space is Tempest in a Teapot?" Fellini asked.

"Large enough," Victoria answered. "We have room for what we want to do."

"Give me dimensions," Fellini insisted. "For my students, of course. It would help to have an idea of how big a stage they might someday be able to perform on."

What difference could that possibly make? Connor shook his head. Good acting was what was needful, not pacing off the stage. Was this man as simple-minded as he appeared, or was there a more sinister purpose to his questions?

Connor studied Victoria as she answered increasingly specific questions about her theater. He learned quite a few things he hadn't known before about Victoria's troupe; he spent many more fruitless moments puzzling over other things he had no familiarity with.

What was hemp and why did Fellini's eyebrows disappear under his hair when Victoria mentioned it growing in pots all about the stage? And why, when Victoria mentioned the rents on her theater being paid through the new year, did Fellini clap his hands together as if in pleasure he could not contain?

And why, after that clapping of his hands, did Fellini resume an attitude of disinterest, as if everything they had spoken about in the preceding half hour had held little interest for him at all?

Baffling.

Connor looked at Victoria. Her expression had shifted from boredom to faint suspicion.

Fellini seemed not to notice.

Connor supposed he wouldn't have noticed, either, had he not become so acquainted so quickly with the myriad appearances of that lovely visage.

The saints preserve him for it.

"You know," Victoria said briskly, "I think I need to get back."

Fellini yawned. "Me, too. I think I'll dash off a letter to a faculty member or two at Juilliard. I'm sure they would be interested in Tempest in a Teapot, as well. You know, in the details you so kindly gave me today. In the interest of our students, of course."

"Of course."

Victoria walked with Fellini back the way they had come. Connor would have thought she hadn't seen him—indeed, he had intended that she not—but to his surprise, she flashed him a look and nodded her head toward the path she and Fellini were taking. As if she wanted him to come along.

He went.

It was likely because he was walking behind her, mesmerized by the cascade of flame curls she sported on her head, that he didn't notice she had stopped until he fair walked through her. He jumped back, startled almost as much by that as by her gasp of surprise.

"Where's my grandmother?"

"She's probably gone on ahead to the inn," Fellini said with a shrug. "Bathroom break, or something like that."

Victoria went very still.

Connor found that her stillness became his quite easily. There was something here that was not right.

Not right at all.

"She wouldn't have gone off without saying something first," Victoria said.

"She knew better than to interrupt me," Fellini said. "Obviously a woman with good sense."

Connor walked around Victoria and looked down at the picnic paraphernalia. The hamper was there, devoid of food thanks to Fellini, of course. Nothing else looked disturbed, however. No signs of a struggle. No blood. No tracks from half a dozen booted ruffian feet. Connor met Victoria's eyes and he grimaced. He should have stayed behind.

Then again, perhaps Fellini had it aright. The habits of an old woman . . .

Victoria took a step closer. "Her knitting bag's gone, but look." She reached down and picked up a room key. "Why would she have left this?"

"I'm sure your grandma just ran off for some incontinence containment and forgot some of her stuff," Fellini said. "Pruitt's got another key."

"I have a feeling something's not right," Victoria said, looking around her.

"You're imagining things," Fellini said.

Victoria reached down and picked up Mary's sunglasses. "She wouldn't leave without these."

"It's cloudy out," Fellini said shortly. "Come on, Victoria. I've got things to do. Grab the stuff and let's go."

Victoria stroked the sunglasses. "This just isn't good. She left her key and her sun—"

"Look," Fellini said curtly, "I'm not going to hang around here and speculate. She's probably at the inn and that's where I'm going to go. And I want to see your theater space when we get back to Manhattan."

Connor watched the man spin on his heel and stride angrily away. If he hadn't known of the man's whereabouts, he might have suspected him of foul play.

He looked at Victoria. "I left her here not a handful of moments ago."

Victoria looked around in consternation. "It doesn't make sense. She wouldn't just . . ."

She stopped speaking and walked a few paces away. She bent and picked something up.

It was a single knitting needle.

She looked at Connor and held it up.

"A long 4.00 mm," he said grimly. "No doubt one of her best weapons."

Victoria looked at the picnic basket, then back at him. "Maybe she did go back to the inn. Maybe she did just lose this . . ."

She turned and bolted for the road.

Connor took one more look at the scene, then sprinted after her. He caught her easily. "We'll find her," he promised, supposing she might be weeping already.

She was dry-eyed.

"I hope," she said.

He ran with her to the inn, then waited whilst she stood outside the front door, leaning against the door frame to catch her breath. She gulped in air for a few moments, then shook her head.

"I need to exercise more," she said. "You would think that yelling at actors all day would be workout enough, wouldn't you?"

"You need time in the lists," Connor said wisely. "It aids not only strength of body, but agility of mind, as well as having the added benefit of according you the useful skill of being able to do someone in."

She blew her hair out of her eyes. "I wish I could get Michael Fellini there. Damn him for not caring!"

"I am unsurprised," Connor said, pursing his lips.

Victoria looked up at him. "You don't like him."

"You know I do not."

She shook her head with a sigh. "You're right about him, of course. I should have seen it earlier." She looked at the front door, then put her hand on the doorknob. "I can only hope we'll find her inside."

Connor nodded, but he held out little hope they would find Victoria's grandmother safely tucked away inside the inn.

They didn't.

Chapter 10

Victoria sat in the chair, staring into the darkened hearth. There was only one lamp on and it did little to relieve the gloom. She wasn't sure what time it was. She suspected it was no longer Saturday, which meant it had to be Sunday. The fact that she could still tell the difference was probably a very good thing.

Yesterday was a blur. She remembered running an abysmal rehearsal in the morning. She remembered a picnic with her granny and Michael's very odd questions. She remembered returning to the blanket and finding her grandmother gone. She remembered a frantic return to the inn, only to have her suspicions confirmed.

The bobbies had been subsequently summoned. She was fairly sure she had answered questions, waited while others answered questions, then answered more questions. It had seemed to take most of the afternoon and quite a bit of the evening. Then the bobbies had gone. More were promised for the morning.

Mrs. Pruitt had deposited a tea tray in the sitting room, lit a single lamp, and left her alone.

Only she hadn't been alone.

She looked away from the cold hearth. There, in a hard chair across the room, sat a dark-haired man, tall and broad-shouldered. His head was bowed, his hands were clasped. He lifted his head and looked at her, silently.

She sighed. "I need to call my family."

He started to rise. "I'll go—"

"Don't," she said quickly, then hesitated. "That is . . . if you wouldn't mind staying . . ."

He sat. "Of course."

She stared at him for several moments in silence, then looked down at her hands. "Thank you," she said.

"For what?"

"For staying. For my granny."

He cleared his throat. "It isn't for her."

Victoria looked up in surprise.

"Well, not entirely," he amended.

She hardly knew what to say to that. Here was a man who a short time ago was ready to scare the living daylights out of her, and now he was . . . well . . . not. She smiled briefly. "Thank you for that, as well," she said. "Laird Mac-Dougal."

"Connor," he said.

She looked up at him, dry-eyed. "Connor?"

"'Tis my pleasure and duty to render aid to you," he said formally, "Mistress—"

"Victoria," she interrupted. "It's just Victoria."

He paused for several moments.

"Victoria," he said, finally.

She shivered. She was certain that shiver had everything to do with the lateness of the hour and absolutely nothing to do with the fact that a man she could never have and probably shouldn't even be talking to had just said her name in a way that sent chills down her spine.

She looked for the phone. She was losing it. She had to get on with the phone calls she dreaded making while she still had some small hold on her sanity.

She never should have allowed her granny to stay in

England. The smartest thing to have done would have been to heave her grandmother's bags back in the taxi and point the driver toward the train station.

Actually, what she should have done was to tell Thomas to take his castle and go to hell. She never would have hired Michael Fellini, never would have had Gerard flee for less-haunted ground, never would have had her grandmother come to rescue her.

She never would have met Connor MacDougal.

She put her face in her hands. It was hopeless . . .

Then she sat up straight and rubbed her hands over her face, as if she had intended to do that all along. Giving in to discouragement was not her habit. She put her shoulders back and turned to face the problem. She also couldn't help a small peek at Connor, just to see if he'd seen her weakness.

He was watching her with a grave expression.

"I'm fine," she said briskly.

"I never doubted it."

"I'm just not sure who to call first." She paused. "I don't think I'm ready to hear what my mother will say."

He cleared his throat. "This is none of my affair," he began slowly, "but . . ." He hesitated, as if he didn't dare speak his mind quite so fully as he would have liked.

"Go ahead," she said, waving him on. "If you have an opinion, offer it. I'm fresh out of ideas."

He chewed on his next words as if he couldn't quite bring himself to give voice to them. "It galls me to admit this, but your brother is . . . um . . . not unwise."

She blinked. "You think I should call Thomas?"

"He is not a complete fool."

"That's high praise."

"If you tell him I said as much, I will deny it."

She smiled in spite of herself, then sobered. "He'll kill me."

Connor frowned. "Why?"

"This is all my fault."

"Victoria, your *grandmère* was a woman of ripe age and well-developed canniness. She could see to herself."

Victoria wanted to believe it. She knew her grandmother was clever. She also knew her grandmother had her
knitting bag and there were at least a few things that might
qualify as a weapon in there. But it was hard to think of her
out on her own.

She shook her head to clear it, then reached for the
phone. She dialed Thomas's number, her hands shaking so
badly she could hardly manage it. It rang three times.
Iolanthe answered.

"Hello?"

Ah, such a lovely Scottish lilt. Victoria closed her eyes
briefly. "Iolanthe, this is Victoria." She wanted to say more,
but found that she couldn't.

Iolanthe was silent for a moment or two, as well. "Is
aught amiss, sister?"

Well, there was no sense in beating around the bush.
"My grandmother has gone missing."

"Missing?"

"Vanished without a trace. Well, not without a trace. She
left her key and sunglasses behind. But there were no signs
of a struggle. And her knitting bag was gone. She never
went anywhere without it, you know, just in case she had a
spare minute to work another row or two." Victoria paused.
"She was working on a sweater."

She knew she was babbling; she couldn't seem to help
herself.

Iolanthe was silent for another eternity. Victoria wondered if her sister-in-law had moved away from morning
sickness and on to all-day sickness and was now struggling
to keep her dinner down.

"I'll fetch Thomas," Iolanthe said suddenly.

Victoria reached for her tea and downed it cold. It didn't
give her any courage, but it did wet her whistle enough that
she thought she might be able to spar verbally with her
brother.

"Vic?"

Then again, maybe not. What she wanted to do was
break down and bawl like a baby. The only thing that kept

her from it was the fact that she would be doing it in front of Connor and Thomas both. She would never live it down. She took a deep breath. "I lost her."

"You lost who?"

"I lost Granny. I left her sitting on a blanket and when I came back, she was gone. It's my fault. I was off making nice to one of my actors."

"Fellini?"

"Thomas," she said, through gritted teeth, "what difference does it make which one?"

"I'm just curious."

"You idiot, I just lost our grandmother!" she bellowed.

"Did you call the cops?"

"Yes, I called the cops."

"Were there signs of foul play?"

Victoria rubbed the spot between her eyes that was starting to throb. "No."

"So, you're telling me she just wandered off?"

"I don't have conclusive evidence to that fact, but all things seem to point to it."

"Vic, you should have been a lawyer."

"Thomas!"

"We'll be there as soon as we can get a flight out."

"Really?" she asked, surprised. "You will?"

"Of course. What else would I do?"

"I don't know," she said with a deep sigh. "But if you're going to come, hurry."

"Get off the phone so I can."

Victoria slammed the phone down. She glared at Connor. "He's a jerk."

Connor rubbed his fingers over his mouth, as if he fought an expression that begged to come out.

"Are you smiling?" she asked suspiciously.

He shook his head. "Nay. It merely warms my heart to hear you give your brother the drubbing he so richly deserves."

"He's coming right away."

"If the straits were not so dire, I would be happy to

welcome him with a few shriek-inducing antics." Connor pursed his lips. "The saints only know what runs through his mind."

"Mindless babble," Victoria said. She was relieved, though. It should have galled her. She was certainly as capable as her brother of handling all kinds of crises. And it wasn't as if Thomas had spent the whole of their youth bailing her out of scrapes. More often than not, he'd been at the bottom of her troubles.

But he had once or twice been there for her when she really needed someone—unasked and without undue I-told-you-so activity afterward. Maybe this would be another thing to add to that very short list.

She sighed. "Well, I guess I have no choice but to call my mom and dad now. I'm not looking forward to this." She looked at him. "My mother will be devastated."

"If your dam is anything like her dam, she will bear it well enough," Connor said. "A right fearsome wench is your granny."

The phone rang. Victoria picked it up out of habit, then wondered if she should have let Mrs. Pruitt do it. Too late now.

"Hello?" she said hesitantly.

"Have you called Mom and Dad?"

She sighed. "No. Do you want to?"

"Sure," Thomas said. "I'll call you right back."

Victoria hung up and looked at Connor. "Thomas is calling my parents. We'll see how they hold up." She paused. "You don't suppose that my granny—"

"I do not," he said sharply. "And neither should you. She is well and sound and counting on you to come fetch her. I daresay the authorities are skilled enough, but they have not our inducement to find her."

Victoria nodded her head and stared at the phone. That didn't keep her from jumping again when it rang. She looked at Connor, then picked up the phone.

"Yes?"

"Mom and Dad are okay."

Victoria let out her breath slowly. "Are they really?"

Thomas laughed a bit. "Mom said not to worry. Dad said, and I quote, 'The woman never goes anywhere without a bag full of steel needles. She even terrorized me a time or two with them. She'll be fine.'"

Victoria managed a wan smile. "I can see Granny taking Dad to task."

"Well, I'm sure she'll show back up to do it again."

"I hope so."

"Dad's booking their flights right now and I'll do the same. Why don't you go get some sleep. We'll all be there, probably the day after tomorrow, and straighten everything out."

Victoria nodded, said her good-byes, and hung up the phone, somehow quite relieved to have Thomas's help. She looked at Connor. "They're all coming."

"As well they should," Connor said gravely.

"I think my mom is okay."

"It must be the MacLeod blood," Connor said, "and that compliment does not come without cost."

She smiled briefly as she pushed the phone away. "She's completely caught up in that Scottish woo-woo-business. Second sight and all that. I'm sure she and Ambrose will get along very well."

"No doubt."

"At least I can guarantee Thomas doesn't know anything about the paranormal." She paused. "Well, outside of you, I suppose."

Connor began to cough, but he managed to gain control of himself eventually. Victoria looked at him suspiciously.

"What is it?"

"An intense desire to do your brother in came over me suddenly," he said, with a minor squirm.

"You probably shouldn't. He's bringing his wife, Iolanthe."

"I imagined he would."

"Have you met her?"

"A time or two," he said evasively.

She wondered at his tone, but didn't have the energy to wonder too hard. There was no doubt some kind of something going on and she would find out about it later.

Maybe when she'd staked Thomas out over a red-ant hill and was using a mirror to shine the sunlight in his eyes. Did they have red ants in England and what would her actors think when she clunked her brother over the head so she could more easily tie his unconscious hands and feet to little tent stakes she would happily spend quite a while securing into the ground?

Probably better not to know.

"Satisfying thoughts?" Connor inquired.

"I'm thinking of ways to torture my brother."

"I have some ideas."

She laughed, then put her hand over her mouth quickly. Laughing wasn't something she could do at present. She sighed and leaned back in the chair. "We'll compare notes later, when my granny's here to listen."

"Aye."

Victoria closed her eyes. "I think I'll be okay if you want to go."

He was silent.

In fact, he was so silent that she finally forced herself to get her eyes back open so she could peer at him blearily.

"Really," she said.

He smiled grimly. "If you want me to be off, I will."

"I don't want to impose."

"You imposed from the first time I saw you. 'Tis a little late for an apology now."

She would have endeavored to unravel that, but she was just too fuzzy around the edges. "So you'll stay?"

"Unless you snore."

Victoria made herself comfortable in that overstuffed chair, the kind you sink into with little hope of getting out of without undignified exertions.

"Wake me if I do," she managed.

It was still dark when she woke. She knew that she'd been asleep only because the arm of the chair was wet. Sleep was probably the only place she could weep.

She opened her eyes and looked around the sitting room, expecting to find herself alone.

Connor was still there, sitting across from her in a hard chair, his arms folded over his chest, his eyes open and watching her.

His expression might have been a gentle one.

It also might have been a trick played on her by the firelight.

"You stayed," she whispered.

"I told you I would."

She closed her eyes and slipped back into peaceful, if not dry-eyed, slumber.

Chapter 11

C onnor worried. It wasn't in his nature to fash himself over anything that wasn't directly related to keeping meat on his supper table or keeping enemies out of his herd of cattle, but drastic times called for drastic measures—and the sight before him was drastic indeed.

Victoria was working.

He suspected that if she worked any harder, or worked her actors any harder, the whole lot of them would have a collapse.

"Again," she barked at Fellini and Mistress Blankenship.

"But Victoria," Cressida complained, "we've done the scene three times already."

"And it stank three times already," Victoria said crisply. "Do you want lousy reviews, Cressida? Your purpose in this scene is to draw the audience into your madness, not shove it down their throats."

Connor looked at Fellini, who had told Cressida more than once that she was not violent enough in her actions. The man stood on the stage with his arms over his chest, watching with angry, glittering eyes.

Cressida, on the other hand, looked as if she might descend into madness truly—likely from trying to decide whose advice she should heed.

Connor could scarce wait to find out whose it would be.

"All right," Cressida whimpered. "I can do it one more time."

"Of course you can," Victoria said. "Just check the ridiculous dramatics at the castle gate, would you?"

Half the cast and most of the crew gasped. Connor pushed away from where he leaned against the wall, certain there would be bloodshed. But Cressida only bowed her head, nodded humbly, and took her place on the stage for the beginning of the scene. Fellini stood at the side of the stage, silent and watchful. Connor went to stand nearby, lest the man mutter something useful under his breath. That put him close to Victoria, on the off chance that she might have a breakdown.

Not that she would.

And that was what worried him the most.

She had woken the previous morning, thanked him most politely for his companionship, then marched briskly from the sitting chamber and on to the business of her Sunday—which fortunately for her actors had not included any rehearsals.

But she had pounded through her own business of production checks with a relentlessness that bespoke heavy suffering. Connor understood that. There was nothing like getting on with doing to keep uncomfortable and unpleasant emotions at bay. He wondered how she managed it, though. She was so slender and lovely; it seemed that the weight of her burden should have simply crushed her asunder.

Not like her brother, who had apparently just arrived from the Colonies. Connor watched Thomas McKinnon walk through Thorpewold's gates as if he owned the place, damn him, with shoulders broad enough to carry any variety of burden. Thomas was alone and Connor wondered where his wife was. Surely Iolanthe MacLeod couldn't have resisted a chance to come and crow about her state of wedded bliss whilst Connor remained quite thoroughly cuckolded and unalive.

Life was, he decided, very strange indeed.

Thomas approached his sister. "Vic?"

Victoria didn't bother to look at him. "Talk to me after."

"After?" Thomas echoed. "I just flew in and all you can say is 'after'?"

"Nice to see you," she amended. "Now, get lost and let me finish here."

Connor snorted out a half laugh. By the saints, 'twas pleasing to see Victoria turn her sharp tongue on someone besides him. And who deserved it more than that arrogant and irritating brother of hers?

Thomas looked at her, then shook his head and sighed. Connor had to admit he understood that, as well. When Victoria was in the heat of battle, there was no conversing with her. He watched Thomas walk across the bailey to join him at the wall.

"MacDougal," Thomas said.

"McKinnon," Connor replied.

"I see my sister is still in full possession of herself and her sanity. I can only assume you haven't begun to terrify her."

Connor grunted. "She promised me a full month of screams if I left her and her company alone for the duration of her play."

Thomas's mouth fell open. "She did?"

"Aye."

"And you agreed?"

"The wench is a canny bargainer."

Thomas looked at him in astonishment. "I can't believe it. I think you're actually getting along with her."

"She is—outside of your fair grandmother and our good Lady Blythwood—the exception in your family. It must be, and this galls me to say as much, the MacLeod blood in her veins."

Thomas's mouth fell open for a moment or two, then he began to grin. "Interesting."

"Interesting would be watching your head leave your shoulders."

"But then who would entertain you?" Thomas asked. "Victoria? She's too busy running her rehearsals. You'll have to settle for me." He paused and looked at his sister. "I can't believe she's at it today."

"What else is she to do? She grieves."

"She doesn't look particularly overwrought."

"Fool," Connor said succinctly. "If she stops moving, she will break her own heart with weeping."

Thomas's mouth fell open again.

Connor glared at him. The man would begin to catch all manner of bug life in that trap if he did not close it soon. Connor felt somewhat compelled to say as much.

Thomas shut his mouth. He managed to maintain a neutral expression, but there was the hint of a twinkle in his eye. "You seem to have a good handle on what she's feeling."

"Go to hell, McKinnon," Connor said. "And leave the keys to my keep behind before you set off. I weary of your kin disturbing my peace."

"Do you?" Thomas asked, beginning to smile. "You don't seem all that tired."

Connor blustered a bit. He examined several lies he could have told, lies about his irritation at having Victoria McKinnon underfoot all day and his weariness over having to look after her at night. But prevarication was not in his nature.

So he settled for a glare.

Thomas laughed. "I'm sure you're just being nice to Vic so you can really give her a good scare later."

There was no good response for that, either.

Thomas laughed. He continued to chuckle until he saw Michael Fellini coming his way. He frowned. "Is that her star?"

"Aye."

"I don't like the look of him."

"I daresay your opinion will not improve upon meeting him."

Thomas seemed to consider Fellini as he walked toward them. Fellini looked about him suspiciously, as if he searched for something he could not see. But by the time he reached them, he had put on a smooth smile. He extended a hand to Thomas.

"You must be Victoria's brother."

"Thomas McKinnon," Thomas said, shaking the man's hand. "You must be Michael Fellini. Victoria sang your praises the last time we talked."

Fellini preened. It was all Connor could do to keep his thoughts, and his sword, to himself.

"Your sister is too kind. But," he said, lowering his voice as if he wished to draw Thomas in, "I have to admit to being worried about her."

Thomas leaned in and put on a greatly exaggerated look of interest. "Really? Why?"

"She's working herself to exhaustion. I'm afraid it's going to damage her health."

Thomas nodded solemnly. "She really gets involved in productions and it's impossible to pry her away from them. Do you have any suggestions?"

"Well, as you probably know, I am a fabulous director," Fellini said helpfully. "I make my living teaching, but I can *do*, as well. If you think it would be helpful, I could offer to take some pressure off Victoria. But only if you think it would help. I certainly wouldn't want to intrude."

"The hell you wouldn't," Connor said distinctly.

Michael blinked, then looked at Thomas in surprise. "Did you say something?"

"It was the wind," Thomas said. "A foul, unpleasant east wind, no doubt. You know, I appreciate the offer and I'll see what I can talk Vic into. She's pretty stubborn."

Fellini smiled pleasantly. "Yes, I've noticed. Just keep in mind that I'll be happy to help if you need it. By directing."

Thomas nodded. Connor stroked the hilt of his sword fondly as he watched Fellini walk off.

"You don't like him, do you?" Thomas asked quietly.

"I do not. I don't trust him, either."

Thomas raised an eyebrow. "This is novel. We two on the same side of a fight."

"When the enemy is a turncoat of that water, what else can we do? But do not expect this happy collaboration to last," Connor warned.

"I wouldn't," Thomas said sincerely. "Oh, look, the crew is packing up. Gotta run."

Connor allowed him to go without offering any post-collaboration threats. If he chose to bedevil Thomas Mc-Kinnon, it would be at a later time. Perhaps he would save such misery as something to be savored after the play was finished. For now, 'twas enough to give it a bit of thought whilst the company went about the business of securing the stage for the night.

Thomas badgered Victoria until she shouted at him to go back to the inn and wait for her to finish. He threw up his hands and walked away. Connor pursed his lips. By the saints, the man had lived with Victoria for years; had he no idea how to manage her?

Connor waited, quite wisely to his mind, until all the work was finished, the crew had departed, and Victoria had given Fred his final instructions for the day before he dared even contemplate leaving his place against the wall. Then he waited for several long moments as she made herself at home on the bench set against the side of the great hall. It was only then that he dared walk over and sit down next to her. But he didn't speak. She was no doubt reviewing her actors' performances in her head and wouldn't wish to be interrupted.

Finally, she lifted her head and looked at him. "Long day," she said wearily.

"Mistress Blankenship is improving," he offered.

"I was too hard on her."

Connor shook his head. "She was overacting. Best to pluck the desire from her before it takes full root. You did no more than you had to."

"Thank you," she said quietly. "For everything."

"A courageous man makes the best of his situation," he

said lightly. "And your actors are more interesting than the tourists who usually drive me to madness during the summer months."

"No, not for letting us inside the castle," she said slowly. "Thank you for last night. And yesterday. And today." She looked down at the dirt between her feet. "I needed a show of support."

"Of course you didn't," he said promptly. "I've never seen a wench soldier on as you do. You didn't need me."

She smiled fleetingly. "Thomas wants to see where we were on Saturday, when I was off yakking with Michael while my granny was going heaven knows where."

"The fault is equally mine. I should have stayed with her," Connor said grimly.

"Thomas wants to go back to the picnic site." She paused. "I wonder if there might be clues we missed."

"'Tis possible," Connor conceded.

She sighed and rose. "I imagine my parents will be here soon. I should go figure out where they're going to sleep."

"No doubt Mrs. Pruitt has matters well in hand."

"That's what I'm afraid of. Let's go."

Connor walked back to the inn with her. The way seemed shorter than ever. Perhaps he had passed too many decades of his undeath denying himself the company of other goodly souls. He was not unhappy to be remedying that. There was much to be said for amiable company and the inn certainly seemed to provide it.

He hadn't put foot to the inn's garden path, however, before he heard quite unwholesome and less-than-friendly sounds coming from inside.

"Trouble," Victoria said with a sigh.

"Fellini," Connor identified.

"Heaven help me."

Connor suspected even heaven couldn't do anything with that miserable excuse for a man, but he followed her to the inn just the same. He passed through the entryway after her and frowned fiercely at the goings on there.

"I will *not* give up my room!" Fellini bellowed. "I don't care who's here!"

"In a time of crisis," Mrs. Pruitt said crisply, "we are all called upon to make sacrifices. Whilst Mistress Victoria's kin are under *me* care, they'll have suitable chambers. There is ample room in the King of Denmark's room for a cot. You and His Majesty may come to blows over who takes it, but do *not* do so in me entryway!"

Fellini was in midscreech as Thomas walked out of the dining room.

Fellini shut his mouth with a snap.

Thomas threw Connor a look before he walked over to the treacherous viper. "Are there problems with the rooms?" he asked in an easy voice.

"No, no, of course not," Fellini said.

Mrs. Pruitt scowled, but said nothing.

"I'm sorry to displace you," Thomas continued, "but Mrs. Pruitt was kind enough to rearrange things so my wife and I could stay here in the inn. You know, this being the site of the tragedy and all."

Fellini nodded, but to Connor's eye seemed to be having a hard time swallowing his rage.

"Let me take you out to dinner tonight in return for your flexibility," Thomas continued with a smile. "I'm interested in how you think the play is going. And I understand from Victoria that you've had an amazing career. If you have the time, I'd like to hear all about it."

Brave man, Connor thought to himself. That would have been a duty far beyond his own capacity to endure.

"I'll go move my stuff, of course," Fellini said, suddenly all smiles and friendliness. "I didn't realize you were the one, um, who would be, you know—"

"Kicking you out?" Thomas said with a conspiratorial smile. "Sorry about it, but I appreciate your understanding."

"Of course. Shall we do an early dinner?"

"That would be great. It'll give us plenty of time to talk. I don't want to rush any of your stories."

And with that, Thomas clapped a companionable hand on Fellini's shoulder and sent him scurrying up the stairs.

"I'll need someone to move my bags," Fellini tossed back down over his shoulder.

Thomas caught Victoria by the elbow before she headed for the staircase. "Don't you dare," he said in a low voice. "He can move them himself." He paused, then smiled at his sister. "Besides, it sounds like Mom and Dad are here. Can't you hear Dad griping already?"

Connor leaned back against the sideboard and waited for the onslaught of the rest of Victoria's family. She looked uneasy, as if she would rather have been anywhere but where she was. Connor caught her eye and nodded for her to join him. She did, looking somewhat relieved.

"Prepare to be outnumbered," she said with a wan smile.

"So many McKinnons, so little time to do them all in," Connor began, but then the door opened, Victoria's parents swept inside, and there was no more time for pleasantries.

Connor looked first at her sire, who enveloped Victoria in a fatherly embrace. He was a large, powerfully built man, not unlike Thomas in stature. He scanned the entryway with a wary eye, though, as if he expected to be assaulted at any moment. Connor stroked his chin thoughtfully. Perhaps the man had had his own experiences with the Boar's Head lads.

Lord McKinnon then turned to Thomas and pulled his son into a brief, manly embrace, taking the opportunity to slap him on the back several times. Connor nodded in approval. He had, once or twice, received the same sort of affection from his own father. It said much about Victoria's sire that he was free with his admiration.

He would have considered that further, but he caught sight of Victoria's mother and found her far more pleasing to look upon than her husband. She was all that a wench of Scottish descent should be: strong, capable, and quite beautiful. 'Twas little wonder Victoria and Megan both were so lovely to look upon.

Though Connor had to admit, he had a preference for the former.

He would have clapped his hand to his forehead to hopefully dislodge a bit of sense, but he was interrupted by the sight of yet another McKinnon wench coming into the inn.

"Jenner!" Victoria said in surprise. "What are you doing here?"

"Offering an extra pair of hands," the young woman said, throwing her arms around Victoria. "You look terrible."

Victoria pulled back and scowled at her. "I open in four days. I always look like this four days before I open."

"That is Victoria's sister, you know. Jennifer."

Connor jumped, then glared at Ambrose, who had appeared next to him. "Would you cease with that business? Announce yourself next time!"

Ambrose only smiled. "She is a brilliant musician, from all accounts, and a very fine actress."

"Why is she not in Victoria's play?"

"She neither acts nor wields her fiddle, but I can't say why not," Ambrose said. "She works with her mother, fashioning clothing for wee ones." He paused. "She is unwed."

Connor looked at Ambrose suspiciously. "The poor wench isn't on your list, is she?"

"Lad, they're *all* on my list."

Connor considered that for quite some time. So, all the McKinnon siblings were on Ambrose's list? Connor could see that Megan had wed quite happily to that de Piaget lad with vats full of funds. He supposed that Thomas was happy enough with Iolanthe MacLeod. Jennifer, that youngest of Thomas's sisters who was so beautiful, had obviously, and no doubt happily, remained beyond Ambrose's clutches—at least up until now.

He paused.

What of Victoria?

He chewed on that thought until he could spew out the question that burned in his mouth like a live coal. "Have you a match in mind for Victoria?" he blurted out.

Ambrose stretched, cracked his knuckles, took an inordinate amount of time examining his fingernails, then smoothed a hand over his silver locks. It was only after he'd settled them to his satisfaction that he turned to Connor.

"Wouldn't you like to know," he said with a wink.

And with that, he disappeared.

Connor was so surprised he found himself quite unable to speak. Damnation, but aye, he would most certainly like to know! And then once he knew the name of the whoreson, he would immediately set about making his life a living hell.

Then he found that his jaw had slid south as if it were unhinged. Why, by all the saints, did he care who Victoria McKinnon wed?

Before he had the chance to truly convince himself of the truth of that disinterest, he was joined by Victoria on one side of him and Thomas on the other. He recaptured his favorite frown, on the off chance that they might read his thoughts in his expression.

"Jen can take the cot in Mom and Dad's room," Victoria said. "You and Iolanthe take Ambrose's bedroom. I'm sure he won't mind."

"We'll be better guests than Fellini," Thomas agreed. "But what about you?"

"Mrs. Pruitt has one more cot. I'll put it in the library. No one goes in there much, anyway. Or at least they won't now." She looked at Connor. "Meet my family."

"A fine group," he managed.

Thomas began to cough. Victoria looked at Connor.

"Excuse me."

She went around and pounded on her brother's back until he held up his hands in surrender.

"I'm all right. I just want to know why this madman here is so nice to you when and he spent half a year trying to chop my head off."

"He's mellowed," Victoria said. "I think Dad wants to go right up to the picnic site. I'll tell you all about Connor's metamorphosis later." She looked at Connor. "Do you want to come?"

"Ah . . ." He still had not recaptured his balance from his conversation with Ambrose. Who was that man who found himself on Ambrose's list for Victoria? Not Fellini. Surely not even Ambrose could be that feeble-minded. But if not Fellini, then who? There were not eligible men within Victoria's cast or crew who were worthy of her. Indeed, Connor was hard pressed to name a man within miles who was not only unwed, but man enough to handle a flame-haired, acid-tongued wench of Victoria's stature.

He paused.

Well, save himself.

"Connor? Are you okay?"

Connor looked at her in shock. Was *he* the man Ambrose and his undead cohorts had chosen?

"Victoria, who are you talking to?"

She looked at her father. "The inn's haunted, Dad, didn't you know? Let's get right on our little walk, shall we?"

Her father looked around frantically. "Where? Where are they?"

"Dad, she's teasing." Thomas tugged his father toward the door. "Let's go. Vic's just hallucinating from lack of sleep. A little fresh air will do her good."

"You said the idyllic countryside would do her good and look at her now," their father said. "Victoria, come along. I'm worried about you . . ."

Victoria threw Connor a look of mild panic before she walked off with her father.

Connor waited until they had all left the inn before he followed at a discreet distance. Indeed, he hung back purposefully, but soon found himself walking next to Victoria's mother. He would have thought it coincidence, but two things convinced him otherwise. One, the woman matched his pace, no matter what that pace was; and two, she could see him.

"Um," he said in consternation.

"I'm Helen McKinnon," she said, with a smile. "You are Laird MacDougal, I assume?"

He cleared his throat uncomfortably. "How did you know?"

"My mother knows how to use the phone."

"She told you of me?" he squeaked. He felt a blush flood his cheeks. By the saints, he never squeaked. Perhaps it hadn't been a squeak, but rather a manly exclamation of surprise and pleasure all rolled into one. After all, he did have quite fond feelings for Mary.

"She described a very tall, exceptionally handsome Highland laird," Helen continued, "youngish but in full command of his surroundings, who was graciously allowing my daughter to use his castle for her production."

"I daresay your son seems to think he owns the bloody place," Connor said, grasping for something to say. Exceptionally handsome? By the saints, were these McKinnon wenches going to forever keep him off balance?

"We know better, now, don't we?" she said with a smooth smile. "I can see that my mother didn't quite give you the credit she should have for graciousness."

"Your mother is kinder to me than I deserve," Connor managed. "She is a lovely woman."

"She is." Helen looked at him for a moment or two longer, then smiled again. "Thank you for watching over Victoria. She needs it, though she'll never admit it. I can see why it would be easy for her to rely on you."

And with that she left him behind, walking on as if she hadn't a care in the world. Of course, it wasn't hard to leave him behind, given that she had fair frozen him in his tracks.

Yet another McKinnon wench to admire.

Surely the world would end soon.

He managed to get himself within several feet of Victoria's family without being noticed. He listened to them discuss the possibilities, the concerns, the complete improbability of their grandmother being kidnapped. Then Victoria's sire apparently wearied of the discussion, for he broke away from the group and started to tramp off over the farmer's field.

Thomas caught him by the arm.

"Don't, Dad."

"Don't what?"

"Look at the flowers in that grass. See how they form a ring? You shouldn't step inside that."

Lord McKinnon looked at his son as if he'd never seen him before. Connor shared his sentiments precisely. Had Thomas gone completely daft? Had marriage to Iolanthe MacLeod been *that* taxing?

"Why not?" Lord McKinnon asked.

"Just trust me," Thomas said.

"What's there? Poisoned oak? Snakes? Aggressive spiders?"

"Nothing so commonplace. Just stand back and let me look around for another minute."

Connor watched as Thomas walked about the flowery ring, studying it here, bending to look at it there, as if he actually found something interesting about weeds growing in a circle.

"Daft," Connor muttered to himself.

Thomas finished with his inspection, then came to put his hand on his father's shoulder. "Let's go back to the inn. I have a friend to call who might know something about this. Actually, he's a relative of Iolanthe's. Let's have him come look at this place before we go trampling all over it."

Connor pursed his lips. Yet another MacLeod in the vicinity. Obviously, he was going to be troubled by them far into his afterlife.

He watched as the entire troupe headed back toward the inn. Victoria seemed to lag behind just a little bit. In time, she was walking a goodly distance behind her family and next to him. She looked up at him.

"Will you keep me company in the sitting room again tonight?" she asked.

"Nay."

She looked up in surprise. At any other time, he might have been somewhat gratified by her look of disappointment. "Oh," she said. "I'm sorry. I obviously misunderstood—"

"I won't sit up with you because you need to sleep and you cannot sleep sitting up in a chair in that sitting chamber. Find a bed, Victoria, and make use of it. You do your granny no service by driving yourself thusly, though I do understand why you do it."

"I don't think I can sleep," she said quietly.

"Come now, woman," he said sternly, "must I threaten you with a proper haunting to force you to obey?"

She smiled wearily. "No. No, that's incentive enough."

He walked on with her, trying not to be overly gratified by her reaction.

The rest of the afternoon passed slowly, as did supper and the final sorting out of the chambers. It was well after dark before Victoria settled into the Boar's Head Inn's finely paneled Elizabethan library. Connor watched her go in, then waited an appropriate amount of time before he poked his head through the door to see that she slept.

She lay there with her hands folded over her chest, staring up at the ceiling, not having snuffed out the faint lamplight first.

He found her in like condition through the first two watches of the night. An hour or two before dawn, he sighed, then walked through the door to sit down in one of the leather chairs before the hearth.

"Bloodshed or haunting?" he asked, resigned.

She turned her head to look at him. Even by the weak light of the lamp he could see that her eyes were quite bright, as if she had tears to shed.

"Am I to be involved in either the bloodshed or the haunting?"

"Normally, I would say you aye, but I fear it would keep you awake. I'm disappointed in your lack of mastery, Victoria McKinnon. You've troops to marshall on the morrow. A commander is not at his best when he's bleary-eyed."

She smiled. "You're right."

"I generally am."

"Then tell me of hauntings," she said, with a yawn. "I

don't want to hear about your life until I'm awake to enjoy it. Bore me with screams of terror."

He hadn't begun but his second tale before he realized that she slept. He stoked a fire with a flick of his wrist and watched her by that light.

By the saints, if he'd had a pair of wits to cast at each other to form a single thought of self-preservation, he would have taken himself and fled for his keep whilst his heart was still intact.

What if he was the match for her?

By the saints, 'twas a mighty thought.

But he couldn't bring himself to think on it more. So he sat and watched her through what was left of the night. Let her think on him as a distraction, or a useful guardsman, or even as an unwanted protector.

Let her think on him at all and it would be enough.

Chapter 12

V*ictoria* suspected the sitting room might be full of one too many Highland lords.

She sat in a chair and looked around her, wondering how it was that two months ago she had been living a perfectly normal existence in Manhattan, thinking about Shakespeare and reminding herself to buy enough Raid on the way home to take care of her perennial cockroach problem, yet now she was sitting in the cozy sitting room in an Elizabethan inn, surrounded by men—some of whom were actually alive— who would have been at home on a medieval movie set.

She first considered the man sitting across the coffee table from her: James MacLeod, Iolanthe's grandfather. Maybe *Grandfather* was just a title of respect. Iolanthe called him *my laird* just as often, so maybe it was a Scottish thing Victoria just didn't get. He was certainly too young to really be her grandfather, so maybe *Grandfather* was what you called a man who looked as if he wielded a sword every day just for fun and probably would have been just as at home if he'd been using it to do business with. He simply reeked of medieval lairdliness. If she'd been casting a *Braveheart* kind of movie, James MacLeod would have been her first choice for the star, regardless of whether or not he could act.

Weird.

Next to him sat her brother—no, never mind there about the Highland lord thing, though she had heard Iolanthe call him *my laird* on more than one occasion. That could be chalked up to morning sickness, no doubt. Thomas was tough enough, she supposed, but he had certainly never wielded a sword and she seriously doubted he'd gotten in any more fights than his barracuda lawyer Jake had gotten him out of. Fisticuffs? Victoria snorted. This was her brother and she knew just what a weenie he could be when he ran out of butter and sour cream.

Besides, a good look at him presently was enough to put the last nail in the coffin. He was wearing an apron and trying to convince Iolanthe to eat the oatmeal he'd made her. And given that just the sight of Thomas's attempt at breakfast made Victoria want to puke, she suspected Thomas's continued flirtation with domesticity wasn't going to fly with his wife.

And it certainly disqualified him for lairdship.

But behind the couch, in a little lairdly row, stood Ambrose, Hugh, Fulbert, and Connor. All with their arms folded over their chests, all with thoughtful frowns on their faces, all looking as if a mere command from them would send lesser mortals scurrying to do their bidding.

Well, Fulbert looked as though he would have preferred to be sitting rather than standing, but he was doing his part.

"'Tis most interesting," Jamie MacLeod was saying. "She simply vanished without a trace."

"Leaving behind things she normally wouldn't have," Thomas said, with a look that spoke volumes.

Victoria wished she knew what books he was referencing. She revisited her plan containing ants and stakes. Iolanthe would survive it if he were in the hospital for a day or two, recovering from his interrogation session. There was something spooky going on.

And it had nothing to do with ghosts.

Jamie stroked his chin thoughtfully. "Well, I canna say for sure until I see the area—"

"Just a minute, if you don't mind," she heard herself say. "I'm a little confused here. Are you some sort of private investigator?"

Jamie smiled at her. "Nay, I'm not. I'm merely kin of Iolanthe's. But I have some experience with the strange happenings in Scotland."

Victoria could believe it. And since he seemed less than interested in telling her what those strange happenings might be, she could see that she would just have to tail him until she found out for herself.

Jamie rose. "Now, if Thomas would humor me—"

"Sure," Thomas said. He turned to Iolanthe, who was curled up in an overstuffed chair, looking as though she'd much rather be in bed. "Will you be okay? I can leave the oatmeal here . . ."

She waved him away. "Take it, I beg you. I canna bear the smell of it."

Thomas hesitated, then gave in. "All right. I'll take this back to the kitchen and meet you guys outside."

Victoria crawled to her feet. "Should I go get Mom and Dad?"

"No," Thomas said quickly, shooting Jamie a look full of meaning. "I mean, let's let them rest for the morning, shall we?" He smiled at Victoria. "Don't you think?"

"I think a lot of things," she began, "and one of them is—"

Thomas held up his hand suddenly. "Quiet," he said urgently.

Victoria frowned. Was he having second thoughts about the oatmeal? Poor Iolanthe. "Thomas," she said with a gusty sigh, "let's just get—"

"Wait. I think I hear something."

"That's your wife moaning. Let's leave her in peace."

He tiptoed, oatmeal in hand, over to the door. He put his ear to it, then jerked it open suddenly.

Michael Fellini came sprawling into the sitting room.

Thomas reached down and helped Michael to his feet.

"Why, Michael," he said in a friendly voice, "what a pleasant surprise."

Michael brushed himself off stiffly. "I'm here because I was concerned that Victoria might be troubled over her grandmother's loss."

"How kind of you. Were you just going to knock?"

"Yes, that's it," Michael said quickly. "I was just about to knock."

"Well," Thomas said, putting his hand on Michael's shoulder, "I'm sorry I opened the door so fast. That must have been a little embarrassing—you know, leaning on the door so hard before knocking that you fell right into the room."

Michael huffed and puffed and came close to passing out from lack of oxygen. He looked at Victoria. "I was just concerned about *you.*"

"I'm fine," she said, frowning. What in the world was he up to? "I appreciate the concern. Maybe you should just go practice your lines."

"I know my lines," Michael said.

"Then get your stuff together."

"Why?"

"Mr. MacLeod needs a place to stay. We're going to have to find another place for you and Denmark."

Michael opened his mouth to protest, but Jamie stepped forward and extended his hand. Michael's jaw continued on its downward course, rendering him, thankfully, quite speechless.

"Good of you," Jamie said, shaking his hand firmly as he towered over Michael. "I'm James MacLeod. I'm here to help out with the search for Victoria's grandmother."

"Mr. Fellini is a very famous drama pedagogue," Thomas said, "as well as a very accommodating human being. He's already given up one room for me."

"Kind of him to make yet another sacrifice," Jamie said. "You didn't hurt yourself falling into the sitting chamber, did you, Master Fellini?"

Michael apparently was incapable of shutting his mouth.

Victoria watched, deeply suspicious, as he finally managed to get hold of himself long enough to leave the room and head back up the stairs, ostensibly to inform the King of Denmark that they were being kicked out yet again.

He did cast one last quite furious look back down the stairs, which he didn't realize would be seen until he connected gazes with her.

He wiped all expression of his face.

She realized that she was very grateful he had been with her when her granny had disappeared. She would have suspected him of foul play otherwise. She wasn't sure she didn't suspect him of it anyway.

She watched him disappear upstairs and cursed herself under her breath. When would she cease to be bamboozled by people? She was a hard-boiled, hard-bitten, steely-eyed New Yorker. She was not taken in by shysters.

Handsome, talented, big-agent-card-carrying actors aside, apparently.

"All right," Thomas said in a low voice, "I'll make my kitchen run and meet you all out in the garden. Try to keep Dad out of this, Vic, would you?"

"Why?"

"It would be too much for him."

And with that cryptic statement, he made tracks for the dining room. Victoria couldn't imagine why they might find something her father couldn't handle, but maybe Thomas knew more than she did.

An alarming trend, to be sure.

She waited outside with Jamie until Thomas rejoined them, then followed the group out the front door—mortal men in front, lairdly ghosts striding behind. She walked behind them all, speculating furiously. There was something fishy going on between Thomas and Jamie, and it was more than a little chitchat over memories of Thomas's wedding.

But before she could really get herself worked up, Ambrose caught up with her. "Granddaughter," he said in a friendly fashion.

Victoria pursed her lips. "Who is James MacLeod?"

"Kin of Iolanthe's," Ambrose said. "He was at Thomas's wedding. Don't you remember him?"

"Sure," Victoria fibbed. Actually, she remembered very little of Thomas's wedding. She'd flown back and forth from Scotland to New York twice in less than a month and that during a rather taxing run of *The Tempest*. She remembered thinking that the MacLeod castle was quite medieval-looking and that Jamie must have had buckets of money to keep it up. But other than that, she'd just been too wrapped up in thinking about how the production couldn't possibly run without her, and worrying about planning productions to come, to really pay attention to anything else.

She paused.

She considered.

Was she too caught up in the theater?

The very thought was almost too shocking to contemplate.

She took a deep breath and let it out. She was no more caught up in her life than anyone else was. She had just managed to overlook Jamie, the very essence of Highland lairdliness, due to jet lag, no doubt.

That Jamie had such a, well, medieval aura about him was something to be investigated another day. Maybe when Iolanthe had stopped spending all her time in the bathroom and was capable of prolonged speech regarding her relatives.

Victoria trailed along after the living as they made their way to the scene of the alleged crime, then found herself standing a little ways off, accompanied by ancestors and, well, Connor.

"Foul deeds afoot," Fulbert said gloomily. "I've little liking for the feel of this place."

"You've little liking for anything that doesn't resemble a pub," Connor snapped. "Be silent and let the lads who know their business be about that business."

Victoria looked at Fulbert, who was fingering the hilt of his sword purposefully. Hugh had backed well out of the way. Ambrose stood next to her, wearing the same sort of easy smile her mother was wont to wear. Victoria frowned at him.

"Is it a MacLeod trait never to panic?" she demanded.

" 'Tis a MacLeod trait to possess an abundance of patience," he said. "All will be well."

"Do you know something I don't?"

"Aye, that you should move, lest Connor cut you in two by mistake."

Victoria whirled around to see Connor with his sword drawn, glaring at Fulbert. "Oh, please," she hissed, "save it for later, would you?"

He turned his glare on her. "He irritated me."

"And you're irritating *me*. Stay on task, would you?"

She turned back to the little tableau in front of her. It was only when Ambrose's soft chuckles became too distracting that she looked at him.

"What?" she demanded.

He nodded toward Connor. Victoria turned to see that Connor had put up his sword and folded his arms over his chest. He shot her a look of disgust before he turned his face forward.

"I've never seen him back away from a fight," Ambrose said conversationally.

"I did not back away," Connor said curtly. "I'm humoring the wench here. She's distraught and not thinking clearly, else she never would have spoken to me in that tone of voice."

"Of course not," Ambrose said, sounding as if he'd swallowed something very large and was having a hard time breathing because of it.

Victoria ignored them all and watched the goings on in front of her. Jamie walked here and there, bent now and then to study the grass, then walked some more.

At length, he talked to Thomas, who nodded, then walked toward Victoria.

"I think you can wait for us back at the inn."

"Wait for you?" Victoria echoed. "Are you telling me I'm being dismissed?"

"Something like that," Thomas said easily.

Victoria hesitated, looked at Thomas to judge his level of stubbornness, then shrugged. "All right."

Thomas blinked. "You'll go?"

"Didn't you just ask me to?"

"I didn't think you'd do it."

Victoria shrugged. "I'll go. We'll all go. *All* of us," she said pointedly.

The Boar's Head Trio seemed willing enough and started back toward the inn. Even Connor stomped off with a curse or two.

Victoria nodded in a friendly fashion to her brother, then trudged along obediently after her ancestors for quite a distance. Then she let out her most artistic expression of dismay.

"My watch!" she exclaimed. "I must have dropped it along the path. You all go along ahead. I'll catch up."

Ambrose frowned. "We can help—"

"I wouldn't dream of it. You should check on Iolanthe."

Ambrose nodded. "Aye, there is that. Come on, lads. Let's be about our business."

The men started back toward the inn. Connor followed them.

"Not you," Victoria whispered fiercely.

Connor looked back over his shoulder at her, then frowned. "Not you, who? Me?"

"Of course, you." She nodded back toward the rise of the hill where on the other side Thomas and Jamie were investigating. "You don't think I'm going to let Thomas be in charge, do you?"

"I knew there was a reason I hadn't terrified you to death already," he said pleasantly as he turned back toward her.

"Well, keep it to yourself and be discreet about this."

"Discreet?"

"Don't let them see you. Thomas is my mother's son, you know. Though I'm not quite sure where Jamie fits in; he's a suspicious character. Now, if I only knew how to sneak up on them—"

"Follow me," Connor said, leading off into the grass.

It was only slightly disconcerting to see none of the local flora and fauna show any trace of his passing. Victoria shivered, then plunged into the field after him.

It seemed an inordinate way out of the way, but she realized he knew what he was doing when they made their way through the trees and wound up within eavesdropping distance of the pair of lunatics standing there stroking their chins and discussing flowers in the grass.

"'Tis a proper fairy ring," Jamie was saying.

"Well, you would know."

Victoria looked at Connor with wide eyes. He was smirking unpleasantly.

"Prissy MacLeod woman," Connor said with a soft snort. "No offense to present company."

"Maybe his wife likes flowers," she offered.

"Perhaps he has plucked too many and the scent has gone to his head and ruined whatever wits he might have once possessed."

Victoria took that under advisement and leaned around the tree to better hear what was being said.

"Do you think it's possible?" Thomas was asking.

"'Tis always possible with these sorts of suspicious bloomings," Jamie said, stroking his chin thoughtfully. "And we *are* in Scotland, never mind that 'tis so close to the English border that the wind blows unpleasantly foul."

Thomas laughed. "Jamie, you're not very tolerant of your southern neighbors."

"I'd spend more time being tolerant if the Inland Revenue spent less time dipping into my coffers."

"Coffers," Victoria echoed. "What a quaint term for it."

Connor grunted. "His speech is passing medieval, if you ask me."

Victoria nodded to herself. She would certainly have some questions for Iolanthe when the time was right.

"So, my laird," Thomas said, jamming his hands into his pockets, "what's your opinion?"

"There is only one way to know for sure," Jamie said.

And with that, he stepped quite deliberately into the fairy ring.

And vanished.

Victoria gasped.

Connor gasped as well.

She sat down hard. Connor jumped aside to avoid her and went sprawling. She was almost speechless. Fortunately, it was a condition that never troubled her for long.

"Did you see what I just saw?" she asked Connor.

"He's a demon," Connor breathed. He crossed himself for good measure.

"Either that, or a damned good magician." Victoria heaved herself to her feet. "Come with me while I torture some answers from my brother."

"Gladly," he replied, leaping with alacrity to his feet. "Pray allow me to inflict some kind of damage upon him, as well."

"Wait your turn."

Thomas turned as they approached. He didn't look all that surprised, either that she was there or that Jamie had disappeared. Victoria stopped in front of him, folded her arms across her chest, and glared at him.

"All right, spill it," she demanded.

"Spill what?"

"Don't be dumb," she snapped. "Jamie was here and now he's not. Where did he go?"

Thomas shrugged. "I have no idea."

"Thomas!"

He put his hand on her shoulder. Connor growled.

"Down, Laird MacDougal," Thomas said. He looked at Victoria with twinkling eyes. "He's quite possessive."

"I'm robbing him of tourists to scare. He's just marking time until the castle is back in his possession. Now, cough up the details before he really does you some damage."

Possessive? Victoria tried not to let that word rattle around in her head. Connor MacDougal had all the time in the world and he was killing it by hanging out with her.

Surely.

Thomas put his arm around her shoulders and pulled her away. "Let's walk. I'll tell you what you want to know. Well, at least most of what you want to know." He looked at Connor. "You should come as well, MacDougal. You've seen enough weird things in your time not to be surprised by any of this. Besides, I'm counting on you to keep my sister in line. You know," he said, leaning over Victoria's head conspiratorially, "she can really come unhinged when it suits her. Has she let you have it yet?"

Victoria elbowed her brother quite forcefully in the ribs.

"I've managed to avoid most of her ire," Connor said easily, "but her cast and crew lives in fear."

"Hey!" Victoria said, glaring up at him. "You're supposed to be on *my* side."

He almost smiled. She could have sworn he had.

He looked at Thomas and shrugged. "Provoke her at your own risk. I daresay I would have to hold you accountable for her suffering."

"How gallant of you," Thomas said, with an unwholesome snort of laughter.

"Shut up," Victoria suggested.

Thomas gave her shoulders a squeeze. "Cut me some slack, sis. Didn't I get you a great castle for your play?"

"Yeah, full of ghosts dying to do me in."

"Laird MacDougal doesn't want to do you in any longer. At least not until after the play's over. Isn't that right, Mac-Dougal?"

Connor only muttered under his breath.

Victoria found herself walking back to the inn with her brother on one side and Connor MacDougal on the other.

And it felt perfectly normal.

"I think I'm sleep deprived," she announced.

Connor grunted. "Now you see the effects of not heeding my advice."

"She never listens," Thomas said. "Don't waste your energy."

"Aye, I have become accustomed to it. How is it you have dealt with this stubbornness? You managed her quite poorly in the keep yesterday and I wondered if you had been at all successful at the task in times past."

"Well, generally I just let her grind herself into the dust. She'll wear out eventually."

"Can't you two find anything else to talk about?" Victoria said briskly. "You know, like where my grandmother went and why James MacLeod just vanished into thin air?"

"We'll get to all that in good time," Thomas assured her.

Victoria wondered if this kind of surreality was what you felt after you'd flown around the world three or four times and could no longer tell what time zone you were in. She looked at her brother blearily. "I think my life is unraveling."

"I think it started a while ago," Thomas suggested.

She felt her eyes narrow. "I think you might have started it all."

"Me?" he asked innocently. "I had nothing to do with it. But aren't you glad anyway?"

Well, she was, but she'd be damned if she would admit it. "You have some answering to do," she said, wagging her finger at him. "You wiggled out of quite a few explanations after you and Iolanthe got married, but that won't happen this time."

"Sure," Thomas said with a smile. "But first, let's go call Jamie's wife. She'll want to know he's off on a little business trip for a while."

"How can you be so cavalier about this!" she exclaimed.

"I know Jamie. He'll be all right."

Victoria looked at Connor. "Are you this relaxed about it?"

Connor lifted one shoulder in a shrug. "I cannot bring James MacLeod back. As I said, there is something different about him." He looked at Thomas pointedly. "Something unsettlingly, medievally different."

"He's a Highlander," Thomas said negligently. "You're all sort of a fierce lot anyway, aren't you?"

"True," Connor agreed, "but that doesn't explain several peculiar things about the man."

"Answers," Victoria demanded. "I want answers."

"And you'll have them," Thomas answered.

"When?"

"Oh, look, there's the inn," Thomas said, quickening his pace. "I'd better see how Iolanthe's doing."

Victoria watched him turn his pace into a flat-out sprint. She looked at Connor.

"He's hiding something."

"Aye."

"I wonder what it is?"

"There's only one way to find out."

"Torture?"

He smiled.

Victoria gasped in spite of herself. "That's a very unpleasant smile."

"I've worked for centuries to perfect it."

"Yeah, well, don't ever look at me like that. But use it on my brother as often as possible. If we're lucky, he might even pee his pants."

"One can dream."

She smiled up at him. "I like you."

His eyes widened in surprise and she realized what she'd said. She quickly ran through all the things she could say that would clarify or downgrade or trivialize what she'd said.

But she couldn't come up with a thing.

"Let's go," she said quickly. "Before he escapes our foul clutches."

Connor nodded. "Aye."

Victoria walked with him the rest of the way to the inn. She vowed to keep a better grip on her tongue, just so she didn't make any more uncomfortable gaffes.

She looked at Connor out of the corner of her eye. He didn't look to be too upset. He looked thoughtful.

He was probably wondering what in the world he was going to do with a woman who was obviously losing her mind.

She wondered the same thing.

Chapter 13

Michael Fellini crouched behind the little stone fence and peered over just far enough to watch Victoria McKinnon and her brother walk down the road in the direction of the inn. Once they were gone, he sat down with a thump on the ground, Mrs. Pruitt's poached binoculars hanging heavily around his neck.

He had just seen a man disappear.

Hadn't he?

He would have thought it was just a nifty special effect, but he was, unfortunately, not starring in a supernatural thriller. He was stuck in rural England with nothing to do but make trouble and let his imagination run away with him.

He crawled unsteadily to his feet and made his way to where he'd last seen that MacLeod character. He approached carefully, though; there was no sense in getting himself into trouble unnecessarily. A cursory look showed him nothing but farmland. Well, except for those flowers in the grass, growing in a circle. What was the deal with that?

No trap door, though. No way to disappear easily and leave the audience fooled.

Well, obviously he was going to have to do more eaves-dropping. He hadn't heard nearly enough with his ear to the door that morning. Maybe Mrs. Pruitt had something he could use to turn up the volume. She certainly had quite a stash of investigative paraphernalia. He couldn't have cared less for the paranormal chicanery, but the listening devices and night-vision goggles could certainly come in handy. Now, if she just didn't keep most of her stash under her pillow, it would be a damned sight easier to steal it.

Then he paused.

Pruitt did paranormal investigating. Did that mean there were ghosts in the inn? Did that mean there were some sort of paranormal shenanigans going on out here in the field?

He considered.

Nah, it was impossible. The old bat had more time on her hands than was good for her. He could certainly give her a few things to do. His room was completely inadequate. Her time would be better spent worrying about the comfort of her guests than looking out for ghosts.

Or disappearing men.

He turned and marched doggedly down the road. He wasn't certain why he was so fixated on the events of the day before. He couldn't have cared less what had happened to Victoria's grandma. She'd probably been abducted, though why anyone would have bothered, he didn't know. But there was something about the way she'd gone and the subsequent activity that had intrigued him. Finding Mrs. Pruitt's gear had only increased his curiosity.

He was certain he could use it somehow to further his own ambitions.

Maybe he would find the old woman, rescue her, then present her to Thomas and collect his fee by taking Victoria's job.

He rubbed his hands together and smiled pleasantly.

Chivalry most certainly wasn't dead.

He was living proof of that.

Chapter 14

Connor leaned back against the wall in the sitting room and watched the goings on with a frown. The chamber was full of McKinnons, MacLeods, and a lone de Piaget. Rehearsals were over for the day, lunch had been consumed, and now Victoria's family and sundry were gathered to enjoy lively conversation. Victoria's kin occupied the couch and a pair of comfortable chairs. The sundry, which included the Boar's Head ghosties, had gathered themselves to the side, though they were listening intently and commenting amongst themselves.

Connor watched the mortals gathered there and thought wistfully of his own family's pleasant conversings involving swords and the effective use of them on enemies. Though the McKinnons only discussed actors and their foibles, Connor enjoyed it greatly.

He wondered how Victoria could keep herself from joining in. He looked at her, sitting apart from the group, poring over lists of costumes and lighting directions and columns of numbers marching down the page. She had been driving herself since dawn, plowing through her rehearsals with ruthless determination. Connor had shadowed her for most of the day already, simply because he feared she would drive herself into a collapse if he did not keep an eye on her.

Well, his reasons for following her might be slightly more complicated than that.

But those reasons aside, he did harbor a goodly amount of concern for her. Though she'd happily whispered threats to her brother the night before, today she had ceased even with that pleasant bit of amusement. She had listened earlier that morning as Thomas had called James MacLeod's wife to give her the tidings of Jamie's disappearance. Lady Elizabeth had been unsurprised, and that had surprised Connor greatly. Though he generally spared no more thought for a MacLeod than to want to be free of them, he had found himself fearing that Jamie's wife might have a collapse. That she apparently expected her husband to return safely boded well not only for him, but for Victoria's grandmother, as well.

Assuming she had disappeared through the flowery ring in like manner.

Victoria had listened to Thomas's recounting of the conversation, then thrown herself back into her work. Not even the distraction of her younger sister Jennifer had brought her out from behind her papers, even though he understood from Thomas that Jennifer was Victoria's especial favorite.

It was not encouraging.

Connor watched as Jennifer rose and went to sit down next to Victoria. He moved closer as casually as he could. He didn't escape the watchful eye and approving smile of Helen MacLeod, but then again, he suspected little escaped her notice.

"Vic, let me have that."

Victoria looked up at her sister. Connor frowned at the sight of the darkened circles under her eyes. All was not well indeed.

"I'm fine," she said.

She was lying, obviously. Perhaps Jamie's journey into the fairy ring had been more distressing to her than she dared admit.

"You're not," Jennifer said.

"I *am*."

Jennifer pursed her lips in a very fair imitation of Victoria. "Let me at least look over the costume lists."

"I am more than capable—"

"I never said you weren't capable—"

"Victoria, you should let your sister look at them," Connor said, finding that his sidling had left him standing quite near the pair.

Jennifer turned around in her chair with a gasp. She gaped at him with wide eyes.

Connor attempted a smile.

Apparently, it hadn't come out quite as pleasantly as he might have hoped.

Jennifer stood up and shrieked—quite nicely to his mind—then her eyes rolled back in her head and she slumped to the floor. Connor did his best to catch her, but he couldn't even slow her descent.

"Good heavens!" Victoria's father exclaimed. "Are there rats in this place?"

Connor stood over Victoria's sister with his hands outstretched uselessly, then met Victoria's eyes.

That she didn't chastise him was worrisome indeed.

"Thomas, come help," she said wearily. "It was probably jet lag. Or too much time surrounded by baby clothes. Mom, when is she going to get a real job? She has a degree in music, for heaven's sake. She should be playing with an orchestra. Or she should have kept up her acting. Did you see the way she fainted? You can't teach that."

"I know, dear," Helen said.

Connor backed away as Thomas roused his youngest sister. She came to, babbling.

"Good grief, Jenner, cease the gibberish," Victoria commanded.

"It's Gaelic," Thomas said, flashing Connor half a smile.

"And how would you know?" Victoria demanded. "As if you can understand it!"

Thomas only smiled, unperturbed. "Io is a Highlander, you know. Doesn't it occur to you that I might have wanted to understand her if she felt the need to swear at me in her mother tongue?"

"It occurs to me that you must be very adept at it, as I'm certain she does *that* quite often," Victoria said with a snort. She looked at Jennifer. "You're hallucinating. Come sit back down and don't scream anymore."

Jennifer allowed Thomas to help her to her feet. Connor found himself being regarded with wide eyes.

"Do you see what I'm seeing?" Jennifer whispered to Thomas.

"Connor MacDougal," Thomas murmured. "He's the wannabe laird of the castle up the way."

Connor couldn't stop himself. He had his sword half drawn from its scabbard before he realized that Jennifer was on the verge of swooning again.

"He's harmless," Thomas whispered.

"He doesn't look harmless," Jennifer said weakly. "He's got a sword."

Thomas turned her around and sat her down in the chair. "I don't think he'll use it on you, but let's talk about that later. Dad wouldn't be able to handle this conversation."

Thomas made loud conversation with his father as he returned to his seat. Jennifer sat uneasily, stared up at Connor just as uneasily, and groped for her sister's hand.

"He has a sword," she whispered frantically.

"Yeah, well, he wasn't waving his sword at you," Victoria said shortly. "He was preparing to do damage to your brother with it."

Connor attempted a smile, but apparently that only made matters worse, because Jennifer now clutched Victoria's hand so tightly Victoria squeaked.

Victoria pulled her hand away. "Get a hold of yourself, Jenner. If you're determined to be useful, check those costume lists. I want to make sure everything's still where it's supposed to be."

Connor considered leaving the chamber. Indeed, he started toward the door.

Victoria cleared her throat pointedly.

He took that to mean she did not wish him to go. He resumed his place against the wall.

Jennifer leaned closer to her sister. "I didn't imagine him, did I? Not really."

"Nope," Victoria said, chewing on a pencil.

"Do you see him, too?"

"We'll talk later."

"Vikki, he's a ghost."

"That, too," Victoria said.

Jennifer put her head between her knees. Victoria looked at Connor.

She smiled.

He had to brace himself against the wall.

Jennifer sat up, wheezing. "Aren't you afraid?"

"Terrified," Victoria said solemnly. "I'll introduce you to him later when Dad's gone up to bed."

Jennifer's head went between her knees again. Victoria smiled to herself, then bent back to her work.

Connor watched for another hour or so as Victoria and Jennifer worked on their papers and the rest of the group talked about nothing in particular. It was truly a day made for easy conversing among family and acquaintances. Thomas, especially, seemed to be in a jovial mood.

Connor studied the man and wondered what it was he knew that none of the rest of them did.

In time, Victoria's parents left the parlor to go for a stroll through the inn's gardens. Iolanthe departed for her bedchamber, no doubt to shore up her strength for the taxing proposition of being Thomas McKinnon's wife.

"You know what," Thomas said, putting his feet up on the coffee table and his hands behind his head, "since all of us, except Vic, of course, speak Gaelic, maybe it would pass the time pleasantly if we had ourselves a day in the native tongue." He smiled at Ambrose. "What say you, my laird?"

"I always find a bit of Gaelic to be quite useful," Ambrose agreed. "But perhaps we should introduce ourselves to your other fair sister first, before we begin this happy exercise."

Connor watched as Jennifer clutched the edges of the table so fiercely her knuckles went white. But she seemed to have quite a bit of her sister's spine, for she did not flee.

"Breathe, Jen," Victoria said dryly, "and prepare to meet your ancestors."

"This is genealogy taken too far," Jennifer said in a low voice.

Ambrose stood and made Jennifer a bow. "I am Ambrose MacLeod, your grandfather from olden times." He gestured to Hugh and Fulbert. "Hugh McKinnon and Fulbert de Piaget. Fulbert is Megan's husband's uncle."

Jennifer's eyes were very wide. "But not all that recently, I'd imagine."

"No indeed, missy," Fulbert said.

"Several generations removed?" Jennifer asked uneasily.

"Several, at least," Fulbert agreed.

Ambrose nodded toward Connor. "And that is Connor MacDougal. He was laird of his own clan during his day, and now watches over Thomas's keep, up the way."

Connor didn't bother to correct anything Ambrose said, which made him wonder how far he had slipped in defending his claims and wreaking havoc. Obviously, he needed a few hours out on the field, hacking at an opponent almost equal to him in skill so that he might remember that he was a warrior and not a ladies' maid.

But there was no sense in terrorizing Victoria's sister, so Connor kept his arguments to himself and tried not to scowl.

"All right," Thomas said, putting his feet on the floor and rubbing his hands together in anticipation, "now that everyone's been introduced, let's get on with this. Vic, you don't have any Gaelic, do you?"

"You know I don't," Victoria said stiffly. "I regret it now, but at the time I had more pressing things on my mind than letting Granny teach me, such as clawing my way through Juilliard's hallowed halls. Just go on without me. I'll suffer the price of my folly."

"No, indeed," Thomas said in mock horror. "I think I have the *perfect* translator for you. Laird MacDougal, will you do the honors?"

"Of course," Connor said quickly. Too quickly, if the satisfied look on Ambrose's face was any indication. Thomas was wearing the same look.

Connor revisited his suspicions of the day before. Was Thomas colluding with Ambrose on these matchmaking ventures? And the next question that begged a definitive answer was: Was the matchmaking for him or for Victoria? Or were they, as he had wondered the day before, match-making for him *and* Victoria?

"Connor?" Thomas prompted.

"I do," he said, then realized what he had said. "I mean, I'll do it if I must."

Thomas burst out laughing.

Connor looked at Victoria to find her looking at him with pursed lips.

"I'm *happy* to do it," he assured her. "To translate for you, that is. In truth, I am."

"I know I should have taken advantage of my granny, but I didn't."

"There's always today," Thomas said, wiping his eyes and letting out a final chuckle. "And think about all the tu-tors you have around you. Ambrose, Hugh, Connor, Jenner. Why, I imagine even Fulbert knows a word or two."

"Mostly insults," Fulbert admitted readily. "Though I could be called on to render a pleasing sentiment or two, if necessary."

"Well, then, let's get to it," Thomas said. He smiled at

Victoria. "You'll be clueless for a little while, but you'll catch on. Maybe Connor will give you private lessons later."

Connor watched Victoria fling one of her writing instruments at her brother. It brushed his ear and stuck itself in a blanket draped over a chair several feet behind the man.

"Well done," he said in admiration. "You would be quite dangerous with a knife."

"My brother should live in fear," she said.

"I do," Thomas said with a laugh.

And then he was off in the mother tongue. Connor listened to him in surprise. Then again, he supposed he shouldn't have been surprised. Thomas was, his offensive self aside, a shrewd man and not one lacking in intelligence. That he should have learned his lady wife's native tongue was no surprise. What did come as a surprise, though, was how well he spoke it. It was as if he'd spent his entire life in the Highlands.

Connor leaned back against the wall and listened with pleasure to the conversation going on around him. Even Jennifer added her part now and again, and quite satisfactorily. As he listened to the talk leap from battle to beautiful locales to visit, to modern things that seemed to be geared to make one daft, he realized that he had, in some unforeseen way, become a part of this group of very fine souls. He added his part when he felt it appropriate and found that his comments were welcome.

Then he realized he was shirking his primary duty. He looked quickly at Victoria to find that she was watching him, resting her chin on her fists with her elbows on the table. She was smiling slightly, as if she found him not unpleasant to look at.

And the saints pity him, he couldn't even muster up a frown in return.

He would have smiled, but that was apparently beyond him. He conjured up a chair and sat down next to her—not because he needed to sit and not because his knees had gone quite unsteady beneath him, but because he desired to save her the kink in her neck looking up at him would induce.

"Where to start?" he asked.

"I'm overwhelmed," she said honestly. "Tell me your favorite words. I'll learn those first."

So he considered, then translated for her a handful of his favorite things: brook, stand of trees, rain, fire, stew, beautiful woman.

She turned her chair so she was sitting next to him instead of facing him. "What are they talking about? And is Thomas holding his own, or is he making a fool of himself?"

"It amazes me to say it," Connor said, feeling quite amazed, "but he speaks perfectly. I don't wonder about it, though. Iolanthe likely has driven him to it."

"Either that, or he did it because he loves her and it's his gift to her."

Connor looked at her in surprise. Victoria appeared to be equally as surprised.

"I haven't slept enough," she said, sounding stunned. "I'm saying nice things about my brother."

"You'll feel more yourself tomorrow," Connor assured her. "Now, do you care to learn more single words or would you rather have things to say?"

She stared thoughtfully at the hearth for a moment or two, then she looked at him. "I wonder if we both could learn to read it and you could teach me to speak on the side. Would Ambrose help us, do you think?"

"You ask," Connor said promptly. "I might be tempted to do him damage if he says nay."

She smiled faintly. "I'll ask him. But later. Now, I think I'll be happy just to listen for a bit."

He looked at her and felt himself falling into her sparkling blue eyes. It was all he could do not to reach out and trail a finger along that perfect cheek, smooth a hand over her riotous hair, slide his hand underneath it, and pull her forward to—

"MacDougal?"

He blinked. "Aye?"

Then he realized it hadn't been Victoria saying his name. She was looking at him with an expression of something that he couldn't quite term lust, but that—he flattered himself to say—he couldn't relegate to disinterest.

"Laird MacDougal?"

Connor tore his gaze away and focused on the little group before the hearth. He realized that it was Thomas McKinnon who called his name.

"A battle story?"

"Aye," Connor managed. "Which one?"

"Any one," Thomas said, without a trace of a smirk on his face. "We're interested in something really gory."

Connor looked at Victoria briefly before he obliged the rest of the company, but in truth, he couldn't have said for certain just what he'd recounted for them.

His eyes were too full of the woman beside him who had wished she'd learned his language whilst she'd had the chance.

For what reason, he did not know and he dared not speculate.

Several hours later, Connor took up his post outside the library door. The afternoon had been passed most agreeably, with tales of victory and glory, and he'd done his best to dutifully translate for Victoria everything that had been said.

Such dutifulness had kept him too busy to really look at her again.

The saints preserve him, *that* would have been a disaster.

Now, evening had fallen and Victoria had retired, leaving him standing outside her door, determined to make certain that she had peace for sleeping.

And, unsurprisingly, who should arrive to disturb that peace but Michael Fellini, slithering down the steps and across the entryway like the snake he was. Connor wouldn't have moved aside for Fellini to knock on Victoria's door, but he couldn't bear the thought of the whoreson knocking through him. He stood aside and put his hand on his sword.

Victoria opened the door and looked at Fellini in surprise. "Michael," she said. "It's late; what do you need?"

Fellini bowed his head. "I have been appallingly unsympathetic about your grandmother. I came to apologize."

"Well," Victoria said, clearly taken aback. "I appreciate that."

Fellini lifted his head and looked at Victoria with an expression of such contrition that Connor almost believed him to be genuine.

If he hadn't been such an accurate diviner of men's characters, that is.

"I also think we got off on the wrong foot," Fellini continued. "What with Bernie and all his rules." He smiled conspiratorially. "You know agents. He's just doing his job."

"Sure," Victoria said. She smiled in a friendly manner. "I understand."

Connor felt his jaw sliding down of its own accord. She was *smiling* at that liar? And it wasn't just a normal, polite smile she was giving him. It was a *welcoming* smile. He thought it almost could have been called an *intimate* smile.

He simply could not believe his eyes.

"I'd like to start over," Fellini said. "Tomorrow, perhaps? It would be an honor to maybe share breakfast and take a walk up to the castle. Or perhaps we could borrow your sister's car and do some sightseeing."

Victoria simpered. Connor watched her do it and felt his astonishment increase at an unpleasant rate. What was the wench thinking? Damn her to hell, she was being taken in by this charlatan all over again!

Connor folded his arms over his chest and reconsidered his vow never to put a woman to the sword.

"Oh," Victoria said with a smile that said she was pleased, flattered, and *perfectly* happy to agree to anything Fellini suggested, "that would be just *wonderful*."

"Good," Fellini said. "I'll pick you up at eight. In the morning," he added with a terribly familiar chuckle.

Victoria almost swooned.

Connor almost retched.

"Go inside," Fellini said, making shooing motions with his hand and smiling. "Get your beauty sleep. Not that you need it."

"Oh," Victoria said again, a little breathlessly. "All right." She put her hand over her heart, as if the bloody thing was about to beat so hard it stood to fling itself out of her chest. She fluttered her eyelashes and gave him a flirtatious smile as if she simply couldn't believe her good fortune in having Michael Fellini appear at her door and request her presence for the next bloody day. "Good night."

And then she closed the door.

Connor watched Fellini slink back across the entryway and slither back up the stairs. He said nothing and cast no looks of triumph to anyone who might be watching.

Connor turned and scowled at the library door. Why, the silly wench was under the impostor's spell yet again! He was terribly disappointed and it took him several moments to discover why. Then he felt an expression descend upon his features that wasn't his normal scowl.

It was an expression of disillusionment.

The door creaked open suddenly. Victoria peered out.

"Is he gone?"

"Do you pine for him already?"

Damn the wench if she didn't look at him as if he'd lost his mind. Connor felt his expression of disillusionment turn to irritation.

"Aye, he is gone," Connor said flatly.

"What's wrong with you?" she asked.

He folded his arms over his chest and glared at her. "If you cannot divine it, then my disappointment in you has reached a new low indeed!"

"Disappointment?"

"Aye, and if you cannot divine the why of that—"

She blinked, then looked at him in surprise. "What? That bit with Michael?"

"Aye, that bit with Michael!"

She looked at him in surprise, then rolled her eyes and opened the door. "Come in."

"I have lost much respect for you—"

"Get in here, would you?"

He got in, only because he suspected she might try to pull him in otherwise, and since that would lead to failure and potential swearing on her part, it was best that he capitulate and allow the rest of the house to remain safely and happily asleep. But as he allowed her to shut the door behind him and take up a place where she could see him, he folded his arms over his chest again and prepared to tell her how he found her lacking in spine.

"Victoria—"

"Spill it," she interrupted.

He scowled at her. "It isn't as if this is any of my affair," he said shortly, "but it is quite a shock to my system to watch you fawn over that . . . that . . ."

"Fawn?"

"You've fallen for him again!"

"But, Connor, I wasn't serious!"

He blinked. "I beg your pardon?"

"That was *acting*," she said, suddenly finding a scowl of her own. "Surely you don't think I am that vapid."

"Well . . ."

"I am, and I say this quite modestly, a damned good actress."

He paused and considered. "Well, aye, I suppose so."

"I can't believe you think so little of me."

"Well," he said finally, "you *were* very convincing."

She smiled. "Maybe I've missed my calling in life. But that uncomfortable subject aside, I have the feeling Michael's up to something and I decided this was the best way to find out what."

"You aren't going to spend the day with him tomorrow, in truth," Connor said in disbelief. "Are you?"

"How else am I to find out anything? Though it's going to take all my self control to make nice." She turned and walked across the room to sit down in front of the hearth.

"I suppose I'll have to at least hang out with him during the morning."

"What will you do to escape his clutches after that?"

"Bore him with production minutiae until he goes away of his own accord."

"I could run him through," Connor offered. "There would be no permanent damage."

"Except to his ego, when he ran screaming the other way." She paused, then shook her head. "I was hoodwinked. And for the longest time, that's the kind of man I thought was the epitome of masculinity."

"Hmmm," he said, stroking his chin as if he were truly surprised that such a man might not be her ideal. "And now?"

The words came out of his mouth and he found that it was, unfortunately, much too late to call them back.

She smiled. "My tastes have changed."

Damn the woman, would she give him no hint as to her thinking? "Have they? Not that I'm really interested," he added quickly, to save his pride, in case she had someone in mind besides him. "I'm just being polite."

She blinked as if she'd been slapped briskly. "Oh. I see."

He wondered if it would disturb her if he cut off his own head. He considered blurting out that he thought her a right fearsome wench and one he would have been honored to guard day and night for the rest of her life. He considered telling her that the foregoing was a load of tripe and that he bloody well had fond feelings for her, and that if she took another serious look in Fellini's direction he bloody well would take his blade to her. He even considered telling her that if she didn't think him all that a man should be, he would walk out of the inn and find another part of England to haunt—

"Connor?"

"Aye?" he snarled.

"I think you need a nap."

"I most certainly do not need a nap!"

She sat back in her chair and studied him. He almost drew his sword in self-defense. At least then she would have been distracted by the glint of steel and ceased with her staring at him. He started a fire in the hearth with a flick of his wrist. Blades were better admired by firelight, he decided.

And damn it, so were red-haired, porcelain-complected women of the kind to steal his breath in spite of his iron self-control.

"Connor?" she asked quietly.

"Hmmm?" He put away his unreasonable and impossible thoughts. He was spirit; she was flesh. There was no circumnavigating that small inconvenience.

Would that he could.

"Thank you," she said.

In Gaelic.

The saints pity him, he thought he just might love her.

"For what?" he asked gruffly.

"For today," she said. "For keeping me company and wanting to avenge my bruised honor."

"A shade's work is never done," he managed.

Her smile faded, but didn't disappear.

"No," she said softly, "I suppose it isn't." She looked at him for several minutes, then rose slowly. "You don't have to stay."

"I ken that well enough, woman," he said gruffly. "Go to bed. I'll make certain Fellini doesn't slip something foul into your tea on the morrow."

She crawled into bed and closed her eyes. "Good night, Connor."

He was a very long time in answering, mostly because he wanted her to be asleep before he did.

"And to you, my lady," he whispered.

Damnation, he was past any hope of reason.

Chapter 15

Victoria walked along the way from the castle back to the inn, cursing in Gaelic. Learning the language was her new obsession and curses were the extent of her vocabulary so far. That was okay. She'd been swearing at Michael Fellini all morning, which was the only thing that had kept her from killing him.

She'd managed to eat breakfast with him that morning without doing him bodily harm. Then she'd bored him to tears with talk of technical things she knew he couldn't possibly have the patience for. He'd lasted until noon, which had been three hours longer than she'd been betting on. She'd learned nothing more than what she should have known from the start, which was that the man was a complete jerk. Why she'd ever found his exuberant, over-the-top, diva-type personality appealing, she would never know . . .

She hesitated.

She had obviously spent too much time around men packing swords.

She shook her head and continued on her way back to

the inn. She no longer recognized her life and that should have sent her speeding off to a therapist's couch. That it didn't was something to be examined another day. For now, she would just go with it. Maybe when she was striking the set after the show was over, she would do an equal amount of tearing down of her own life.

So many things she had taken for granted.

So little time spent on what really mattered.

Not that she was going to quit the theater and start making baby clothes any time soon. Jennifer could lose her mind that way, but Victoria had no intentions of doing the same thing. But balance? Yes, balance was something she could definitely stand to find.

She walked along the path up through the garden and smiled with the pleasure of sniffing Mrs. Pruitt's quite lovely-smelling flowers. There was also the fact that another day had been successfully conquered to savor. And that was no small feat. With only two days remaining until opening night, she was past being nervous. There was nothing else she could do at this point. Her actors knew their lines; they had their blocking down; they knew where to find the castle; no one was sick.

And no one was being haunted, either, at least today. Even the Boar's Head Trio had deserted her. She hadn't seen a one of them all day, not during the morning when Michael had been hanging onto her like a limpet, nor when her rehearsal had flown by during the afternoon.

She hadn't seen Connor, either. She'd grown so accustomed to him hanging around the stage or waiting to walk her back to the inn that it seemed strange to have seen nothing of him. What was he, a fair-weather ghost only willing to make an appearance if there was a good scream in it for him? Too busy with his afterlife to show up for five minutes and say hello?

She went immediately into the library. Connor sat there before the fire, poring with furrowed brow over a Gaelic version of *Thomas the Tank Engine*.

"Interesting book?" she asked.

He looked up at her and shrugged. "There are fewer letters in my language."

"You weren't at the castle today," she said briskly, putting her hands on her hips before she thought better of it.

He looked as shocked as she had ever seen him. "I was there this afternoon."

"Were you?"

"Aye, I was. Don't you remember?"

She rubbed her eyes, then sighed. "I'm sorry. It's been a long day."

"You should go in to supper," he said, folding up his book and sending it into oblivion. "I should likely come, as well. The saints only know what Fellini will be about."

"He's probably still recovering from this morning," she said. "I kept him busy at the castle this afternoon, but I didn't follow him when he left."

"I should have done so," Connor said. "I would have, but you bellowed at me to leave and I thought it best to comply."

She blinked. "Did I? Bellow at you?"

He lifted one eyebrow. "Can you not remember it?"

"Opening night is two days away," she explained.

"Will this condition of yours grow worse?"

"It always does."

"The saints preserve us," he said, with feeling. He rose and nodded toward the door. "Let us be away. Supper will do you good."

Victoria made her way to the dining room. It was packed to the gills. Mrs. Pruitt had apparently been forced to feed the King of Denmark and Gertrude in the kitchen, due to the new company, but the rest of the cast and Victoria's family found places at tables. She contented herself with a plate on her lap while she sat on a chair set up against the wall. She looked around to see if anyone else was as on-edge as she was.

Her parents were quiet, but not unsettled. Jennifer was listening, with glazed-over eyes, to Michael going on about heaven only knew what. Thomas and Iolanthe were as they always were: delighted beyond measure to gaze deeply into each other's eyes and ignore everyone around them.

No one seemed to be worried that Granny was gone or that James MacLeod had disappeared in like manner. Victoria felt as if she were in a terribly written play, portraying a character that she loathed and living for the moment when she could get offstage.

She choked down lukewarm vegetables and tried to keep a stiff upper lip. Everything would be okay. Jamie would show back up from wherever he'd gone. Her granny would pop back in the same way.

One could hope.

She was working on very dry bread when the door to the dining room burst open. She fully expected to see one of the ghosts burst in to put Michael to shame. But it wasn't a ghost. It wasn't even an actor.

It was James MacLeod.

Dressed in head-to-toe Elizabethan gear.

"Wannabe," Cressida said with a sniff. "The local costume shop hasn't got a clue and he hasn't got a talented bone in his body."

Victoria heard a crash. She realized as she stood up in surprise and felt something squish beneath her shoe that the crash had been her dinner landing on the floor. But before she could say anything, Thomas had risen and gone to welcome Jamie into the dining room. Victoria wanted to begin the grilling right then, but she was distracted by the food on her shoe and the necessity of cleaning it up. Mrs. Pruitt arrived with a dish towel and helped her. It was just as well, as Victoria found herself without the presence of mind to do it.

Jamie was back.

And Thomas didn't look at all surprised to see him.

Victoria leaned back against the wall, having given up any thought of eating. "Thomas knows something," she murmured.

Connor grunted. "I daresay."

"Did you know him when he was remodeling Thorpewold?" she asked out of the side of her mouth.

"Aye, you know I did."

"Why didn't you do him in when you had the chance?"

Connor snorted out a half laugh. "I should have."

"If you have the chance again, don't be such a gentleman. But let me use the thumbscrews on him first. I have a few answers to pry out of him."

"As you will, lady."

Jamie wasted no time ingesting quite a substantial dinner. Victoria considered while Jamie inhaled. Why did Thomas look so unsurprised? Had he expected Jamie to return? It wasn't possible that her brother had done his own hopping in and out of fairy rings.

Was it?

She let that percolate for a moment or two in her head, then dismissed it out of hand. This was Thomas she was thinking about. He was great with money, great with power tools, and spectacular with a pair of crampons on his boots, but anything to do with a sword? Ha! He would probably trip and impale himself on it, thereby saving his foe the trouble.

She turned her attention back to the known quantity. Jamie wasn't wasting any time with his meal and she was grateful for that. She was chafing at the bit to know what he'd found out.

Unfortunately, her actors were dawdling over their damned desserts. She tapped her foot impatiently. When they showed signs of lingering over coffee, she reached over and thumped her brother on the back of the head. He scowled at her as he rubbed the spot, but the wordless communication did the trick.

"Well, good night everyone," Thomas said, rising. "A family conference in the sitting room?"

Her family rose, and Michael rose along with them. Victoria strode over to him.

"Good night, Michael," she said with a smile. "I'm sure we'll see you in the morning."

He looked primed and ready to protest. Victoria opened her mouth to speak, but found that unnecessary.

"Sit down, you bloody bugger," Connor said sternly from behind him.

Michael shivered, then sat. "You don't have to be nasty about it," he groused. He looked at Victoria. "I suggest you don't use that tone with me again."

"Pre-performance stress," Thomas said, shaking Michael's hand.

"Whatever," Victoria said, brushing past him and Thomas both and heading toward the sitting room. She got there first so she could stake out her territory and have a good place to pace at the back of the room.

Her family took an inordinate amount of time lingering outside the sitting room. She tapped her foot, counted to ten, and scowled.

"They live to torment me," she said to Connor, who had joined her near the wall.

He lifted one eyebrow. "I can believe anything of your brother, but your parents seem quite lovely. Especially your mother. She has your grandmother's eyes."

"She has you under her spell, as well, I see."

He went so far as to duck his head a little. "Aye, likely so." Then he cleared his throat roughly. "Both she and your granny have been very kind to me."

Victoria studied him. It seemed preposterous that she should be entertaining such thoughts at a time like this, but she found herself unable to restrain them.

"Was no one kind to you before?"

He lifted his head with a snap and looked at her darkly. "Daft wench, I'm a warrior, not a bairn. What need have I for kindness?"

"I see."

"I daresay you do not."

She folded her arms over her chest. "Connor MacDougal, you're a fraud."

"A fraud? How dare you—"

"You're right. You aren't a fraud."

He nodded stiffly. "I accept the apology."

"You're a marshmallow."

"A . . . a what?"

"Marshmallow. It's something that's very soft in the middle. Some people even call it food."

His eyes were very wide. "You compare me to food?"

"I didn't call you a haggis now, did I?"

He began to splutter. She would have given him a more thorough explanation of why she considered him soft inside, but she was distracted by the entrance of her family. The Boar's Head Trio came in first, taking up their places against the back wall. Thomas came in and claimed a prime spot on the couch without delay. Jennifer followed him, scanning the room until her gaze fell on Connor. She walked over to him in a daze. Victoria watched as her sister stopped before him, then looked up at him and gaped.

"Jenner," Victoria said sharply, "nothing to see here. Keep moving."

"Vikki," Jennifer whispered, pointing at Connor, "do you realize—"

"Yes, I realize," she hissed.

"But . . ."

"Look," Victoria said impatiently, "buck up, will you? For pity's sake, Jennifer, too much time fondling fleece and fingering baby yarn has ruined you. You were, before your descent into baby-clothes madness, a professional violinist and a damned good actress. Dig up some of that professionalism and put it to good use."

Jennifer shut her mouth and looked for a chair. It was occupied by Fulbert. She squeaked, then looked around desperately for somewhere else to sit. In the end, she collapsed next to Thomas on the couch. Victoria supposed she was probably safer there.

Jamie came in and sat down with a flourish in a soft chair near the hearth.

Victoria waited, but the door was shut and no more family was entering. "Thomas, where are Mom and Dad?"

"I figured this wasn't a conversation Dad could handle," Thomas said, looking back over his shoulder at her. "Io's tired as well, and Mom offered to get her upstairs. It's just us here."

"And the ghosts," Jennifer said faintly.

Thomas put his arm around her. "That won't be the weirdest thing you hear tonight, Jenner. Hang on for the ride."

Victoria shot Connor a brief look of disgust before she went to sit down in a chair across the coffee table from Jamie. "I'm dying to hear what happened."

Jamie smiled in satisfaction. "Well, the first thing to tell is that the gate works."

"The gate?" Victoria echoed. "What gate?"

"The time gate in Farris's fairy ring," Jamie said simply.

Victoria wondered if it was possible to tell from just looking at Jamie whether or not he had lost all his marbles or just a few of them. She glanced at Thomas.

"Are you buying this?"

"I'd buy quite a bit if it explained where Granny had gone," Thomas said easily.

"But time travel!" Victoria exclaimed. She looked at Jamie. "This is time travel you're talking about, isn't it?"

"Aye, it is, Mistress Victoria," Jamie said. He smiled. "Perhaps a little proof would sit well with you."

He pulled coins out of a purse at his belt, then drew a dagger from his boot. He put all his booty onto the coffee table, as well as a sheaf or two of very new-looking parchment with very antique-looking writing on it.

"Interesting," Thomas said, leaning forward. "Where did you go and what did you see?"

"The fairy ring leads to Elizabethan England," Jamie said. "At least it did for me, but I was determined to bend its power to my will. Where it would take someone else is anyone's guess. My desire was to go where your grandmother had gone and off I went." He stroked the ruff around his neck. "Hence my sixteenth-century gear. I canna say I cared overmuch for the food. Or perhaps that was merely because I was in Renaissance London. The food is better in the country."

"It cannot be worse than medieval Scotland," Connor muttered.

Jamie looked at him and laughed. "Nay, it was not, Laird MacDougal."

Victoria wanted desperately to interrupt and ask how the hell James MacLeod would know anything about Renaissance country food or medieval chow, but she couldn't get her mouth shut and a useful swallow down before Jamie was off again, describing the delights of Renaissance London. And then he sobered.

"I must bring the disappointing tidings that I did not find Mistress Granny," he finished, "though I looked diligently for her."

"But you think that's where she went," Thomas stated.

"Aye, wouldn't you?"

Thomas nodded wisely.

Victoria suppressed the urge to bludgeon her brother with questions, as well. Who did he think he was, nodding in that knowing way as if he'd experienced time travel for himself?

Time travel?

Ha!

"That simplifies things," Thomas said.

"That simplifies things," Victoria echoed, finally finding her voice. "What do you mean by that?"

"It means now we know where to go get her."

"Go get her," Victoria wheezed. "Go *get* her?"

"Yes," Thomas said easily. "We follow Granny back to Elizabethan England, get her, and come home."

Victoria's first instinct was to reach over and thump her brother on the head to restore good sense to him. But then she realized what Jamie had said.

Elizabethan England?

Despite herself, she was intrigued.

She looked over her shoulder and motioned for Connor to come and sit next to her in the hard chair by the fire. The Boar's Head Trio was also soon seated there in front of a fire that did nothing to warm the room. She wouldn't have been surprised to have seen Shakespeare make an appearance.

But maybe that was asking too much.

"Even so," Jamie said, "it will not be an easy journey. We can assume your grandmother is there, but finding her is a different matter entirely. We've no idea where she would have wandered off to."

"Well, at least we know where that gate leads," Thomas said, leaning forward with his knees on his elbows. "It's a start."

"It would have come as a shock to her, doubtless," Jamie said, stroking the fabric of his shirt. "Wandering unknowing through that gate and finding herself in Shakespeare's London."

London. Victoria shivered in spite of herself. Modern-day London was rough enough. How in the world would her grandmother survive London in any other century? She looked at Thomas. "I'm hearing all this, but I can't quite believe it."

"Life's weird," he offered.

Jamie yawned suddenly. "Forgive me. I've had a very long se'nnight. We should speak more of this on the morrow. There is much to be discussed and many plans to make." He looked at Thomas seriously. "The gates can be very unpredictable. Even I, who have extensive experience with them, have found them from time to time to be unresponsive to my will. There is very real danger involved in this journey."

Victoria saw that Jamie and Thomas were still speaking, but she couldn't hear their words any longer. Her mind was reeling with two things she'd just heard.

Jamie had extensive experience with time gates and even he, who had used those gates apparently quite a bit, thought the journey was a dangerous one.

Maybe time travel wasn't as improbable as she thought.

It was the second item that clamored for her attention, though. If the trip was as dangerous as it sounded, it would be better made by someone with the least amount to lose.

Jamie had a family and he had already risked his life once to investigate. Her dad probably wouldn't get the gate to work for him because he was a confirmed skeptic. Thomas and Iolanthe were expecting a baby in the fall and there was no way Thomas could leave Iolanthe now.

They needed an unentangled person to go. Someone who knew something about Elizabethan England. Someone who could blend in, don an authentic-looking costume, and pull it off. Someone who could at least get by with the language.

Someone like her.

Jamie yawned again and rose. "I am weary. Let us converse again on the morrow and make our plans."

He left. Jennifer followed. Victoria looked at Thomas suspiciously, but decided that the interrogation could wait. She had things to think about and her own plans to make.

"I'm going to bed," she said, crawling to her feet. " 'Night, all."

Connor rose and followed her.

"MacDougal, you can stay," Thomas said.

"Aye, I could," he agreed.

"Manly talk," Thomas offered. "You might enjoy it."

"I don't trust Fellini," Connor answered crisply. "I will go stand guard outside Victoria's door."

"Of course," Thomas said.

He sounded like he was trying very hard not to laugh. Victoria cursed him thoroughly under her breath as she nodded to Connor and went to get ready for bed.

She managed to get in and out of Mrs. Pruitt's guest bathroom without incident and quickly escaped to the library.

Connor was sitting inside in his accustomed place before the fire. She took the seat opposite him.

"Well?" she asked. "What do you think?"

" 'Tis madness," he said promptly.

She smiled. "And my having this conversation with you isn't?"

He looked at her gravely. "Perhaps there is more to it that we suspect."

"'There are more things in heaven and earth, Horatio, than are dreamt of in your philosophy.'"

"Hamlet," he said.

"The very same."

"Mayhap he knew of what he spoke."

"But London, Connor," she said faintly. "A trained private investigator could spend years looking and never find her." She leaned her head back against the chair. "I can't talk about this anymore. I can't even think about it."

She would think about it plenty when she had some privacy, but not now. She'd already made up her mind about going. What she didn't need was Connor talking her out of it.

She looked at him sitting across from her, the firelight playing across his face, and felt for the first time in her life as if she truly had a friend. She smiled. "Do you still want to do me in?"

He grunted. "Did I ever?"

"Yes, you did, and that isn't an answer."

"Go to sleep, Victoria."

"You're hedging."

"You're vexing me." He looked at her, clear-eyed and peaceful, clearly unvexed.

"Thank you."

"For what?" he asked.

"For the lessons in Gaelic. For letting me drag actors into your castle. For standing outside my door and protecting me." She listened to what was coming out of her mouth and wondered when the stream of very personal revelations was going to end. "For sitting here and being my friend."

Apparently, the stream wasn't going to end soon.

"Friend?" he repeated, looking somewhat horrified.

"Is that so bad?" she asked, feeling her eyelids becoming very heavy. Maybe she was sleep-talking. Yes, that would be her excuse. *I was baring my soul late last night, but it was really just me babbling in my dreams.*

Would anyone, namely Connor, buy that?

He was silent for so long she wondered if she had fallen asleep truly.

"It will suffice for the moment, but by the saints it will not do forever."

She realized she was asleep only because her chin eventually hit her chest. She jerked her head back and it snapped smartly against the wooden chair. She forced her eyes to open. It took her a moment or two to focus on Connor.

He was watching her with a smile.

Which he quickly wiped off, of course.

"I'm hallucinating," she slurred. "You're smiling."

"And you're drooling," he returned. "Go to bed before you wrench your neck overmuch."

She nodded and managed to get herself to bed before she fell asleep on her feet. She managed to get the covers up to her ears before she felt herself slipping into oblivion.

"Friends? Ha!" There was the sound of a manly snort accompanying that declaration.

Then again, she could have been dreaming it.

Chapter 16

C onnor used a goodly amount of his strength to lock Victoria's door before he walked through it and made his way to the kitchen. Dawn was still an hour or two off, but he had the feeling there would be deeds afoot.

He was correct, as he assumed he would be. Ambrose, Hugh, and Fulbert were sitting at the table in the kitchen, a cheery fire burning in the Aga behind them, and comforting mugs of ale littering the table. Ambrose looked up as Connor walked in from the dining chamber.

"Connor," he said with a smile. "We expected you."

Connor sat down and conjured up his own mug. "And I expected you wouldn't be sleeping through matters of this import. Well, what have you discussed?"

"Someone has to go fetch Mary," Hugh said. "I say 'tis our duty to go."

"And *I* say you'll make a great hash of the plans," Fulbert grumbled. "*I* should go alone. 'Tis my century, after all."

Connor looked at Ambrose to see him stroking his chin in a most James MacLeod–like manner.

"I daresay Fulbert does have a thought worthy of consideration," Ambrose said, "though he should include me as a creature of that particular age."

"You're a Scot," Fulbert said with a snort. "What do you know of Elizabeth's London?"

"As much as you, likely," Ambrose said. "I did my share of traveling and spent my share of time in the London of those days."

Connor listened to them argue the merits of their particular experiences versus what Hugh, as Victoria's grandfather might bring to the venture. He drained his cup, then tortured it as he considered the conversation he'd had with Victoria several hours earlier.

Friend.

Damn her, what was she thinking?

She was thinking that he was hardly a man she would look at twice for anything else.

"Connor?"

Connor blinked and looked at Ambrose. "Aye?"

"What are your thoughts on this?"

"My thoughts?" Connor mused. "I wouldn't be surprised if Victoria vowed to go on her own. Indeed, I would only be surprised if she did not take on this task."

"And if she does?" Ambrose said. "And I agree with you, by the way, that she will believe herself responsible. If she does make the attempt, will you go with her?"

Connor nodded. "I had already planned to. I daresay she'll need all the *friends* she can bring along."

Ambrose looked at him in surprise for a moment or two, then he began to smirk. Not much and only for the time it took him to put his hand over his mouth as if he yawned, but it was enough. Ambrose held out his hand in a calming motion before Connor could remember where he'd put his damned sword.

Propped up by his chair by the fire in the library, apparently.

"Does she consider you such?" Ambrose asked.

"Apparently."

"I doubt she means it as an insult," Ambrose offered.

"I—"

"Though it surely wouldn't trouble you if she did," Ambrose interrupted quickly. "Of course. And who's to say that she'll wish to go? Indeed, it might be quite ill-advised."

"Who else is to go?" Hugh asked, cupping his hands about his mug protectively. "Jamie has a wife and bairns; 'twas dangerous enough for him to be about the journey once. Thomas is likewise a lad with a family and cannot leave them."

"Victoria's sire could go," Ambrose said slowly.

Connor snorted. "The man is perfectly blind to what goes on beneath his nose. It must be the McKinnon in him."

Hugh bristled.

Connor shot him a look that had him reaching for a sheaf of papers and taking refuge behind them.

"What are you reading now?" Fulbert asked.

"The Merry Wives of Windsor," Hugh responded, peering over the top. "I'll let you know how it ends."

Connor had a flash of envy run through him. Even Hugh, coward that he was, could read, while he himself still struggled with it. It would take time, or so Victoria assured him. He could only hope that his future wouldn't hinge upon his being able to read, or that her future wouldn't hinge upon her being able to speak Gaelic.

The saints preserve them both if either should be the case.

The debate continued, but with no useful results. The sun still slept as the dining chamber door opened and Thomas walked in. He sat down next to Ambrose.

"Well, laddie," Ambrose said with a smile, "you're awake early."

"I couldn't sleep," Thomas said, yawning widely. "Any answers yet?"

"Nay, but many questions."

Connor sat and contemplated the strangeness of sitting companionably at a table with men he had considered his enemies not two months earlier. He was still thinking on that when James MacLeod walked in and took the seat at the head of the table.

"How did you find sixteenth-century England, in truth?" Ambrose asked him.

"The food was vile," Jamie said bluntly, "and given what I've eaten in my time, that says much. I suppose that could have been my lack of funds, though. Is the larder full here, do you suppose?"

Thomas laughed and went to make breakfast. By the time he and Jamie were tucking in to something substantial, the door to the dining chamber creaked open again. Fulbert and Hugh vanished. Ambrose looked primed to flee, but sat back down when he saw it was only Victoria.

Only Victoria.

Connor looked at her and felt his mouth go dry.

By the saints, the wench was fetching, even with her hair slept on and in wild disarray.

And she sat, without even the barest of hesitations, next to him.

It wasn't as if there weren't other places vacant. Of course, Hugh and Fulbert took care of those other empty seats immediately after she sat down, but no matter. She had chosen the place next to him.

And then she smiled at him. "You're awake early."

Thomas spewed his tea all over his breakfast. "And how," he gurgled unattractively, "would you know that?"

Victoria looked at her brother with distaste. "Clean up the table, would you?"

"How would you know that his appearance at breakfast today is any earlier than any other day?"

"I know just because I know and the how of it is none of your business."

Thomas fetched a rag and returned with it, his eyes twinkling with an unholy amusement. "I see."

Victoria took the rag from him, cleaned the table, then flung the sopping wet cloth with great force into Thomas's face.

"Well done," Connor said approvingly.

Thomas grinned unrepentantly. "She's not usually this friendly with her bodyguards."

Friendly. There went that word again. Connor looked at Victoria. "Bodyguard?"

"You know," Thomas said, "like a garrison knight committed to looking after only one person until he's relieved of his duties. Bodyguard."

Bodyguard. Connor turned the word over in his mind. Was that how she considered him? Then again, hadn't he only offered to protect her?

Nothing more . . .

"Connor's not my bodyguard," she snapped.

"Then what is he?"

She seemed to be having trouble speaking. Connor watched her and wondered at the sudden redness of her cheeks.

"Are you unwell?" he demanded. "Poisoned?"

"At a loss for words?" Thomas asked politely.

She took a deep breath. "I'm fine," she said, looking at Connor. "Thank you for your concern." She turned to her brother. "If you want to be alive to see that baby be born, you'll cease and desist. There's a sword out in the hallway and I can figure out how to use it."

Connor frowned. He had seen Thomas McKinnon wield a sword. "Victoria," he said slowly, "I think you should choose another threat."

She looked up at him in surprise. "Why?"

"Your brother would best you in a sword fight. And saying that does not come without cost."

"Never let it be said that Connor MacDougal was stingy with his praise," Thomas said with a grin. "Now, moving right along before my sister thinks of other ways to do me in, what ground have you already covered?"

Connor listened intently, for there was no aid to be offered where there had not been attention paid to the plans, but at the same time he managed to skillfully be aware of everything the woman beside him was doing. First she drummed her fingers on the table. Then she picked at some tea-free bits of her brother's toasted bread. Then she merely took a knife and began to torture the rest of the bread in earnest.

Connor looked at her face to find she was watching him.

She smiled tremulously, as if she fought tears.

By the saints, he would have given centuries of his afterlife to have held her but once and lent her some of his own strength.

"All will be well," he said softly.

She nodded with another unsteady smile.

He put his hand over hers on the table before he realized what he was doing, or the futile nature of that gesture. Victoria saw it, though, and looked up at him.

Her eyes were full of tears.

She blinked quite suddenly, then rose. "Anyone need anything else to eat?" she asked briskly.

"Anything," Jamie said promptly. "Everything."

Connor watched her take the man's plate and look for something to put on it. He wondered who had noticed his *faux pas*. James MacLeod hadn't. Ambrose was listening intently to Fulbert babble on about which streets to avoid in Renaissance London and Hugh was still buried behind his *Merry Wives*. Then Connor looked at Thomas.

The fool was looking at him with something akin to pity on his face.

Connor drew himself up and frowned fiercely, his warning frown that always left those thusly frowned upon backing up swiftly before turning tail and fleeing.

Thomas McKinnon only smiled what he no doubt deemed to be an understanding smile. Then he turned to Ambrose and asked questions that gave no indication that he hadn't been listening fully and without distraction.

Connor looked over Thomas's head to find Victoria watching him as well. She looked at him gravely for a moment or two before she turned back to the stove.

Friends?

The saints pity him, he was past that.

He thought to examine when and where that might have happened, but he was interrupted by the back door flinging open.

Hugh and Fulbert disappeared with a squeak.

Mrs. Pruitt stood there, dressed in black, her ample bosom heaving.

"He's gone," she blurted out.

"What?" Thomas asked.

"Who is gone?" Ambrose asked, then he froze, as if he realized that he had made a grave tactical error.

Mrs. Pruitt fixed her frantic gaze upon Ambrose and her eyes widened even more, if possible. She felt her way across the kitchen and sank into the chair next to him.

"Laird MacLeod," she said reverently.

"Ah," Ambrose said, looking around wildly for an escape.

"I can hardly believe 'tis you," she said, patting her hair quickly. "And me so undone."

"Good woman, what did you say earlier," Ambrose said, sounding quite desperate. "Something about someone being gone?"

"Oh, I did, didn't I?" she said, surreptitiously checking the corners of her mouth.

For froth, apparently, Connor thought sourly.

"Aye, you did," Ambrose said politely. "Didn't she, Thomas? And you've met Laird MacDougal, haven't you?"

Connor glared at Ambrose, then turned his least ferocious frown on the innkeeper. "Good morn to you, Mistress Pruitt," he said.

Mrs. Pruitt seemed to be having trouble breathing.

"Mrs. Pruitt, can I get you a glass of something?" Thomas asked.

Victoria rose and disappeared into the dining room. She came back a moment or two later with a small glass of something Connor suspected was not tea. She handed it to Mrs. Pruitt without delay.

Mrs. Pruitt tossed it back without a flinch.

"Mr. Fellini is gone," she said, dragging her sleeve across her mouth in a businesslike fashion. "And I would have it on tape, but the blighter seems to have made off with me equipment!"

Victoria sank back down into her chair. "Michael is gone?"

"Popped through that fairy ring, he did," Mrs. Pruitt said with a nod. "Just as familiarly as ye please."

Jamie cleared his throat. "Fairy ring?"

"Aye," she said easily. "The one up the way in Farris's potato field. I daresay I don't believe all the rumors, but 'tis said that steppin' in a ring will carry ye off where ye've no mind to go. I know I'd never venture in one."

"And Michael did?" Victoria managed. "You saw him?"

"With me high-powered night goggles," Mrs. Pruitt said. "And the only reason I have those left is that I keep them under me pillow in case I need them at a moment's notice." She slid Ambrose a look. "Never know when they'll come in handy."

Ambrose shivered.

"I followed 'im," Mrs. Pruitt continued, "because he seemed so suspicious and I feared he was about to make mischief up the way at the castle."

"That was masterfully done," Thomas said approvingly. "We never would have known else."

"Wonderful," Victoria said with a sigh.

"He'll need to be fetched," Connor said.

"Why?" Victoria asked. "Maybe he took a turn at the Inquisition."

"You have a keen sense of retribution," Connor said admiringly.

"What goes around, comes around," she agreed. She sighed and looked at Thomas. "Well, I guess we're off for double duty."

"Off where?" Mrs. Pruitt asked.

Connor watched everyone at the table go still. Then Thomas cleared his throat.

"Off to the village," he said easily. "Unfortunately, we probably won't be able to dig up any decent rumors about that fairy ring. I think if we had an idea of what's possible, we might be able to figure out just what Mr. Fellini was up to. It's just too bad we don't have anyone with village connections—"

"I'll go," Mrs. Pruitt said, leaping to her feet and saluting. "And not only will I ferret out all the rumors, I'll capture them on me video camera."

"But I thought you said Michael had poached it," Victoria reminded her.

Mrs. Pruitt sniffed. "Aye, me old one. A newfangled digital recorder arrived this morning. I'll be about reading the directions for it forthwith, then make me way stealthily down to the village later this afternoon, if that suits?"

"Wonderful, my good woman," Ambrose said, bestowing a pleased smile upon her.

Mrs. Pruitt fluttered her eyelashes.

Connor recoiled in spite of himself. Why, the woman could terrify the most stern of souls with that bit of business.

He wondered, absently, if he could use a like technique and achieve the same results.

"I am away," Mrs. Pruitt said, with one last lingering look of pure, unabashed desire cast Ambrose's way before she exited stage left.

The dining room door closed behind her.

Connor looked at Ambrose. "Are you afraid?"

"Terrified," Ambrose said frankly.

"You should have parleyed with her during the winter," Fulbert said, reappearing suddenly.

"Aye," Hugh agreed, coming in behind him. "Mayhap the chill would have cooled her ardor."

"I doubt that," Thomas said with a laugh. "Ambrose has met his doom and she prefers pink fluffy slippers and state-of-the-art electronic gear."

Ambrose buried his response in his cup.

"Perhaps we should send Mrs. Pruitt to Elizabethan England," Thomas said.

"The saints preserve us all," Connor exclaimed.

Ambrose shivered. "The saints only know what sort of

trouble that would stir up. Like as not, she would take her wee video camera with her and record Shakespeare at his work." He shook his head. "Nay, she cannot go."

"Then who?" Fulbert asked darkly. "Who will do this thing?"

"I'll go," Victoria said.

Connor was unsurprised. It was as he had suspected.

"No, you won't," Thomas said, just as firmly. "You have no idea what you're getting in to."

"And you do?"

Thomas seemed unwilling to answer that. Connor studied him and wondered just what experience the man had with these sorts of gates. There had been rumors, of course, that he had gone back in time to rescue Iolanthe before her untimely murder, but Connor had never been certain he believed it.

Of course there was a goodly bit of mystery surrounding Iolanthe MacLeod McKinnon that even a casual observer might find irresistible, but Connor had resisted. Iolanthe was well wed and out from underfoot at Thorpewold. Connor cared little for how she had managed it.

At least he supposed he cared little for it.

It might behoove him at some point to look into it a little more closely.

"I, at least, do know of what I speak," Jamie said. His expression was serious. "'Tis a most dangerous business, Mistress Victoria, and you must be prepared for an immediate entry into a world which is not your own. The language, the dress, the customs—"

"It's Shakespeare's time," Victoria said. "How much more convenient can it be than that?"

"I don't think *everyone* spoke in iambic pentameter, Vic," Thomas said dryly.

"Don't be obtuse," she threw at him. She turned back to Jamie. "I think I could take weeks to prepare and it wouldn't help. I'll just go, be discreet, find Granny and that bloody egoist, and get back. How hard can that be?"

"You can't go alone," Thomas said with a sigh.

"She wouldn't be going alone," Connor put in.

He felt Victoria look at him, but he didn't dare return the look. The saints only knew what kind of expression she would be wearing.

"And can you protect her?" Thomas asked quietly. "Should a band of drunken men bent on mischief accost her, could you rescue her? Besides terrifying them into insensibility, of course, but what if they're not the terrifying kind?"

Connor had several nasty replies come to mind, but before he could sort them out and choose the worst of them, Thomas continued on.

"I don't doubt your skill, which is formidable, or your commitment, which is equally impressive. What I doubt is just the reality of your situation, which, unfortunately, leaves my sister, for all intents and purposes, on her own in a century that is not hers, with no skills to survive it."

"I'll come along to help," came a voice from behind them.

Connor turned in his chair to see Jennifer standing just inside the doorway. She came in farther and let the door close behind her.

"No, you won't," Victoria said firmly.

"I will," Jennifer said calmly. "I'll distract the locals with troubadour songs while you investigate."

Victoria looked a wee bit indecisive.

"I'll earn some money and keep us fed," Jennifer continued. "You'll be happy you brought me along."

Thomas rolled his eyes. "Great. Two sisters and a ghost. If that isn't the most impossible trio I've ever heard of—"

"I took a self-defense class," Jennifer offered.

"Oh, well, that clinches it," Thomas said grimly. "By all means, but please dress up as boys, will you?"

"And how will that serve them?" Connor asked pointedly. "Look at them both. Only a fool wouldn't recognize them for what they are."

"People look for what they expect to see," Thomas said. "If they dress like men and act like men, it's possible they could pass as men."

Victoria put her hands on the table and rose. "I have to get on with my day. You guys can argue all you like over our costumes; I'm going to go take a shower." She looked at Connor. "Are you coming with me?"

"To the shower?" Thomas choked, spewing tea all over the table again.

"To the castle, Thomas, to the castle!" She looked at Connor. "I'll be on my way in half an hour." She glared at her brother briefly, then stomped from the kitchen.

Connor looked at Thomas narrowly. "You insult her," he said. "I will see you repaid."

"It wasn't intentional," Thomas said. "I didn't actually think—well, never mind."

"Was that an apology?" Connor asked.

"It wasn't. Add it to the list of things you want to repay me for and we'll deal with it later." He mopped up the table slowly. "You know, MacDougal," he said finally, "I don't know how either of you will manage this."

"The journey to find your grandmother?"

"That, too."

Connor looked at Thomas in surprise, was momentarily tempted to say something unpleasant, then decided perhaps 'twas better to let that go. He took a deep breath. "If I had a life to give, I would protect her with it. As it is, I will do everything in my power to keep her safe." He glanced at Jennifer. "I will protect your youngest sister, as well."

The thought crossed his mind that it would have been passing convenient if he could have had some sort of change wrought upon him as he went through that time gate, a change that would have restored to him the life he lost through treachery.

He looked at Thomas. "I will do all within my power."

"I know you will."

Connor rose, bowed to Jennifer, nodded to the men remaining there, and left the kitchen. He wandered through the dining room and took up a post in the entryway to wait for Victoria to finish her preparations for the day.

If only a trip into the past might be that which would give him back an existence he could bear . . .

He bowed his head.

The saints pity him for wanting it so much.

Chapter 17

Victoria stood in the inner bailey of the castle, faint from the surprisingly intense morning sunlight, and watched *Hamlet* progress from beginning to deathly end.

She sincerely hoped it wasn't an omen.

Michael's understudy was doing surprisingly well. It helped that he was even more handsome than Michael and that Cressida couldn't seem to keep her eyes off him. She descended quite happily into madness for him.

Fred was directing. He was not at all pleased by the turn of events, but he'd acquiesced, especially after she'd given him the choice of being in charge of the actors or being in charge of the costumes. He'd accepted her scribbled-on script with loud complaints, but he'd done it, and she couldn't have asked for more than that. But the fact that she was deserting her play in its perfect location two days before it was supposed to open was indicative of the way her life was going at present.

Not under her control.

She didn't want to say she was getting used to it. Resigned might have been a better word—resigned to the thought that in the morning she was going to be heading to Renaissance England, where her grandmother and Michael had supposedly gone. At least she had the proper costumes for the trip. Hopefully, none of the Elizabethans would get close enough to her to see the Velcro.

She sighed and walked away to go lean against the wall in the shade. She watched her cast and crew pack up. She'd made a bogus announcement about having to go to London and be interviewed by the authorities. Apparently, Michael had also been called away on important business. She hoped to be back in time for opening night. She had announced that she was assuming Michael would be back as well, which had caused his understudy (and Cressida) serious disappointment.

She was lying so often and so convincingly, she was starting to worry about herself.

There was a little paranormal kerfuffle over by the castle gates. Victoria watched Connor attempt to whip his troops into shape before he bellowed at them in disgust and strode across the bailey toward her.

He was, she had to admit, quite an impressive sight.

He would have made a magnificent Hamlet.

She nodded to herself firmly over that observation. After all, how could she be blamed for looking at the man as potential star material? It was what she did best.

But, generally, leading men did not leave her wishing desperately for something to drink to cure the sudden dryness of her mouth and inability to swallow normally.

Connor looked down at her with a frown. "Nervous?"

"Me?" she rasped. "Never. I'm always up for a challenge. *Advance* is my favorite word, followed closely by *impossible*, *ill-advised*, and *insane*. Does that do it for you?"

"Hmmm," was all he said.

Victoria was afraid to say anything else because if she opened her mouth again, she just might blurt out that she was growing far too accustomed to Connor's solid, dependable companionship. Her life was completely unraveling around her and apparently her North Star was a grumpy, medieval highland laird.

She shouldn't have been surprised.

"I suppose I can understand your unease," he continued conversationally. "The unknown is daunting. I was not un-accustomed to a feeling of apprehension each time I went into battle."

She looked at him and wondered how it was any group of Highlanders managed not to pee their kilts and run off the other way with their tails between their legs whenever Connor MacDougal walked onto the field.

"You?" she managed.

He paused. "*Small* amounts of apprehension, of course."

"Imagine what everyone else was feeling."

"Likely something akin to unease," he conceded. "In my case, I found that such discomfort forced me to take greater care than I might have otherwise. I imagine that your actors feel something like it before they perform. Or you, when the play is about to begin."

"Somehow, what we're contemplating makes opening night look like a trip to the bathroom."

He snorted. It sounded almost like a laugh.

"I think you laughed," she said.

"Never."

"Connor, if I'm going to die in Renaissance England, I would like to see you smile once before I do."

"You won't die if I can prevent it."

"You're changing the subject."

"Aye."

She sighed. "At least you're honest."

"If death is near, I will smile for you. But do not hold out much hope for that. We'll fetch your granny and be back in time for the curtain to part here."

"Michael, too," she reminded him.

He pursed his lips. "Aye, well, I suppose we'll need to look for him, as well. I daresay we'll find him wherever we find our good Master Shakespeare, wouldn't you think? Or perhaps not. I suggest we first try the locales where over-acting is appreciated."

She suspected he might be right. Unfortunately, she couldn't, in good conscience, leave Michael to his performing stunts. She could only hope that the job would be done quickly and she would get back home with her runaways intact.

She didn't want to contemplate the alternative.

She spent the rest of the day trying not to think about what she was planning. By the time night had fallen, she had finished up her theater business and raided the costume shed for costumes that seemed appropriate for two lads journeying through sixteenth-century London. Connor was shown several alternatives, which he managed to recreate without trouble, though he did insist on changing his ghostly garb in private. The first time he came back into the sitting room in poufy trousers and a velvet doublet, Thomas almost choked to death.

"Something less conspicuous," Victoria suggested.

He glared at her, stomped from the room, then came back a moment or two later dressed in more conservative, guild-member gear. No poufs, less brocade, and fewer baubles. It actually suited him quite well.

"Perfect," she pronounced.

"What it does is make me your servant," he groused, gesturing to her finery.

"Not by much. I will trade you, if you like."

"Trade what for what?" her father asked as he walked into the sitting room. He swept them all with a look. "Are you all fitting yourself in understudy roles?"

Victoria thought it best not to say anything.

Dinner dragged on far too long and she excused herself as soon as was polite. She didn't usually care about being polite, but she thought that the less her actors were panicked about the upcoming events, the better. All she needed was to have the whole gaggle of them taking flight.

She used her parents' bathroom, bid them a good night, allowed her father to chalk her red eyes up to opening night stress, and kissed her mother good night.

Mary was unfooled. "I know what you're doing," she murmured.

Victoria would have stopped and gaped, but her mother continued to propel her across the room.

"Be careful," she said as she walked Victoria to the door.

Victoria paused in the doorway. "Have you been talking to Thomas?"

Helen shook her head. "Ambrose."

"Oh, Mom, not you, too."

Helen smiled. "It's in the blood, love. And I appreciate the sacrifice you're making for your granny."

"I'll be okay."

"Connor will see to it," Helen said confidently.

"Hmmm," was all Victoria could manage as she nodded, then walked away down the hall. She didn't bother to ask how her mother knew what Connor might or might not be capable of. For all she knew, her mother had been grilling him while Victoria had been working out the final production kinks.

She continued to reflect on the complete improbability of the whole escapade until she reached the downstairs and had made her way to the library door.

Connor stood there, looking as real and corporeal as any man she'd ever seen.

Maybe it would work.

Then again, since she was the one who had to turn the door handle to get them inside, maybe things would be a little dicey after all.

She pulled her robe tighter around herself and sat down in front of the fire he made with a flick of his wrist.

"How do you do that?" she asked, marveling.

"'Tis just my own artistic nature venting itself in the building of illusionary fires, the creation of high-quality ghostly ale, and designing of incomparable imaginary gear for the Renaissance gentleman with less than he might like in his purse."

She laughed. "You've been consorting with actors for too long."

"I've become a windbag," he agreed, sitting down across from her. "I vow my men hardly knew what to make of me this morning. My frowns have given way to too much verbiage. I'll need to remedy it eventually."

"I like it, actually. Especially when you go on in English and not Gaelic. My head hurts less that way."

"I don't suppose you've the stomach for it tonight, do you?" he asked, tilting his head to look at her. "Or do you need a distraction from tomorrow's journey?"

She sighed and looked into the fire. "It just seems so impossible. I saw Jamie disappear, then I saw him come into the dining room several days later dressed in clothes that weren't his. I've sat in the kitchen with my ancestors and chatted about current events." She looked at him. "And then there is you. I sometimes wonder if I'm dreaming it all. And perhaps I don't need to tell you that I'm not one to waste much time dreaming."

He only stared back at her, solemn and silent.

"Don't you feel that way sometimes?" she asked wistfully.

"The last eight centuries have felt like a dream," he answered slowly. "But for me, I feel as if I have just recently awakened."

And then he looked at her.

And she wasn't sure if she should be happy or devastated that he was a ghost.

"Shakespeare will do that to you," she managed.

He grunted at her, then looked into the fire. "I imagine he does many things, but this is a change he cannot claim credit for." He looked at her then, started to say something, then shook his head. " 'Tis late, woman. You should be abed. Who knows when we will sleep next?"

"I'll try."

"I could sing."

"I suddenly feel I won't have trouble at all, thanks just the same."

He pursed his lips. "I sing very well."

"Sure, depressing songs about bloodshed and cattle raiding."

"They are rousing anthems guaranteed to put spine into the weakest of fighting men."

"Favor me tomorrow, then. Right now, read me something in Gaelic."

He considered. *"Thomas the Tank Engine?"*

She laughed. "I was just about to suggest it." She paused. "You know, you really are doing well. It can be difficult to learn to read when you're an adult. And you're learning to do so in two languages at once."

He pulled the book out of thin air. "Many no doubt envy my skill. Be abed with you, mouthy wench, before all this talking wearies me as well."

Victoria crawled into bed, pulled the covers up to her neck, and turned toward the fire.

She fell asleep to the deep voice of a Highland laird reading in his native tongue as if he'd been doing it his entire life.

The sun was barely up when Victoria stood with Jennifer and Connor on the edge of the fairy ring. Thomas was there, as was Jamie. They'd managed to ditch Mrs. Pruitt by sending her, with almost all her paranormal equipment strapped to her person, off on a wild goose chase. Jamie had been certain direct contact with the fairy ring could only be a bad thing where the innkeeper was concerned.

Victoria had agreed heartily.

Her parents were not there and Victoria felt that was just as well. Her dad would have had a fit, or leaped forward to stop her, or fallen into the fairy ring of his own accord, and then they really would have been in trouble.

The Boar's Head Trio was there, though, offering moral support and, in the case of Fulbert, friendly scowls.

Some things never changed, apparently.

Victoria looked at her sister to see how she was handling things. Jennifer looked serene.

"Are you sure?" Victoria began.

"I have a reproduction fife in my bag," Jennifer said easily. "It'll be great for earning lunch money. Besides, it can double as a weapon. I thought that made more sense than bringing a violin."

Victoria frowned. "Tell me again why you gave up such a promising career in the arts to make baby clothes?"

"I don't like musicians."

"No, you don't like to *date* musicians," Victoria corrected. "You could easily perform with them. What you should do is marry yourself a nice attorney who plays the guitar for fun and won't mind when you go to rehearsals three days a week and have a crushing concert schedule. I don't suppose you play your violin anymore, do you?"

"Now and then. When I get tired of chenille."

Victoria threw up her hands and scowled at Connor. "She makes me crazy."

"She may be the only way you eat for the next few days," he pointed out. "I wouldn't irritate her overmuch."

Victoria pursed her lips. "I suppose. But, Jennifer, I want to have a talk with you about your life goals when we get back," she said. "A very long talk."

"Well," Thomas said, coming to stand next to them, "it's now or never, I suppose. Who knows when Mrs. Pruitt will come rushing our way, ready to document the attempt on tape. Are you ready?"

"Ready as we're going to be," Victoria said. She looked at her sister. "Shall we?"

"Good luck," Thomas said, giving Victoria a quick hug, then doing the same to Jennifer. "Let Connor protect you as much as he can."

He stepped away.

Victoria looked around once more, then took Jennifer's hand. She reached for Connor's, as well, as she stepped forward.

She could have sworn she held onto something.

She looked up at him in surprise.

But then the feeling was gone. When she had digested that and was prepared to really get down to the business of wishing herself back to Elizabethan England, she found that they were no longer in Farris's field.

They were in an alley in a city.

"So far, so good," she ventured.

"I don't know about that," Jennifer said warily. "You'd better turn around."

Victoria turned around.

Half a dozen thugs stood there. In broad daylight. She cursed under her breath. Maybe this wasn't the best part of town. She should have wished them to a more well-heeled alleyway.

She put her hands on her hips and dredged up her most impressive frown. "Begone, curs," she said firmly.

The men looked unimpressed.

"Knavish brigands," she called in a more insulting tone.

"Knavish brigands?" Jennifer complained. "Couldn't you have come up with something better?"

"I don't know if it will matter," Victoria said. "I don't think they care what we call them."

"Excuse me," came a voice from behind them.

Victoria ducked and pulled Jennifer out of the way before Connor stepped past them and drew his sword with a ferocious war cry.

Three men screamed, turned tail, and fled.

The remaining three blinked almost in unison, then two drew swords and grinned happily. The third hung back to watch the melee.

"Great," Victoria said.

"It's not bad," Jennifer offered. "There are only three left."

"I don't think this is going to work," Victoria said grimly.

Connor tossed a curse at her over his shoulder and

threw himself into the fray with all the enthusiasm of a medieval Highlander bent on mayhem. Victoria reconsidered her doubts. Connor was indeed something to see. He was very loud and quite fierce.

He was also not wielding a sword that made any noise when it connected with those of his opponents.

They noticed this, too, after a few moments.

"Oy," said one. "He's not the lad we think he is."

"Let's 'ave at 'im."

"He's powerful large," the first said doubtfully. "No matter that his sword makes no noise."

"Wha' are we gonna do, then?" asked the second.

"Fight him?" suggested the first.

"Aye, you should," Connor said.

And then he took his head off and tucked it into the crook of his arm.

The two men screamed, dropped their swords, and ran away. Victoria realized after they had exited the alleyway that Jennifer was screaming, as well. She had to admit to a moment of alarm seeing Connor without his head, but she quickly overcame that.

"Jenner, be quiet!" she exclaimed. "Connor's fine. He just scared the men away."

Well, all but one.

The final thug looked at Connor with a sneer, then walked through him. Victoria found herself face to face with one of the most unpleasant-looking characters she had ever seen. His teeth were rotten, his breath vile, and his personal grooming habits left everything to be desired.

He resheathed a very long sword. Instead, he drew out an equally wicked looking dagger.

Jennifer jumped between them and shouted "No!" at the top of her lungs.

He backhanded her and she went sprawling. Victoria looked down at her sister. She didn't move.

Victoria threw herself at her attacker, intending to at least gouge his eyes out. The next thing she knew, she had been turned and slammed up against the wall. When the man began to grope her, she knew she was in big trouble. Well, at least he wasn't going to slit her throat first. That had to be a bonus.

She wondered if this was what hysterical felt like.

But the next thing she knew, she wasn't being accosted anymore.

She felt her attacker back away. She hardly dared look over her shoulder. When she heard a thud, she turned around and looked. He was lying on the ground next to Jennifer.

He had a sword protruding from his back.

Connor was on his knees, his chest heaving.

"Wake Jennifer," he gasped. "You must away before anyone comes."

Victoria dragged her sister bodily to her feet and pulled Jennifer's arm over her shoulders.

"I don't feel so good," Jennifer managed.

"Feel crappy later. We've got to go now."

She helped Jennifer over the slain assailant and looked at Connor. "And what of you?"

"No one will see me," he said weakly. "The sword belonged to one of his fellows. Go secure lodgings. I'll find you."

Victoria would have asked him how in the world he intended to do that, but the look he gave her made her shut her mouth.

Victoria dragged Jennifer from the little alleyway and onto a main street. That not a soul stopped to inquire why she and Jen were in such awful shape was likely a good indication of their location. Victoria had glanced at a map of Renaissance London but only long enough to ascertain where the Globe found itself. Unfortunately, the theater wasn't exactly entertainment for the upper crust, and actors and their ilk weren't exactly members of that upper crust, which left her with the choice of either taking a room in a less-than-desirable establishment or forcing Jennifer to walk for miles.

She was so desperately tempted to just stand in the street and gape at her surroundings that she could hardly stand it. She was in the midst of Elizabethan-looking souls going about their business with very King-James-English kinds of accents.

It was like dreaming, only it smelled much worse.

"I'm better now," Jennifer said, managing to straighten up. She put her hand to her cut lip. "This will look authentic, don't you think? I doubt anyone will mess with us now that they see what a brawler I am."

"We can hope."

Jennifer fell silent. Victoria strode along in the most manly fashion she could devise, thinking about nothing more than finding somewhere safe to stay, when she realized that her sister hadn't said anything for quite some time. She looked at her.

"What?"

Jennifer was wide-eyed. "Can you believe this?" she whispered. "Where we are?"

"Without a can of Lilt in sight," Victoria said crisply. "I doubt we can even find any chocolate. It's a catastrophe."

"Where's Connor?"

"He's coming."

Jennifer nodded, but said nothing more. They walked until the surroundings began to look a little more reputable. Victoria stopped at the first likely place.

She paid for a week's lodging out of the money Jamie had given her. She hadn't thought to ask him how he'd come by it.

In fact, there were several questions she hadn't thought to ask him, such as how had he returned from his little jaunt to Elizabeth's England without so much as a flicker of unease. Just how much experience did he have with these sorts of gates? Why was it he had that rough, medieval lairdliness that Connor had? And why was her brother thick as thieves with the man—outside of the fact that Iolanthe was related to him?

Grandfather.

There was something very fishy about that.

She made herself a mental note to determine the answers to those questions just as soon as she got home. But for now she was happy to drag her sister up the stairs and hope that both Connor and lunch would arrive at the same time.

She let the maid make up a fire for them in the hearth, then waited until food was brought before she bolted the door and sat down at a little table with her sister.

"How did you meet Connor?"

Victoria looked at her sister in surprise. "What?"

"How did you meet him? You never told me."

Victoria pursed her lips. "Don't beat around the bush, Jenner. Why don't you ask me what you really want to know?"

Jennifer smiled, then winced at her cut lip. "I'm curious about him. I can't imagine you brought him over from the States with you unless I'm hanging out in the wrong part of Manhattan."

"It's a very long story."

"I have lots of time."

Victoria sighed. She looked around, but there seemed to be nothing else to distract her sister with besides lunch, and she wasn't all that sure that lunch looked edible. She found that Jennifer was still waiting, rather expectantly, and decided that there was no reason not to answer her.

"All right," she said with a deep sigh, "here's the deal."

She outlined her entire paranormal experience, beginning with Hugh in the prop room and ending with Connor trying out Renaissance outfits in the sitting room.

"Unbelievable," Jennifer said when Victoria finished. "I wouldn't have believed it if I hadn't seen him for myself."

"I wouldn't have believed a lot of things if I hadn't seen them for myself," Victoria agreed.

"What now?" Jennifer asked. "We find Granny, find Michael, go home, then what?"

Victoria blinked. "Then what, what?"

"What are you and Connor going to do?"

Victoria very rarely found herself without something to say. But the fact that her sister had so deftly and with such little mercy cut right to the heart of her most desperate concern was enough to leave her speechless.

"Ah," she managed.

"It isn't as if you can marry a ghost," Jennifer said.

"Marry!" Victoria exclaimed. She blushed furiously and began to babble.

She never blushed.

She never, ever babbled.

It was at that moment that Connor chose to walk through the door.

Jennifer squeaked. "Oh," she managed, putting her hand to her chest. Then she jumped to her feet. "Vikki . . ."

Victoria saw. She jumped up, as well, but found quite quickly that there was absolutely nothing she could do. Connor fell. It was probably a good thing he wasn't precisely corporeal; he probably would have gone through the planks. Victoria knelt down next to him as he lay with his cheek against the floor.

"Connor," she said uneasily, "what happened? Was it the knife in the man's back? Did he hurt you?"

Connor shook his head. "He couldn't. But for me to wound him . . . took all my strength." He closed his eyes. "I'll need to rest. Wielding things . . . from the mortal world . . . very taxing."

"Take the bed," Victoria said promptly.

He grunted weakly. "Won't know the . . . difference."

And with that, he closed his eyes firmly and fell asleep. Victoria knew this because he began to snore.

"Well," Jennifer said, "at least we'll know when he's awake."

Victoria looked up at her from where she knelt next to him. "I think we should wait for him to . . . um . . . recover."

"I think so, too. We can get some details of where we

are from the servants, I imagine. Too bad we don't have a map."

"We can probably get that, too, for a price." She looked at her sister. "I think I need a nap, but we should sleep in shifts. You go first."

"No—"

"Yes. I didn't just get popped in the mouth. Go to bed."

"All right," Jennifer said slowly. "Maybe we should practice your Gaelic this afternoon when I wake up. You really should put some more effort into it."

"I'm sure it will be incredibly useful here," Victoria replied.

Jennifer smiled gingerly. "I wasn't thinking about here. I can't imagine any Highland laird resisting being wooed in his native tongue."

Victoria only half heard the last. But when she realized what her sister had said, protestations rose and fell off her lips.

Jennifer had a point.

Victoria looked at her sister, who was playing possum, then looked at her laird, who was definitely not, and decided that perhaps her time could be used well that afternoon.

She went to sit back at the table, then looked around the room and started naming all the things she could under her breath.

In Connor's native tongue.

On the off chance it would make a difference to him someday.

Chapter 18

C onnor sat up with a groan. He felt much more himself, but he supposed that was nothing to rejoice over.
He looked around the chamber and found himself somewhat surprised he was where he was. There had been a part
of him that feared the time gates would not work for him.

They had worked in transporting him to another age.

They had not restored him to life.

He hadn't expected that they would. Not truly.

He looked around the very sixteenth-century chamber
and marveled at the construction. It looked somewhat like
the Boar's Head Inn, though 'twas obvious to him that this
chamber was far newer.

It was currently being used not only by him but by Victoria and Jennifer, both of whom were unconscious on the
bed. Connor would have feared for their safety, but Jennifer
was talking in her sleep and Victoria was reaching over to
give her a shove. Obviously, they lived still.

Connor had to admit to being somewhat fascinated by
the interaction between the two sisters. He'd had little to do
with women as he grew to manhood, having no sisters and

a mother who had died in his youth. Victoria and Jennifer were a revelation to him. Neither was shy about expressing opinions on the other's conduct or business. Connor had learned quite quickly that Victoria thought Jennifer should be earning her bread playing music and Jennifer thought Victoria should be finding herself a husband and settling down.

Connor wondered, absently, why Victoria hadn't.

He found it not an unhappy state of affairs, though he certainly couldn't have said why. It wasn't as if he could do a bloody thing about it save dance at her wedding to some lad from her time.

He got to his feet, swayed, then steadied himself as best he could. He wished grimly that he had brought someone else along. How he was going to protect these two women with naught but his wits was beyond him. Then again, hadn't he done as much the night before?

But had it been the night before, or had he been senseless for days?

He would have given that more thought, but a knock sounded on the door, interrupting him.

Victoria sat up with a start, caught sight of him, then relaxed and smiled. "You look better."

"Did I look so ill before?" he asked.

"Well, yes, you did." She rose and went to answer the door. Food arrived and Connor looked at the window to see what the time might be. Daylight again. Well, perhaps he had only slept through the night.

Victoria gestured to the table. "There, if you please," she said with a decidedly French accent.

The maidservant obeyed, bobbed a curtsey, and left with alacrity. Connor looked at Victoria.

"French?"

She shrugged. "I thought Scottish, but I wasn't sure how that would play here."

"And what, pray, am I to do, mistress?" he asked archly. "I cannot be what I am not."

"You just be quiet," she said easily, "and let me do the

talking. Jennifer speaks quite a bit of French, so if things really go south, we'll let her see what she can do. But I'm hoping we won't run into any more problems."

"Aye," he said, with feeling. He sat down across the table from her. "Are you recovered?"

"From the sight of you without your head, or the feeling of that now-dead Londoner groping me?"

He couldn't smile. "The latter, surely."

"I'll survive. You can't imagine how I appreciated the rescue, though."

"I daresay I can."

She smiled and began to study breakfast. Connor watched her with her hair loose about her shoulders and her features not overwrought with anything but choosing from the offerings before her. How he wished he could have pulled that hair back from her face, brushed it for her, braided it if she pleased.

By the saints, the sight of that whoreson attacking her had made his heart stop.

If he'd had a heart to behave in such a fashion.

The rage that had rushed through him had surprised him, but not rendered him useless. It had given him strength beyond what he should have had, strength enough to raise a sword and plunge it into the man's back. He supposed he was fortunate he hadn't impaled Victoria, as well.

"Connor, are you all right?"

He rubbed his hands over his face and gave her a weak smile. "I am well enough."

"I would comment on that pleasant expression you're wearing, but I'm trying to be discreet."

"Does it make me look less fierce?" he inquired politely.

"Definitely."

"Then you see why I do not wear it often."

She smiled at him and a dimple appeared in her cheek. Connor fought not to wheeze.

"Aren't you past trying to intimidate me?" she asked. "I think I'm immune."

"What a failure I am as a shade."

"But a success as a fr—"

"By the saints, Victoria McKinnon, if you call me friend one more time, I will produce frown enough to leave you screaming for days."

Then he realized what he'd said.

His mouth fell open.

Oddly enough, so did hers.

"Ah," he scrambled.

"Um," she attempted.

"Breakfast?" came a cheery voice from the other side of the suddenly quite small chamber. "Wonderful!"

Connor had never been so happy to see anyone as he was to see Jennifer McKinnon, who looked enough like her sister that she should have given him pause. He vacated his chair for another flame-haired beauty who smiled in a most pleasant, nay, sisterly manner at him, and commented quite complimentarily on his conduct the morning previous.

"So, what are we up to today?" Jennifer asked brightly. "Do we dare venture out? Are we French lads on a lark, or Scots looking for action? Do we actually have any idea where we're supposed to be going? Victoria, eat. It looks good."

Connor looked at Victoria, who was most definitely not looking at him. He conjured up a chair only because he thought he needed something useful beneath his backside. He sat and listened to Jennifer carry on enough conversation for the three of them, acutely aware of Victoria McKinnon sitting next to him, pretending to break her fast.

"Victoria," Jennifer said sharply, "eat."

Victoria ate.

Connor plucked a mug of ale out of invisibility and applied himself diligently to emptying its contents.

Time passed.

Eventually, Jennifer informed them that she had an engagement with the chamber pot and asked if they would be so good as to give her a bit of privacy. Victoria went with him to stand outside the bedchamber, though Connor supposed there had been no need for her to leave. But he wasn't displeased with the chance to speak with her.

"Victoria," he began.

She looked up at him quickly. "I won't use that word again."

He opened his mouth to speak, but found there was nothing to say, short of blurting out sentiments that likely would leave her fleeing the other way. He settled for looking at her with the friendliest expression he could muster.

Friendliest. Was there no end to the indignities he would suffer for this wench?

"Connor?"

He shook his head. "I am well."

"Well . . . good."

He nodded.

Time passed.

Not soon enough, the door opened behind them.

"Your turn," Jennifer said to her sister. "I'll wait outside with Connor."

Victoria nodded and went inside. Connor sighed and looked down at Victoria's sister. Why had no man managed to capture the heart of either of them? Both women were beautiful, both spirited, both possessed that flame-colored hair and porcelain skin. Jennifer's eyes were green, not blue, but she looked to have quite a bit of Victoria's fire. Connor had to admit he couldn't understand why she chose to make clothing for bairns, either. Surely she should have been making music somewhere, or making some man's life a bit of heaven. Perhaps Victoria wouldn't be remiss in having speech with her about that.

"How are you doing?" Jennifer asked sympathetically.

He blinked. "I beg your pardon?"

"You know, that thing between you and Vikki. How are you doing with that?"

A denial was on the tip of his tongue, but he couldn't seem to get it to come off. He blew out his breath. "I have had better centuries," he said finally.

She smiled gravely. "I'm really sorry it has to be this way."

To his horror, he felt his eyes begin to burn. Bloody dusty inn . . .

"I'm certain it was accidental on your granny's part to step into that fairy ring," Connor said, desperate to change the subject. By the saints, that was all he needed—to weep in front of not one, but *two* McKinnon wenches!

Jennifer was obviously far too observant for her own good. "Right," she said slowly. "Okay, we can move on to Granny and her whereabouts. Where do you think she could be?"

"I've no idea," he said quickly. "All we can do, I suppose, is take up our quest. We have gold enough to keep on with a lengthy search."

"Let's hope it isn't too lengthy. My repertoire of Renaissance music isn't what it should be." She smiled. "I just hope this whole adventure works out in the end. You know, the thing with Granny."

"Hmmm," he said, swallowing with difficulty.

She only looked at him as if she pitied the hell out of him.

He felt the same way. By the saints, 'twas an impossible tangle and he became more enmeshed in it with each passing day. Rescuing Mary MacLeod Davidson seemed a simple thing when compared to rescuing his poor heart—

"Oh, hey, Vikki. Are you ready to go?"

Connor heaved a great sigh of relief. Now they could march forward and concentrate on a task he could manage.

Victoria shut the door behind her. "I'm as ready as I'm going to be," she said. She looked up at Connor. "Shall we go for a little explore?"

Well, that was what they were there for. Connor put his shoulders back. "Aye, let us see what the day has lying in wait for us. Have you any thoughts on where to begin the search?"

"I say we start with the theater district. If nothing else, we'll probably find Michael there." She paused for a moment or two. "I don't have any good ideas on where to look for Granny."

"Near yarn," Jennifer suggested. "Let's track Michael down, then head to wherever knitters go. Granny would have needed a way to feed herself."

Connor nodded. "To the Globe, then, then onward. With any luck, we'll find Mary quickly and be on our way just as quickly."

Victoria smiled faintly. "We can hope. Let's go."

Connor followed her sister down the stairs and through the great room of the inn, trying to look as servantlike as possible. No one troubled them and Connor managed to not walk through anyone and set them to screaming.

It was an auspicious sign.

Victoria stopped and had a conversation with the inn-keeper, using hand signs and very accented English to inquire about where Master Shakespeare did his plays. She joined them at the door with a sigh.

"This is going to be interesting."

"Did he tell you where to go?" Jennifer asked.

"Sort of," Victoria said ruefully. "I think I know the general direction. We'll just have to ask for specifics the closer we get." She looked at Connor. "Ready?"

He put his hand on his sword. "Aye."

She blinked. "That's not your usual sword."

"I conjured up a more modest, Elizabethan edition for our current circumstances."

She smiled at him. "You're very prepared."

"A good warrior always is."

"Well, let's hope you won't need to do any more warrior stuff any time soon. Let's find Granny and get out of here. Among other things, I'm just not all that sure about the quality of the water."

"It's probably better not to think about that," Jennifer agreed with a smile.

Connor followed after the two of them with their hair stuffed up under caps and wondered how in the hell anyone would see them as anything but what they were. Thomas had been right. They were far too beautiful to be mistaken for lads.

And he was far too uncorporeal to be of much use. He spent most of his time glaring at men who took second looks at the sisters. If he could intimidate by his sheer presence alone—which he was certain he could and had done on many occasions in the past—then he would do so and be content with that. He didn't want to think about what might happen otherwise—especially given that he'd found that out firsthand in their first moments back in time. But he'd conquered that test in his usual fashion.

The saints preserve him should he have to, with his feeble, ghostly strength, keep Victoria and her sister safe.

He turned his mind away from those unproductive thoughts and set himself to watching for danger. He would at least be able to warn the sisters about coming trouble.

A pity he hadn't been able to do so for his own heart.

Chapter 19

Victoria swaggered down the street with her sister and her . . . well, her not-friend, and wondered at the strangeness of her life. The sights, sounds, and most definitely the smells of Elizabethan London assailed her from every direction. Oddly enough, it didn't smell all that different from some parts of Manhattan, especially in the height of summer. The sights, however, were another thing entirely. It was like a Renaissance Faire, only this was real.

And she was taking part in it with a medieval Highlander.

She was tempted to cue *Twilight Zone* music, but she forbore. For one thing, she didn't want to draw any attention to herself. For another, she didn't think her poor heart could take any teasing about her situation.

Having feelings for a man who was real but not?

Ridiculous.

But as she walked next to him and listened to him banter with her sister in Gaelic, it didn't seem quite so ridiculous.

Her father would have had a fit if he'd known. Her mother would have quietly suggested that even though it was most likely Fate putting in its oar, she was probably better off resigning herself to the fact that she'd lost her mind. Her grandmother would only have looked on with raised eyebrows, then suggested a trip to some trendy Manhattan boutique for a funky wedding dress. Thomas would have laughed his bloody head off. She wondered, absently, what James MacLeod—he of the not-so-casual acquaintance with time-traveling gates—would have said.

One thing she did know: Mrs. Pruitt would want to get whatever happened with Connor all on tape.

"Are you picking up any of this?" Jennifer asked.

Victoria looked at her. "Picking up what?"

"Our Gaelic."

"No," Victoria said shortly. "I'm concentrating."

"She's distracted," Jennifer said to Connor.

"I'm trying to keep us from getting lost. When was the last time you got directions in pre-King-James–Bible English?" She scowled at her sister. "Go back to your chatting in the native tongue and let me keep us from getting lost."

"You know," Jennifer said pleasantly, "you really should be paying attention. We could be talking about you."

"Heaven help me," Victoria muttered. But she looked up at Connor and smiled faintly.

He looked at her with something akin to friendliness. Then his expression changed to one of panic. "Duck!" he shouted.

Victoria ducked, but apparently not quite far enough. She straightened up and looked down at her sleeve.

"Well," she said finally, "now I'll at least smell like the locals."

Jennifer wrinkled her nose. "You should wash that off. *Eau de chamberpot* is highly unpleasant."

"Jenner, it isn't as if the water is any better," Victoria pointed out. "Did you see the washing water this morning? I think I would have been better off washing in beer."

"You would have smelled better than you do now—"

"Duck!"

Victoria shoved her sister over toward the wall of the

closest building. Connor leaped aside agilely and avoided the recent drenching Victoria had received. Not that it would have done him any damage. Victoria looked at him and could not believe how real he looked. If she hadn't known better . . .

She took a deep breath and nodded in a forward direction. It was all that would save her from really losing it. "Down by the Thames," she instructed. "The Globe is supposedly across the water from St. Paul's. We'll make it there if we can keep from getting mugged."

"Connor will protect us," Jennifer said confidently. She smiled easily at him. "You're really intimidating."

"Aye," he agreed with a modest smile.

Victoria wondered how it was he could smile so easily at her sister and not at her.

Life was complicated.

The fact that she was a twenty-first century kind of gal traipsing around in Elizabethan England with her equally modern sister and a medieval ghost was proof enough of that.

She was torn between savoring the delights of a Renaissance Faire on steroids and worrying that someone would figure out she didn't belong and boot her out the front gates. Here, though, it wouldn't be just an ejection from the festival, it would be a little Elizabethan justice. Time in the stocks? A burning at the stake? A beheading?

Or maybe she would get lucky and just spend the rest of her life in the Tower of London. Were there any time gates in the Tower of London?

She suspected there weren't.

She happily contemplated that for quite some time as she threaded her way through the crowds and did her best to follow the directions she'd been given. And then, quite suddenly, she found that she didn't have to follow directions anymore.

"Oh," Jennifer whispered. "Vikki, is that—"

"Yes," Victoria said breathlessly. "The Globe."

She walked forward in a daze. It was yet another in a

long line of things that were just too unreal to get a handle on. The Globe Theater. Where Shakespeare had produced a great portion of his plays. Where he had starred himself in numerous productions.

Amazing.

"Victoria?"

She looked at Connor. "Yes?"

"You weren't moving."

"I'm absorbing."

"Aye, well, perhaps you should absorb later. It looks as if a play is about to begin. Do you care to go watch?"

Victoria was horribly torn. What she needed to be doing was looking for her grandmother. Yet there, right in front of her, was the Globe Theater. She might even see Shakespeare on stage.

She chewed on her bottom lip for quite some time.

"I say we go inside," Jennifer said suddenly. "Who knows who we might see? Maybe Michael got a part. That would at least solve one problem."

Victoria exchanged a brief glance with Connor, then nodded. "All right, let's go. It can't hurt."

"It can't," Jennifer agreed. "Come on."

Victoria walked with her sister and her . . . friend across to the theater. But as she became part of the crowd, she found she could no longer ignore the reality of her situation. She was looking for her granny in a city of tens of thousands. It was exactly like looking for a needle in a haystack. She found that she could no longer ignore her very real doubts that they would be successful.

"Victoria?"

Victoria dragged her sleeve across her eyes. "What?"

"Crumble later. Buck up now."

"Why did I bring you?" Victoria asked, blinking furiously. "I could have been happily having a nervous breakdown right about now if you weren't here interrupting me."

"Let's go catch the play," Jennifer said. "I have a good feeling about this."

"You don't smell like chamber pot."

"I don't, but I'm assuming everyone in the cheap seats will, so you'll fit right in. Should I go sit up in the boxes with the somewhat-washed?"

"No, you should come stand with us," Victoria said. "And you can walk on the outside on the way back to the inn and maybe you'll be treated to the initiation rite."

"Can't wait," Jennifer said cheerfully. "Let's go."

Victoria led the way. She paid, watching her hand as it handed over the coins and wondering why she felt as if she'd never seen it before. So she was hanging out with a ghost. That was one thing. Time-traveling was another thing entirely. Her hand shook as she pulled it back. She clenched it into a fist and tried to give the usher a manly smile as she led her little crew into the theater. She was sure she would get it together very soon—

But not today. She stood at the very back of the crowd standing on the floor of the Globe Theater and couldn't help a brief, hysterical gasp of laughter.

Good heavens, she was in the *Globe*.

It was truly theater in the round. The stage jutted out into the crowd that was gathered on the floor in the cheap, standing-room-only area. Up above and behind her were boxes in which she could see men and women showing off their Elizabethan finery. But as fine as these accommodations were, they weren't the ones for the super rich. Those folks were sitting behind the stage. Victoria knew that such was the case, but it was one thing to read about it in a dry historical treatise; it was another thing entirely to look back behind the stage and see lords and ladies wearing clothing that cost probably the equivalent of a year's wages for all the plebeians standing on the floor.

They were certainly on display and, given that Shake-speare could be enjoyed just as much by the words alone, without any complicated scenery, Victoria supposed they were happy enough in their location.

It beat the floor. In the area for the huddled masses, there were no bathrooms, no garbage cans, and no in-between-the-movie workers to give the place a little tidy-up. Did the stench bother the actors? Victoria vowed to give her cast a serious lecture on the ease of their lives the next chance she had.

"What is this play?" Connor asked from behind her.

Victoria realized she had completely forgotten about him. She'd forgotten about Jennifer, too, so she suffered no pangs of guilt. She looked over her shoulder at him.

"I don't know yet. How are you doing?"

"No one is screaming yet," Connor answered grimly. "But the press is rather too close in here. We may yet find ourselves in a delicate situation if someone steps through me."

"Let's hope not." She turned back to the stage. "Oh, here comes someone. Three someones." She caught her breath. "It's the Scottish play."

"What?" Connor said.

"The Scottish play," Victoria whispered over her shoulder. "Can't say the name; can't quote it unless you're acting in it. It's bad luck."

"It's *MacBeth*," Jennifer said dryly. "I'm not an actor, so the dictum does not apply to me."

"*MacBeth*," Connor said thoughtfully. "Interesting."

"And it's beginning," Victoria said. "Can you two be quiet, please?"

"Can you believe this?" Jennifer said in her best stage whisper. "At the Globe? In the cheap seats?"

"Standing through three hours of play," Victoria pointed out. "Save your strength; stop using it to converse."

The play began. Victoria, in spite of herself, felt the magic come over her. Great theater was great theater, no matter the century. But to see one of Shakespeare's plays in the original venue with an all-male cast . . .

Mind-blowing.

And then Connor laughed.

It was a soft laugh, but it was definitely a laugh and not a chuckle. Victoria turned and looked at him in astonishment. He was smiling.

He was, put simply, drop-dead gorgeous.

Maybe this was why there weren't dozens of women in his keep. They hadn't seen what she was seeing.

Lucky for them.

Desperately bad for her.

"What?" she whispered.

He leaned down close to her and pointed to the stage. "Look," he said, sounding actually quite delighted. "Cast your gaze upon yon witch to the left."

Victoria turned back around and looked. And she caught her breath.

"'Tis an awfully big needle that auld witch uses to stir her pot, aye?" he whispered. "Likely a size fifteen—and bamboo. I daresay she had one in her bag that afternoon. I fear such a needle would snap did it come into contact with a lad's sternum, but that is my opinion only."

"Perhaps she was knitting with big wool," Jennifer suggested.

"Och, I suppose that might be true," he said doubtfully. "Though I thought she preferred a finer gauge. Well, whatever the case, we now know where your granny is."

"How did she get this gig?" Jennifer asked. "I thought only men got to act during Shakespeare's time."

"She's Granny," Victoria said. "How could they resist her?"

"Size four, aluminum," Connor said wisely. "That would convince me of quite a few things."

Victoria felt her knees grow quite unsteady beneath her. Her relief was complete and so overwhelming she wasn't at all sure how she was going to manage to get through the rest of the play. She felt Jennifer's arm go around her briefly and was grateful for it. She watched the first several acts of the play unfold without truly seeing them. She would have given quite a bit for a chair, but there was no hope of even pulling up a handy bit of floor.

The first chance they had to sneak out, she turned to Jennifer and Connor. "Let's get out of here and wait for her at the stage entrance. I'm assuming they have a stage entrance."

"Don't you know?" Jennifer asked.

"I've never been here before," Victoria muttered as she threaded her way through the crowd.

She waited with Connor and her sister until the play was over, then waited a bit more as the cast and crew left the building. And when her granny came out, Victoria threw herself at her with a glad cry.

"Victoria!" Mary said, staggering in surprise. "Connor, as well. Jennifer, you, too! How did you all get here?"

"The same way you did, lady," Connor said with a smile.

"Yes, well, that was quite a surprise, wasn't it?" Mary said, smiling. "I had just gotten up to go stretch my legs, paused to admire those interesting flowers in the grass, and subsequently found myself somewhere I never intended to be."

"It's a good thing you never go anywhere without your knitting bag," Jennifer said, giving Mary a hug.

"You never know when you'll be stuck in a line," Mary said.

"Well, it's a good thing it wasn't a line to the Tower's dungeon," Victoria said, feeling almost giddy with relief. "Come on, Granny, let's go."

"Oh," Mary said with a slight frown, "but I can't go yet."

Victoria frowned, as well. "What do you mean you can't go yet? Let's get out of here before someone figures out we're not locals!"

"But, Vikki, honey, I couldn't disappoint William."

"William?" Victoria echoed. "William who?"

"Who do you think?" her grandmother asked smoothly.

Victoria felt faint. She'd bypassed woozy, barreled through unsteady, and plowed right into reeling. "Shakespeare?" she managed in a very garbled voice.

Her grandmother took her by the arm. "Let's go sit over there on that little wall. I have an hour or two before I have to be off for supper."

"Off for supper," Victoria repeated weakly. "Off for supper with whom?"

"Vikki, are you not feeling well?"

Jennifer laughed. "Granny, I think Vikki's having withdrawal symptoms. You know, being separated from her production of *Hamlet* by, oh, four hundred years or so. Cut her some slack."

Victoria found herself deposited on a little brick wall. Her grandmother sat down next to her, took her hand, and patted it. Victoria had a hard time not bursting into tears.

"I'm all right," Mary said, smiling sympathetically. "I appreciate you coming all this way to get me. Now, give me a few days to wrap things up and I'll be ready to go home."

"Shakespeare," Victoria whispered. "You met Shakespeare? Where are you staying? How did you get a part in his play?"

Her grandmother laughed. "So many questions, so little time before I'm due for supper with William. He finds my accent charming, you know. Scottish with a tinge of something he's still trying to identify."

"Is that so," Victoria managed.

Mary put her arm around Victoria. "Yes, it is. Now, I have a thousand things to tell you and some gossip as well. Where are you staying?"

"In the seedy part of town," Jennifer offered. "How about you?"

"Dear William found me a little room in Lord Mountjoy's house."

"Granny," Victoria said, stunned, "do you have any idea whom you're hobnobbing with?"

"I'm an old woman," Mary said with a smile, "so titles don't impress me. But a soft bed does. You know, the pub behind us is quite nice. Let's go chat, shall we? I have some interesting news for you."

Victoria managed to get to her feet and trail after her sister and her grandmother. She looked up at Connor.

"Well," she said.

He shrugged with half a smile. "As I said, a most canny wench. I am unsurprised."

"But Connor, she met *Shakespeare*."

"Maybe he was impressed by her knitting needles."

He wouldn't have been the first person, Victoria supposed. Mary seemed to know the proprietor of the pub, who subsequently offered them fine seats near a window. Victoria waited until everyone was seated before she turned to her granny and began the grilling.

"All right, now spill the details," Victoria said.

"Are you feeling better, dear?" Mary asked.

"Much, and don't hedge. How in the world did you get that gig? In the Scottish play, no less!"

Mary smiled. "It's a rather long story, but since I assume you found yourselves here in the same way I did, I'll spare you the details of my trip. I should probably also spare you the details of my encounter with a ne'er-do-well or two who felt the bite of my needles."

"How did they serve you, those needles?" Connor asked politely.

"You would have been impressed, Connor," Mary said, her eyes twinkling. "Since I did not have a strapping, braw Highland lord at my disposal, I did what an old woman has to do to get along. Now, as you might imagine, I was slightly disconcerted to find myself so far out of my normal routine, but—"

"Being Granny, you made do," Jennifer finished with a smile.

Mary smiled modestly. "I do what I can."

"But, Granny," Victoria said impatiently, "how did you meet Shakespeare?"

"Apparently, he was off on a little walk to meet a new actor when he saw me and felt compelled to approach."

"How fortunate," Connor offered.

"He needed a new witch," Mary continued, "and liked the look of my needles."

"But, Granny," Victoria said again, "you're a woman. They didn't let women act during Elizabeth's day."

"It's 1606, love, and James is king. William saw that I was perfect for the role and decided that what the Master of the Revels didn't know wouldn't hurt him. Besides, it's only for another week. He's staging something else then and I'll be free to do whatever suits me."

"But we came to take you home," Victoria pointed out.

Mary smiled. "In a week, love?"

Victoria sighed. "I suppose if you're safe, we can spend a week looking for Michael. Who knows, it may take us that long to find him. I hope not longer," she added darkly.

Mary leaned forward. "I might be able to help you there, as well."

Victoria caught her breath. "Can you?"

"Finish your lunch, love, and then we'll see what appears in the little square across the road."

"Granny, what's across the road is the Globe," Victoria said. "If Michael Fellini has gotten a gig there, I'm going to kill myself."

"Hold that thought, love, until after you've eaten."

Victoria found that she just couldn't bear even that long a wait. "Are you telling me that Michael's acting at the Globe?"

Mary laughed. "In his dreams, dear." She waited until lunch had been served before she continued. "He's holding court every couple of days on the stepes of those hallowed boards, trying to get people to pay attention to him."

Jennifer sniffed suspiciously at her cup. "And are they? Paying attention, I mean. By the way, what do you think this stuff is?"

"Wine," Mary said. "Safest thing on the menu. And, no, the people aren't really paying attention. He's trying to pass off *Othello* as his own. What he can apparently remember of it, which according to my memory, is not very much."

"But *Othello* was written in 1605," Victoria said. "And you said it is 1606."

"Exactly," Mary said. Then she shrugged. "He's staying at The Gander's Goose. It's not a particularly nice inn, but it's what he can afford." She paused. "He doesn't sound well. I wonder if the shock has done him in or if it's something else."

"Let's figure it out right away," Victoria said. "Let's get him right now and be on our way."

"My run," Mary reminded her. "I can't disappoint the Bard."

Victoria was horribly torn. Jennifer and Connor, she could tell, would have happily stayed for quite some time, but she did have her play at home to be taking care of. Then again, this was Elizabethan London and her granny had a part as one of the witches in a genuine Shakespearean production.

"All right," Victoria said. "You finish your run and we'll keep tabs on Michael and make sure he doesn't get into any trouble."

"I want to sightsee," Jennifer said.

"Might as well," Victoria said, resigning herself to really not being in control of her life. "Granny, are you safe?"

Mary patted her knitting bag. "Perfectly. Besides, one of Will's most lethal actors has been assigned as my bodyguard. He's hanging around outside, waiting to escort me wherever I want to go." She smiled modestly. "I finished the Fair Isle sweater for him."

"A fortunate lad, indeed," Connor said, sounding just a little bit envious.

"He apparently thought so," Mary agreed. She dabbed at her mouth with her napkin. "I'm sorry to dash, but I'm expected at Lord Mountjoy's. A witch's work is never done, I suppose."

Jennifer laughed. "Granny, I can't believe you. You'd think you had lived in this century forever!"

"I'm flexible, love. 'Bloom where you're planted' is my motto."

Jennifer shook her head. "I could never live without modern conveniences."

"Never say never, love," Mary said, patting Jennifer's hand. She looked at Victoria. "You'll be all right? Can you amuse yourselves for a few days?"

Victoria blinked. "You mean, you're ditching us until your run is over? I don't get to meet the man?"

"Yes, I'm ditching you, and yes, I'll see what I can arrange with William." Mary paused. "I can't exactly tell him that you've been producing his plays for years, can I? I suppose I can tell him that you're a huge fan and want his autograph."

Victoria felt a little faint. "I suppose you could."

"I could," Mary agreed. "All right, today's Saturday. Meet me after the show on Tuesday and hopefully I'll have a famous playwright in tow."

Victoria was very glad she was sitting down.

"And Michael?" Mary asked.

"Mayhap we will be forced to resort to violence," Connor said, not looking unhappy at the thought of that possibility.

Victoria gave her grandmother a kiss and watched her sashay out of the darkened pub. She sat back and looked at her companions. "Can you believe it?"

"I believe anything of your *grandmère*," Connor said. "A formidable woman, that one."

"Hobnobbing with William Shakespeare," Victoria squeaked. "How did she manage that?"

"Like you said, she's Granny," Jennifer said. "Well, at least we know where she is. We probably should go find Diva Fellini and see about damage control."

"Heaven help us," Victoria muttered as she rose, left money on the table, and headed out of the pub with her companions.

They hadn't walked ten feet out of the door before she heard Connor swear.

She ducked, just on principle.

"There he is, the rat," Jennifer said.

Victoria folded her arms over her chest and looked at Michael Fellini standing across the muddy street, arms flung out wide, reciting lines from *Othello* as if he stood on the Drury Lane stage.

Reciting them badly, truth be told.

Victoria looked at him more closely. "Well," she said finally, "I think he could have benefitted from a trip or two to a Renaissance Faire. Look at his clothes."

"Sneakers with tights," Jennifer said in disgust. "I mean, really. I could have done better than that."

"Of course you could have," Victoria said crisply. "You're a fabulous actress, something we *will* discuss when we return home." She looked up at Connor. "What do you think?"

"What I think isn't fit for a lady's ear."

She smiled. There were just so many things to like about Connor MacDougal. "Well, we could just sit here and watch until he gets tired and goes home so we're sure of where he's staying, or we could go sightseeing."

"I vote for sightseeing," Jennifer said.

Connor stroked his chin thoughtfully. "And if he flees? 'Twill be a hard thing indeed to find him again."

"Flee?" Victoria said doubtfully. "I don't think he will. He's standing ten feet from the Globe Theater. He's probably having delusions of grandeur even as we speak. If I were Shakespeare, I'd be watching my back."

"I'm certain he trembles in fear," Connor said dryly. "Very well, Mistress Jennifer, where is it you care to go?"

"The Tower," Jennifer said with bright eyes.

"I doubt there will be a tour of the Crown Jewels," Victoria said. "We can only hope we won't have a personal tour of the dungeons."

Connor shivered. "The saints preserve us," he said with feeling. He put his hand on his sword and looked at Victoria. "After you, my lady."

Jennifer gave Victoria a knowing look that made Victoria want to smack her, but she refrained. Who knew but what police frowned on that sort of thing, and then they really would find themselves in the Tower's pokey.

My lady.

She followed her sister, Connor's words ringing in her ears.

Chapter 20

Michael Fellini sat at a wobbly table in the garret of an equally unstable inn and stared at the business end of a quill, wondering if he should dip it again into the inkwell or just poke himself in the eye with it.

He paused.

He was fairly sure he had a fever.

He was almost equally sure he had seen Victoria the day before.

But given that he thought his fever might be causing hallucinations, it was possible that he was imagining the last.

He pulled up the sleeve of his stolen tunic and looked at the slash on his bicep. It was red and angry. As the man who had given him that slice had been red and angry, as well, maybe it was fitting. All he really knew was that it was probably infected and that wasn't good.

He'd get it fixed later, when he'd sold his play and gotten some money. He looked at the little pouch of gold on his table, hefted it, then decided it was most definitely not enough. He'd clunked someone over the head and poached his clothing on his first day in Renaissance England, but the guy hadn't been all that well-heeled, so Michael had had to make do with a cheap room and meager supplies. At this point, paper and writing gear was on his list; a doctor wasn't.

Damn it, where was Bernie when he needed him?

He looked at his quill again and decided on writing instead of damaging. After all, who knew if, when he finished his new play, he might be called upon to take the lead role and a missing eye might disqualify him for that. He wasn't about to let that happen, given that the play he was about to write was going to be something that would make Elizabethan England stand up and take notice.

Othello, Moor of Venice.

He paused and frowned. The only problem was, he could only remember Othello's part.

He shrugged. It wouldn't be hard to make up the rest. Shakespeare had done it, hadn't he?

He tickled his nose with the feather end of the quill in an effort to keep himself awake. What he wanted to do was sleep. He was achy, feverish, and really could have used some antibiotics. That, coupled with the last two days he'd spent in front of the Globe trying to attract attention out in the disgusting London air, left him not wondering at all why he felt so bad.

That had gone pretty well, all things considered. He'd had some donations of food while he'd been standing there, and he really couldn't complain about the ripeness of the treats tossed his way. After all, the local yokels probably didn't have a whole lot of extra cash. That they'd been willing to part with parts of their lunch said a lot about how much they liked his performances. Of course, some of the locals had parted with their lunches a little more enthusiastically than others, but he hadn't complained. Food was food, whether it was scraped off the floor or off your shirt.

Too bad no one had wanted to contribute any doctor's fees to the cause. He supposed he might have been able to pop back through that time gate, grab some stuff out of

Mrs. Pruitt's medicine chest, then get right back to business on the seedy side of the Thames. Then again, he might not have managed that, so there was really no sense in trying.

Besides, *Othello* was going to be a smash hit and then he'd have all the fame and fortune he could handle. He'd hire the best damned doctor in all of Elizabethan London.

He stared off into space for a moment and tilted his head at the best angle to contemplate that amazing bit of sorcery. Who would have thought an innocent tramp through innocent-looking grass could transport a man back centuries in time to the precise place where he could best become a star.

Unbelievable.

He realized, after a while, that he was still staring off into space and that it was becoming all he could do.

This was not good.

He forced himself to lower his aching arm to the really crappy paper he'd been able to afford and begin the first and only draft of his genius.

He could hear the applause already.

Chapter 21

Connor stood in the shadows of a very lovely, very recently built Tudor building and considered the past se'nnight. It had been strange, somehow, to pass time into a century that wasn't his own. True, he had lived through these times once already, but he hadn't come to London. He'd had enough to do terrorizing souls at Thorpewold, which, having been built in the late fourteenth century, had just begun to boast proper hauntings.

He wondered if James MacLeod did this often, this tromping about in a time that wasn't his own. It would have been interesting, to see a different world, but Connor suspected that the novelty of it would have worn quite thin for him after just a time or two. Truth be told, what he had wished for in life had been home and hearth.

A pity he found a wench he would have gladly shared the like with seven centuries past his expiration date.

As it were.

He looked at the woman in question. She was currently standing with her sister, watching events going on across the street. Connor found it in him to smile. Jennifer had spent the previous few days traipsing happily about London, blending in with the natives as if she'd been born in their century. Victoria had scowled at everyone as if they'd been actors performing poorly on her stage, then spent any left-over time warning her sister about the condition of the water.

And judging by the condition of the sewage in the street, Connor had been inclined to agree with Victoria.

But the se'nnight had been survived and there they were, standing across the way from the infamous Globe and pondering their next move. Connor put his hand on his sword, wishing that it was tangible. He would have used it without hesitation on Michael Fellini, who was holding court in front of the theater, carrying on in a most unhinged fashion.

"Well," Victoria said, taking a deep breath, "let's go get him."

"Vikki, I don't think he's all there," Jennifer warned.

"I agree," Mary said. "Let's be careful."

"We just have to get him pointed in the right direction and Connor can terrify him into moving forward."

Connor nodded and hoped that would be the case. Fellini did not look well, but Connor supposed that could have come from the layer of food that seemed to encrust the man. Had he been pelted with rotten food, or was he dressing that way for effect? Hard to say.

Victoria led the way across the street. She stopped in front of Fellini.

"Michael, you don't look well," Victoria said bluntly. "Let me get you a doctor."

"No!" Fellini bellowed, wrenching away from her. He pointed a shaking finger at her. "I thought I saw you before."

"I hired you to do my play, remember?"

"No, here," he snapped, then weaved unsteadily. "I saw you here."

"Yes, you did. Right now. Now, come with me—"

"I'm not leaving!" he shouted. He looked around him wildly. "I'm going to be a famous playwright."

Victoria rolled her eyes. "Sure you are. But let's get you to the doctor first."

"Shakespeare had better watch his back," Fellini said, lowering his voice suddenly. "I'm having inspiration."

"I think you're having a hallucination," Victoria muttered. "You know, if you don't come with us, the king's men are going to come and throw you in the Tower of London to rot."

Connor refrained from commenting on the potential enjoyment he might have had from the sight of that.

"The King's Men," Fellini said, his ears perking up. "Shakespeare was one of them. Good company—"

Victoria punched him in the nose.

Fellini fell backward, cracked his head on the side of a low brick wall, and slipped into oblivion.

Connor stared at Victoria in amazement. Why, there were few men of his clan who could have dealt such a blow.

"Well done," he praised.

"Yes," Jennifer said, "but now that he's unconscious, how do we haul him?"

"I have a cart waiting in an alley," Mary said. "Girls, can you get him that far?"

"You bet," Victoria said. "He's a welterweight." She looked at Connor. "I'm glad I'm not hauling you."

"You wouldn't manage it," he said. "You'd be dragging me by the heels and then I would wake very cross indeed." He stood idly by and watched as Jennifer and Victoria wrestled Fellini across the street to the cart that Mary had so kindly provided. The lout remained senseless through the entire exercise—unsurprising, and a boon to all involved.

It was probably just as well for Fellini, given the cart Mary provided had, by the looks of it, recently carried quite a bit of refuse.

"Nasty," Connor commented happily as Victoria and Jennifer heaved Fellini into the depths of it.

"I do what I can for the cause," Mary said. "Now, shall we be going?"

Victoria took several deep breaths, wrinkling her nose as she did so. "Are you finished with your business here? Finally?"

"Why are you complaining?" Mary asked, giving Victoria an affectionate pinch on the cheek. "You lifted a glass with William Shakespeare yesterday. Aren't you satisfied?"

Jennifer laughed. "She's still speechless. If she were ever speechless, that is."

Connor looked at Victoria and found that aye, indeed she seemed to have little to say. She'd had little to say the day before, as well, when her grandmother had appeared with Master Shakespeare escorting her. Connor had stood back and listened to Mary and Shakespeare carry on an animated discussion of women and their rights to liberty and happiness, while Victoria looked on as if she hadn't an intelligent thought in her fair head.

In the end, duty had called, and Shakespeare had been off to another rehearsal. He'd kissed Mary on both cheeks. He'd gallantly if not slightly uneasily kissed Victoria on the hand. He had then treated Jennifer to the same affection he had their grandmother before he'd trotted out of the pub.

Jennifer had managed to keep her mouth closed and her drool checked during the interview.

Unlike her sister.

It had taken hours before Victoria had regained her powers of speech. She'd said pithy bits, such as *wow* and *unbelievable* and *great*.

Connor had begun to fret a bit over what would be left of her if she didn't regain her sensibilities.

Fortunately sleep seemed to have restored some of them. Seeing Fellini on the street corner, babbling about his new play and demanding to see Shakespeare as quickly as possible, had put Victoria back in fighting form.

For the most part. Now that she was face-to-face with the infamous Globe, she had gone a bit daft in the head again.

"We'll let her ruminate a bit longer," Mary said. "For now, let's get this pile of crap—"

"Granny!" Jennifer exclaimed.

"An apt description," Mary said unrepentantly. "He hasn't bathed in days and I think he's had a douse or two of chamber-pot water. But, however he smells, I suppose we must get him home."

Connor sighed as he watched the three women pull the cart between them. Mary looked at him once and clucked her tongue at him. He understood. It wasn't his fault that he couldn't help, so there was no use in berating himself for it.

He berated himself just the same.

He also spent his share of time frowning fiercely at those who looked tempted to question them. Most looked with pity on them for having a drunken fool to cart about through public streets. Connor exchanged a glance of commiseration with a likely lad or two and found himself somewhat thankful he wasn't kin to Michael Fellini, though less for his imbibing habits than just on general purposes.

And then he realized, as they turned into the little close where they had used the time gate, that Fellini might not be intoxicated.

"Victoria," he said, "look at his arm."

She put her end of the cart down and looked Fellini over. "What are you seeing?"

Connor leaned closer. "Look at his upper arm. I daresay that has made him out of his head."

"Good heavens," she gasped. "Look at that cut. It's oozing green stuff." She looked up at Connor. "I'm no doctor, but—"

"This is dire," Connor said. "Let us return him to the inn as quickly as may be."

"Here?" she asked in astonishment. "The inn here?"

"Nay, the Boar's Head," Connor said. "They will have nothing here to cure that infection save bleeding him, and that will likely kill him."

"And I suppose we can't let that happen," she said, sounding as if she didn't find it such an unappealing alternative after all.

"Let us be away," Connor said. "While we can manage it."

Victoria nodded and entered the alleyway unwillingly, but whether that was due to leaving Shakespeare's environs or because she had foul memories of the place, Connor couldn't have said. Connor waited until the women were safely in the spot they had determined a day or two earlier, then he drew his sword and approached. He ascertained that the close was empty save for them, then he turned his back on his ladies and stood with his face forward, his sword bare in his hand, and a fierce frown on his face.

"All right," Mary said, "how is it we go about this again?"

"Think about the Boar's Head Inn in 2005," Victoria said. "And don't think about anything else. Jamie says the way to get the gate to work is to focus your mind on where you want to go."

"If he says so," Mary said easily.

"Granny, what were you thinking about when you wandered into the fairy ring?" Jennifer asked.

Mary seemed to give that a bit of thought. "I was thinking about what a tremendous bore Michael Fellini is and how I wished I could see Shakespeare for myself to see how it had been done originally."

"Well, there you go," Victoria said. "Let's have equally interesting thoughts about getting this tremendous bore back to a doctor so I'm not accused of murdering him."

Connor wondered if he should close his eyes and say a little prayer, but thought that might be sacrilegious.

But nothing seemed to be happening.

He was reconsidering his doubts when Fellini awoke and began squealing in the manner of a skewered pig. Connor turned, prepared to deliver a stern lecture or a purposeful blow, but he was distracted by Victoria's gasp.

"Look!" she exclaimed.

Connor saw the grass beneath his feet before he turned and saw what a more hopeful man might have called Farris's field.

"Think we made it?" Jennifer asked.

"There's only one way to tell," Victoria said, sounding rather relieved. "Let's see if the inn is where it should be." She paused. "I suppose we'll have to take Michael with us."

"We should," Mary said with a smile. "Well, shall we chance it?"

"If there's the potential of a hot shower down the road, you bet," Jennifer said with feeling. "I'd settle for clean water of any temperature at this point."

"I would like some tea," Mary said with a contented sigh.

"I would like my master list of things to do," Victoria said, taking a determined hold on the cart. "Michael, shut up. We're taking you to the doctor."

"But I need to go back to the Globe," Fellini muttered. "I have a mission there, to bring great acting to the people of Renaissance London! Hey," he complained, rubbing his face, "my nose hurts."

"Don't talk too much, dear," Mary said soothingly. "Save your strength."

He looked up at her with very bleary eyes. "Should I?"

"You should," Mary said, giving him a pat. "Don't talk, don't fret. In fact, I would do my best to remain completely still until the doctor tells you differently."

"You're right," Fellini said in a very weak voice. "I should conserve what strength I have. It's the right thing to do."

"Of course, dear."

Connor looked at Victoria who was rolling her eyes quite vigorously. He shared her sentiments perfectly. Now, if they could have, in good conscience, left Fellini to his fate in Renaissance London, he would have been content. But they couldn't have, again in good conscience, left him to rot in some madhouse—which was where he would have found himself if he had at some point begun to make any sense to the Elizabethans.

Connor sighed. It looked as if more overacting would be the dish of the day, as it were, for as long as Michael was serving things up on the boards of Thorpewold Castle.

Connor walked along behind the cart, feeling more confident with every step that they had come back to the proper point in time. He had almost decided to run ahead for help when help arrived in the persons of James MacLeod and Thomas McKinnon.

"We'll carry him," Thomas said. Then he came to an abrupt halt some ten paces away. "Then again, maybe we'll watch you keep pulling him. He reeks."

"Nice to see you, too," Victoria said tartly. "Yes, we had a successful trip, yes, we found Michael and Granny, and yes, I saw the Globe and met Shakespeare."

Thomas looked at her in shock. "You're kidding."

Connor watched as she suddenly broke into a smile such as he had never seen before. It was one of wonder, disbelief, and elation.

"I did," she said, sounding almost giddy.

"What did you say to him?"

"Not a thing," she said happily. "I just listened to him shoot the breeze with Mary. But he kissed my hand."

"He kissed my hand *and* both my cheeks," Jennifer put in, grinning. "I think Vikki scared him. She was totally starstruck."

"I'll just bet," Thomas said, looking equally pleased. He gave Mary a big hug. "Granny, good to see you."

"You too, love," Mary said. "Thanks for the cavalry. Our good Laird MacDougal was fierce enough to keep all thugs at bay and we're very grateful to him."

Connor waved her words aside dismissively. There was so much more he could have done, but it was behind them and he was damned grateful for it. He watched Victoria, Jennifer, and Mary walk ahead while Thomas pulled Fellini. He hung back, to give them time to celebrate their successful mission. James MacLeod fell back to walk along with him.

"How was it?" Jamie asked.

"Difficult," Connor said quietly. "Frustrating. Dangerous for the women. They were accosted the moment we arrived and though I used my fierceness to its utmost advantage, the ruffians soon saw what I really was."

"How did you best them?"

"I used what poor strength I have with things from the mortal world and managed to plunge a sword into the leader's back." He paused. "'Tis a miracle I didn't stab Victoria, as well."

"Let us hope such heroism is not called for again any time soon. Though I daresay you would be equal to it in any case."

Connor looked at James MacLeod and allowed himself—now that the danger had passed—to wonder. The man certainly seemed comfortable in his modern clothing, but there was something about him that hinted at a life lived in more primitive circumstances. He cleared his throat.

"You aren't modern, are you?"

Jamie only lifted one eyebrow and smiled. "What do you think?"

"I suspect . . . thirteenth century. Late thirteenth century. Perhaps early fourteenth."

Jamie shrugged, with another easy smile. "Very perceptive."

"But you came to the Future."

"I did. I married a girl from the Future. She had accidently, or fortuitously if you prefer, traveled back to my time. We loved, wed, and planned to live out our lives in my day. But when I escaped death at the hands of my enemies, I saw that there was no reason for me not to come forward with her."

"Hence your experience with the time gates."

Jamie grinned. "Och, but that would imply I'd used them but once and you *know* that cannot possibly be the case."

Connor found himself smiling, as well. "Where have you gone?"

"Where haven't I gone?"

Connor laughed in spite of himself. "That poor wench you wed. How she must fret."

"Aye, well, she's come along on enough adventures of her own. Not so often now that we have wee bairns, but there will no doubt come a day when she joins me again."

Connor sighed. "It must be a pleasant life."

Jamie nodded. "It is and I'm grateful for it."

"How did you find the modern world?" Connor asked. "At first?"

" 'Twas startling at first," Jamie said with a smile. "But I've accustomed myself far too quickly to its wonders. I'm equally curious how you have found watching the events of history parade before you in all their glory."

"Startling at first," Connor repeated easily. "I wished I could have done more than terrify the occasional Englishman. I was there at the '45, but the Highlanders were so overwhelmed, there was little I could do. For the most part, I have stayed at Thorpewold." He paused. "I wish I had traveled more. I could have been more use to my country thusly."

"We all have regrets," Jamie agreed. "You were of great service to Victoria just recently. That counts for much."

Connor nodded, and supposed there was truth to that.

It was cold comfort, though.

"I would trade it all," he said, half to himself, "for an hour, nay, but a handful of moments . . ."

"I'm sorry for that," Jamie said quietly.

Connor nodded in acknowledgment of the understanding, then blew out his breath. There was no sense in thinking on it. He was what he was and could not change it, no matter how much he might have wanted to. He continued down the road with Jamie, glad for the companionship and the silence.

It was quite some time later that Thomas and Jamie both managed to get Fellini to the front door. Mrs. Pruitt met them there but refused to allow him inside.

"I will not allow something that smells thus into me fresh-smelling entryway. Take him away and hose him off." She looked at Jennifer. "Ye don't smell very nice, either. Nor," she said, sniffing in Victoria's direction, "do ye."

"We could use showers," Victoria conceded. "Can we come in if we promise not to touch anything and swear to put our clothes into the dustbin after we've changed?"

Mrs. Pruitt considered. "I'll find plastic bags for ye to lay your gear on. Don't lay anything on the carpets." She looked at Mary. "Dear Mary, ye look a sight. You may come into the kitchen and I'll be about fixing ye a lovely tea. How is it ye're so clean?"

"I stayed with nobility," Mary said easily, going inside the inn. "Knitting is a passport to all sorts of things, apparently. Do you knit, dear?"

"I tat," Mrs. Pruitt said. "So easy to tuck into a pocket and work on when time permits. So, they were kind to ye?"

"Young William was wonderful," Mary said as she disappeared into the dining room with Mrs. Pruitt. "Shakespeare, you know . . ."

Connor watched them go, then looked at the rest of the Renaissance contingent standing stranded in the doorway. "I say we heave Fellini into the bushes and be about our business."

"Don't tempt me," Victoria said. "Thomas, what time is it?"

"A little after noon."

"I need to shower and get with Fred and see how things have gone."

"The play's been fabulous," Thomas said. "I've watched every night while you were gone—just to make certain no one flubbed their lines."

"Or stuck their fingers up their noses," Victoria said pointedly.

Connor clasped his hands behind his back. Fingers up noses? Embarrassing and likely career-ending. He wondered which actor in Victoria's past had made such a grievous *faux pas* and ruined his chances to be her star.

"I don't suppose you would deal with Michael," Victoria said with a frown.

"Is he going to be angry he was fetched from Renaissance England?"

"Enormously."

Thomas smiled. "I'll take care of him, then. He won't dare say anything nasty to me and it will be fun watching his head explode from the effort."

Victoria looked at him closely. "Do you know something I don't?"

"I think he harbors a secret desire to direct."

She rolled her eyes. "Heaven help us. Connor?"

Connor found that she was looking at him. "Aye?"

"I'm going to get cleaned up, then head up to the castle. Do you want to come with me?"

Connor realized with a start that everyone was looking at him to see what he would say. Well, everyone except James MacLeod, who was allowing him some lairdly privacy.

He frowned. "I should go up to the castle myself," he blustered. "To see how my garrison fares."

"Great," Victoria said with a yawn. "See you in a few."

Thomas's sense of decency apparently was only within reach until his sister disappeared inside. Then he turned to Connor and smiled pleasantly.

"She needs an escort. Apparently, you're it."

"You know," Connor said conversationally, "I can wield a knife from your world. It would make quite a large hole in your chest."

"Then you'd have to deal with Iolanthe, Victoria, and Fellini. I'd go wait for Vic and stay out of harm's way if I were you."

Connor snorted. "You have a reprieve, not a stay."

Thomas made him a little bow. "Good of you. Now, I'll go find a doctor. Let's leave the heap out here until we absolutely can't any longer. I don't think he'll get too sunburned. It is England, after all."

Connor left him to it. He made Jennifer a low bow, thanked her for her company, thanked Jamie for his kind words, bestowed a hearty glare on Thomas, then walked around the side of the inn, where he could wait for Victoria in peace.

The saints preserve him.

He could attempt to fool her kin, but there was no fooling his heart.

He was lost . . .

Chapter 22

What a difference a day made.

Or two, or maybe three. Victoria yawned as she opened the library door and peered into the darkened entryway. She was having the same feeling of jet lag she'd had on her initial arrival in England. Maybe time-traveling was harder on a person than advertised. Jamie never looked anything but perky and well-rested, but she suspected that there wasn't much that slowed him down. And he probably had spent his time in Elizabethan England frowning away bad guys instead of trying to corral a feverish, whining nutcase. And a bombastic, feverish nutcase at that.

And speaking of that nutcase, Michael Fellini was upstairs recuperating. Bombastically, if anyone cared.

It was enough to drive all sensible guests from the inn. The exodus had already begun the day before. Jamie had left for Scotland, no doubt anxious to be back home amid the heather instead of on the border amid the chaos. Victoria's parents and her grandmother had gone with him to take in the sights.

Thomas and Iolanthe hadn't ventured that far. They'd gone on a little sightseeing trip to Artane, a castle on the coast. They seemed to have been unusually eager to see it—and for Iolanthe and her pregnant self, that was saying something. Victoria had wanted to get to the bottom of it, but she'd had her hands so full keeping Michael under control that she hadn't been able to investigate as she would have liked.

Jennifer had taken a train south to London, no doubt to regale Megan with all sorts of tales Megan would immediately and completely believe without question.

That those tales might be true was really beyond the scope of the argument at present.

Whatever the case, it left Victoria all alone in the inn, and for the first time in her life she wished she weren't. Alone, that is. Alone with ghosts. Alone with ghosts that were most definitely not going to become anything but ghosts in the foreseeable future.

She paused. Perhaps she wasn't as alone as she thought. Yes, there he went again. The lunatic upstairs to whom someone had mistakenly given a little servants' bell.

"Doesn't anyone down there hear me?" a faint, though surprisingly strong voice called plaintively.

Victoria jumped at a movement to her left. There, in the gloom, hovered Mrs. Pruitt's face, lit from below by a single weak light, like something out of a spooky movie.

"I think," Mrs. Pruitt said in a low voice, "that I might have to stab meself an actor."

"*I* didn't give him the bloody bell," Victoria pointed out.

"Dr. Morris told me to," Mrs. Pruitt said. She paused. "I'm finding the good doctor less attractive by the ring." She considered that for a moment or two longer. "Distressing, as I found him quite to me taste a few days ago."

"I thought you were sweet on Ambrose," Victoria said.

"I'm hedging me bets," Mrs. Pruitt said.

Then she smiled.

It wasn't a pretty sight in the glow of the flashlight.

"I might," she continued, "just have to call the good

doctor and have him sedate the patient. For his own good."
She patted her hair self-consciously. "How do I look?"

"Ravishing," Victoria said promptly. "Even better if you
can get Michael to shut up. He's ruining everyone's sleep."

"I'll call the doctor," Mrs. Pruitt said, pulling a mobile
phone out of her pocket and heading upstairs with it.

Victoria wondered briefly if she intended to bean
Michael with the phone, or phone the good doctor and let
him do the honors. She stood in the middle of the entryway
and listened closely.

The door opened.

Complaints wafted downward.

There was a screech cut artistically short.

Apparently Mrs. Pruitt was wielding her cell phone
with great success. Victoria had no complaints. In fact, she
was sick of complaints, and considering that's all she'd had
from Michael for the last indeterminate amount of time,
she was happy to have him silenced for a bit. Ignoring the
fact that a Kathy Bates *Misery* moment might be taking
place upstairs, she moved toward the kitchen for a little
something to help her sleep.

She walked through the dining room and paused at the
sound of low voices coming from the kitchen. She didn't
hear any cursing or the loud, declarative type of thing that
bespoke insults being delivered between Highlanders or
between Highlander and late medieval Englishman, so she
assumed it was safe to enter.

But as she stood at the door, she heard the strains of
something far more interesting than threats of bodily harm.

" 'My hour is almost come, when I to sulphurous and
tormenting flames must render up myself '," Ambrose
quoted.

" 'Alas! poor ghost,' " said Connor sympathetically.

Victoria felt her jaw slide a little south. Ambrose and
Connor, reading lines?

" 'Pity me not,' " Ambrose said, " 'but lend thy serious
hearing to what I shall unfold.' "

" 'Speak, I am bound to hear.' " Connor snorted. "And

that, my laird, is the first and last time you shall hear me beg to hear you blather on at length without interruption."

"My good Connor," said Ambrose, "I am only repeating the lines of the play."

"At least you are not bleating them like that pitiful excuse for a ghost Victoria finds herself saddled with. I vow, if he bellows *adieu* once more in that groaning fashion, I will clout him over the head with a dirk myself!"

"Then I thank you, lad, for the compliment on my acting. Let us continue, shall we?"

"Aye," Connor said, "but let us make haste in this runthrough. The night will not last forever and I wish Victoria to have no idea that I waste my time thusly."

There was silence for quite a lengthy period of time. Victoria wondered if she'd made a noise to alert them to her presence, or if Connor was pausing to count all the reasons why spending his night practicing Shakespeare was less useful than grinding guardsmen into the dust.

"Connor, my lad," Ambrose said slowly, "this is not a waste of time. You've learned a goodly number of Hamlet's lines—a not unworthy accomplishment. You'll find that it will aid you in learning to read them. And there is more to a full, rich life than the ability to best any soul on the field."

"I daresay," Connor said with a snort.

"I daresay," Ambrose countered. "Young William Shakespeare was full of large, profound thoughts."

"And many bawdy ones."

"A happy marriage of both. Soon, you will be able to read all his plays yourself. Time spent with great thinkers is never wasted. Consider what a connoisseur of human nature he was. How much time you will save when you can label a man a Rosencrantz, or an Iago, or a MacBeth and be done with them." Then Ambrose made a dismissive noise. "But what am I lecturing you for? You have a keen eye and a mighty intellect, else you would not have learned so many lines already. Victoria will be impressed."

There was another pregnant pause.

"Think you?"

"A man who can quote Shakespeare is always in fashion."

"In court circles, perhaps, but not on a windswept moor. But I am not above learning a thing or two if it will aid me in my reading. Let us continue."

Victoria backed away, then backed into something solid. She turned around and screamed.

Mrs. Pruitt stood there, flashlight under her chin again.

"Only me," she whispered.

The lights went on in the dining room and Victoria whirled around to find Connor, Ambrose, Hugh, and Fulbert in a little cluster at the kitchen door.

"Oh," Mrs. Pruitt purred.

Ambrose disappeared.

"Why does he do that?" Mrs. Pruitt asked.

Victoria turned around and gave her a fake smile. "Maybe he thinks you've transferred your affections to Dr. Morris. You know those Highland lairds."

"I would certainly be happy to." She sighed and clicked off her flashlight. "And now look; there go the other ones. Perhaps they've not the spine to face a mature woman with a mind of her own."

"I'm sure that's probably it. What did Dr. Morris say?"

"He's on his way." Mrs. Pruitt patted her hair. "I'm off to do me curls."

"Still hedging your bets?" Victoria asked.

"Och, aye, lass."

Victoria watched her turn and make tracks out of the dining room. Then she went back to see if anyone was left in the kitchen. The stove was lit, the lights were on, and the four ghosts in question sat around the table, playing cards.

Interesting.

"A good game?" she asked.

"Quite," Ambrose said. "It passes the time pleasantly between sword fights."

Victoria looked at Connor. "You're chummy with these three."

"I'm regaling them with tales of Elizabeth's London,"

Connor said, stroking his throat gingerly as if he feared his lie might get stuck there. "Quite interesting."

"I'll bet. Mrs. Pruitt's off to wait for the doctor to come and sedate Michael."

"How lovely," Ambrose said. "He is rather ruining our game with his endless complaining."

"Well, you boys don't lose your shirts gambling here," Victoria said, backing out of the kitchen. "Good night."

"Good night," came the rather casual chorus.

Victoria hadn't been a damned good actress herself without good reason. She made noises as if she walked across the room when in reality she remained by the door.

"Lose our shirts?" Fulbert huffed. "What the devil does that mean?"

"Nothing personal," Ambrose said. "A term from the Old West. Apparently Victoria doesn't want us gaming overmuch. Now, let us put away our ruse and be about our true work. Connor, where were we?"

"The ghost was on the verge of describing his own murder. I do not like this part, by the way."

"You're not reciting the lines," Ambrose said pointedly, "you're just listening."

"I'm not all that fond of *listening* to this part," Connor grumbled.

"Make do," Ambrose suggested. "Think on why you're doing this and let us be about it."

Victoria snuck away before she could hear any more of Connor's grumbles. She walked back to the library without encountering either Mrs. Pruitt or Dr. Morris. She sat down in one of the chairs in front of the fire and closed her eyes briefly.

Was it possible that three days ago she had been in another world with no running water and no toilets but really great theater? And now, there she was, in her sister's comfortable inn, safe and well-fed.

With theater going on in the kitchen.

Amazing.

Now, if she could just assure herself of good theater at

Thorpewold. Michael's understudy was doing a great job, but Victoria couldn't help but chafe at the fact that Michael was lying uselessly upstairs, when he should have been doing his job up at the castle. She had contracted to pay him for a certain number of performances. If he couldn't be bothered to show up, she wouldn't be bothered to pay him.

Or, at least she *thought* she wouldn't be bothered. She could hardly bear to think about what Bernie the Bardmaker would do if she dared.

She contemplated this for several more minutes until she heard a discreet knock on the front door. Well, at least she would have one distraction removed for a while. What would happen when Michael was more himself was another thing to worry about, but later, when she had to.

She sighed. Michael would need hand-holding, and though she was tempted to relegate that job to Mrs. Pruitt, she was half afraid to do so, lest Michael find himself with more injuries than he'd started with.

She rose and went to make certain her star would survive his medical attention.

Chapter 23

I*n my heart there was a kind of fighting that would not let me sleep . . .*

Connor had finished the rest of his lines in the last scene, but those were the words that haunted him as he listened to the rest of his little band of players do their final bits. There was truth in what Shakespeare had written, just as Ambrose had said. But of late, in his heart, there was very little fighting indeed.

Longing was what had taken the fighting's place.

He sat down at the table and conjured up the final page of Shakespeare's play of life and death. He was, quite frankly, surprised by how many of the words he could read. Apparently his time in the inn's kitchen with Ambrose hadn't been time wasted. If nothing else, he was beginning to read things that pleased him.

It did little to assuage the sorry condition of his poor heart, but perhaps he should have been grateful for what he did have instead of longing for what he didn't.

Hugh and Fulbert sat down at the table with hefty

tankards of ale and began discussing the strengths and weaknesses of their performances.

"Nay, you were not so bad," Fulbert conceded to Hugh. "You have that annoying, cloying superiority that so suits Polonius."

Hugh's ale sloshed over the side of his mug with the force of him slamming it down. "I beg your pardon! I was playing the part—and quite well, I'd say."

"And *I* say you don't need to act," Fulbert said, shoving aside his own ale and glaring at Hugh. "And I say as well that if you tell me once more how it is I'm to play Claudius, I will draw my sword and teach you a thing or two about kingly executions!"

Hugh leaped to his feet, his chair crashing down behind him. "Draw your sword and let us see who has more nobility in their breeding!"

"Outside," Ambrose barked.

Hugh stopped in middraw and looked at Fulbert. "I suppose the garden will suit."

Fulbert shrugged and had one last gulp of ale. "Well enough, as usual." He gestured politely to the door. "After you."

"Nay, you."

"I insist."

"I wouldn't dream—"

"Go!" Ambrose bellowed.

Hugh and Fulbert went. Connor sighed and put his book away. He fussed with his own ale for several minutes before he looked at Ambrose.

"Why did you choose me?"

Ambrose blinked. "Choose you? You mean to play Hamlet in our little company?"

"Nay," Connor said impatiently. "Why did you choose me for Victoria?"

Ambrose smiled faintly. "Well, she needed a man equal to her in ferocity and determination. 'Twas a certainty no man with those qualities existed in Manhattan. You were the obvious choice."

Connor glared at him. "Damn you."

"Damn me?" Ambrose asked in surprise. "Why?"

"Because you've thrown us together and now look where we are!"

"You weren't without choice," Ambrose said placidly. "Neither was Victoria."

"She hasn't made a choice."

"Hasn't she?" Ambrose shrugged. "I daresay you shouldn't decide that until you've asked her."

Connor would have drawn his sword and taken Ambrose to task, but he was too sick at heart. "She has made no choice," he said flatly. "I daresay what she feels for me is . . . friendship." By the saints, even saying the word made him want to grind his teeth. "Unfortunately, that is not the case for me."

"Well," Ambrose said, "what are you going to do about that?"

"I daresay stabbing you repeatedly each and every day for a few centuries might keep me occupied."

Ambrose laughed. "As entertaining as that might be for you, perhaps you should consider other alternatives. I wouldn't discredit Victoria's feelings—or your own. Why don't you take yourself off to the keep and see if you can't discover a way to make both your lives tolerable. Woo her. Befriend her. Make her life better than it was when she came here with only Michael Fellini to love."

"The saints preserve her," Connor said grimly. He rose and looked at Ambrose with a scowl. "You and your matches. Have you never considered that some of them might be attempted where they should not be?"

"Aye."

Connor folded his arms over his chest. "But you've no apology to offer?"

Ambrose looked up at him, untroubled. "Are you worse off than you were at the beginning of the summer? Have you not made friendships that you did not have before? Have you not found a purpose to your days that did not exist before Victoria came?"

"I am still lacking a bloody captain," Connor grumbled.

"Aye, well, there isn't a man alive or dead equal to that duty, so perhaps that is not a good way to measure your success."

Connor pursed his lips. It was the best way to disguise the fact that he couldn't deny that Ambrose was right. He had formed a friendship with Victoria's granny. He had passed the occasional moment in less-than-unpleasant conversation with Thomas McKinnon. He had even found comrades in the Boar's Head Trio—a thing he never would have suspected could be possible. He had learned to read. He had discovered that there was a world that existed outside himself and his fury over his own life cut short.

And he had met Victoria.

For that alone, he would be forever indebted to the shade before him.

He grunted. "I'm off to the keep. I have things to see to before the sun rises."

Ambrose raised his cup. "Until sunset, then."

Connor left the kitchen before he did the unthinkable and thanked Ambrose for his bloody interference.

He walked up to the keep in predawn calm, surprisingly light of heart and step. His life, such as it was, could have been worse. It *had* been worse.

He hoped it wouldn't get worse than it had been.

He walked into the keep just as the sky was beginning to lighten. There was no activity in the inner bailey. Well, except for the man up on the stage, striding about, reciting his lines with vigor.

Connor swallowed his surprise and walked over to the stage to look up at Roderick St. Claire, who was dressed in a rather finely made costume and seemed to be perfectly comfortable exhibiting his acting talents, which were not unworthy.

Roderick paused, then turned and bowed. "My laird."

"What are you doing?"

"Playing Laertes," Roderick said, straightening. "How do you find it?"

"Surprisingly good," Connor said honestly. "I would not be unhappy to be in the same production with you."

Roderick stumbled backward in apparent shock. It took him several moments to regain his feet, and during that time Connor wondered if he had been that unpleasant to be around for all those centuries.

He suspected that he had been.

Roderick straightened his clothing. "Unfortunately for me, I've no connections with any who might be in this business of acting. I would be content with even a few suggestions from one who might know her . . . er . . . his business."

Connor considered. He considered quite a few things, actually.

He wanted to woo Victoria, the saints pity him. Roderick wanted to meet Victoria. Roderick, in spite of his flounces, was a man of his time and well-versed in the wooing practices of Victorian England. Surely those would translate well enough into modern times.

Perhaps Ambrose's suggestions weren't without merit after all.

"I'll introduce you to Victoria McKinnon," Connor offered suddenly, before he thought better of it.

Roderick smiled, looking as delighted as Connor had ever seen him. "Would you? Would you indeed? Why, that is simply capital of you, old man."

"*If* you give me wooing ideas."

Roderick gaped for a moment, then shut his mouth with a snap. "Of course. Yes, yes, of course I will. Immediately." He sat down on the edge of the stage. "Let us discuss where you've been in regards to women, shall we?"

Connor's first instinct was to draw his sword and let it tell the tale, but he did want a few answers out of the fop, so he ignored the insult to his dignity. He hopped up on the stage next to his Victorian compatriot and decided to do his best to answer the question honestly.

"Women?" he mused. "In truth, I've no experience with wooing them."

"But you were married."

"Aye, but there was no need to woo her."

"What was her name?"

"Morag McKinnon."

It took Roderick several minutes to recover from his fit of coughing. "A McKinnon?"

"Ironic, isn't it?"

Roderick laughed. "Dear boy, you've no idea. Very well, so you wed yourself a McKinnon lass, but you had no need to woo her—"

"Her father wished for peace with my clan. I grew weary of his clan trying unsuccessfully to poach my cattle—even though the cessation of that would have robbed my kinsmen of opportunities to better their killing skills." Connor shrugged. "It seemed a simple way to end the troubles."

"No other wenches who fell victim to your charm?"

Connor scowled fiercely—in spite of his vow to be pleasant.

"Ah, I see," Roderick said quickly. "Never mind. Very well, we'll move on. I have, as you might imagine, quite a bit of experience in this area."

"Wooing wenches? Or blinding them with your bright clothing?"

"It works for peacocks, my friend; it worked for me. And yes, I wooed them, as well."

Connor chewed on his words for a moment or two. "Were you wed?"

"Ah." Roderick sighed lightly. "Now, there is a tale. I was betrothed, it is true, but she died of consumption a month before she was to be mine. I must admit that it did cause me grief. Indeed, 'tis possible to say that my subsequent life of complete debauchery was due to the loss of the love of my heart."

"Weren't you killed in a duel?"

Roderick nodded. "Yes, thanks to yet another episode of debauching. I had been about the business with an enemy's wife, which perhaps made it more taxing than it might have been otherwise. Of course," he added quickly, "the wife was more than willing. Indeed, all that passed between us was her suggestion. But I was caught in a bit of a compromising situation."

"I daresay," Connor said with a snort. "What happened then?"

"I was called out, as I expected I would be. It was my honor to appear the next day at the appointed place. It was there that I met my end."

"Are you so poor a marksman?"

Roderick smiled a smile that even Connor had to admire. "Would you believe his second shot me while the lord in question fired early and managed to do naught but serious damage to a tree behind me? And yet," he said, brushing a bit of lint off his clothes, "I managed to catch the gun my second threw at me and put a ball into my murderer's gut before I fell."

"Well," Connor said with a nod, "that was nicely done."

"Leaving me centuries to ruminate on my wooing techniques," Roderick said pleasantly.

Connor hesitated. "And you are not bitter that your life was ended whilst you were so young?"

Roderick shrugged. "Life ends when it does and all one can do is hope that his life has been well-lived. I had love and more than enough of other things. I have no regrets. And fortunately for you, I am here for you to benefit from my great expertise." He looked off thoughtfully into the bailey. "Indeed, I have often thought I should offer my services to the trio down at the inn. I know they are matchmakers by trade, but surely they could make use of my vast stores of romantic experience. On a strictly case-by-case basis, of course."

"I'll ask them when next we meet," Connor promised. "Now, about these wooing ideas . . ."

"In your case, verse," Roderick said. "Flowery sentiments. Pleasing words against the feminine ear. Nothing about death, destruction, or sword fights well executed."

Connor frowned. "In truth? Why not?"

"Because you want to woo the lady in question, not terrify her. I suggest Shakespeare, for a start. I'll think of other things as we go on."

Connor cleared his throat. "I might be able to read a few things if you could write them down for me."

"Indeed," Roderick said, sounding genuinely pleased. "Well, then, indeed I will, old man. I'll give voice to a thing or two now, and you let me know what strikes you as something your lady might like. Then I'll put pen to paper and scratch it out for you."

Connor nodded, squelching the feeling of pleasure it gave him to be able to say he could actually make out words on the page.

He spent the next half an hour listening to Roderick recite several of his favorite Bardly passages, found several to his liking, and sent the Victorian Fop off to scribble them down so he could learn them more quickly.

He took another look at the keep, then decided perhaps 'twas past time he made for the inn to see what Victoria was about. He hopped off the stage and walked toward the gates. He was intercepted not five paces from them by Robbie McKinnon, the current aspirant to the lofty position of captain of his guard.

Connor frowned. "Aye?"

"My laird, I have been keeping an eye on things whilst you've been about your business."

Connor looked about him and found that, indeed, there was some truth in that. "I see we haven't been overrun by ruffians."

"Except actors," Robbie offered.

Connor started to smile in agreement, then remembered himself just in time. He coughed roughly. "Well, be that as it may, I'll still expect the keep to be run as I would run it. Discipline. Order. Terror, when called for."

Robbie put his shoulders back. "Of course, my laird."

Connor frowned. "Don't accustom yourself to the position. I've still not made my final decision."

Robbie bowed and scraped and made for safer ground

as quickly as possible. Connor supposed he couldn't blame the lad, given that Robbie was Morag's brother and had waited centuries before he'd even dared show his face at Thorpewold. Connor shrugged with a sigh. The lad had showed himself well so far. Perhaps it was time to let the past be in the past.

He started down the path, Shakespeare's words floating pleasingly through his mind.

> *Let me not to the marriage of true minds*
> *Admit impediments. Love is not love*
> *Which alters when it alteration finds . . .*
> *Love's not Time's fool . . .*

He returned to the inn, surprisingly contented.

Chapter 24

Victoria looked in the mirror and pinched her cheeks to try to bring some color to them. She was wearing makeup, but she doubted anyone could have told as much, thanks to the pasty complexion she was currently sporting. Being a redhead left her fair-skinned enough as it was, but closing-night jitters had exacerbated the condition beyond reason. She usually had a small case of nerves, but tonight those nerves had morphed into full-blown panic. She laid the blame for that at Thomas's feet.

Her family had returned to the inn the day before, arriving from their various destinations well-rested and ready to celebrate the closing night of a successful run. Victoria had shared a late-night snack with Jennifer and their grandmother, during which they had spent quite some time determining all the sights in Scotland they would have to see before Victoria had to return to Manhattan to start rehearsals for her fall schedule. They had been joined eventually by the usual suspects and the evening had passed most pleasantly with conversation including a discussion of the state of the National Trust of Scotland's care of important historical landmarks.

Of course, all those warm and fuzzy feelings had disappeared earlier that morning at breakfast when Thomas had told her that Megan's father-in-law, the current Earl of Artane, was theater-mad and would be arriving later that day to catch her last performance. It was possible that, based upon loving her show, the earl would be willing to make all her theater dreams come true.

Victoria had thought she just might throw up.

She wasn't one to get nervous. She'd rubbed shoulders with the rich and the wish-they-were-famous and had no especial regard for deep pockets. But she didn't have a theater space to return to.

And she was desperate for a reason to stay in England.

She took a deep breath. She didn't take a second one, though. The last thing she needed was to greet her potential backer with a paper bag over her mouth and nose.

Besides, he was probably just all bluster, anyway. She'd had plenty of people over the years frothing at the mouth with enthusiasm until it came time to pony up the cash. No offense to Megan's father-in-law, but Victoria had learned never to count her monetary chickens until they'd hatched in her bank account.

She dragged a brush through her hair, pinched her cheeks one more time, then left the bathroom and headed for the kitchen. She nodded to the men there lingering over their drinks. Connor rose when she came into the chamber. She paused and looked at him with a frown.

"What?"

"A gentleman stands when a lady enters the chamber," he said with a pointed look thrown at his companions.

Ambrose popped up immediately, as did Hugh. Fulbert crawled to his feet with a heavy sigh and a hearty rolling of his eyes.

"Oh," Victoria said. "Well. Thank you. I'm heading up to the castle for a last light check."

"But, my dear," Ambrose said, "the curtain isn't until eight o'clock tonight."

"Closing-night jitters," Fulbert said wisely, sitting back down with another gusty sigh. "Be off with ye, then, gel, and do your last check. We'll keep an eye on things this afternoon for ye."

"Thank you, Fulbert," Victoria said, surprised and gratified. "That's very nice."

"Parting is such sweet sorrow," Connor blurted out.

Victoria looked at him with consternation. "Are you sick?"

He scowled. "I'm being *polite*."

"Oh. Well, thanks." She nodded to them, then made her way out of the kitchen, through the garden, and up the way to the castle. Obviously, she wasn't the only one with a case of nerves.

She took a few deep breaths, because she couldn't help herself. Everything would be okay. All her actors were in perfect health. She'd been tempted to lock them all in their rooms, but that had seemed like overkill, even for her. They had every reason to want to finish strongly, for their own sakes. Even Michael was back to fighting form. The doctor had been there the day before and given him a clean bill of health. Victoria had spent most of yesterday fetching and carrying for him, just so he didn't strain himself too soon.

One more day, and then she could tell him to go to hell. Which she would do. Silently. She didn't want repercussions from Bernie the Bardmaker, after all.

"Victoria."

She stopped two hundred yards from her destination, surprised to find Michael lurking along the side of the road.

"Michael," she said with a smile. "How are you? You're up and wandering around. Feeling strong?"

He shoved a piece of paper at her. "Here. Sign this."

"What is it?" she asked. Good heavens, what next? Was Bernie faxing post-illness nursing demands now?

"Just sign it."

She looked at him in surprise. Gone was the smooth, suave actor she had thought was so perfect on so many levels. In his place was a man who looked just the slightest bit wild-eyed. Was he still delirious from his Elizabethan fever, or was he just freaked out for general reasons? Victoria wondered why she hadn't thought to bring along a ghostly bodyguard or two. Would they hear her if she started to scream?

"I don't have a pen," she stalled.

He threw one at her. She caught it and did her best to fumble around with it for a moment or two until she had her feet back under her. She looked at the contract-weight set of papers she had in her hand.

"A contract?" she asked in surprise. "Do you want to sign on for an entire season?"

"No, I don't want to sign *on*," he said disdainfully. "I want you to sign *over*."

"Sign over? Sign over what?"

"Your theater troupe."

Victoria knew she had to look as completely baffled as she felt. "My troupe?"

"Yes," he said impatiently. "Sign it over or I don't go on tonight."

"I'll have you blacklisted," she said immediately, before she thought better of it.

He only laughed.

It wasn't a pleasant laugh.

"Will you?" he said scornfully. "Try it and see what Bernie leaves of you—if he leaves anything at all. Now, don't be dumb. Just sign the damn paper and let's get this business behind us." He gestured impatiently at the contract she held. "Put the name of the company down and sign it."

"But," she said slowly, "my troupe doesn't have a name."

"It has to have a name, stupid, because the name has to go right there." He reached out and tapped the top sheaf impatiently. "On that blank line there."

Victoria looked at the blank line. Sure enough, it looked

ready for something to be written there. She looked at
Michael. He seemed to be fully *compos mentis,* yet there
was something that didn't quite fit.

"You want Tempest in a Teapot?" she asked.

"What do you think?" he asked archly.

I think you're an idiot, she thought immediately, but there
was no sense in telling him that. If he believed her venue
came with her, more power to him. She had long since
resigned herself to the thought that where just desserts were
concerned, Michael Fellini had long avoided his serving.

She considered.

It took quite some time, but in the end, she took the pen
and wrote something down. She flipped to the end of the
contract and scrawled illegible characters where her name
should have gone. She handed the contract back to
Michael.

"There you go," she said, wondering if this was how it
felt to cut off your nose to spite your face.

Michael grabbed it eagerly and began to read. Then he
began to frown.

"The name of your troupe is Go to Hell You Overacting
Windbag?" He flipped to the back and frowned again. "Is
that your signature?"

She smiled without humor. "You figure it out."

It took him quite some time. But realization came eventually. She watched it happen, like the first rays of dawn
touching the morning sky. Slowly, at first, then more
quickly, the truth hit him.

"Overacting windbag?" he wheezed.

"If the shoe fits, bucko."

He spluttered quite unattractively for quite a long time.

"I'll walk!" he thundered finally. "I'll take the whole
cast with me!"

"Go ahead," she shouted back. "And watch me sue them
all for breach of contract!"

He crumpled the contract in his hands. "You'll regret
this."

"Will I?"

"Watch and see," he snarled, then stomped off back toward the inn. Victoria watched him go, then shrugged and headed up toward the castle. He wouldn't take her entire cast. She would do her quick check, then hurry back to the inn and tell Cressida that English nobility was going to be in the audience scoping out talent. Michael would find himself and his miserable personality alone at Heathrow. No one else would dare jump ship.

She oversaw the testing of her equipment, dawdled for a bit, then sighed and walked back to the inn.

The inn was unsettlingly quiet when she opened the front door. Maybe everyone was having a last-minute nap. She was about to go do a room check when Thomas opened the door to the sitting room.

"Vic," he said with a smile, "I have someone you're going to want to meet."

Victoria smiled, a little sickly, to her mind, but she managed it.

"The Earl of Artane," Thomas whispered. "Make a good impression. Your career no doubt depends on it."

After the morning she'd had, Victoria didn't doubt it.

The only upside she could see was that she wouldn't have much time for chitchat. She needed to go let Michael's understudy know he was going on, and she needed to be up at the castle in an hour.

But money called first. She put her best business face on and walked into the sitting room with the same amount of enthusiasm she might have a deluxe room in the Tower of London.

*C*onnor stood in the inner bailey, looking wistfully at the stage, counting up all the nights he'd watched *Hamlet* performed there, all the nights he'd either watched or stood next to Victoria as she stood against the castle wall watching the play proceed as she had directed.

He could scarce believe those nights were soon to be nothing but a memory.

He walked slowly into the great hall. He crossed over to the dais and turned around to face the door, placing himself in the spot where he'd stood two months ago, waiting for V. McKinnon to walk through the ruined entryway and earn the fright of his life. Only V. had turned out to be Victoria.

And he'd been lost from the moment he'd clapped eyes on her.

As if history were repeating itself, in came Victoria McKinnon, only this time she rushed in, her hair in wild disarray, her very stance bespeaking tumult and uproar.

Connor looked at her in astonishment. Was she over-wrought that her play was ending? He would have thought that now was the time for a bit of wistfulness, reminiscence, even perhaps a bit of regret that the labors of the past pair of months were over. But this wildness? Surely there was something amiss.

Victoria saw him and dashed across the great hall. She came to a teetering halt before him. Connor reached out instinctively to steady her, then realized the gesture was useless. He clenched his hands at his sides.

"What ails you?" he asked, gritting his teeth. "Are you ill?"

"He's gone."

Connor blinked. "Who's gone?"

She cursed. "Michael's gone and he took the whole damn cast with him."

"He did *what?*"

"You heard me. He walked off the job because I wouldn't sell him the rights to my company and now I'm left with a closing night, important guests in the audience, and no players. I can't believe he talked them all into going with him. Heads will roll, I promise you."

Connor was rarely stunned, and even less rarely without a helpful bit of advice in a crisis, even if it was limited to "strangle the fool with his own entrails and put his head on a pike outside the gates as warning to other disobedient leading men," but at the moment, he found himself with no useful thing to offer but an expression of shock.

"Can you do Hamlet?" Victoria asked suddenly.

He stuck his fingers in his ears and wiggled them. "I beg your pardon?"

"The role. Can you do it?"

He felt a chill slide down to his very vitals. Never in his life had he experienced such a feeling of sheer terror. Not when it had been him alone at ten-and-eight facing a half dozen fierce McKinnons, not when he'd been set against bloodthirsty MacDonalds with only a handful of half-grown lads at his back, not even when he'd seen the flash of the Frenchman's sword out of the corner of his eye—too late to avoid it—and known he was going to die.

"Hamlet?" he croaked.

"Yes."

He looked closely at her. There was no doubt in her eye. He considered a bit more. Surely, she wouldn't have asked him if she'd thought him unequal to the task. And if he peed his kilt onstage, no one would be the wiser.

Reason enough to go forward.

"Aye," he said with a confidence he didn't quite feel.

"Good. Be on stage in ten minutes. I've got to run back to the inn and find more players. And get that Roderick St. Claire for me if you can. I'll need him for Laertes."

And with that, she turned and left him standing in his great hall, speechless.

Hamlet?

He took a deep breath. " 'For these are actions that a man might play,' " he whispered, " 'but I have that within which passeth show.' "

A body could hope, at least.

He took a deep breath, blew out it, indulged in a brief fervent prayer, then left the great hall to await the rest of a cast he was certain would be the oddest of Victoria's long and illustrious career.

He didn't have to wait long.

Ambrose, Hugh, and Fulbert came rushing into the bailey and jostled each other in their haste to leap up on the stage. Connor leaped up on the stage with like athleticism, bowling Roderick over in the execution of his jump.

"Does she need me?" Roderick asked breathlessly from where he lay sprawled on the deck.

"Aye," Connor said simply. "Dispense with the lace, however. We are wearing a more medieval look tonight."

Roderick leaped to his feet. He fondled the lace at his throat one more time before he exchanged it, in the blink of an eye, for a rough tunic, worn hose, and scuffed boots.

"Will this suit?" he asked.

"Victoria will tell you if it does not."

Roderick laughed. "Yes, I imagine she will. How can you not love that woman? She is formidable on every level."

Connor would have asked Roderick how in the hell he knew that, and repaid him properly for his answers, but he was distracted by Victoria's arrival. Jennifer trotted along at her heels.

"All right," Victoria said, motioning for the cast to join her on the ground in front of the stage. "Here's the thing. We've never rehearsed this and we don't have time. We're on in less than an hour. Is there anyone here who does not know their lines or, heaven forbid, what part they're playing?"

Ambrose smoothed over the front of his tunic. "I will play the deceased King of Denmark, Fulbert will play Hamlet's uncle Claudius, and Hugh will delight us with his pedantic and irritating Polonius. Hugh, do not overact when Hamlet stabs you during the scene with Gertrude. By the way, Victoria dear, who will play Gertrude?"

"Jenner," Victoria said.

"How will she know the lines?" Connor ventured.

"She's done it before," Victoria said. "She has a photographic memory; she'll remember the lines."

Ambrose leaned close to Connor. "What that means is that once she reads something, she can always remember it. A handy talent, aye?"

Connor hesitated to say that he could, at present, see any of the pages of Shakespeare he'd read swimming before his eyes as he willed, so perhaps he had that skill as well. But he would discuss it with Ambrose later, when the show was finished.

"Horatio will be played by Thomas," Victoria said, checking her list. "Fred and Megan's husband Gideon will do their best with the rest of the minor characters. If they forget their lines, we'll sack them after the show is over."

Connor listened to her finalize all her preparations with a commander's control. He nodded to himself as she voiced appreciation for their willingness to salvage the night. He admired her calm in the face of admittedly amateur actors who, in the persons of Gideon and Thomas, hoped they could get their lines down—or keep their gorge down, whatever the case might be.

But as he listened, he realized that something was missing.

"Victoria?" he asked, finally.

She looked at him. "Yes?"

"Who will play Ophelia?"

Silence descended.

"Oh," Jennifer said quietly. "That is a problem."

Victoria stared at him in mute distress.

Connor felt, after a moment or two, that there were none others there but he himself and Victoria, staring at each other, as if time had ceased to be.

"You know the part," he said quietly. "Don't you?"

She closed her eyes briefly and swallowed convulsively. "Yes."

"Then that solves that," Jennifer said brightly. "Let's all go raid the costume shed. Well, except for those of you who can conjure up your own."

Connor continued to look at Victoria as the others set off for the gates. He smiled encouragingly. "You will be wonderful," he said confidently.

"I think I might be sick," she replied.

"Retch later. Go choose a costume now. You will do the role justice as Mistress Blankenship never could have."

Victoria nodded and turned toward the gate. She stopped, though, after a pace or two, and turned back to look at him.

"Thank you."

"For what?"

She smiled, albeit a little weakly. "For all your work on the part." She paused. "I couldn't put on the show without you tonight."

"I will do my best not to disappoint."

She looked at him for so long in silence that he began to fear that she thought him unequal to the task and was afraid to say as much. Then she shook her head.

"Connor MacDougal, I don't think you *could* disappoint." Then she smiled briefly. "But I will, if I don't find a costume that fits. Cressida probably has sucker goo spilled all down the front of hers. I swear, if I'd seen that girl with one more Tootsie Pop in her mouth, I would have hosed her down."

And with that, she was gone.

Connor looked heavenward briefly, then turned toward the stage to concentrate on what he had to do that night.

The evening passed for him as if it had been a dream. Shakespeare's words came from his mouth as if they had been created for just that moment in time, to be whispered or shouted or crisply spoken as if they'd been swords meant to cut through the webs of deceit woven around him.

He remembered wordplay with Victoria as Ophelia. He sparred verbally with Hugh, listened raptly to Ambrose tell the sorry tale of the late king's murder, tried to reason with Jennifer as Gertrude. He let Hamlet's words become his own and speculated aloud as to the meaning of life and death.

Then he stood in the wings and watched Victoria descend into madness as if she'd done it every day of her life and found the journey too exquisite not to be shared with anyone who would pay her heed.

She was, in a word, breathtaking.

He found himself, finally, crossing swords with Roderick, who seemed to dredge up from some hidden wellspring of skill enough ability to actually seem as if he might be Connor's equal.

In the end, there was death, as usual.

But this time, death was followed by a curtain call and thunderous applause.

Connor took his own bow as he'd seen Fellini do numerous times. He found himself a little startled and not just a little surprised by the applause he received.

He understood why Fellini liked performing so much.

But when the curtain pulled together and he stood in a huddle with his fellow actors, watching tears of relief course down Victoria's cheeks, he found that he was almost tempted to do the same. Victoria turned to look at him.

"Amazing," she breathed.

He laughed. He simply couldn't help himself.

"Heaven help me," she said with a laugh of her own, "Connor MacDougal just laughed. I think it's time for a swoon."

"After everyone's gone," Jennifer said, throwing an arm around her sister. "You were brilliant. Connor was, well, there are no words to describe it. I've never seen Hamlet done better."

Connor would have thought she was exaggerating, but she was equally quick to point out that Thomas had flubbed several of his lines but that she loved him anyway, so Connor found himself with no choice but to take her words as she spoke them.

"Vikki? Gideon's dad wants to come backstage." Megan was peeking under the curtain. "He especially wants to meet Hamlet." She smiled at Connor. "Hi, Laird MacDougal. You were wonderful, by the way."

Connor would have nodded in thanks, but he was too startled. He looked at Victoria. "What now, Captain McKinnon?"

"Well, you certainly can't shake his hand. Say hello from a distance. Claim a cold, or strep, or the plague."

Connor grunted. "Not amusing."

"Yes, but necessary." She slipped through the curtain and soon was calling his name.

Connor looked at Thomas. "Your aid, McKinnon?"

"For the man who drove my sister to madness? Anything." Thomas pulled the curtain back and waited.

Connor found himself looking at the Earl of Artane, a rather unassuming man as earls went, but then again, the man likely wasn't training with a broadsword every day.

"Megan told me that there was a bit of a muddle with some of the cast having transportation difficulties," the earl said, all smiles, "but I daresay that was fortuitous. A fabulous performance, sir, I must say!"

Connor bowed low. "I thank you for that, my lord. But it is Mistress McKinnon who deserves the credit. There is not a better director in all of the Apple."

"The Big Apple," Thomas whispered from behind him.

"Manhattan," Connor clarified, remembering suddenly what Victoria had called it more than once. "And I daresay England has never seen her like."

"My dear," the earl said to Victoria, "you are truly a treasure. I don't suppose there might be time in your schedule tonight to discuss what you've done in the past. We didn't have nearly enough time this afternoon."

"I would love to discuss it," Victoria said. "If you would give me half an hour to close up the set?"

"Of course." Artane looked up at Connor. "Truly a pleasure, sir. I don't think I've enjoyed a performance more."

Connor bowed again, unable to think of a single reply that would have done the compliment justice. He retreated back behind the curtain and kept himself out of the way as the crew arranged scenery and weatherproofed it. Sound and lights were put away, along with the accompanying gear. Once that was all finished to Victoria's satisfaction, she came to stand near him.

"Well, that's over," she said with a sigh.

"Are you content?"

She smiled. "I can't talk about it tonight. Let me humor

Megan's father-in-law, have something to eat now I'm certain I won't immediately throw it back up, and then get a good night's sleep. I'll know tomorrow what I thought."

"Shall I wait for you?" he asked. "In the library?"

"Do," she said. "I won't be long. Well," she amended, "that may not be true. It depends on the earl. Thomas said he might be looking for a theater company to fund and I can never say no to conversations of those sorts."

"I'll wait," he said.

"I'll be there eventually."

He watched her walk off with her brother and sister and stood on the edge of the stage, continuing to watch them as they left through the gate. Victoria turned back once to wave, then went on her way.

"I think that performance definitely could be considered wooing verse."

Connor looked at Roderick, who had come to stand next to him. "Think you?"

"I do. Well done, indeed. The garrison is, I believe, speechless to a man."

"Hmmm," Connor said thoughtfully. He bid Roderick a peaceful night and left the castle himself, slowly making his way toward the inn.

He went in through the front door and walked over to the sitting room. He put an ear to the door and listened for a moment or two to the conversation going on therein, but found that his emotions were so strong, he simply had to have privacy before they overcame him and unmanned him in the eyes of all.

He went into the library, stoked up a fire in the fireplace, and sat in his accustomed chair.

He never wept. He never allowed himself to even entertain regret. But there, in the dark, he couldn't help but consider shedding a tear or two for what might have been.

And for the radiant, gifted woman he might have shared it with.

By the saints, she was luminous.

He would have given anything to have called her his.

Chapter 25

V ictoria walked up the way to the castle, feeling as if she'd been doing it all her life, not just the better part of the summer. It was hard to believe that her run was over and she had no further reason to remain in England. The earl had made vague noises about having her do something else at the castle at his expense, but he'd said nothing definite enough for her to count on. Connor would now go back to his hauntings; she would soon go back to her rehearsals. He would remain in England; she would go back to Manhattan. All that had happened over the past two months would be relegated to memory, and life would go on. Only she suspected she would have a hard time going on.

Then again, what else was she to do? Connor was a ghost; she was a mortal. There wasn't exactly a manual for dealing successfully with this kind of relationship, even if Connor had been interested in any kind of relationship.

She paused, blew out her breath, and suppressed the urge to walk immediately to a handy wall and bang her head repeatedly against it until she found sense again.

She entered the bailey to find Connor sitting on the stage,

staring off thoughtfully into the distance. She took a deep breath. She'd seen him the night before in the library, but she'd been so tired, she'd hardly managed to tell him good night before she'd fallen into bed and passed out. Now was the chance to tell him how wonderful he'd been, tell him of her plans to do a little sightseeing, then see what he thought of her heading back to Manhattan in a couple of weeks.

Unless he wanted her to make good on her promise to let him haunt her for a month.

Heaven help her.

She crossed the dirt to stand in front of him. "How are you?" she asked.

He pulled himself away from his musings and looked at her with a faint smile. "I'm still not quite sure what it is I think."

"Stardom does that to a person," she said, hopping up on the stage to sit next to him. He was wearing his hose and tunic from the night before, as if he couldn't quite bear to change it. Victoria smiled. "I think you have a new calling in life."

"Me?" he answered, looking surprised. "What?"

"Actor. Your Hamlet was truly breathtaking. I could watch you do it every night for years."

He shifted. "Thank you. Your Ophelia was heart-stopping, as well." He paused. "I must admit to being baffled as to why they did not wed, those two."

She shrugged. "Circumstances, I suppose."

"Circumstances," he repeated quietly.

He glanced her way.

And her heart almost stopped.

"It seems a poor reason to forgo something that seems so perfect," he said slowly. "Think you?"

She swallowed convulsively. She had the feeling that he wasn't talking about Shakespeare any longer. "There were things they could not change," she said, feeling a little desperate. "He was a prince; she was below him in station. A world of convention stood between them. It was impossible."

"I care not for that word."

"I'm not a big fan of it, either."

He swung his feet back and forth under the edge of the stage and looked down at the ground.

Then he looked at her.

"I want you."

She would have fallen off the stage, but she had already done that years ago in school. Instead, she clutched the wood and hoped it would help her world stop spinning.

"You what?" she managed.

"You heard me."

"I want to be clear on what you mean." She paused. "You want me to do what? Direct you on stage? Find you a publicist? Scream for you for a month—"

"I want you," he repeated slowly. "In my bed. In my life. At my side from dawn to dawn and all the hours between them." He paused. "I believe the term for it is marriage."

She felt tears well up in her eyes. One of them fell down her cheek with an authenticity Cressida could never have matched on her best day.

"Marriage?" she whispered.

"Aye."

She looked at him simply because she could not look away. And then she put her face in her hands and cried.

He let her weep. She would have tried to make the downpour as quick a one as possible, but once she got going it was hard to stop. She bawled like a baby until she had no more blubbering to do, then she dragged her sleeve across her eyes and looked at him. He was smiling grimly.

"Is it so terrifying a thought?"

"No," she sniffed. "But Connor, it's impossible."

He looked at her for several moments in silence, then hopped off the stage. "Come with me."

She got off the stage much less gracefully, but managed to land on her feet just the same. "Where are we going?"

"To talk to your brother."

"Are you going to ask his permission? My dad's at the inn as well, you know, though apparently he and Mom are headed to London with Megan tomorrow for more sight-seeing, so if you—"

"I'll talk to your father later. 'Tis your brother I will have answers from now."

"Answers? Answers to what sorts of questions?" She was already out of breath and she supposed it would have been convenient to blame it on the fact that Connor was striding down the pathway with very long legs and she was running to keep up. In truth, she suspected it was just because she'd never been proposed to before. By the one man whose proposal she would have accepted.

And the one man she could never have.

"Questions about several things," Connor said briskly. "Questions about some of the inhabitants of Thorpewold over the years."

"What do those questions have to do with us?"

"You will soon see."

Victoria trotted alongside Connor as he made his way to the inn. He walked through the front door; she ran into it. She backed up with a curse. He appeared instantly back through the door.

"My apologies."

"See," she said crossly, "it wouldn't work. I'd be nothing but a bruise."

He stopped and looked at her. "Your eyes are leaking."

"It's the flowers. They make me sneeze."

"Then let us be away from the garden. Open the door, love, if you will."

She obeyed, then froze halfway over the threshold. "What did you call me?"

"The first of countless endearments if you'll but stir yourself to hold to our current course."

She folded her arms over her chest. Actually, she hugged herself so she wouldn't shatter into a million pieces. "Say it again."

"Move your fetching arse, *love*," he said impatiently, "before we find Thomas and Iolanthe napping where I daren't disturb them."

She opened the front door. "You know, you could use some work on your love language."

He grunted at her as he strode into the inn. "Keep up," he instructed.

And so she did, past an incredulous Mrs. Pruitt at the reception desk, in and out of the kitchen very briefly to find the Boar's Head Trio looking equally as surprised, and back into the sitting room, where Iolanthe was stretched out on the couch groaning and Thomas was hovering.

Victoria would have been groaning too with that nursemaid attending her.

"Good grief, Thomas," she exclaimed, "give the poor woman room to breathe."

Thomas scowled at her, but he ceased with his hovering and sat down on the arm of the couch. "That was quite a night last night, wasn't it? Are you here for a debriefing?"

"Not exactly," Victoria said.

"Post-performance letdown?"

"Connor has a question or two for you."

Thomas paused, then looked at them both assessingly. "Well," he said. "What is it?"

Connor looked at Victoria and gestured to the empty chair next to the couch. "Sit. My love," he added.

"Oh," Thomas said, drawing the word out for quite a while. "So, that's how it is."

"It's your fault," Victoria said promptly.

"Hey, I just sent you here to torment him," Thomas said with a grin. "I didn't intend for you to fall in love with him."

"Maybe you should have thought about that before you started meddling," Victoria said.

The look Connor gave her made her quite relieved to be sitting down.

Connor sat, as well, and looked at Thomas. "I've questions to put to you."

"I think I may hesitate to give you answers," Thomas said frankly.

Victoria watched Connor open his mouth, no doubt to retort with something nasty, then he stopped, took a deep breath, and looked at her brother with what he obviously thought would pass for a pleasant expression.

"Please," he said simply.

Thomas blinked in surprise. "Hell," he said finally.

"Nay, I'm hoping for somewhere else," Connor said. "Now, in order to make that so, I need you to tell us your tale."

Thomas shifted uncomfortably. "I have lots of tales—"

"Jerk," Victoria said, before she thought better of it. She marshalled all the resources of her patience. "I mean, please Thomas, humor this very large, very fierce Highland laird who has humbled himself at great personal cost to come and politely ask for your help because, thanks to you, he had the great misfortune to meet me and beyond all reason and no doubt against his better judgment, decide that he wanted to marry me!"

"Well, when you put it that way—"

"It wasn't a misfortune," Connor said quietly.

Victoria didn't dare look at him. His words were enough to make her eyes burn. Heaven only knew what a look would do.

"But I *am* asking politely," Connor added.

"Besides, he left his sword by the front door," Victoria muttered. "I'm almost sure of it."

Thomas looked at them both, shared a long look with Iolanthe, then sighed. "Well, since you asked so nicely, yes, I will tell you what you want to know. But I suggest you let me finish before you yell at me, Vic, for not telling you this sooner."

Victoria shrugged. "You're entitled to your privacy."

"Yeah, well, hold that thought." He shared one last look with his wife before he took a seat on a chair next to the couch and looked at Connor and Victoria. "You remember that I bought Thorpewold a few years ago."

"I remember that I was doing King Lear a few years ago," Victoria said. "I don't remember anything else."

"Answer enough. But you do remember that I came over to remodel last summer."

"Yes," Victoria said. "I thought you had lost your mind."

Thomas smiled. "Thank you. I began to think so, as well, once I found out the place was haunted."

Victoria snorted. "That serves you right for several things. I hope you had several hair-raising episodes. Do I dare speculate on the identity of those ghosts?"

"There were several shades hanging around you might recognize," Thomas said. He nodded toward Connor. "Your fierce friend there was one of them."

"You shouldn't use that word," Victoria advised. "Friend. He doesn't like it."

Thomas smiled briefly. "I imagine he doesn't like it from either of us, but for far different reasons. But since I'm the one he wants answers from—and Laird MacDougal, I know the questions you have already—I suppose he'll make nice for the afternoon."

Connor grunted, but said nothing.

Thomas nodded. "As I was saying, I came and found the castle haunted by a rabble of Scots, but that wasn't the most surprising thing. It was haunted also by an exquisitely beautiful woman."

"A real ghost," Victoria asked, "or just a figment of your overactive imagination?"

"A real ghost."

Victoria wondered how Iolanthe would react to that news. She looked at her sister-in-law, but Iolanthe was lying on the couch with her arm over her eyes, barely breathing. Maybe deep breaths stirred up more than just air. Victoria looked at her brother. "Well, what does that have to do with us? So, you met a good-looking ghost? I'm sure it was entertaining for you, but I don't understand what it has to do with anything." She shifted uncomfortably. "In fact, I don't know why we're even talking about any of this. It's an impossible tangle—"

"I wouldn't say impossible," Thomas interrupted.

"Then pick another word that means the same thing."

Iolanthe cleared her throat weakly. "Ask your brother the name of that poor ghostly wench."

"What good—"

"Ask him, Victoria," Connor said quietly.

"All right," she said, startled briefly by the seriousness of his tone. She looked at her brother. "Who was that gorgeous ghost that kept you awake at night for months?"

Thomas smiled faintly. "Iolanthe MacLeod."

"Right," Victoria said. "Well, that's just plain spooky. I mean, how strange that your wife should have the same . . . name . . ."

She realized she had stopped talking only because her brain apparently had finally engaged itself.

"Iolanthe MacLeod?" she whispered.

Thomas shrugged helplessly, still smiling just a little. "As fate would have it."

Victoria looked at Iolanthe, green with morning sickness, then at Thomas, who looked as if he'd never felt sorrier for anyone than he did his sister, who was so incredibly dense, then at Connor, who met her gaze expressionlessly.

"You knew?" she managed.

Connor lifted one shoulder in a faint shrug. "Aye."

"This same . . . that same . . ." Victoria couldn't manage to say it, but she did manage to point at the woman laid low on the couch.

"Aye," Connor said. "The very same."

"But . . . but how?" Victoria looked at Iolanthe, then Thomas. "How? It's a fairy tale, impossible, beyond belief—"

"It is quite possible," Iolanthe said quietly, pushing herself up unsteadily. "I was indeed that poor, unhappy ghost who dared your brother to come and take my castle from me. Now, Thomas, tell her the rest of the tale and don't make her suffer through a long recounting. I won't last—" She put her hand over her mouth.

"Are you going to be sick?" he asked quickly, halfway to his feet.

"She will be if you don't hurry," Victoria said tartly. "Spit it out!"

Iolanthe waved him away and resumed her prone position with her arm over her eyes. Thomas sat down uneasily.

"Here's the condensed version, then, before Io loses her breakfast," he said. "I met her, fell in love with her, and decided that if I could go back in time and rescue her before her untimely end, I might be able to bring her forward to the future."

"Through a time gate," Victoria said.

"Well, yes, of course," Thomas said. "How else?"

"Then that's how you know Jamie MacLeod."

"Yes to that, too."

"And you pretended not to know anything about what had happened to Granny!" Victoria exclaimed.

"I don't remember pretending anything one way or another," Thomas said with a smile. " 'The better part of valor is discretion,' as the Bard would say."

"Yeah, except when it comes to matters of this kind of import," Victoria said in irritation. "You could have told me!"

"Why?"

Victoria growled in frustration and turned to Iolanthe. "Is Jamie really your grandfather? Does that make him medieval? Are you medieval? Damn it, I need dates!"

She realized that she was starting to lose it.

Iolanthe took a deep breathe, groaned, then rolled over to look at Victoria. "I was born during the fourteenth century. Jamie is my great-great grandfather. He first discovered the time gates because his brother had traveled to the future through them. It was something of a family secret and 'twas for the refusal to tell that secret that I was murdered. Your brother risked all to come and rescue me before that murder took place."

Victoria had to take a few minutes to digest that. She was looking at an honest-to-goodness medieval gal who had obviously lost her mind while going through a time gate. It was surely the only way she'd managed to convince herself to marry Thomas.

"You couldn't have liked him," Victoria said with a frown. "Did you?"

"I thought he was a demon," Iolanthe volunteered. "When I met him back in time."

Victoria nodded in satisfaction. "I would have been surprised by anything else."

"Thank you so much," Thomas said with a laugh. "It's all true, though. Even though I'd known Iolanthe—and loved her—as a ghost, she didn't recognize me when I first found her. And she didn't like me after she got to know me." He reached over and put his hand on her head. "But eventually, she remembered all those years of her other life and we worked things out."

"Poor woman," Victoria muttered, then she fell silent.

Not because she didn't have anything to say, but because the import of what she had heard had finally sunk in.

Iolanthe MacLeod McKinnon had been a ghost in that castle up the way. Thomas McKinnon had gone back in time, rescued her from an untimely death, and brought her back to the future. Brought her to the future as a living, corporeal being. And if Iolanthe could be rescued, so could Connor. He could be brought back to the twenty-first century. If it were possible, there would be only one person able to do it.

And that person was her.

She felt her mouth hanging opening very unattractively. She shut it with a snap and looked at Connor.

He returned her look for a very long moment before he stood and made Thomas a small bow.

"My thanks for the tale. Any more personal details will not be necessary."

"Wait a minute," Victoria said, standing, as well. "The personal details will too be necessary."

"Nay, they will not."

"Yes, they will! How else am I going to pull this off without knowing what Thomas did?"

"I've no intention of you 'pulling this off,'" Connor said firmly.

"But—"

"Are you daft, woman? You, traipsing through the centuries back to a time where you cannot speak the language, defend yourself, or throw yourself into my arms and have me welcome you there? 'Tis absolute madness!"

"I can do it," she said, feeling a rush of stubbornness flow through her. "I went back and got Granny, didn't I? I can do this, too."

"You cannot and you *will* not."

Victoria felt a frown begin. "Excuse me?"

Connor leaned forward and looked at her with a matching frown. "I forbid it."

Thomas whistled softly and rose. "Io, I think we should be moseying along now. Before the fireworks start."

Victoria didn't see them go. She supposed it was for the best. Iolanthe was probably not up to listening to what would no doubt be a watershed moment in ghost/ mortal relationships. She glared at Connor. "You cannot stop me."

"Oh, can I not?" he asked in a very soft, very dangerous tone.

She looked at him for a moment or two, then took an unsteady step backward. "It's lunchtime. I'm starved."

He folded his arms over his chest. "You will not do this thing," he said flatly.

She started to retort, then shut her mouth and looked at him for several moments in silence. She stared up into his beautiful face and marveled that this man, who had had centuries to find someone to love, had picked her.

Well, sort of.

He stared at her, his jaw set, silent and unmoving. Then he let his hands drop down by his sides and took a step backward. He unclenched his jaw. Then he looked at her pleasantly.

Or what he obviously thought might pass for pleasantly.

"I do not want you to do this," he said.

"Connor—"

He turned away. "Nay, Victoria."

She stared at his broad back for several minutes in silence, then sighed. "I'm going to go get lunch. And then I'm going to start my Gaelic lessons, because I love you."

He didn't move, didn't speak, didn't give any indication he had heard her.

But he had to know he not changed her mind.

Victoria left the sitting room and headed for the kitchen. The Boar's Head Trio was sitting there, partaking of a healthy repast. Thomas was there, cooking something for someone—no doubt poor Iolanthe—and all of them chatting quite happily together.

In Gaelic, as fate would have it.

Victoria greeted the four men with a smile, fetched herself something she would no doubt not manage to eat, then sat down at the table with the Trio.

"I'm going to go rescue Connor," she announced.

They looked at her blankly.

"You know," she said impatiently. "Like Thomas did Iolanthe."

Fulbert gasped. Hugh's mouth dropped open and he made inarticulate sounds of horror. Ambrose looked unsurprised. Thomas turned around from the stove and smiled.

"Well," he said, drawing the word out quite a bit, "you are a seasoned time-traveler, I suppose."

"Damn straight," she said.

But she quaked a little as she said it. It was one thing to go back to a place where she could almost speak the language, with her sister for company and a big, strapping six-foot-four Highland ghost as protection. It was another thing entirely to go on her own. To a time she knew nothing of. To a place where she wouldn't be able to understand anything. To rescue a man who, if Thomas's experience was any indication, wouldn't know her from Adam. Or Eve.

And he probably wouldn't like her, in either case.

"It is impossible," she whispered. She looked at her brother. "It *is* impossible, isn't it?"

"*Impossible* is a powerful word," Thomas said, setting a plate down on the table. "I wouldn't use it lightly."

She blew her hair out of her face and looked up at the ceiling. It was a futile effort to try to keep the tears in her eyes. She looked at Thomas and let them slide down her cheeks.

"I can't imagine my future without him," she said finally.

"Now, that, my dear, is a better sentiment," Ambrose said approvingly. "You know, Connor has grown on me of late, as well. I find many things to recommend his character."

"Me, too," she said, dragging her sleeve across her eyes. She looked at Thomas. "Will you help me? Or are you headed back home soon?"

"We can stay for another couple of months," Thomas said. "You'll want to head to Scotland soon, I imagine. Jamie can give you a crash course in medieval survival skills. His brother and cousin live nearby. You'll need them, as well."

"A veritable colony of reenactment whackos, hmmm?" she asked.

"Oddly enough," Thomas said with a smile.

"Or are they all of the same vintage?"

"Might be," Thomas conceded.

"All right," she said, rubbing her hands together briskly. "I'll make a more complete to-do list later, but for now, what do you suggest?"

"Gaelic," Ambrose said without hesitation. "Perhaps a bit of knifework, lest you meet a lad or two short on chivalry."

Fulbert snorted. "Knife work, to be sure. History, customs, local politics—if you can stomach them."

"And you'll want to know Connor's particulars," Thomas added, "though I suspect he may be unwilling to give them."

Victoria sighed. "He won't remember me, will he? Since I would be preventing him from being a ghost for eight hundred years—"

"Well," Thomas said with a smile, "that is a matter of opinion. We'll have a very long discussion about remembering the future on our way to Jamie's."

"I can hardly wait."

"You can talk to Iolanthe about it later. For now, I'll give Jamie a call and see if he can help you. He's generally willing to make time for this kind of thing. How soon do you want to leave?"

"Fred's overseeing the storing of our gear. If Mrs. Pruitt lets me keep the costumes in the shed, I won't have to deal with that until right before I go back to the States." She considered. "I suppose I could leave day after tomorrow. Monday," she clarified. "Maybe Tuesday."

"Tuesday it is," Thomas said.

Victoria nodded, struggling to swallow past the lump in her throat.

She would do this and hope that Connor would change his mind.

She couldn't bear to think about the alternative.

Several hours later, she staggered to the library, wondering if she might not quite be equal to the task before her.

She had passed the morning in Gaelic-land, learning the depth and breadth of her lack. Even Thomas sounded like a native—an annoying fact in and of itself. She'd begged, after a couple of hours, to go deal with the post-production details she normally detested.

Unfortunately, those had been wrapped up far too soon for her taste, and without a Connor sighting for the whole of the afternoon.

She'd discussed defenses with Ambrose and Thomas over dinner, with a few mutterings from Fulbert thrown in for good measure. By bedtime, she was past being tired. And far past being overwhelmed.

She was numb.

She entered the library and closed the door behind her. She was surprised to see a fire in the hearth. She was even more surprised to see Connor sitting in his accustomed chair. He rose at once and waited until she had taken the seat across from him before he sat.

And then he merely stared at her for an eternity in silence.

She had nothing to say. What was there to say? How could she convince him to agree with her? And what was the point if he didn't want her to go and get him?

Connor closed his eyes and bowed his head for several minutes. Then he lifted his head and opened his eyes to look at her.

His eyes were moist.

"I love you," he said quietly.

She started to cry. She didn't mean to, but when it came right down to it, she simply couldn't help herself.

"Please," he pleaded, leaning forward and looking at her with tears in his eyes. "Please do not do this thing."

She would have taken his hands if she could have. Instead, all she could do was look at him with tears streaming down her face.

"Please don't ask me not to."

"Victoria, you cannot fathom the danger."

"You're right," she said. "But I can fathom the misery if I don't try."

He bowed his head for several minutes, then he sighed deeply. "Can you imagine how this galls me? The only way I can have you is to allow you to risk your life for mine. How can I tell you that I agree with this? By the saints, Victoria, how can I help you find your way to hell?"

"Is medieval Scotland that bad?" she asked lightly.

"I was talking about myself."

"Are you telling me I'm going back in time to rescue a jerk?"

"I was . . . difficult."

"You're difficult now. Big deal. I'm a pain, too."

He smiled briefly, then sobered. "Nay, my love, you are all that I could wish for and more. Should I spend the rest of my days simply loving you from afar, I would be content."

She snorted. "You wouldn't be and neither would I. Now, if you'll excuse me, I have more Gaelic lessons in the morning and I don't want to be bleary-eyed."

He looked heavenward for a moment, then met her eyes. "I do not like this."

She waited.

"My pride will suffer."

She waited a bit more.

"I want you to understand that when we succeed, and when we return to your day, *I* will be the one seeing to you."

"Head of the house? Breadwinner? Presiding officer?" she said with a smile.

"I am in earnest."

"And I'm just thrilled you want to come back to my day."

"Indoor plumbing," he said succinctly. "French wines, French cooking, French chocolate." He paused. "I've heard rumors."

She rose and smiled down at him. "Good night, my laird. Are you going to bed?"

"I'll keep watch over you, if it doesn't trouble you."

She felt a moment of awkwardness when she would have preferred to kiss him senseless, but considering that she couldn't even shake his hand politely, she settled for a smile and a hasty retreat to her bed.

"A tale?" he asked when she was comfortably ensconced under her covers.

"A song, instead."

"All right."

It was a love song. She only recognized a few words, but *battle* and *death* weren't among them.

Love and *forever* certainly were.

She would have to have him translate the whole thing in the morning.

She fell asleep smiling.

Chapter 26

Three weeks later, Connor stood on the edge of James MacLeod's garden and considered several things.

First, there was the complete improbability of standing on MacLeod soil without a sword in his hand and death on his mind. It never would have happened during his lifetime. He supposed he shouldn't have been surprised that it happened during his death.

Second was the somewhat surreal experience of being back in the Highlands. It had been, literally, centuries since he had walked over his native land. That he should be there seven hundred years after his death was almost too much to be believed.

Victoria had come with Thomas and Iolanthe in Thomas's car; Connor had made his way at a more leisurely pace with the Boar's Head Trio. Even Fulbert had been rendered mute by some of the scenes they had viewed on the way. There was nothing quite like Scotland during high summer to leave a man sorry that he had to return any time soon to anywhere south of Hadrian's Wall.

Last on his list of things that consumed his attention

was the consummate dread he felt watching Victoria try to make herself over into some sort of medieval Highland warrior lass.

By the saints, she would never manage it.

That wasn't because Jamie's facilities were lacking. The MacLeod castle was nothing short of spectacular and the surrounding environs were just as lovely. The keep itself lacked nothing in the way of modern conveniences, which made for a good rest after a hard day of training. There was ample room near the garden for training and large expanses of countryside for the mastery of horsemanship. Jamie seemed to have all manner of family with medievalness clinging to them like perfume, who seemed to be more than happy to provide any sort of training a body might desire.

Unfortunately, in spite of her enthusiasm, Victoria hadn't been very successful at learning what her masters had endeavored to teach her. Though she had made some progress in her speech and now knew what end of the dirk to point away from herself, her ability to reduce a man to tears with anything but her sharp tongue was indeed lacking.

"Well?"

Connor jumped slightly and turned to find Thomas McKinnon standing next to him. "Well, what?"

"I imagine I know what you're thinking," Thomas said.

And he said it in Gaelic. Connor wondered about that. "How is it that you speak my mother tongue so well?"

"It's a gift," Thomas said modestly.

"Why can't your sister do the same?"

"She's only been at it a month. Give her some time."

"She doesn't have time," Connor said grimly.

Thomas smiled suddenly. "I have an idea. Why doesn't Vic take Jennifer along as a translator?"

"The saints preserve me," Connor said with horror. "You wish to have the blood of *two* of your sisters on my hands?"

Thomas laughed. "No, I think Vic's will be quite

enough for the time being." He looked at his sister, who was trying to stab Ian MacLeod with a dirk and failing gloriously. "I think we're in trouble."

Connor could only grunt in agreement.

"Maybe she just needs a bigger sword. I'm sure she had fencing lessons somewhere along the way." He looked at Connor. "Would anyone notice a woman with a very long sword, do you think?"

"Anyone with eyes will notice your sister. Her beauty alone will be a beacon which will call any and all males in the area to her, all with no doubt less-than-noble designs upon her person. If she lives to see my hall, it will be a miracle. If she survives an encounter with me, she will have accomplished what few other souls have—be they wenches or men."

"It doesn't sound promising."

"Did you ever consider that it did?" Connor exclaimed. "Did I not say it was folly? Did I not endeavor to convince her it was madness?"

"She doesn't listen very well."

"She does not listen at all!"

Thomas shook his head. "She really must like you, to be doing this."

"Daft wench," Connor muttered.

"Well, she's also a determined one, so since you can't do anything about the former, maybe you should do something about the latter."

Connor folded his arms across his chest and donned his fiercest frown. If he offered Victoria aid, that meant he agreed with her decision.

But if he didn't offer her aid, he would quite possibly be condemning her to a horrible fate of some unthinkable kind in the wilds of medieval Scotland, with him being the only one capable of rescuing her, but likely—as much as it galled him to admit it—too stupid to do so.

He sighed deeply. It was the kind of sigh that came straight from a man's toes when he resigned himself to the fact that, in the matter at hand, he was not going to be master of his own fate.

"Very well," he said. "I will aid her."

Thomas was too wise to smile. "I imagine she will appreciate it."

"It does not mean I agree with her decision, nor do I approve of her plan."

"I never would have thought either was the case."

Connor grunted at him. "Well? Any suggestions?"

"A longer sword and a few insights into your medieval persona might be a good place to start."

Connor chewed on his lip for a moment or two. "It galls me to admit it, but in life, there was not much at all to recommend me."

Thomas did smile. "There wasn't much to recommend you last summer, either, but look what a charmer you've become. Vic'll work on you."

"You assume I'll allow myself to be worked on."

"It's Victoria. Even I, as her jaded and skeptical brother, have to admit she's gorgeous. And she's just as bad-tempered as you are. I imagine you'll take one look at her and fall madly in love."

"Ha," Connor said grimly. "I wish I could credit my mortal self with such good sense, but I cannot. Your sister will be fortunate indeed if she doesn't see the inside of my dungeon before she can spew out her message to me."

"Connor, my friend, give yourself some credit."

Connor looked at Victoria's brother for a moment or two in silence, then spoke. "Would you allow your lady to do this for you?"

Thomas McKinnon was, mercifully, silent.

Indeed, he looked as if Connor had jarred him quite forcefully in the gut. It took him several moments before he could recapture his breath.

"I see," he said finally.

"Now you do."

"I'll work on her Gaelic; you work on her swordplay and landmark-reading skills."

"I suppose I can do nothing less," Connor said. "Unless I could find a way to thwart her plans."

Thomas shook his head. "Don't think it. Let's go prepare her as best we can. The rest will take care of itself."

"As it did during your trip to the past?"

"We'll talk about that after it's all over." Thomas smiled. "I think Vic's beginning to tax Ian's patience and that's saying something. Start making your list of what she should know and I'll get with the language."

Connor nodded and wished he could pour his whole heart into the idea. All he could think about was Victoria, alone and unprotected in the wilds of medieval Scotland. Or, worse yet, in the wilds of his hall, with him never the wiser and ready as he had always been to toss out of his hall anyone who displeased him.

The saints pity them both.

*T*o his surprise, the longer sword proved to be a great success. Connor stood in Jamie's garden a day or two later and watched Victoria spar with Ian—Ian who was apparently the resident swordmaster to women who had lost all sense and were determined to pursue a course of madness. She was not only holding her own, she was forcing Ian to actually exert himself to maintain his dignity.

"Peace," Ian exclaimed with a laugh. "This is a more delicate and refined fighting that I am used to and it taxes me greatly."

Victoria dragged her sleeve across her brow. "Then go get your broadsword and hack at someone else for a while. It will make you feel better."

Ian made her a low bow, swished his rapier through the air with a delightful sound, then took Victoria's advice and sought out a different blade and a sturdier partner. Connor waited for Victoria to have a drink before he began peppering her with questions.

"How do you find west?"

She sighed. "Take a stick, mark the shadow. Wait fifteen minutes and put another stick where the shadow has moved to. Draw a line between the two. That points east and west."

"And if it's too cloudy for a shadow?"

"Pray."

He pursed his lips. "And if ruffians come upon you?"

"Kill first, be polite later."

He grunted. "And if your horse falls lame?"

"Connor, my horse will be fine. I will be fine. I'll find your hall, tell you what's up, and convince you to come back with me." She smiled. "It's all going to work out just fine."

If only he could be so convinced. Well, at least her Gaelic wasn't as dreadful as he had first thought. He would not mistake her for a Scot, but she was almost intelligible. Perhaps even fluency would come in time. He could only hope it wouldn't come thanks to time spent in his dungeon, consorting with the other prisoners he had tended to toss in and forget about.

"Iolanthe and Elizabeth are working on some clothes for me," she said with a bright smile. "I think I should probably go try them on. Later, I should walk and see if I can recognize all the edible plants Patrick told me about. He's Jamie's brother, you know, and quite adept at eating all kinds of things you wouldn't think you could."

Connor sighed. Aye, he knew Patrick and had found him to be just as lethal and fierce as his older brother, though perhaps a little more jovial. Connor wasn't surprised by Patrick's resourcefulness. He had been surprised, however, at the pleasure he'd taken in conversing with both MacLeod brothers.

Miracles never ceased, apparently.

"Do you want to come with me later?" she asked.

"Aye," he said with a sigh. "I will await you in the meadow."

"Great," she said brightly and turned to walk across the garden and into the hall.

She didn't look afeared by what she intended to do.

That troubled him.

But he said nothing about it as the afternoon wore on. He took no notice of her excessive cheerfulness as she scouted out things she could eat in a moment of need. He even managed to ignore her exaggerated yawn after supper, as if the day had been just so full of delights that she could do nothing but seek out her bed and recover. He watched her go.

She was acting.

Poorly.

It did not bode well, somehow.

After supper, he found himself sitting alone before the fire in the great hall. He wasn't without companionship for long, though. James MacLeod joined him after the household had gone to sleep. He sat down in a chair opposite Connor and stared into the fire for quite some time.

Connor marveled at the strangeness of it all. To think it had taken him seven centuries to realize that he could befriend clansmen he would have killed without thinking during life. He had to admit that in Jamie's case at least, he would have made a mistake.

"Well?" Connor said. "What do you think?"

Jamie looked at him. "What do *you* think?"

"What I think isn't fit to utter."

Jamie's expression didn't change. " 'Tis a very great risk she takes for you."

"I begged her not to."

"And it no doubt takes a goodly bit of humility on your part to accept that risk."

"More than I possess."

Jamie smiled faintly. "I daresay I can understand that. I cannot say that I wouldn't feel the same in your place. To have my woman do for me what I could not . . . it would be difficult."

"It galls me deeply. I have no means of protecting her when she goes."

"Can you now?" Jamie asked.

"In some small measure, aye," Connor said.

"But you cannot wed her, give her children, or see to her as you would wish." He smiled gravely. "You are in an untenable position, my friend. If you allow her to do this thing, you cannot protect her. If you do not allow her to do this thing, you cannot give her what your heart desires."

"She will go over my protests."

"Will she?" Jamie mused. "Despite her determination, I daresay she feels somehow that you disapprove of her choice. It robs her of the benefit and comfort you might offer her and I suspect it keeps her from throwing her whole heart into her training. In spite of your pride and because of your affection for her."

Connor found that it was quite some time before he could rid himself of all the uncomplimentary things he wanted to call James MacLeod. Because of his words. Because he had it all aright.

He sighed. "I fear for her."

"Then prepare her for the worst. We both know how dire her straits could become."

Connor nodded wearily. "I will."

"I had a thought earlier," Jamie began.

"Another one?" Connor asked sourly. "Have you not bludgeoned me with enough of them already tonight?"

Jamie smiled easily. "I was thinking that if you would care to write down your memories, I could aid you in that. I did the like for Iolanthe and it was of great comfort to her."

Connor considered, then shook his head. "I couldn't read at all in the past, so words will not serve me if I come to the Future. Nay, I'll simply be forced to rely on my superior intelligence and flexible imagination."

"And hope you lose your sword on the way through the gate?" Jamie asked with a hint of a smile.

"I'll be far less tempted to use it that way, I suppose," Connor agreed.

"Well, then perhaps we will find another way to stir your memories when Victoria brings you home."

"If she manages—"

"I would cease with that sort of talk if I were you," Jamie interrupted sharply. "It will do nothing to give your lady the confidence she needs."

Connor sighed gustily and rose. "Thank you, my laird, for the advice and the censure. I will take both to heart."

"All will be well," Jamie said, standing and taking Connor's hand. "She is strong."

"Headstrong," Connor muttered, then he looked at Jamie quickly. "It is a fine attribute that will aid her well in her task."

Jamie laughed. "Well said."

Connor nodded absently, bid Jamie a good e'en, and went on his way. His first thought was to escape from any more of Jamie's piercing truths, but he soon found himself climbing the stairs and walking down the passageway to the chamber where he knew Victoria slept. He put his ear to the door and listened.

Within was the sound of quiet weeping.

"Ach, by the saints," he said, then knocked.

Victoria opened the door shortly thereafter, blowing her nose. "A cold," she said, then she realized it was he. "You knocked."

"I didn't want to disturb you unnecessarily."

"You did that from day one." She stepped back a pace or two. "Please, come in."

He went inside and perched on a very feminine-looking chair. He waited until Victoria was seated nearby before he took a deep breath. Her cheeks were tearstained and her eyes very red. He cursed himself silently, then sighed. "I am here to apologize," he said.

"Apologize?"

He scowled at her. "You needn't sound so surprised. I am capable, you know."

She smiled wanly. "Then by all means, go on."

"I have not been enthusiastic about this plan of yours and it has no doubt hampered your efforts. You are sacrificing everything to save my sorry arse and instead of gratitude, I've shown you an appalling lack of succor."

She stared at him in astonishment.

"Well," he said defensively, "I have."

"I'm not quite sure what to say."

"Say, 'My, what a flowery bit of rubbish that was,' and let's get on with your preparations. I suggest a good night's rest tonight, for on the morrow we train in earnest."

A tear or two ran down her cheeks. "Thank you."

He waved her thanks away. "'Twas nothing. Least I could do. I would recite verse for you, as well, but I don't want to reduce you to tears again." He stood. "To bed with you, woman. I'll guard your door outside."

She nodded. He supposed if she could have, she might have clasped hands with him, or even gone so far as to have kissed his cheek.

He made her a low bow and disappeared before he could consider either of those things further.

He took up a post outside her door and forced away his worry. There was, in truth, little else to be done and no pleasing alternatives to consider. If Victoria was successful in saving his life but he refused to go to the Future with her, he wouldn't be a restless spirit haunting Thorpewold and he would lose what little he had with her.

But if he didn't allow her to try, he was quite certain he would lose her just the same. It was easy at present to suppose that she would stay forever, but the truth was, there would come a time when even the most stoic and committed of wenches would want a real man in her bed.

Nay, he would have to let her go, even if only for that small possibility that she might succeed.

He could only hope he wouldn't be a complete horse's arse when she showed up at his gates.

That was a probability of which he was all too certain.

Chapter 27

V ictoria stood several feet away from what they had affectionately come to call Farris's Fairy Ring and took three long, slow breaths. It was what she did before performances to still her nerves. It was those quick breaths that tended to get her in trouble, but the long ones—no, those were the life-saving, heart-calming ones. Unfortunately, they weren't working all that well at present.

Damn. She should have taken Moonbat Murphy up on those yoga lessons while she'd had the chance.

Yet another thing she wished she'd done that she hadn't.

In her defense, she *had* done several things over the past six weeks that she never would have dreamed she would manage. She had learned to ride a horse and eat grass, thanks to James MacLeod's very handsome brother Patrick. She had brushed up her rapier skills and acquired a decent bit of knife skill, thanks to Jamie's dapper and jovial cousin Ian. She had acquired an entirely new understanding of medieval Highland politics, thanks to James MacLeod himself.

She had also learned more than she'd ever wanted to about Jamie's infamous map with Xs marking the time gates scattered over Scotland and northern England. She'd asked him how he knew where those Xs were located and where they led.

He'd only smiled.

She'd felt a sudden rush of sympathy for Elizabeth. Good heavens, no wonder the woman only rolled her eyes when she heard Jamie was off on another adventure.

But that education from Jamie had paled in comparison to the conversations she'd had with Connor. Who would have thought he had survived such a brutal world? It made her wonder, quite briefly, what she was thinking to even consider going back to that world.

By herself.

Taking the risk that she might wind up in some other world and get stuck there without friends or family.

She shook aside those thoughts before they overwhelmed her. She was doing what she had to do. And if she was successful, it would all be worth it. She refused to consider what she would do if she failed.

She thought again about all the things she had learned from Jamie about the time gates, more particularly the gate before her. According to Jamie, the Farris Fairy Ring was a gate of a most peculiar potency, leaving the time-traveler with many options for destinations. She hadn't asked him how he knew this, though she could bring to mind a handful of times during his stay at the inn when he had been AWOL.

Testing out his theories, apparently.

Well, if the gate was as powerful as Jamie claimed, it would take her where she wanted to go. Or, at least, it would if she could manage to stop the colossal argument going on behind her so she could concentrate and give it a try.

She took a firmer grip on the horse Mrs. Pruitt had rounded up for her and turned to look at the altercators.

"I will," Connor said, his hand twitching toward his sword as he glared at Thomas.

"And I say you shouldn't," Thomas returned in frustration. "It's crazy!"

Victoria cleared her throat pointedly. "Will you both

just be done!" she exclaimed. "I can't listen to either of you any longer!"

Connor and Thomas exchanged a final glare before they turned to her.

"We're discussing," Connor said.

"I think you've discussed enough," she said shortly. "Thomas, let Connor do what he wants to do."

"Vic, he *can't* come with you. It doesn't make any sense. What is he going to do, defend you from his mortal self?"

"I *am* going," Connor said. He moved to stand next to Victoria. "I will at least see her safely to my hall. I can likely do nothing for her after that, but I will do what I can for her until that time."

Thomas threw up his hands in despair. "This is nuts, but I'm officially done fighting it." He looked at her and scowled. "You're as prepared as you probably can be and if you have this foul-tempered nut tagging along with you, you'll probably be just fine. But it doesn't make sense for him to go back to a time when he was alive."

"Why not?" she asked.

"It's spooky, that's why not."

Victoria walked over to give her brother a tight hug, then followed it up with a shove. "Get out of here. I'll be back in a day or two. I'm sure it won't take long."

"One could hope," Thomas said. "Now, what are your three key phrases again?"

Victoria sighed. " 'I'm not a witch,' 'I don't have much Gaelic because I'm French royalty,' and 'There's a fairy ring down the road I think you really need to come look at.' " She looked at her brother. "Good enough?"

"Perfect."

Victoria peered over the top of her horse to look at Connor, who stood on the other side. She wasn't all that sure about the advisability of taking him back to a point in time where he was alive, either, but he didn't look to be in the mood to be argued with. "Ready?" she asked brightly.

"Very," he said, apparently trying to sound enthusiastic.

Victoria took stock once more of her supplies. She had camping gear, extra clothes, and food strapped to the horse. She was wearing a backpack with essentials, in case of emergency—though she was planning on things going smoothly. An extended stay was not really in her plans, though she supposed it was possible that Connor would take one look at her and invite her to be his guest for an indeterminate amount of time.

Stranger things had happened.

Well, there was no time like the present to get on with it. She nodded to her brother, nodded to Connor, took a firm grip on her reins, and pulled her horse into the ring. Once she was standing inside that spooky bit of fauna, she focused her thoughts on Connor and everything she'd learned about his fourteenth-century self. She willed herself to see the land he'd described as his holdings to the south, where only the brave went after dark because of the harrowing tales associated with the area. She even closed her eyes for good measure, not because she thought it would help, but because it seemed like the right thing to do.

But before she could really bring the impressive powers of her formidable imagination to bear on the current task, the damned horse Mrs. Pruitt had given her whinnied in fear and reared up, wrenching the reins from Victoria's fingers.

"Hey!" she exclaimed.

The next thing she knew, the horse was off like a shot, carrying with it most of her gear and all hope of non-perambulating travel.

"Can you believe that?" she said to Connor.

Only Connor wasn't there.

Neither was that little grove of trees she had hidden behind with Connor when they'd been spying on Thomas and Jamie. Thomas was gone, as well.

"Oh," she wheezed. "Not in Kansas anymore, I guess."

"Witch! Fairy! Sorceress!"

She whirled around to see two very filthy, very terrified children hiding in another species of trees and pointing at her while they called her names.

Dangerous names.

Names Thomas and Jamie had insisted she learn in Gaelic so she would be prepared for the worst. Victoria thought it might be best to run before she met up with any parents with pitchforks. She didn't have fifteen minutes to determine where west was, so she checked the handy compass she'd bought two days earlier and tucked in her sock, then made tracks north.

She ran until she couldn't run anymore and she thought she might have left the name-callers behind. She hunched over with her hands on her thighs and sucked in air— fortunately not as desperately as she might have six weeks ago. Time at Jamie's in that respect had not been wasted. Ian had seemed to take an inordinate pleasure in being her personal trainer. She had thought at the time that he just had a sadistic streak, but now she suspected he did it so she would actually manage to make it through medieval Scotland alive. Then she would have a tale to entertain his family with in front of his shiny red Aga stove.

She was grateful that she at least had on her backpack and that Connor had insisted she keep her sword strapped to her person and not her horse. She would thank him for that advice the next time she saw him.

"Och, but yer a fetchin' wench."

Victoria spun around, drawing her rapier at the same time. A bedraggled, though surprisingly bright-eyed man stood there, leering at her. He flicked away the point of her sword.

"I'm not afeared of your puny wench's blade," he said scornfully.

"Perhaps you should be," she said. She moved to one side.

He blocked her.

She resheathed her sword and folded her arms over her chest. "Get out of my way."

"Och, but where's the sport in that?" he asked, grinning as he reached out for her.

"Oh, well, maybe you're right." She smiled encouragingly. And then once he had his hands on her arms, she kneed him sharply in the groin. While he was dealing with that, she took her steel-toed army boot and smashed it down on the top of his foot, just where Jenner had once taught her was the premier disabling spot for a guy wearing rags on his feet.

While the man was hopping and shrieking, apparently unable even to curse her properly, she gave him a good push and dashed away.

Damn. Ten minutes into medieval-looking Scotland and already she'd had trouble. Well, at least there was no crashing of underbrush behind her and the shrieks faded eventually in an authentic way, so Victoria counted that one hurdle overcome. She continued her all-out sprint for Connor's hall.

She did have to slow to a jog at times, but she didn't stop. It was a gloomy day, perfect weather for trying to blend into the countryside. She held onto her compass with one hand and a borrowed dagger from Jamie with the other as she made her way north. Connor had said the fairy ring was a couple of miles south of his home. With any luck, it would take her twenty minutes to get to Connor's hall.

She was surprised by the forest, but knew she shouldn't have been. All the Highlands had been forested at one time. She couldn't remember when the English had cleared them, but apparently that hadn't happened yet in Connor's day. They were beautiful, those trees, but gave her no clue as to how much progress she had made. It felt as if she had been running forever. Her lungs burned. Her legs were rubber. Her hands were shaking.

She dropped her compass and hunched over again, gasping until she thought she could straighten and take a normal breath. She picked up the compass and managed to heave herself upright. And then she lost her breath all over again.

Apparently the forest did have an end.

She stood there and gaped at the castle in the clearing

in front of her. It wasn't that she hadn't seen castles before, but she hadn't seen a medieval one operating in its proper time period. At least she hoped it was the proper time period.

And the proper castle.

She stood there for several minutes, wondering at the lack of activity outside and debating her next move. Her plan had been to show up, talk to Connor, and then see what happened. She was hoping to charm him, or at least unsettle him enough that he would take the time to listen to her. She sincerely hoped she wouldn't be invited to take up residence in his dungeon.

Maybe this wasn't the right castle. Worse yet, maybe she hadn't come back to the right time. What would she do if Connor came out that front door, but he was still toddling around in diapers—

Bagpipe music started up suddenly.

She listened, open-mouthed, to renditions of the songs Connor had sung too many times to count. She had a momentary flash of hope, but that was quickly extinguished. Jamie had known some of the same songs, so she supposed it was possible that she was in the wrong part of Scotland. The piper faltered and the music faded.

Victoria held her breath.

The piper took another stab at things. Another song soon floated to her on the wind. It was Connor's favorite battle dirge, the one he considered to be quite rousing.

It was the one tune Jamie hadn't known.

"Well," she said out loud, "that's a good sign." She put her compass back in her sock, resheathed Jamie's dagger, and started toward the castle. She made it almost all the way to the front door before a clansman of some sort came rushing outside. He came to an abrupt halt, looked at her in surprise, then drew his sword and pointed it at her. "Who are you?" he demanded.

He looked so much like Connor, she smiled. "French nobility," she said promptly. "I'm hear to see the laird, Connor."

He looked about her in puzzlement. "Alone? Where are your men?"

Well, at least he wasn't telling her she was asking for the wrong guy. Things were looking brighter by the heartbeat.

"My men were slain," she said. "By Campbells."

"Damn the wretches," the man said perfunctorily. He put up his sword and nodded toward the hall. "Well, come inside then. You don't look all that fierce, so I don't feel the need to disarm you."

"Thanks so much," she said politely.

He shrugged and grinned. "Anything for a fetching wench." He paused. "What's yer name, fetching wench?"

"Victoria McKinnon," she said.

His eyes widened briefly. "Indeed."

"I'm sure I'm not related to the McKinnons you don't like."

"The laird dislikes *all* McKinnons," he said, "so I'd keep my clan name to myself."

"Thanks for the advice. What was your name again?"

"Cormac MacDougal." He smiled. "I'm the laird's cousin."

"How fortunate for you. Let's go see him, shall we?"

Cormac nodded and led her into the hall. Victoria found that she was having a little trouble making her legs move. Her feet seemed to have an overwhelming desire just to plant themselves somewhere until her brain began working again. Not that the floor was anything to want to stay still in. She looked down.

"Eeuww," she said involuntarily.

"I know," Cormac said. "Damned lazy servants. When the rushes are this fresh, I've no liking for them, either. Give me a floor that's seen a good bit of hard living and I'm content."

Victoria found herself quite content to be wearing boots that kept her delicate toes off that fresh floor. She had no idea what was squirming around under the hay, nor did she want to find out. She could only imagine what the dungeon looked like.

She didn't want to know for sure.

She followed Cormac across the hall and did her best to keep her boots out of the worst of the goo as she did so. It was no easy task and she found that it took all her powers of concentration just to put one foot in front of the other and keep going.

And then her forward motion was stopped abruptly.

It was as if she had run into a wall.

She realized, as she looked up, that she had run into a Connor MacDougal instead.

"Oh," she breathed, looking up into his stormy gray eyes and feeling her eyes burn suddenly. "Oh, my."

He grasped her by the arms, presumably to keep her up on her feet. All she knew was that he was touching her.

"What do you want?" he demanded. "And be quick about it. I've business to see to."

He was touching her. It was more than she could take in. She stammered and stuttered and, in the end, failed miserably to articulate anything useful. She was standing a hand's breadth from the man she loved and he was *alive*. Nothing Thomas or Iolanthe had said had come close to preparing her for it. In her own mind, she had suspected it would be earth-shattering.

She hadn't expected it to be heartbreaking.

"Oh," she said again, breathlessly. "Well."

He rolled his eyes impatiently. "Daft wench," he muttered.

In much the same way he'd been saying it to her all summer.

He released her abruptly and turned away in disgust.

Well, at least he hadn't thrown her into his pit. "Laird MacDougal," she said, taking a step toward him, "I have things I need to tell you."

He turned back around and frowned at her. "Who are you and whence do you hail? Your Gaelic is terrible."

Victoria had been preparing for just those sorts of questions, and practicing her answers, for weeks. Connor had even given her several ideas of what to say and how to phrase it so he wouldn't immediately label her a witch.

"My name is Victoria." When he didn't immediately reach for his sword, she pressed on. "I have come from a great distance to warn you about events to come."

The storm clouds began to gather.

"I'm not a witch," she said quickly. "Do not put me in your dungeon."

"By the saints, woman, I think that is the place for you."

She found that a crowd was gathering so she leaned in closer. "Is there a place where we could talk in private?"

"Aye, my dungeon."

She expected that. She expected that he wouldn't want to talk and that he would impatiently or with incredulity brush aside what she wanted to say. She hadn't expected that standing so close to him would turn her brain to mush.

"Ah," she attempted, "I think you'll want to hear what I have to say."

He folded his arms over his chest and frowned down at her. "'Tis only because you are a damned fetching wench that I take the time to listen. And I like your red hair, though you look a fair sight too much like those damned McKinnons. Are you a McKinnon?"

"Would I be here in your hall if I were?" she hedged. She shot Cormac a look, but he only watched with his arms folded over his chest, a thoughtful frown on his face, and his sword safely tucked in its scabbard. So far, so good.

"Hmmm," he said doubtfully. "I'll have that answer in time, I daresay, and throw you in my pit if you answer amiss. But get on with your business and let me be about mine."

She chose her words carefully. "A question first, if you don't mind. Do you have a French minstrel in your hall?"

His expression darkened considerably. "Why do you ask?" he asked in that low, dangerous voice she'd heard a time or two before. Only seven hundred years in the future, he hadn't had that enormous, imminently real broadsword strapped to his back.

"I ask," she said, lowering her voice as well, "because there is a fairy ring through the forest, over the hill, and down into the glade. It is a gate to the Future. I came

through it to tell you that I know what will happen when
the Frenchman leaves with your wife and children and you
go to search for them."

Connor had warned her that such a statement would not
sit well with his medieval self.

A pity he hadn't warned her just what kind of reaction it
would provoke.

The Connor presently standing in front of her roared.
He roared again for good measure, then drew his sword
and swung. Blessing Ian MacLeod for his brutal training
regimen, Victoria managed to duck just in time.

"Wait," she said from her crouched position at his feet.

"Begone, you vile wench!"

"But I have more to tell you—"

"Get out of my hall or leap into my pit!" he thundered.
"I'll hear no more of this mad speech!"

"His wife left a se'nnight ago," Cormac offered helpfully.

"Damn ye to hell," Connor snarled at him. "Must you
tell the entire bloody keep?"

"But, Connor," Cormac said reasonably, "everyone
knows already."

Connor turned to vent his frustrations on his cousin.
Cormac must have been accustomed to it because he
merely drew his sword in an instant and was fighting fire
with fire, as it were. Victoria stood and watched, hoping
she hadn't caused a fracas where she shouldn't have. Then
again, Connor was going after his cousin and not her. That
had to be a good thing.

Now, if she could just get him to listen to her while he
was otherwise engaged.

"The Frenchman will send for you," she shouted over
Connor and Cormac's cursing. "His messenger will promise to tell you where to find your children."

"Be silent!" Connor thundered.

She waited until he'd taken a bit more of his irritation
out on his cousin before she attempted anything else.

"Beware the Frenchman," she said. "He will murder you
in the clearing near the stream—"

Connor growled and pointed his sword at her. "If you say one more word, I will pull out your entrails and strangle you with them."

She blinked. "You will?"

"Well," he conceded reluctantly, "likely not, you being a woman and all."

"Could we sit and visit, then?" she asked.

He swore in disgust. "Nay, we may *not*! Woman, I've *business* to see to that does not include listening to some strange, daft wench who would be better served by being silenced permanently!"

"But—"

"Be*gone,* ye silly wench!"

"We can't chat over a cup of ale?"

Connor swore viciously and took her by the arm. He dragged her to the front door.

"Wait," she said, digging her heels into his floor. This wasn't going at all how she'd planned. It wasn't even going according to her worst-case scenario. She had to at least blurt out a warning or two. Maybe then something would click with him and he would stop long enough to listen to everything she had to say. She suspected that convincing him he wanted to have dinner with her might be asking too much.

She took a deep breath. "The arrow will come at you. Your horse will crush you beneath it and then the Frenchman will come and finish you," she said quickly.

He growled.

"He will tell you as you die that your bairns and your wife died of the ague because he dragged them through the wet for days on end—"

She found, quite suddenly, that she was flying down the front steps. Fortunately, there were only four of them. Even more providential was the fact that one of Ian's first lessons had been the tuck and roll. She stumbled down the stairs, tucked, and rolled. She came back up onto her feet and turned to look back at the hall.

Connor stood there, his chest heaving, and glared at her a final time.

Then he slammed the door and didn't open it again.

Victoria brushed herself off and took a good long look at Connor's medieval home. It was gray, unforgiving, built to withstand assaults of all kinds. Sort of like Connor himself.

Well, things had certainly not gone as planned.

She stood there for several minutes and simply stared at the keep. She could go back and try again. Maybe if she tackled Connor to the ground and sat on him, she might be able to keep him immobile enough to make him listen to her.

Somehow, though, she doubted it.

It was with great reluctance that she realized the most unfortunate truth of all.

Her trip to the past had been a bust.

She thought about Connor, his beautiful, mortal self, and realized that perhaps she had leaped where she should have looked. Never mind that he had told her unequivocally not to try to rescue him, that he was not reasonable as a mortal, that he would not listen to her, that it was very likely that he would do her harm.

Had she listened?

No, she had not.

Suddenly, unpleasant and uncomfortable realizations washed over her. There might be, she conceded, parts of herself that were not very likeable. One of those parts might possibly have been her need to control everything and everyone around her. Looking at her life from her current perspective in the past, she could see that she had spent almost the whole of her adult life micromanaging the lives of the actors who worked for her, demanding commitments far and beyond what other directors demanded. She realized with an equal and sudden clarity that she did so because she desperately feared that if she let people act the way they wanted to, they might do something she didn't like.

As Connor just had.

She wanted to sit down, but there was nowhere to go but the ground, and heaven only knew what kind of response that would bring from Connor's clan. It was difficult to come to terms with it, but she realized that she had no choice but to accept that she simply could not save Connor's life. She couldn't fix him, she couldn't control him, she couldn't help him when he didn't want to be helped. She couldn't write his script for him.

More importantly, she realized that she had no right to try.

She heard the door open behind her. She almost didn't turn around, but her curiosity got the better of her.

Cormac came loping down the steps, mopping up the blood dripping from his nose with the hem of his tunic. He stopped in front of her and smiled.

She was almost sure he'd had more teeth ten minutes ago.

"Where will you go?" he asked.

She smiled faintly. "Home."

"Don't you have a horse?"

"It ran away."

He lifted both eyebrows in surprise. "Indeed. I vow I do not like the thought of you wandering about without protection."

"Don't worry; I have a sword."

"Can you use it?"

"If I have to." She paused. All right, so she couldn't save Connor. That didn't mean she couldn't make one last effort to warn him. "You know, Cormac, there is something you could do for me."

"Name it."

She smiled truly. What a gallant soul. "Convince Connor to be careful in dealing with the Frenchman. He is not to be trusted."

"How do you know? Are you in league with him?"

"No. I have the Second Sight."

"Aaahh," Cormac said, satisfied. "Our grandmother had it as well. I daresay if you had told Connor as much, he would have listened to you."

She shook her head. "I've told him all he needs to know. Just help him, if you can."

He looked at her for several minutes in silence. "Did

you come through the fairy ring in truth, Victoria McKinnon?"

She hesitated. "That would be difficult to believe, wouldn't it?"

"Scotland is a magical place, my lady."

Victoria was just certain she'd heard that somewhere before. She suspected James MacLeod carved it into big rocks in every century he visited. "Well, magical it may be, but the Scotland of your day is no longer the place for me." She smiled. "Keep Connor safe. That's all that matters."

He stared at her in amazement, and that was the sight she carried with her as she walked from the hall and made her way back through the forest.

Fortunately, not much time had passed inside the hall, so it was still near noon when she started through the forest. It was fortunate, because it made it quite easy to find her path back through the trees. And given that she could hardly see for her tears, that was a very good thing, indeed.

She had done the right thing. Not the easy thing, but the right thing.

She wondered what Connor would say when she saw him in the future. Maybe that was why he had been so vocal in his insistence that she not try. Maybe he had known she would come and he would ignore her and be killed just the same.

But how could that be, when she hadn't met him until after he'd been dead for centuries?

She decided to try and sort it out later. For now, she could carry with her the knowledge that she had tried and that she had walked away. Hopefully that counted for something in the grander scheme of things.

She turned back for one final glimpse of Connor's forest, then turned away and trudged off toward the fairy ring.

Chapter 28

Connor paced about his great hall, wishing desperately that someone would enter those doors and tell him that there were enemies tampering with the cattle, or crofters needing a rescue from unruly neighboring clans, or perhaps even the stray band of Englishmen lost in the north and desiring a quick send-off to the next life.

Unfortunately, all he had was his very pleasant, very reasonable cousin coming inside to be further tormented.

"You should have listened to her," Cormac said easily.

Connor growled at him, but his cousin only smiled, unafraid. And given that the responsibility for his bloody nose could be laid at Connor's feet, along with that tooth that had been rotting out of his head an hour earlier and now seemed to have migrated to the floor, Connor refrained from further comment with his fists.

"She was daft," Connor muttered. "Me, slain? Ha!"

"She seemed in full possession of her senses. Besides, why would a McKinnon want to do you a good turn? I vow, Connor, she was in earnest."

"She was a McKinnon?" Connor exclaimed. "I *knew* it."

Then he paused. "But why would a McKinnon want to enter my hall? Surely that she did so is proof enough that she had lost all her wits."

"You're an untrusting whoreson."

"Can you fault me for it?"

Cormac sighed. "Nay, I cannot. But," he added, "I think you should consider her words. You know, she had the Sight."

Connor pursed his lips and turned away. Victoria McKinnon might have been beautiful, but she was daft, spouting all that nonsense about him being killed—

He looked back over his shoulder at his cousin. "The Sight?"

"Aye, so she claimed."

Connor turned away and reluctantly gave that some thought. His grandmother had possessed the Sight and she had certainly predicted more than one thing over the course of her life that had come to pass in its own time.

He considered what the McKinnon wench had spewed at him. His wife had indeed left him a fortnight ago, taking his bairns with him and casting in her lot with that cuckolding Frenchman, but that was common knowledge.

Connor turned and looked into the fire. It wasn't in his nature to ruminate overmuch on things he had decided he had no time for, but even so, there was something almost familiar about that wench. As if he'd dreamed of her but only just remembered that at this moment.

He frowned. He was quite certain he wasn't feuding with McKinnons at present. Then why did her name raise his hackles?

He rubbed his hands over his face vigorously. He was having a damned unpleasant se'nnight.

The door burst open. Connor looked, hoping foolishly that it might be that feisty redheaded wench come back to torment him a bit more.

Instead, it was a man, filthy and drenched, gasping for breath. He fell to his knees just inside the doorway. Connor strode over to him, but stopped a handful of paces away. He heard Victoria McKinnon's words whisper in his mind.

Beware the Frenchman. He will murder you in the clearing near the stream . . .

He considered, then shook his head with a snort. Impossible. He didn't consider himself above death, but he was well aware of his own fierceness and prowess as a scout. No one would catch him unawares.

Well, unless Victoria McKinnon was the one to murder him, but somehow he suspected she was not capable of that. Besides, what reason would she have for it? He could think of several who might want him dead, but he could not list that flame-haired wench among them.

He looked at the man kneeling on the floor in front of him. "Aye?"

"I bring you tidings of your lady, my laird," the man gasped.

The hair on the back of his neck stood up. It was as Victoria McKinnon had predicted.

Then again, perhaps she *was* in league with the Frenchman and she had known this fool would come to bring his tidings.

"What tidings?" Connor asked flatly. "That she is fled?"

"She dies, my laird. She calls for you."

"Why?" Connor asked. "That she might again remind me of my condition as cuckold?"

The man shook his head. "She bid me say she will tell you where your children lay."

Connor caught his breath. Ach, but if there was one thing that would have induced him to leave his home, 'twas that.

Beware . . .

He shrugged aside the warning. "I will come," he said shortly. "Are you alone?"

"Aye, my laird."

"Refresh yourself whilst I fetch my gear."

The man nodded, accepted drink, and was waiting when Connor came back with his sword and cloak. They walked

down the steps to the ground, where Connor found his
horse waiting for him.

"What is your name?" he asked the messenger.

"MacDuff."

"Well, then, lead on, MacDuff." Connor paused, then
frowned. By the saints, was he losing his mind? Lay on?
Lead on? The words swirled in his head. He had a vague
memory of having a ferocious fight with someone over
which it was.

He'd fought with that red-haired wench. He was almost
certain of it.

But how was that possible? He'd just clapped eyes on
her but an hour ago. Was he having a vision of something
else?

By the saints, was his *grandmère*'s Sight coming home
to roost in him?

He put his hands to his head and held it for a moment
until the fog receded. Obviously, breakfast's vile smell
should have signed that something was amiss with it. Next
time, he wouldn't ignore his nose in favor of his belly.

He vaulted up into the saddle.

"Let us be off," he said curtly. "MacDuff."

The man took the lead and they set off. They hadn't left
the castle behind before it began to rain. Connor cursed.
The day was doomed.

He paused. Doomed?

The hair on the back of his neck rose in direct propor-
tion to how far away from his keep he rode. The man in
front of him looked back now and again, as if he made certain Connor was still there.

"I'm not going anywhere," Connor barked.

The man jumped as if he'd been pricked with a dirk. He
nodded nervously and continued on.

Beware the clearing. The Frenchman will attack you . . .

He watched his surroundings with a piercing eye, all his
senses on alert. His horse was skittish. Connor cursed.
Damned beast. He would have been better served to have
purchased that ugly thing that had greeted him pleasantly

rather than this prancing ninny who had blinded him with his beauty.

"Just up ahead," the messenger said, plunging into the trees. "There is a clearing up ahead. She awaits us there."

Connor caught his breath. The glade? Would his death await him there?

He rode slowly, fighting his horse and his suspicions both. He saw the clearing up ahead. The messenger slowed down and looked back over his shoulder as if he feared Connor would not come along.

Connor hesitated at the edge of the forest. He saw nothing.

But that made him no less suspicious.

The arrow will come at you from the east. Your horse will crush you beneath it and then the Frenchman will come and finish you. He will tell you as your die that your bairns and your wife died of the ague because he dragged them through the wet for days on end . . .

There was no reason to believe that would happen. There was also no reason to believe it wouldn't.

Connor rode out into the glade.

The sound of an arrow leaving a bow came from his left.

His horse reared. Slipped. Went down.

Connor's feet were out of the stirrups already, though, as he had been anticipating the like. He went down with the horse, but instead of being crushed beneath it, he dropped to a crouch beside it. He quickly flattened himself on his back and waited.

And the Frenchman came, just as Victoria had predicted.

Was she a witch, then, or in league with this devil? Or did she indeed possess the Sight?

Connor feigned groans of anguish.

"I see you are almost finished," the Frenchman said with a smile. "I will help you along, *mon ami*, but first let me tell you a small tale that will interest you greatly."

"Will it?" Connor groaned. "More than the stealing of my children and bedding of my wife?"

"Your children died of the ague," the Frenchman said

with a negligent shrug. "I did not want them, anyway, so it grieved me naught. But your lady is dead as well. A pity. She was, how do you say it, quite spirited in bed—"

And then he began to gurgle. Connor drove his sword harder into the man's belly and twisted. The man gasped in agony, then slowly and satisfactorily died a most uncomfortable death. Connor shoved him over, then stood, wrenching his sword from the man's belly.

"For my children," he said bitterly. "Braw Donaldbain and bonny Heather. Perhaps now you will join their dam in hell."

The Frenchman wheezed out one last breath and died.

Connor looked at his horse, which was thrashing about. Broken leg, the damned beast. Connor did what was necessary, then looked about for the messenger. He saw the flash of clothes in the forest. He threw his sword with all his strength. There was a cry, then nothing. Connor strode into the forest and found the man who was now carrying it in his back. He wrenched it out and rolled the messenger over.

"Where are my bairns?" he asked coldly.

"Never—"

"Tell me!" Connor roared.

"Day's ride east," the messenger wheezed. "Abandoned crofter's . . ."

He said no more. Connor cleaned his sword and stood. Then he turned and walked away, wondering what he was to do now. His wife and children were dead. His enemy was dead. He paused in the middle of the glade and looked at the scene of death.

It could have been him there, lying with his life ebbed from him, his eyes staring unseeing at the sky. And it would have been, if not for Victoria McKinnon.

There is a fairy ring through the forest, over the hill and down into a glade. It is a gate to the Future . . .

The Future? What, by all the saints, did that mean? The Future was ever before him and he needed no gate to get there. It would arrive as surely as the sunrise without him doing aught to invite it.

But the fairy ring was another thing entirely. He knew where it was. Indeed, he'd even had a look at it once or twice, but that had been years ago when he'd been young and willing to be afrighted by tales of ghosties and boggles and other otherworldly creatures who were rumored to haunt the place. But to give it serious thought now?

Ridiculous.

As if in agreement, rain began to fall. He shook aside his unproductive ruminations and strode back through the forest. By the time he reached his hall, the rain had plastered his hair to his head and his plaid bore a fine sheen of drizzle. He shook himself off like a hound and walked inside his keep.

There was nothing out of the ordinary therein. Cormac stood by the fire, listening to one of their more witless clansmen spewing out some sort of problem that required all the laird's time and attention. Connor would have tossed the fool out his door.

But Cormac listened gravely, then gave the man a small list of things he should do to see the problem solved by himself, then yet another list of things Cormac would do for him after those had been done.

Connor considered. That was well done, to be sure. Indeed, the crofter had certainly fared better with Cormac than he would have if Connor himself had listened to his sorry tale.

The fairy ring . . .

Connor wondered if he could drown out Victoria McKinnon's words with vast quantities of ale. It was tempting to try, but he had other things to see to before he indulged in that. Besides, he wasn't one to blot out his troubles with strong drink. Better to face them with his sword drawn and ready. The thing to do now was find his bairns and bury them properly. He would give thought to the rest of his future after that was done.

A future that he had thanks to Victoria McKinnon.

"Connor?"

Connor blinked and looked at his cousin. "Aye?"

"You've returned. I didn't expect you back for days. Ho, Angus, go see to the laird's horse—"

"My horse is slain," Connor said briskly. "My gear could be fetched, though. There are two dead assassins there, as well. They can rot in the rain, for all I care."

Cormac's eyes bulged. "The McKinnon wench was right?"

"Aye."

"Then the bairns are—"

"Dead."

Cormac closed his eyes briefly, then looked at his cousin. "What will you do now?"

"I must bury my children."

"That is as it should be." Cormac paused. "And while you're gone?"

"You will see to the keep and the clan."

"But what of Robert and Gordon—"

"My brothers are fools. I'll see that our people know to follow you." He cursed. "Damn that useless horse. If it hadn't broken its leg—"

"Take mine."

Connor sigh. "I'll pay you for him."

Cormac smiled. "Connor, there is no need. You have been brother and father both to me all these years. 'Tis but a small thing in return."

Connor was not given to displays of affection, but he thought a hand placed briefly on his cousin's shoulder was not inappropriate, given the seriousness of the moment.

"My gratitude," he said. "I will fetch supplies and be on my way."

"So soon?"

Connor looked for a way to explain how uncomfortable he suddenly felt walking about his hall when he should have been dead. It was not at all the same feeling he'd had countless other times when he'd cheated death thanks to his prowess. In this case, he had the very cold, unyielding suspicion that he would have met his end, were it not for

Victoria McKinnon seeking him out and delivering a warning to him.

Why had she?

I came because I know what will happen . . .

He considered that for several minutes. She had come because she knew what would happen? Why had she cared? What had she hoped to gain? What if she had come not expecting anything at all?

He could scarce fathom that. But all things seemed to point to it.

"Connor?"

Connor looked at his cousin. "I need to go. Today."

"Of course."

Connor left his cousin standing there watching him and went to fetch himself some food for his journey.

It took him a handful of hours to prepare, which did not please him. His supplies were gathered quickly, but 'twas the business of the clan that delayed him. In the end, he had to draw his sword to cow his brothers into obedience, and he suspected it would last no longer than the time it took for him to ride out of sight, but that would not be his affair then. Cormac could keep them in check until he returned.

If he returned.

He stopped still as he was preparing to swing himself up onto his cousin's horse. Not return? Where had that daft idea come from?

Connor, your path will lead you where no other MacDougal has ever set foot . . .

His grandmother's parting words came back to him forcefully, though not unexpectedly. He tended to think on them before each setting out, especially if he was off on a long journey. He'd always assumed that she meant he would be the first to rout out that pesky group of Gordons to the west, but now he began to think differently.

Had she suspected he might travel to the Future?

Could he travel to the Future?

"Connor, are you unwell?"

Connor looked at Cormac and felt as if he'd never seen him before. Or perhaps it wasn't that; it was that he might never see him again.

" 'Tis Victoria McKinnon," Connor managed. "Her daft words have affected me adversely."

"Have a good long ride," Cormac advised. "Perhaps some cattle-raiding on your way home." He rubbed his arms for emphasis. "A hard winter's coming."

Connor almost smiled. It wasn't his habit to smile, but his cousin almost inspired it in him now and again. He swung up into the saddle feeling quite a bit more himself.

"Until we meet again," he said, then wondered where those words had come from. His usual sentiment at parting was a grunt and a nod.

Cormac looked equally shocked. He nodded, wide-eyed.

Connor rode off before he did anything else unsettling, such as burst into tears.

His first destination was the last croft he knew had sheltered the fugitives. The Frenchman had threatened the poor couple with death if they made known anything about their unwelcome guests, but Connor's former minstrel obviously had no concept of clan loyalty. Connor had received the message not an hour after his wife and her lover had taken his bairns farther away.

He should have ridden off after them then, but he had foolishly assumed Morag would see the error she had made and return with all haste. That, and the fact that Campbells had attacked that eve from the west, had taken too much of his time.

He would have to live with that misjudgment for the rest of his life.

He sighed deeply. He would find his children and bury them. And then perhaps he would seek out that ring in the grass and see where it took him. Perhaps it would take him off to Titania's lair, where she would force him to be her lover for centuries. He supposed a body might be subjected to worse fates.

Aye, he would try that haunted bit of ground and see

what happened to him. If he was carried off to the Fairy realm, he would survive it. If he was carried off to the Future, he would find Victoria McKinnon, offer his thanks, and return home as quickly as he could.

And if none of it worked as promised, he would take a day or two and go fishing.

At least he would have a full belly when he went home.

Chapter 29

Victoria stood on the stage and wondered if she would ever be able to look at any part of Thomas's castle again without weeping. She folded her arms over herself and looked heavenward. She wept anyway, no matter how she tried to thwart gravity and her own broken heart.

Time-traveling did that to a person.

She was really going to have to give it up someday.

She walked the boards, from one end of the stage to the other. There was no scenery left. That had long since been put into storage for use in some other production. Lights and sound had also been put into storage for use in some other production.

She wondered if she would ever be able to stage another production.

She stopped in the middle of the stage and frowned as she looked around her. Not only was all the stage paraphernalia gone, the ghosts were gone, as well. She'd been back almost a week and nary a sight of a single one. She suspected the Boar's Head Trio had decamped for France, leaving her time to deal with her grief on her own.

She hoped they were planning on staying a good, long time.

Connor was probably giving ghostly thought to what a jerk he'd been during her visit to the past and was wisely giving her time to cool off before he showed his face again.

She couldn't blame him.

Though she would be the first to admit that she hadn't been angry at that point. She hadn't even cried—not at first. She'd stumbled out of the fairy ring one afternoon a week ago and somehow managed to make her way back to the inn. Thomas had been standing at the end of the driveway, as if he expected to see her. He'd made her eat, then put her to bed without asking any questions.

She'd needed to tell Iolanthe that her husband wasn't such a bad nursemaid after all.

Fortunately for her, the rest of her family had left for London before she'd even attempted her trip to the past, so she'd had no questions to answer upon her return. Thomas, she supposed, had just assumed that since she hadn't returned with Connor, she hadn't been successful.

"I warned him," she said at supper, five days later.

Thomas had looked at her for several moments in silence, then picked up his fork and dug into Mrs. Pruitt's meat pie. "You couldn't do more than that."

She hadn't talked to either Thomas or Iolanthe much since then. They had departed the day before for another visit to Artane. Perhaps they had grown tired of her silence.

She hadn't minded. She'd spent most of her days up at the castle, sitting on the stage, wondering what she would now do with the rest of her life. Wondering if she would ever see Connor again.

Wondering if she wanted to.

She sighed. She supposed Thomas had called Jamie to let him know that things hadn't gone as planned. Would Jamie mind if she came up and camped with them for a few days? She felt a longing well up in her to stay again at

Ian's, enclosed in that family circle, listening to Ian and Jane's children wreak havoc and fight over Legos.

Maybe she would go. After all, what else did she have to do? Remain at Thorpewold and just soldier on? Fly back to Manhattan and try to pick up the pieces of her shattered life? Find a new venue for her company? Spend more time flattering big bucks, soliciting sponsors, begging for funds?

After she'd seen Connor MacDougal in the flesh?

After she'd tasted the heady intoxication of becoming Shakespeare's words on stage?

She couldn't. She couldn't go back. She could only go forward, only she had no idea where *forward* would lead. But she suspected it wouldn't lead to another stint as director of her own troupe.

She began to walk around in a circle, slowly, with her eyes open and watching the floorboards. She walked faster, then faster still, until she was running.

And then she closed her eyes.

She didn't care if she fell. Maybe she would fall forever and find herself back in medieval Scotland, where she could have all the time in the world to persuade a certain laird that she was desperately in love with him and if he could just remember the future, he would find he felt the same.

She suddenly felt nothing under her feet, just as she had twelve years earlier when the circle of actors had broken and she'd had no one to keep her from falling into the orchestra pit.

"By the saints, woman!"

She opened her eyes the split second before she landed.

In Connor MacDougal's arms.

In his arms.

She must have been cruising at quite a clip. He stumbled backward and landed quite firmly on his backside, still clutching her to him.

She could only stare at him, amazed beyond all reason, unable to form a coherent thought.

She supposed, absently, that she should have been

happy he hadn't broken her back with how tightly he was holding onto her.

"Are you daft?" he exclaimed.

"Ah . . ."

He pushed her away from him and crawled to his feet, where he could, apparently, more easily glare down at her.

"Where am I?" he demanded.

It might have been the strain of her rigorous training at Jamie's. It might have been that brush with death on her way to castle MacDougal in the thirteenth century. It could have been the fright she'd had when encountering Connor MacDougal on his home turf, very much alive and very much irritated by her interruption. It could have been all the sleepless nights, all the headache-inducing dreams in Gaelic, all the horrible imaginings of things to go wrong. Or it could have been that she hadn't had any breakfast and was now succumbing to a hypoglycemic episode.

Whatever the case, she did the most sensible thing she'd done in weeks.

She fainted.

And she realized, as the numbness started at the top of her head and worked its way down, that things had most definitely changed. Normally, she would have fought the feeling, fought the loss of control, fought the descent into uncertainty.

Not now.

"Bring it on, baby," she murmured happily as she plunged into oblivion.

She woke. She wasn't sure how long she'd been out. She did know, however, that Connor was leaning over her with his hand raised, as if he contemplated briskly bringing her back to her senses. That he was staring at his hand as if using it for such harsh purposes was a bad thing was a promising sign.

He looked at her and a look of relief crossed his beautiful face.

His beautiful, mortal face.

Victoria closed her eyes and tried not to weep.

"Ach, nay," he exclaimed, "do not faint again, ye weak-stomached wench!"

She opened her eyes and looked at him. "I won't faint," she said faintly.

"See that you do not," he grumbled. "I've enough to see to without fretting over you."

"Of course," she said, closing her eyes to better memorize how it felt to have his hands holding onto her arm.

"Victoria McKinnon!"

She opened her eyes immediately. "What?"

"You were going to faint yet again!"

"I wasn't. I was . . . well, never mind what I was doing." She sat up gingerly. "I'm fine."

He grunted and sat back on his heels. Victoria clenched her hands in her lap. Otherwise, she might have been tempted to reach out and touch his dirty kilt, his smudged face, his glorious hair . . .

"Where am I?" he demanded. "I've little liking for this place. I had planned on Faery, or perhaps even the Future, but this looks far too much like the Lowlands for my taste." He looked around for a moment or two, then scowled again. "I'll be going now."

She gaped at him. "Going?"

"Aye," he said shortly, rising and walking away. "I've lost my cousin Cormac's horse. I must go find it."

Victoria scrambled to her feet and stumbled after him, trying to see him through the sheets of stars flashing before her eyes. "Wait," she managed.

He turned and looked at her. "Aye?"

It was all she could do not to tackle him and keep him where he was.

Safely in the Future.

She had to close her eyes again, briefly, and get her bearings.

"Do not faint!"

She opened her eyes quickly. "I wasn't going to. Um, how would you . . . yes, how would you like some food? Before you go," she added.

He pursed his lips. "Your Gaelic is awful."

"You've said that before."

"Hmmm," he said, frowning. "At my hall. It was awful then." He paused. "It hasn't improved here. You've a Sassenach tinge to it."

"I was late in learning it."

"You're a McKinnon. You should have been speaking it from birth."

"I know. Sometimes things don't go as you plan."

He grunted. "Indeed, that is truth." He looked at her. "Your parents taught you ill, then."

No, you can blame James MacLeod, she thought sourly. Well, she probably couldn't in good conscience blame Jamie. He had done his best. *She* had done her best. That she could understand half of what Connor was saying and manage to make herself partway understood after little more than a couple of months spent at the task was nothing short of a miracle.

He looked around him. "Where am I? Where is here?" he asked. "Heaven?"

"Not even close."

"Faery?"

"Not there, either."

"Damnation."

She smiled, trying to make it an unassuming and friendly smile. "I'm thinking you must be hungry."

He looked at her for a moment, then nodded. "Aye, I am. Is your hall nearby, or is this crumbling wreck all you have?"

"This is my brother's hall," she said. "There is an inn down the road."

"To the inn, then," he instructed. "But make haste. I want to be home before the sun sets. This is not at all what I had expected when I stepped into the fairy ring near my home."

"I'll just bet," she muttered under her breath.

Connor set off. It was all she could do not to take his hand. It was even harder not to cry. Ambrose had warned her. Thomas had warned her. Hell, even Iolanthe had warned her.

He won't remember you, they had said as she went through MacLeod boot camp. *He won't remember you at first. Give him time. Don't pressure him.*

"Don't bean him over the head with a rock to bring sense back," she grumbled.

"Eh?" Connor said, frowning down at her.

"Nothing," she said, smiling in her most undemanding manner. She pointed down the path toward the road. "Food is that way."

He grunted and walked with her.

And he hummed depressing battle dirges as he went.

She almost wept.

They reached the inn soon enough, mostly because Connor was using his long legs to their best advantage. Victoria gasped for breath as he came to a sudden halt. Good grief, she'd been through Jamie and Ian's training course, managed to survive medieval Scotland and get home again, yet a little run from the castle was leaving her in this kind of shape?

She supposed it might have something to do with a mild case of shock.

She took a sideways glance at Connor. He was staring at the inn with his mouth hanging open and his eyes huge in his face. He turned to her, astonished.

"This is a familiar place."

"Is it?"

His eyes narrowed. "Did you bring me here?"

"To the inn or to the Future?" she asked.

"The Future. Nay, this inn." He frowned. "Both."

"No, I didn't. You came yourself, remember?"

Blessed, wonderful, baffled man.

He gestured imperiously. "I've dreamed this."

"Do you dream often?"

He corrected her Gaelic automatically, then gestured to the path. "Aye, I do, but we won't speak of that." He drew his sword with a soft hiss. "You go first. I will follow."

"Do not stab me," she instructed firmly. That, at least, was one phrase she had practiced to perfection.

His frown lightened just the slightest bit. "I will not. I might need you to ransom to the fairies to let me go home."

"We're not in Faery."

"So you say, but I have my doubts." He looked at her. "Aye, I think I am beginning to rethink this all. Consider your beauty. You claim to be a McKinnon, but no McKinnon I've ever met could possibly have produced a wench as fetching as you. Ergo, you must be a fairy."

"Um, sure," she said, and for the first time, she wondered if this had been such a good idea.

Never mind that he'd just called her fetching enough to be a fairy.

And then he put his hand on her back and gave her just the slightest of nudges forward.

It almost brought her to her knees.

She took a deep breath and went ahead of him. She walked to the door and opened it. Then she looked over her shoulder.

"Are you coming?"

He hung back. "I do not care to admit weakness, but this place gives me pause."

"It's haunted," she said easily, "but the ghosts are away. It's just the innkeeper inside and she's a *very* good cook."

He looked at her assessingly. "You look as if you possess all your wits, yet you spout madness."

She wasn't going to touch that one with a ten-foot pole. At least not yet. "You should eat. You'll feel better after you do."

"Will it be poisoned?"

"I'll taste everything for you first."

"Sporting of you."

"I do what I can for the cause."

He lifted one eyebrow and almost smiled.

She almost wept.

But before she made a bigger fool of herself than she had already, she walked through the door. She could feel him following her. Mrs. Pruitt came out of the dining room, wiping her hands on her apron. She smiled.

"Mistress Victoria," she said. "Laird MacDougal."

"Does she ken me?" he exclaimed. "How comes this wonder?"

Mrs. Pruitt frowned. "I'm well acquainted with all the inhabitants hereabouts, be they corporeal or not—"

"Mrs. Pruitt," Victoria interrupted politely, "is there anything to eat? We're a little on the hungry side."

Mrs. Pruitt frowned, then shrugged. "Of course, lass. Come on, and I'll make ye something."

Victoria nodded for Connor to follow her. He hesitated. She turned to see what had stopped him. He was staring, frozen in place, at the library door. He looked at it for a brief eternity, then drew his hand over his eyes and shook his head.

"Now *I'm* going daft," he muttered.

Victoria pretended not to notice. She led him though the dining room and pulled out a chair for him in the kitchen. She sat next to him and had to clasp her hands together on the table to keep them from reaching for him.

Mrs. Pruitt whipped up eggs, fried tomatoes and potatoes, sausage, and the obligatory cold toast. It smelled heavenly. Connor's stomach growled.

"In a minute, Mistress Victoria," Mrs. Pruitt said with a brief laugh. "I'm hurrying."

Victoria cleared her throat. "Could we have two plates, Mrs. Pruitt?"

Mrs. Pruitt turned around, her spatula in hand, and frowned. "Why two?"

"One for Laird MacDougal, as well."

"What does he need with a plate? Beggin' yer pardon, my laird."

Connor's frown was equally puzzled. "How will I eat without food, good woman?"

"Well, for obvious reasons," Mrs. Pruitt said, frowning more deeply.

Victoria wanted to head off this discussion before it really picked up steam and ended up with Mrs. Pruitt poking Connor to convince him that he really wasn't corporeal. She cleared her throat. "Humor him, if you could, Mrs. Pruitt."

"Yer stint on the boards has had a deleterious effect on yer wits, lass," Mrs. Pruitt said disapprovingly, but she obligingly prepared two plates. She set the second down in front of Connor with a heavy sigh. "The things I do . . ."

Connor picked up the fork, looked at it with a frown, then shrugged and used it for its intended purpose.

Mrs. Pruitt gaped.

Connor chewed.

Mrs. Pruitt's eyes rolled back in her head and she slumped to the ground.

"What is it with you wenches here in Faery?" Connor asked through a mouthful of egg and tomato. "Fine victuals, though, even if her constitution is passing weak."

Victoria rose and went to bring Mrs. Pruitt back to her senses. The stalwart innkeeper's eyelids fluttered, then she sat up with a squeak. She peeked over the edge of the table.

"He's eating," she whispered loudly.

"That he is," Victoria agreed.

"But . . ."

"I know," Victoria said.

"Ye didn't . . ."

"That, too."

Mrs. Pruitt looked at her. "Did he come today, then?"

"Apparently."

"Is he real?"

"He's eating, isn't he?"

Mrs. Pruitt rose and gaped at Connor until he frowned so fiercely that she shut her mouth and looked at Victoria.

"I should make up the guest room, hadn't I better?"

"He wants to go home."

"Oh," Mrs. Pruitt said in a small voice.

Victoria understood completely.

"But just in case," Mrs. Pruitt offered.

"Just in case," Victoria agreed.

Mrs. Pruitt took another very long look at Connor, then left the kitchen as quickly as possible. Victoria came around and sat down next to her laird and applied herself to breakfast.

She didn't taste a thing.

Connor inhaled all of his, then looked around for more. When he saw that she wasn't eating her meal, he commandeered it.

"Anything else?" he asked, licking his fork, after polishing off what she hadn't.

"I'll see."

She raided Mrs. Pruitt's larder and began to cook. Connor consumed half a dozen more eggs, several more tomatoes, and all the rest of the sausages in the refrigerator before he sat back and belched heartily.

"You're a passing fair cook yourself," he said, dabbing the corners of his mouth with a napkin. "Passing fair."

"Thank you."

He pushed his chair back and rose. "As interesting a place as this is, I've no stomach for the rest of my days spent with fairies and their ilk. I'm not certain where you fit in, but as fetching as you are, I'm for home."

"Do you want company on your way back to the fairy ring?" she asked.

"Nay, I'll be fine." He made her a small bow, turned, and walked through the kitchen, swearing at the swinging door and cursing further as something else troubled him on the way through the dining room.

Victoria stood in the kitchen and wondered if now would be a good time to cry.

He didn't want her to follow him.

That pretty much said it all, didn't it?

He would find his way back to the fairy ring, pop back

through time to medieval Scotland, go and live out the rest of his life in an unmurdered state. He would probably marry again. He would have more children. He would raid cattle, learn more depressing battle dirges, and use the pointy end of his sword to make pincushions out of more men who displeased him.

And she would be in the future.

Very alone.

Without even his ghost to keep her company.

It was for the best, she decided briskly. Now, at least, she knew what had happened to his ghost. Since he hadn't been murdered, he had no reason to haunt the castle, and she would never see him again.

No matter, she reminded herself. She didn't really like him that much, anyway. He was loud, ill-mannered, and short-tempered.

Magnificent. Talented. Gentle.

And in love with her when he'd been a ghost.

She washed the dishes. She scrubbed the pans until they cried out for mercy. She dried everything and tried not to break it as she put it away. And then she sat at the table. Mrs. Pruitt came into the kitchen, took one look at her, and departed for safer ground. Victoria sat until it occurred to her that she could be sitting and grieving in a more comfortable chair. She got up and went into the library.

She sat in her accustomed chair, with only the light coming in from the window to keep her company until that light began to fade.

He was probably walking into his keep by now.

She was momentarily tempted to follow him, in spite of her freshly made vow not run other people's lives. But even if she hadn't been determined to live and let live, she wasn't sure she could get back to Connor's time again even if she tried. Jamie said he had never been to the same place twice. What, was she to try again and wind up twenty years from her target date? Twenty years after Connor had found someone else to marry and have kids with? Hundreds of years before he had ever met and loved her?

And what if she made it back to medieval Scotland and couldn't get back home? The fact that she'd simply traipsed there and back was something of a miracle in itself. Of course, she'd been crying so hard when she'd stumbled into the fairy ring that she wouldn't have noticed if it had dumped her into the wrong century or not.

It was over.

She'd gone, she'd seen, she'd come home empty-handed.

She wondered, absently, if there would be a lower point in her life than at that moment. She was too tired to move; too tired to weep; too tired to breathe. She sat and let the tears trickle down her cheeks because she couldn't muster up the energy to wipe them away.

It grew dark. In fact, it grew so dark that she couldn't see her hand before her face. That frightened her for some reason. She didn't want to be someone who sat in the dark and didn't care. So her life was ruined. At least she could have some light while she was examining the breadth of the destruction.

She reached over and turned on the lamp that sat on the little table next to her. She sat back with a sigh.

Then she sat bolt upright in her chair and shrieked.

Connor stood just inside the door. He was holding up his hands. "I mean you no harm."

"Oh," she said weakly, slumping back and putting her hand over her heart. Sure. That's why he was carrying that enormous sword unsheathed in his hand. "You scared me."

He blinked. "What did you say?"

She tried in Gaelic. "You frightened me." She paused. "I didn't hear you come in."

"You were weeping."

"Yes."

He looked at her, looked at the chair across from her, then looked at her again for a very, very long time. And then he closed the door behind him.

"May I?" he asked, nodding toward the chair.

It wouldn't be the first time. She smiled as unassumingly as she could. "Please."

He resheathed his sword and walked toward her, but had to stop several times, as if he couldn't believe what he was doing and had to complete a few spot checks to make sure he wasn't losing his mind. She knew this because he kept stopping, then shaking his head, then continuing on another step, only to stop and repeat the cycle.

He finally sat. He laid his sheathed sword across his knees and looked at her.

"I failed."

Thank heavens. "You failed?" she asked sympathetically.

"I tried to go home. Your fairy world won't release me."

"This isn't Faery," she said slowly.

"I wonder." He looked at her assessingly. "If I were a superstitious man, I would say you had cast a spell over me and carried me off to your world."

I would have tried that if I'd thought it would have worked. "I'm not a witch," she said. "It really is the Future."

He pursed his lips thoughtfully and looked at the light next to her. Then he looked at her. "I find it difficult to believe."

"There will probably be many things you'll find difficult to believe." She paused. "For as long as you're here."

He chewed on that one for a while. "I will go home," he said finally. "But later. For now, I will stay and see your land."

Victoria managed a nod. "If you like."

He studied her. "You saved my life. Why?"

Where to start? She considered several options for answers, then shook her head. "It is too long a tale for tonight."

He nodded. "Very well. But I will have it tomorrow." He looked around. "Your floor is very clean. If I may sleep there?" He pointed over to the door.

"You don't have to sleep on the floor," she said. "We have beds upstairs."

"I prefer to sleep by the door," he said. "Unless I will trouble you?"

Trouble her? Disturb her? Plunge a dagger into her heart and break it off so it could do the most damage?

She managed to shake her head no. "I'm going to go to the bathroom and get ready for bed. Do you want me to show you one you can use?"

"Bathroom?"

"A fancy garderobe."

"Very well. Shall I bring my sword?"

"Why not?"

She rose and walked over to the door. He followed her. Victoria knew this because she was excruciatingly aware of him but a single step behind her. And when he put his hand on her shoulder, she shivered.

"Are you unwell?" came the deep voice from behind her.

Just out of my mind to sleep with you anywhere near me. "No," she managed.

He took his hand away. "I didn't thank you."

She turned to look at him. "For what?"

He frowned. "I do not accept favors easily. But I thank you for my life." He took a step backward and made her a low bow. "I am in your debt."

"It was my pleasure," she managed. "Bathroom now?"

He straightened and looked at her for a long moment, then nodded. "Please."

She left the library in front of him and picked up her sanity right there where she'd left it in front of the buffet, the morning she'd left to go to Jamie's. Connor would stay the night, have another mighty breakfast, then be on his way. He would go back to the wilds of medieval Scotland. She would go back to the wilds of Manhattan.

Life would go on.

And at some point, she would think about living again, because it was for damned sure she wouldn't be doing much of it at first.

She sighed and led Connor down the hall to Mrs. Pruitt's extra-fancy, use-only-if-she-really-liked-you modern garderobe.

Chapter 30

Connor woke. He realized immediately that he was not on his own bed filled with crunchy straw in his own bedchamber that smelled faintly of wet dog in his own hall that smelled much worse than that. He was on a floor. He sniffed. A not-unpleasant smelling floor.

Damnation, he was still trapped in Faery!

He had assumed he would go to sleep and wake up where he was supposed to be. Apparently, his escape would take more cunning and a bit more effort than collapsing on the floor and hoping for the best.

Then again, perhaps he really wasn't in Faery, he was actually in the Future. Victoria McKinnon had said as much. He suspected she might be telling the truth. Faery had to be more, well, flowery. To be certain, there were flowers aplenty on either side of the pathway leading up to the inn, but they were flowers that looked quite ordinary. And he had seen no small sprites dancing amongst them the day before.

He was quite certain there had to be sprites in Faery.

He sat up. It was not full light yet, but there was light enough that he could see the contents of the chamber he was in. Not that he needed to see the contents. He knew what they were. How he knew that, he wasn't sure. He was, he had to admit modestly, quite a vivid dreamer. But that Victoria McKinnon should find herself in his dreams was something else indeed.

Nay, he had to admit to himself, he was not dreaming. Somehow, beyond reason, he had ventured forth into the Future.

It was sobering, indeed.

He rolled to his feet and stretched silently. Then he walked over to look down at his hostess curled up on a small cot, her riotous hair spread out behind her and her face peaceful and untroubled in sleep. By the saints, he had never before seen such a beautiful woman. Surely that had to count against her. Her beauty was put there to tempt him.

Then again, he had never once heard of a fetching witch.

He retrieved his sword, took one last look at Mistress McKinnon, and left the chamber. He found the doors strange and difficult. It would have been so much easier to have merely walked through them.

He froze. Was he losing his wits as well, then? Since when could a man walk through doors?

He shook his head and made his way down the passage-way to the garderobe. To call it that was to truly minimize its splendor. He opened the door, pushed the switch down to kindle the lights, and merely stared in fascination at the luxury that greeted his eyes.

Never mind that said luxury was displayed mostly in pink.

He looked first at the lights. He was not as troubled by them this morning as he had been the night before. Victoria had assured him they were a Future marvel and not small fairies trapped inside little glass bulbs—fairies who had displeased their queen and were paying a heavy price. He walked over to the lights and stared up at them. Nay, no creatures inside; just strings and such.

He looked at the mirror and that brought him face to face with . . . himself. He looked at his unshaven face, examined his jaw, looked deeply into his own eyes, and inspected his hair. He wondered, absently, why his late wife had found him so much less appealing than the Frenchman.

He paused and considered. The Frenchman had possessed a certain, well, *je ne sais quois*. And even Connor could admit that the Frenchman had, before his timely and well-deserved end, sported not unhandsome French features and a fine French form. Surely by now that Gallic form was beginning to rot, but perhaps that was a pleasant eventuality, to be examined at a later time.

Nay, Morag had never found him to be pleasing and he'd been a fool to wed with her. She had come unwillingly to his bed, borne him children begrudgingly, and eagerly sought any excuse to flee his arms and his keep. He was well rid of her.

His bairns were another tale entirely.

But as the very thought of them made his eyes look suspiciously moist, he turned his attentions to something else. He took his knife and shaved, feeling a bit more in control of his emotions by the time he finished. He explored the marvels of the sink, but stopped short of taking it apart. He'd done that to the shower the night before and found himself facing a very annoyed yet still slack-jawed Mrs. Pruitt, whom he had apparently awoken with his cursing.

Today, he knew better. He purloined a pink towel of uncommon softness, stripped, and stepped into a shower made for a man much smaller than he. But it was a miracle of cleanliness and he indulged in it happily.

Mrs. Pruitt had been willing to explain many things during the middle of the night when sleep had eluded him and he'd been itching to explore the garderobe. She'd shown him how the shower worked, explained again what did and did not go down the toilet—but in less patient tones than Victoria had used, to be sure. She had left him with a selection of things in bottles that smelled and bid him briskly to keep his cursing to a minimum before she had retreated to her quarters and left him to his experiments.

He dried himself off and looked at his clothes. Well, those could do with a bit of a wash. He picked them up with one hand, took his towel in the other, and left the bathroom in search of a washerwoman.

He strode out into the entryway. A man and a woman stood there, corralling a handful of small lassies. The woman took a single look at him and shrieked.

Connor shrieked as well, then gasped that such an unmanly sound of surprise should come from him.

"Laird MacDougal!" Mrs. Pruitt exclaimed.

He turned to look at her. "Aye?"

More shrieks ensued from behind him.

Mrs. Pruitt gestured impatiently to his nether regions. "Cover yerself, if ye please!"

Lowlander Gaelic, he thought with a patient sigh. But he did as she bid, realizing that he should have thought of it himself. He handed his clothes to her.

"Wash these," he instructed.

And with that, he turned about and nodded to the inn's new guests, who were gaping at him with truly unwarranted consternation.

"My apologies," he said politely. "I'm new here in the Future."

They looked at him blankly, as if they couldn't understand a word he said. He looked at the little girls, three of them, who were standing all in a row. The smallest one smiled.

Well, those certainly didn't look like Faery children. Perhaps Victoria was telling him the truth. Stranger things had no doubt happened than for a man to find himself in the Future.

No matter. He would be home soon enough. Yet, for now, he couldn't deny that he was intrigued by the chance to do a bit more exploring.

He knocked before he entered the library. Victoria wasn't there. He felt his heart lurch, but he quickly remedied that. By the saints, it wasn't as if he cared about the wench . . .

A vision of her washed over him: Victoria with her hair

undone, sitting in that chair before a fire, looking at him with tears in her eyes and pleading with him to . . . to . . .

"Oh, I'm sorry."

Connor turned around and saw her standing at the door. He realized then that he was halfway across the room. He managed a formal nod.

"The fault is mine," he said. "I was . . . I seem to be having these, well, waking dreams." He paused and looked at her. "I've no other way to describe it."

"Waking dreams," she repeated. "How interesting."

He frowned. "Do you think me daft?"

"No," she said. "But you do need some clothes."

He looked down at his pink towel, then back up at her. "I frightened the guests."

"Were you wearing the towel?"

"Not at first."

She laughed.

And Connor was tempted to find somewhere he could sit.

By the saints, the wench was breathtaking. He felt his way down into his chair before the hearth and looked at her. Her hair was loose. She was wearing those strange blue trews he had seen her in . . .

In his dreams.

He shook his head sharply, but the image did not cease to place itself upon her person. He blinked a time or two, then surrendered. If his poor fogged brain wished to believe that he had dreamed her, he would not fight it.

Blue trews and a white tunic with buttons down the front. Ah, buttons. He'd heard tell of them. He would have to examine them later, when he thought he could get close enough to look without hauling her into his arms and kissing her senseless.

He felt his jaw slide down. By the saints, where had that come from?

"Laird MacDougal?" she asked. "Are you unwell?"

"Connor," he said, hearing the name come out of his mouth and no longer wondering why it was he had no control over his life. He never allowed anyone to use his given name. It had taken him years to unbend enough to let his wife use it.

He had been, he supposed thoughtfully, a bit of a bastard now and then.

"Connor," she said slowly. "May I call you that?"

"May I call you Victoria?"

She smiled again and it smote him to the heart. "I would like that."

"As would I." He felt his head for fever. None. Perhaps the shower had been too much for him. He would settle for a bath the next time and use fewer of those soaps that smelled of fruit.

"My brother probably has clothes upstairs. Do you want to come look?"

"Of course."

"They might be too small, but we can try."

"As you will. Anything will improve upon this pink wrap."

"I doubt that," she said with another smile, but led him to the door just the same.

And so he found himself following Mistress Victoria McKinnon up the stairs and down the passageway to a very, very fine chamber filled with furniture the likes of which he had never before seen. It belonged in a palace with a king placing his royal arse upon it.

He put his own less-than-royal behind on the bed and bounced a time or two just because, apparently, he was allowed to.

Victoria laughed at him again.

He thought there might be quite a few things he would do to hear that laugh.

"Fancy, isn't it?" she asked, stroking one of the bedposts.

"Aye, very."

"It's sixteenth century."

He blinked. "I beg your pardon?"

"Made during the time when Elizabeth Tudor was queen." She looked at him. "Four hundred years ago." She paused. "She had no children so James the Sixth of Scotland became both James of Scotland and England."

He listened and wished desperately for a drink. A strong one. "'Tis good that a Scot sat on the English throne," he managed.

"There is a great deal of history you might find interesting."

"History?"

"Things that have happened from the time you were laird until, well, the present day. But clothes first." She turned and rummaged about in an armoire. She came up with some clothes and handed them to him. "Here. I think you can figure it out."

Figure it out was beyond his experience, but he gathered the gist of it. He looked at the clothes in his hands. Blue trews, the same as Victoria wore . . .

Ah, buttons! Connor looked at the ones on the shirt with pleasure. He experimented with them for several minutes, then looked up to thank Victoria, but she was gone and the door was closed. Connor put the shirt and the long-legged trews aside, then stared at what was left.

Undergarments, he supposed. He put the things on his feet and drew up the short trews where he supposed they should go. Next came the long-legged . . . He paused and stared off into space.

Jeans.

The word came to him out of that same place from where his dreams were wont to ooze. He shrugged. Jeans they would be. He pulled them up, fastened the buttons as if he'd been doing the like his whole life, then applied himself to the shirt. It was bested in the same quick fashion. Then he sought out a polished glass.

He frowned. The shirt did not reach where he supposed it should on his wrists, and strained across his chest. The jeans came above his ankles, which did not trouble him, but they were passing tight and he wondered if he might actually be able to sit without damaging important parts of himself.

Well, he would stand until his own clothing was clean. Satisfied that he would not terrify the locals, he opened the door and stepped into the passageway.

And he stopped still.

Victoria stood there, several paces away, leaning back against the wall, her head bowed, her hair swept over her shoulder and cascading before her face. She lifted her head and turned to look at him.

He staggered. Damned uneven doorways. Who had built the bloody inn so poorly?

She was staring at him as if she'd never seen a man before. He scowled.

"Have I dressed myself amiss?"

She shook her head silently, still staring at him in shock. Or perhaps it wasn't shock.

Lust? Lust was not undesirable. Admiration? Not as complimentary as lust, but it would do in a pinch.

She quickly whipped her hair back into some kind of horse's tail and looked at him with a decidedly pleasant look.

He frowned. What was she hiding?

"Breakfast?"

"What do you conceal?" he demanded.

She blinked. "Conceal?"

"Hide, woman. You hide your thoughts. I demand you cease with that and tell me honestly what you think."

"Oh," she said, but she made little sound doing it. She smiled uneasily. "I was just thinking that it is a pity you have to return home so soon."

"Because I have dressed in your Future clothes?"

She seemed to give that some thought, then shook her head. "I will miss seeing my time through your eyes," she said finally.

"Your eyes are leaking."

"Allergies."

"Allergies?"

"Flowers make me sneeze."

"Well, then do not sniff any more of them." That problem solved, he took the opportunity to gesture toward the stairs. "Breakfast, if you please. Then we will take the day and investigate your wonders. I'll need to go home tonight."

"Of course."

"I want my other clothes as soon as may be. These are a little small."

"My brother isn't as tall as you are. But since your other choice was something of mine, I thought these would do."

"They are a great improvement on the pink towel—which I left upon the bed." He fetched it, then returned to Victoria. "Food?"

"Always."

He followed her down to the kitchen, handed Mrs. Pruitt the towel, and sat down to a hearty meal. He enjoyed it as much as he had the day before. Victoria ate today and only sniffed suspiciously in his direction once.

He made a solemn vow: No more fruity soaps.

Once he was finished, he sat back and looked at Victoria. "I wish to see the castle."

"Of course."

But as he followed her out from the inn, he wondered why she was being so accommodating. He remembered her as being quite a bit more stubborn.

The thought caught him halfway down the path to the road. He stopped, shook his head, and looked at Victoria.

"I fear if I stay here overlong, I will lose my wits."

"Go when you need to," she said quietly.

"But you'll remain with me until that time?"

"If you wish it."

"I wish it."

He found himself with his arm quite suddenly outstretched and bent, in the attitude of escorting a fine lady at an even finer occasion. He gaped at his arm, wondering how it was that even his limbs seemed to now be acting independently of his will and his better sense.

By the saints, he was on the verge of madness.

The saints preserve him if there was no point in trying to rein in any part of his traitorous form. The next thing he knew, his tongue would be spouting flowery compliments to her goodness and singing lays to her beauty.

She put her hand on his arm. He caught his breath.

In a manly fashion, of course.

She looked up at him. Tears were standing in her eyes. He winced.

"By the saints, Victoria McKinnon," he said, shaking his head, "if it pains you to touch me, you may decline my offer."

"It doesn't pain me."

He grunted. "Then cease with that weeping. I vow you'll have me unsure of my own appeal soon, and then the angels will be weeping with you."

She smiled up at him. "I'll try to stop."

He nodded and walked with her down the path. They came to the road and turned to go up to the castle. He realized as he was walking along that road that it felt as if he had done it hundreds of times. That wasn't possible, so he began to look for other explanations. Bad food? Poison? Too little sleep?

Future magic?

By the time he reached the castle gates, he found that he was having trouble breathing.

"Connor, are you all right?"

He looked at Victoria. She was swimming before his eyes, and he realized with horror that he was on the verge of swooning like a weak-kneed woman.

"Come with me," Victoria commanded. "Connor!"

He snapped to himself and obeyed out of habit. He forced himself to keep up with her as she marched across the inner bailey. He plopped gratefully down onto a stone bench, then leaned his head back against the castle wall.

But when he opened his eyes, it was no better. He could have sworn he saw men gathered in front of him, peering at him with their mouths all agape.

"By the saints!" he thundered. "Begone with you all!"

The lads scattered. Most of them scattered into thin air. Connor stared at a lone straggler, who looked at him, crossed himself, then disappeared. Connor turned to look at Victoria. She was watching him with worry in her eyes.

"What spell is this?" he asked hoarsely. "What devilish work is this I see before me?"

"The stage?"

"Do not jest," he said roughly. He pointed to where he'd seen the men. Highlanders they had been, for the most part. He was almost certain he recognized Morag's brother amongst them. "Those men. Who were they?"

Victoria took a deep breath. "Ghosts."

"Ghosts," he repeated. He looked at her, then found that his fine form had not deserted him after all. He gave vent to a mighty snort of derision. "I do not believe in ghosts."

She looked at him in surprise, then smiled wryly. "I didn't, either. Before."

"Do you now?"

She shrugged. "We're in Scotland."

"The Lowlands," he reminded her.

"Well, it's still Scotland and Scotland is a magical place." She tilted her head to look at him. "Remember the fairy ring?"

He pursed his lips. "Aye, there is that."

"I don't think that's the only gate between the Past and the Future here in Scotland."

"Don't you?"

She shook her head slowly. "I don't believe easily in things I can't see," she said. "But I've seen those ghosts before. And I told you the inn is haunted, didn't I?"

"I haven't seen any ghosts there," he blustered.

"I think they're on holiday."

"Foolishness."

"Whatever you say," she said with a smile.

He studied her for a moment. "Your Gaelic has improved."

"I was nervous there at your hall." She shrugged and looked down at her feet.

"Why did you bother?"

"So I could warn you."

"Indeed?" He looked at her in surprise. "No other reason?"

"No other reason."

He pondered that for a moment or two, then rose and made her a low bow. "Then I thank you, Victoria McKinnon, for my life. Now, let us be away from here. This quarterdeck here makes me uneasy. It tugs at me in a way I do not care for."

"Then what about supper?"

"A wonderful idea," he agreed. Then he paused. "Is it too soon?"

"It's never too soon for a meal. Especially when you compliment Mrs. Pruitt on her cooking."

"Then I will endeavor to dredge up a nice word or two." He offered her his arm again, but this time it did not feel strange. Indeed, it seemed as if it was something he had wanted to do for a very long time. He looked at her.

"I will go home," he said, realizing that he sounded a bit desperate. "Soon."

"I know," she said softly.

"I think I will be sorry not to see you anymore."

She looked up at him. He frowned.

"You're weeping again."

"Allergies."

"Hmmm," he said, nodding. He walked with her away from the castle, not giving in to the impulse to look back and see if he could see the ghosts again. The path to the inn was shorter this time and he knew what to expect when he got there.

Except there was a shiny box with wheels sitting before the inn now. Perhaps it had been there the last time and he hadn't noticed it. He was halfway up the path when the door to the inn opened and a dark-haired man stepped out. Connor came to a standstill so quickly that he almost jerked Victoria off her feet. He reached out to steady her, then realized he had forgotten his sword.

By the saints, if that wasn't indication of his pitiful state, he didn't know what would be.

"Fetch me my sword," he hissed. "Go 'round to the kitchen. I'll distract this one with my bare hands."

"Connor—"

"Go!"

She sighed and went.

"Run!" he bellowed.

She ran, but without enthusiasm. Connor stood there tapping his foot, swearing, and wondering if he should just do in the man facing him with the knife in his boot. It took far too long, but finally Victoria came back out the front door, damn her for a silly wench, and brushed past the man, who stood there with his arms folded, watching Connor with no expression on his face. Victoria handed him his sword.

"There. Now what?"

Connor shrugged. "I know not. I feel this overwhelming desire to kill that man."

"You're wearing his clothes."

"They're too small. That must be part of it."

"That's my brother, Thomas."

"That could be adding to it."

Her brother, Thomas, pushed away from the door. "Vic, get my sword, will you?" he said in a friendly voice. "It's propped up against the reception desk. I just had the feeling I might need it."

"Are you out of your mind?" she demanded, turning to look at him.

Connor admired the way she put her hands on her hips and bellowed. She was a formidable wench. But now she was standing in the way of his swordplay, so he nudged her forward with a gentle push.

"Fetch his sword. Let us see if it is sharp."

She looked at him, looked back at her brother, then threw up her hands and went into the house.

Connor grinned.

The other man grinned in return.

Connor reconsidered. Maybe his time in the Future would be more worthwhile and exciting than he dared hope. Victoria McKinnon and her beauty, Thomas McKinnon and his sword. Connor flexed his fingers and chortled happily. If nothing else, he would have a pleasant afternoon.

He would think about returning home later.

Chapter 31

Victoria spotted Thomas's sword leaning against Mrs. Pruitt's reception desk. She picked it up and admired it. It looked to have seen a bit of action, probably when he'd gone back to rescue Iolanthe. She should have grilled him more about his escapades in the past while she'd had the chance at Camp Medieval. Unfortunately, she'd been too busy trying to develop her own skill set so that she didn't get her throat slit ten minutes into the Past to ask him too many questions about the mileage on his blade. She would take him to task later—maybe after Connor went back home and she was wallowing in despair. It would take her mind off her misery.

She marched out the front door and threw her brother's sword at him, hoping it would plunk him between the eyes and knock him out, thereby avoiding what she was certain would be a bloodbath.

She retreated to the safety of a side path to watch. She wasn't sure what she worried about more—that Thomas would kill Connor or that Connor would kill Thomas. She was pretty sure she knew what Connor was capable of.

Of course, she'd also watched her brother train with Jamie, Patrick, and Ian, and noticed impassively that he wasn't far behind any of them in skill. Well, except Jamie. Jamie lacked nothing and augmented his skill with sheer presence.

Sort of like Connor.

She came to the conclusion that the battle due to begin any moment might just be a draw.

They crossed swords. There was a shriek from one of the upper windows. Their blows rang out again.

"By the saints, will ye move yerself?" a weak, feminine voice demanded crossly.

"Oh, sorry, love," Thomas said, standing aside so Iolanthe could come outside. "The best seats are over there."

Iolanthe had brought a little folding camp stool, which she immediately made use of behind a clutch of lavender. Then she put her hand over her nose.

"Och, the smell," she moaned.

"Maybe you should go back inside," Victoria suggested.

"And miss this? I'll puke my guts out into the delphiniums, thank ye just the same, just for the pleasure."

Victoria laughed, then she caught wind of what the combatants were saying and stopped laughing abruptly.

"I feel I have much to repay you for," Connor said, pausing to scratch his head. "But damn me if I can remember what."

"Do you want to know?" Thomas asked.

Victoria pursed her lips. His Gaelic was very good. Perhaps that came from living with a medieval Scot. It could also have come from his time-traveling. Or it might have had something to do with hanging out with medieval ghosts. Good heavens, they were popping up like mushrooms. She wondered if the Inland Revenue would have to develop a new department soon just to track down those pesky time-travelers. Would a former ghost have the same status?

Then she found she had no more time for thinking of implausible scenarios, because the battle raging through Mrs. Pruitt's garden demanded her full attention. Apparently, it demanded Mrs. Pruitt's attention, as well.

"Me petunias!" the innkeeper bellowed from the door. "Me violas! Damn ye both to hell, be off to trample some other garden!"

Both men looked at her, made profuse apologies, and then walked off down the path, chatting companionably.

"Come on," Victoria said, pulling Iolanthe's seat from underneath her. "Let's go. We can't miss this."

Iolanthe groaned and stumbled after her stool.

Victoria set Iolanthe up in the car park and stood next to her as the men fought. Nothing much was sacred, including a black Sterling that soon acquired dusty footprints as it was used for a launching pad.

More shrieks, of the male kind, ensued from the inn for that outrage.

"I've wanted to kill you for quite some time," Connor said, his chest heaving. "The opportunity to do so is very pleasing, even if I can't remember what you've done." He paused. "I don't suppose you have any idea."

"You didn't like me changing the castle up the way," Thomas said pleasantly.

"Why would I have cared?"

"Thomas . . ." Victoria warned.

Connor pointed briefly at Iolanthe with his sword before he used it for more immediate business. "You know, I've a wealth of irritation for that wench there, as well. I wonder why."

"You can ask her later, but be careful. She's my wife."

"Your wife. She wasn't always your wife, though, was she?" Connor paused in midswing and looked at Thomas. "I knew her before you wed her, didn't I?"

Thomas nodded seriously. "You did."

"But 'tis impossible. I just arrived in the Future yester-morn."

"Iolanthe lived in the castle up the way for quite some time," Thomas said carefully.

"Thomas," Victoria warned, more loudly this time.

Connor stared off into the distance for a moment or two, then looked at Thomas. "How can I know these things?"

"It's a bit of a tale."

"Tell me."

"Here?"

"Here."

"Thomas!" Victoria exclaimed.

Thomas ignored her. Connor was ignoring her, as well. She was tempted to take both their swords away and clout them over the head with them. Thomas went to lean against the hood of the Sterling, propping his sword up against his hip. Connor did the same.

Protests ensued from inside the inn, but the two men ignored those as well.

"Would you rather sit down?" Thomas asked politely.

"Will I wish to at some future point?"

"Probably."

Connor waved the idea away. "I'll content myself with this beast, for now. If I find myself truly irritated, I'll move on with trying to kill you again. You may proceed."

"Well, this is the story." Thomas smiled easily. "I bought Thorpewold castle a few years ago. I came over last summer to repair it, but found out that it was haunted."

Connor's eyes widened. "Then you saw them, too? The men up the way?"

"Yes."

"Just those lads?"

"No."

Connor paused. "Who else, then?"

"Two others."

Connor became very still. Victoria watched him clutch his sword. His knuckles were white.

"Two others?" he asked carefully. "Who?"

Thomas nodded toward Iolanthe. "That lovely woman there."

"But she is a spirit no longer."

"No, she isn't, is she?"

Connor seemed to digest that for quite some time. Then he took a deep breath. "The other shade? Who was it?"

Thomas looked at Connor. Victoria wondered if she

would ever forget the moment, frozen in time, when her brother looked at her love and said the one word that would change everything.

"You," he said finally.

Connor looked at him in shock. Then he looked at Victoria. He looked at Iolanthe. Then he looked at Thomas again, in horror this time.

Victoria would have said something, but the warning look on Thomas's face stopped her.

Connor took his sword in his hands. Victoria wasn't sure if he was going to stab Thomas, stab Iolanthe, or just fling it at her to make himself feel better. Instead, he jammed it into the gravel and strode away.

The sword quivered for quite a long time before the motion stopped.

Iolanthe leaped up suddenly and bolted for the house. Victoria assumed that she knew where all the bathrooms were and felt no compunction about not helping her, nor about swiping her chair. She sat and looked at her brother.

"Thanks," she said sarcastically.

He put his sword up on his shoulder like a rifle and walked over to her. "You will. Later."

"Did you have to?" she asked plaintively. "Couldn't you have just zipped your lips and thrown away the key?"

Thomas squatted down in front of her. "Your eyes are leaking."

"Damn it, it's allergies!"

He smiled. "Vic, he had to know."

"He would have figured it out in time."

"Yeah, eventually. But I thought you might want a fall wedding."

She dragged her sleeve across her eyes. "He's probably gone home."

"Without his sword? Sis, you don't know anything about Highlanders if you think that." He rose and pulled her up with him. "Let's go in. He'll come back eventually, when he's come to terms with it all."

"He'll probably never come to terms with it all."

"Then he'll go back to his miserable life and you'll go back to yours. Did I tell you what a great Ophelia you were? Think of all the misery and madness you'll be able to put into your characters, thanks to Connor dumping you and heading home. I'd thank me if I were you."

"Thomas?"

"Yes?"

"You suck."

He laughed and slung his arm around her. "Ah, that's music to my ears. You'll be fine."

"But will he be?" she muttered. "I doubt it."

And she did. She doubted it even more when she looked out the front door at one point during the afternoon and found that Connor's sword was no longer in the driveway. She glared at Thomas.

"Theft or Return to Neverland; you decide."

"Patience."

"I have none."

"You'll have some after this is over."

She went back to brooding in the library.

By the time the afternoon, and her fledgling patience, had worn very thin, she put herself out of everyones misery and went for a walk. She was going to go to the castle, but she found herself continuing on past it. The sun was setting and the air was still.

Well, except for that dry rain that cropped up, but she was in England; she expected no less.

By the time she had cursed her way to Granny's picnic spot and farther, she realized she was not alone.

Connor stood on the edge of the fairy ring.

She came to a teetering halt, then turned and prepared to tiptoe away.

"Victoria."

She took a deep breath, then turned back around to face him. "Yes?"

"Does your brother speak the truth?"

There was no denying it now. She took another deep breath. She was going to be hyperventilating soon if this kind of thing didn't stop. "Yes."

He looked at the fairy ring for a very long time, then looked at her.

She wondered if she would forget that moment, either.

There stood a proud, undeniably gorgeous Highland laird, in clothes that were just a little too small, holding his enormous sword like a walking stick, looking at her as if he thought looking long enough would reveal all her secrets, making a decision that would affect them both forever.

And then he took his own deep breath and stepped away from the ring in the grass.

He came to a halt in front of her. "I have dreams," he said quietly.

"Do you?"

"Dreams of another life."

She nodded, shaking. "Interesting."

He considered. "They may be of my life as a ghost."

"It's possible."

He looked at her searchingly. "Did I know you?"

"You did."

"Did I love you?"

She had to gather courage to answer that. "You said you did."

"Did I ask you to rescue me from death?"

Ah, there was the rub. "Your forbade me."

He looked at her in surprise, then his expression lightened. "Aye, that sounds like me."

"If it makes you feel any better, I think you wanted to kill me at first, too," she offered. "You know, when you were a . . ."

"Did I?" he mused. "I daresay, not." He put his sword over his shoulder and took her hand. "I must walk," he said easily. "If I do not walk, I will drop to my knees and weep."

"Oh," she managed.

"I will not go home now," he announced. He looked at her briefly. "But I will later."

"Of course," she said gamely.

He walked with her back to the inn, then paused at the front door. "There are several people I wish to question about this whole ghostly business, which I most definitely do not believe."

"Sure," she said with a nod. "Make a list. I'll see they show up."

He looked at her searchingly for quite some time before he spoke. "Do *you* believe, Victoria?"

She took an equal amount of time to answer. "I lived a little of it with you, my laird. I can't not believe."

He was silent for several minutes, then he grunted. "I want the lads from the castle first."

"Do you want to interview them down here or terrorize them up there?"

He frowned at her. "Jesting in this matter is not appreciated."

Well, it beat the hell out of weeping. Victoria put on a businesslike look. "You might have more success getting them to show up if you made the concession of setting up your audience chamber in the bailey. Then you could come down here and question the inn's ghosts."

"The inn is haunted, as well?"

"Haven't I told you that already?"

"I dismissed it as the ramblings of a madwoman, but now I see I was too hasty. Very well. Tomorrow at first light we will away to the castle, then return here for supper and more questions for these lads at the inn. Three of them, are there?"

"There are."

He paused. "Did you tell me that?"

Poor man. Victoria smiled sadly. "I didn't."

He took a deep breath. "Supper. I daresay I'm losing my wits due to lack of strength. I will be fully myself afterward, I assure you."

"I wouldn't expect anything less."

But as she led him into the inn, she wondered if she dared expect anything more.

Chapter 32

Connor sat in the inner bailey of Thorpewold castle and thought that if this had been the state of his reputed afterlife, 'twas no wonder he'd been so foul. He looked at Victoria, who sat on the stage and swung her legs back and forth. She yawned hugely, realized he was observing her, then smiled weakly.

He frowned. So, he was not the only one having trouble listening to these goings on with any seriousness.

Aye, my laird, I did ken ye from centuries past. From before the '45, actually.

The '45? Connor had little liking for those numbers, but he hadn't pressed the man on what they meant. He would ask Victoria about them later.

Laird MacDougal, I aided ye in routing out those pesky Brits when that Tudor wench sat the English throne. What a day that was, with us havin' our heads tucked beneath our arms!

Routing out and *pesky* in the same breath were always good, but Connor had been afforded little time to truly enjoy them. Instead, he'd listened, open-mouthed, to the horrors he had perpetrated, apparently, upon hapless mortals whilst he was, reputedly, a disembodied spirit.

Horrors, he had to admit, that were masterfully executed. Even if he did say so himself.

Sword fights, loud *boos*, ghostly wails, headlessness, armlessness, blood spurting, goo oozing, entrails trailing . . . aye, the tales he had listened to that morn were indeed something.

And all the while, Victoria McKinnon had either sat upon that stage and listened with raised eyebrows or paced about, fighting a smile.

Was it possible that it was true?

And then a man sauntered up to him, dressed in velvets, with enough lace at his wrists and neck to leave a gaggle of Highland lassies drooling for a fortnight. Connor gaped at him in astonishment.

"Roderick St. Claire," the man said with a low bow.

"So I see," Connor said, wide-eyed.

"We've played cards together on more than one occasion," the shade continued. "I have many tales to tell you, old man, when you would care to tear a pheasant together and break open a bottle of claret. Of course," he smiled faintly, "you can indulge. I'll just pretend."

"Old man?" Connor repeated. "Old man?"

"A term of respect," Victoria called helpfully.

Connor looked at Roderick St. Claire and wondered why it was he felt such a strong urge to run the man through. He frowned. "You irritate me."

"I have for decades."

Connor rubbed the space between his eyes. "Decades?"

"I came to Thorpewold after my untimely demise during Queen Victoria's rule."

"Another woman on the English throne?"

"I fear, old chap, that it's all too true."

Connor rubbed his hands over his face. "I think I must have a few moments to think."

Roderick made him a low, flourishy bow better suited to a player on stage, then disappeared.

Connor jumped, in spite of himself. Would he ever accustom himself to this appearing and disappearing these shades did? He suspected not. He dismissed the rest of the garrison with a sharp movement of his hand. They vanished with alacrity. He sighed, stood, and went over to Victoria.

"I am hearing these tales and finding them difficult to believe," he said bluntly.

"I imagine you are," she agreed.

He paused and considered. "I see no reason why these lads would perjure themselves."

She smiled sadly. "I can't, either."

He grunted, then nodded to her before he took himself off to investigate the nooks and crannies of Thorpewold Castle proper. He walked to the one wall that seemed to be the least crumbling of all the walls. To his left was a quite well-preserved tower. Connor approached, but the closer he came, the more dread he felt.

He stood at the bottom and looked up the steps. There was evil there. He wasn't certain what had happened, but it was not of his making, and he had no desire to investigate. He turned away and walked along the wall to the far tower.

It was newly reconstructed. He admired the lower floor, with Victoria's theater equipment still contained therein. He could remember the day—and it hadn't been all that long ago—when the place had been nothing but a shell. But, by the saints, that Thomas McKinnon had been a royal pain in the arse, hammering and banging at all hours, day in and . . . day . . .

Out.

Connor looked at the tower and wondered how in the hell he knew that.

He turned to see how Victoria was viewing his lunacy. She was sitting on the stage still, but she was looking toward the gates, no doubt leaving him privacy to descend into madness. He looked at the corner tower again, shivered once, then moved away before he had any more incomprehensible reactions.

He roamed over the castle, scaling what steps he dared

and leaving alone the ones he didn't. He walked through what was left of the great hall. He stepped into the garden, which was now nothing more than a grassy field. He knew it had not always been so. He could see it as a garden full of flowers and a training field full of men with swords. He watched monks coming and making offerings of plants to a woman he was most startled to recognize.

Iolanthe MacLeod.

But why would they have done that? And when?

Connor leaned on his hand against the wall and let things wash over him. He couldn't call them memories. He wasn't sure what to name them, but he knew he could not call them lies.

Mayhem, terror, decapitations. And that had just been his activities with other men in the keep. But those lads popped their heads right back atop their shoulders and brushed aside killing wounds as if they had been mere stings.

He would have suspected his reign of terror was merely happy recollections of his time as laird of the clan Mac-Dougal, but two things stopped him. One, he hadn't been drenched by the dry Scottish rain; and two, he hadn't been cold.

Odd.

He pushed away from the wall and strode back into the bailey. He looked for Victoria, then nodded sharply at her. She lifted one eyebrow at him, but hopped off the stage just the same. She joined him at the gates and trotted alongside him as he strode away from the castle and its uncomfortable revelations.

He shook his head as he walked. Was it possible? That he had been a specter for several centuries, privy to ghostly counsels, tormenting hapless mortals simply because he could?

He considered the last. Perhaps he had been irritated at his ghostly state. And given that it would have been the Frenchman to plunge him into such a state, mayhap he had good reason to be other than his normally sunny self.

Aye, 'twas possible.

But he simply could not wrap his poor, weary mind around the thought that perhaps he had indeed been a shade for centuries.

If that was so, why was he alive now?

He was alive because Victoria McKinnon had braved medieval Scotland to tell him things he never would have known on his own.

"Who do you want to see down at the inn?" she asked, interrupting his thoughts.

He sighed. "I've no desire to see anyone else, but I daresay I must."

She nodded and walked alongside him without saying anything else for some time. Connor studied her surreptitiously. Had she truly learned Gaelic to save his life? But why? Surely there was little to recommend him here in her Future. In the past, aye, perhaps there was a bit. He was laird there, laird of a fierce and honorable clan. It had at least meant something to Morag, though for considerably less honorable reasons.

He grieved afresh for his children.

But not for the life he had left behind.

That surprised him, though the longer he thought about it, the more it rang true. What life was there to go back to? If the Frenchman had ended his life in truth, his clan would be no worse off than they were now. His cousin was quick witted enough to lead the clan in Connor's absence. Indeed, hadn't he instructed Cormac to do just that? Connor had assumed his absence would not be more than a day or two.

Now, he wondered.

He wondered about a great many things, actually.

Was it possible? Could he have lived centuries as a ghost, haunting the castle behind him, wreaking havoc upon those who dared enter and doing his damndest to make everyone who knew him as miserable as he?

He paused in midstep.

It sounded quite a bit like him in life, actually.

"Connor?"

Connor looked at the woman next to him, who had

stopped as well and was looking up at him in faint consternation. Now, here was a wench for you. Handsome, fearless, red-haired, with a temper to match. She reacted to his frowns with a mere lifting of one eyebrow, as if she thought them interesting, but not too worrying. She treated his demands lightly. She honored his requests when she apparently thought them worth the effort. She only yawned when he bellowed.

Aye, what was not to like about a wench such as she?

" 'Tis naught," he said. "Lead on, MacDuff."

"Lay on," she corrected, then walked away.

He frowned and caught up with her in a pair of strides. "Aye, I suppose it is. Isn't it?"

"It is."

"It feels a familiar phrase."

"It's a phrase from Shakespeare. From the Scottish play."

He looked down at the ground as they walked. "The Scottish play? That is the name of it?"

"No, but you never say the name of it unless you're acting in it. It's bad luck."

"Is it?" he mused. "I daresay I do not fear bad luck. I survived a Frenchman's would-be killing blow and the loss of my bairns. Perhaps things will go well for me from now on."

She looked at him with a faint smile. "I hope so. For your sake."

And for her sake, as well. He was tempted to ask her what she thought of everything she had seen that morning, but he found himself distracted by the sight of Thomas McKinnon coming down the inn's stairs. His hand went to his sword before he could stop it. Thomas only smiled.

"Laird MacDougal."

"McKinnon," Connor growled.

"Oh, good grief," Victoria said. "Didn't you two have enough yesterday?"

"I daresay we did not finish our argument," Connor said, throwing Thomas a look full of promise.

Thomas only smiled. "Whenever it suits you."

"Don't bring that MacLeod wench you wed along to watch. She irritates me overmuch."

"Don't worry," Victoria muttered. "She's sick with Thomas's first child, poor woman."

"Oh, she's much better," Thomas assured her. "But she's having a nap. I was just looking for some way to get a little exercise. How kind of your friend here to offer me that opportunity."

"*Friend?*" Connor repeated. He turned the word over in his mind and found it easily as irritating as looking at Thomas McKinnon was. "Do not use that word again. It makes me desire to run something through."

"As long as that something isn't my sister, I'm all right," Thomas laughed. "I imagine you all are looking for a snack. I think Mrs. Pruitt's still on duty in the kitchen. Besides, who knows what else you'll find in there besides food?"

Connor looked at Thomas and frowned. "Not more ghosties."

Thomas shrugged. "Let's just go and see. Then I'll trample a few of the weeds down the way from Mrs. Pruitt's garden with you if you like."

Connor grunted his assent and gestured for Victoria to lead the way into the kitchen.

And there, sitting at the table as innocently as you pleased, were three hale and hearty men enjoying their own repast. Two were Scots, that he could see readily. The other was an Englishman; that he could tell just as readily.

Victoria made introductions. "My grandfathers from both sides, Ambrose MacLeod and Hugh McKinnon."

"A MacLeod *and* a McKinnon?" Connor echoed in surprise. "What next?"

"Fulbert de Piaget. He's kin to my younger sister's husband."

"An Englishman?"

"I'm afraid so."

Fulbert de Piaget opened his mouth, no doubt to retort as he saw fit, but Connor growled at him before he could begin.

Fulbert disappeared with a curse.

Connor had to sit down. He held on to the table for support and looked at Victoria. "Inn ghosts?"

"Back from their holiday, apparently," Victoria said, sitting down next to Connor.

He turned his attentions to the flame-haired ghost. "You're the McKinnon."

Hugh nodded proudly. "Aye. Grandfather several times removed to young Victoria. And a fine lass she is," he said, as if he dared Connor to disagree with him.

"Spirited," Connor said, finding he had no reason to argue the point. "Beautiful, as well."

A wheezing noise came from next to him. He looked to find Victoria turning quite red.

"Breathe, Vic," Thomas suggested.

"Shut up, Thomas."

Thomas calmly handed her a plate full of very interesting things. Connor watched her sort through the vegetables, then continued to watch as she flung a particularly plump something at her brother. It landed with a satisfying splat in between his eyes.

"What was that?" he asked in wonder.

"Brussels sprout," she said curtly. "I only wish I had more."

"I would give you mine," Connor said as Mrs. Pruitt set an overflowing plate before him, "but I might find them to my liking." He applied himself to a goodly bit of his repast, then realized he was being watched. He looked up to find the other Scottish ghost staring at him. "Who are you?" Connor asked.

"Ambrose MacLeod."

Connor studied Ambrose's clothing. "When did you die?"

"Sixteenth century."

"And you've been here how long?"

"Long enough," Ambrose said, "to make several interesting matches."

"Matches?" Connor gaped. "You make matches?" He looked at Thomas in shock. "Is this a manly business to be engaged in?"

Thomas shrugged. "They brought me together with Iolanthe. I can't complain."

Connor grunted and looked at Ambrose. "I want to approve whomever you choose for Victoria. I daresay she would take a particular kind of man."

"I daresay," Ambrose said dryly.

Connor almost questioned what that might mean, then decided against it. He looked at Victoria. "I think I have eaten enough. I will go train with your brother. It will soothe me."

"Well, don't kill each other," she said.

Connor rose and looked at her. "Thank you for your aid this day, Mistress Victoria. I think I must think about returning home, though."

"Of course."

He wondered why her eyes were so bright. Perhaps one too many Brussels sprouts. He put his hand on her head briefly, then nodded to Thomas. "Let us go."

"Of course."

Connor wondered at the look Thomas exchanged with his sister, as well, but decided that could wait to be unraveled until he had Thomas at sword point. He walked with the man past Mrs. Pruitt's most delicate flowers and looked for a likely spot in the gravelly place where the cars were parked.

Cars. If that wasn't enough to tell a man he had come centuries into the Future, he didn't know what was. He stroked his chin thoughtfully as he admired a pair of the beasts, wondering what it might be like to travel about in one. He looked at Thomas, who regarded him with a smile.

"You know," Thomas said slowly, "you might want to purchase different jeans."

Connor realized his mistake immediately. "I apologize. I have used your clothing without giving you thanks for it."

"It wasn't that," Thomas said easily. "I just thought finding clothes would be a good excuse to go for a long ride in a car."

"A ride in one of those?" Connor asked, feeling a goodly bit of enthusiasm rush through him. "Aye, I would like to do that before I go."

"Are you still going to go?" Thomas asked.

"Certainly," Connor said. But he suddenly felt quite uncertain. "I left my cousin in charge during my absence," he managed.

"Did you?" Thomas asked, leaning on his sword. "Interesting."

Connor considered. "I did see to something else before I left." He paused. "I buried my children."

"I would have done the same," Thomas said quietly.

Connor rested his sword in the dirt and put both hands on the hilt. It was a familiar thing to do, that motion. He had done it countless times; on the field, resting in battle, in his own garden whilst enjoying the hint of fall tingeing the air. It made him feel more himself, that small gesture he had carried with him through the ages.

He felt that same hint of fall blow over him suddenly, that hint of change, that whisper of something coming that might be more lovely than what had come before.

Something in the Future.

Connor looked at Thomas. "If I were to stay," he began slowly, "what would I do here? If it is, as Victoria has claimed, hundreds of years away from my clan, whom would I lead? How would I conduct my manly labors each day, and where? There at this castle, which is nigh on to crumbling to ruins?" He frowned. "Victoria says you own the keep."

"I bought it," Thomas said with a shrug. "I could sell it again just as easily. To you, if you like."

"That is something to consider," Connor agreed. "It would help if I had a bloody pair of coins to rub together. Unfortunately, I've nothing but my sword and my wits."

"Men have made do with less," Thomas said with a smile. "And given that you have those two things in abundance, I wouldn't worry."

"But I do worry. It worries me enough that I suspect that there is not future for me here. In your Future." He frowned. "Damn me if that doesn't give me pains in the head to think on it."

"Then let us be about something less painful," Thomas said, drawing his sword. "Shall we?"

"And you think a little light exercise with me will be painless?" Connor asked, feeling the thrill of potentially using his sword for nefarious purposes rush through him. "I could slay you by accident."

"I wouldn't," Thomas said with a grin. "My wife is quite handy with a blade and she's damned stealthy."

"Your babe leaves her puking her guts up at each turn."

"Ah, but that was yesterday. Today she's much more herself. I daresay she will only become more trouble as time goes on."

"They always do," Connor said wisely, drawing his own sword and tossing the scabbard atop the feed end of what should have been a horse but wasn't. 'Twas a shiny blue car that looked as if it might go very fast. "Is this yours?"

"For a bit," Thomas said. "We'll take it for a ride later. It will make you forget your humiliation at my hands this morning."

"Ha!" Connor said with a ferocious grin. "Engage me, if you dare, you womanly McKinnon."

Fortunately for them both and the state of entertainment that morn, Thomas McKinnon was as skilled a swordsman as Connor could have wished for.

Of course, that didn't mean that Thomas would best him, but he would certainly be sport enough for the morning.

Connor threw himself joyously into the fray and let all thoughts of his future slide away, where a sensible man would have let them go.

There would be time enough for thinking later.

Chapter 33

Victoria sat on the front step of the inn and looked out over Mrs. Pruitt's garden. It was a peaceful place, really, with bees buzzing here and there and the sweet, heady smells of dozens of varieties of flowers wafting through the air. She took a deep breath and, well, sneezed, of course. Zinnias were, in reality, the bane of her existence.

But the lavender and roses more than made up for that. She concentrated on them and tried to block out what was troubling her. If only she could have managed that so easily in other aspects of her life.

The door opened behind her. So Mrs. Pruitt wasn't going to give up on pawning that afternoon snack off on her. Victoria sighed and turned, prepared to offer a polite thanks followed by a firm refusal, but it wasn't Mrs. Pruitt.

"Oh," Victoria said. "Iolanthe."

Iolanthe came unsteadily out the door and sat down gingerly. "Sister."

"Are you sure you should be out here? You know, the smells and all."

"I feel much more myself."

Victoria smiled gravely. "You know, Iolanthe, I hate to say it, but you don't look any better."

"It will end, eventually," Iolanthe groaned. "Or so I've been told."

"Yeah, when the baby's born."

Iolanthe scowled at her and Victoria laughed.

"Now, that's a look that rings true. I'm sure you won't have to wait that long to feel better again. That would just be wrong."

Iolanthe put her hand over her nose and nodded. "Aye, it would."

Victoria nodded as well, then resumed her admiring of the garden. Mrs. Pruitt either had a small army of weeders, or she spent far more time digging in the dirt than she let on. The place was perfect. It was worthy of a great deal of time spent appreciating it. And given that such appreciating took her mind off Connor's indecision, she indulged in it fully.

"Hey," she said suddenly, sitting up straight, "Thomas's car is gone."

"He and Connor went to Jedburgh."

"Thomas took Connor with him in a *car*?" Victoria said incredulously.

Iolanthe nodded gingerly.

"He's out of his mind."

"He's done it before."

"Been out of his mind?"

"Nay, taken a nervous passenger clothes-shopping in Jedburgh."

Victoria realized that she'd hit the motherlode. Iolanthe could provide her with all the answers she needed to exactly when and how she had regained her memories. The question was: Did she want those answers?

She was afraid of what she would learn.

"He took you?" Victoria asked, finally.

"Aye."

"Did you enjoy the trip?"

Iolanthe hesitantly took her hand away from her nose. When she seemed to think it would not go ill for her, literally, she smiled. "I was still at the point where I wasn't completely convinced that your brother was not a demon."

"And you've changed your mind since then?"

Iolanthe laughed easily. "Oh, aye. I've found him to be passing tolerable."

Victoria shifted to more easily look Iolanthe full in the face. "How long did it take you to remember?" She paused. "You know, your other life."

Iolanthe sobered. "Weeks."

Victoria felt herself pale. "Weeks?"

"But I did remember," Iolanthe added quickly. She paused. "Eventually."

Victoria sighed and looked back over the garden. "It's all very strange to me. I don't know how a person can remember an afterlife they once lived then subsequently didn't get to live." She looked at her sister-in-law. "I don't get it."

"Time is not our natural element," Iolanthe said slowly. "Who's to say how its strands weave together to make the tapestries of our lives? The paths we took and those we might have but didn't . . ." She shrugged. "Thomas says those who study space vow that time goes forward and backward at the same time. Perhaps that applies to our memories, as well."

Victoria gave that some thought, then shook her head. "I can believe a lot of things, but I don't know about that."

"Sister, you had best learn to believe if you have any hope of the MacDougal remembering what he had with you."

Victoria's eyes burned suddenly. She dug the heels of her hands into her eyes until she thought she could look at Iolanthe without weeping.

"I suppose so," she said quietly.

"Give him time," Iolanthe said. "He will remember."

"You would know."

"Aye, I would. Besides, for all we ken, the MacDougal won't be such a hard case. I am powerfully stubborn."

"And he isn't?"

Iolanthe smiled. "Aye, he is. But he's also had the testimony of many ghosts in the past day or so, regaling him with deeds of great glory during his years as a shade. That will flatter his vanity, which may well be so pleasing to him that he will welcome those other memories when they come."

"Didn't you?"

"It shames me to admit that I didn't. I fought them and your brother each step of the way. I would not even heed Megan when she tried to aid me after my return to the Future." She smiled ruefully. "I daresay I was not so polite to you, either, when we met at Ian's before Christmas."

Victoria waved away the apology. "I wasn't in the best frame of mind to make friends, either." She hesitated. "But with Connor . . . do you think he will remember? Eventually?"

"I would imagine so." Iolanthe paused for a long moment. "But I cannot speak for him."

Victoria sighed. "It took you weeks."

"Aye."

"It might take him weeks."

"It might."

"If it happens at all."

Iolanthe smiled wanly. "It was a risk you took."

"I'm getting my just deserts," Victoria said grimly. And she was. All her fine talk about living and letting live. Ha! Besides, she knew how that lack of control played out. "Look, Ma, no hands!" generally resulted in chipped front teeth.

She wasn't quite sure what that kind of letting-go would result in when it came to interpersonal relationships. But what she did know was that she couldn't force Connor to remember; she couldn't force him to stay.

Damn it, anyway.

"But how could I not have taken that risk?" she asked Iolanthe glumly.

"You had to." She paused, then smiled. "Look, Thomas

is coming up the lane. Perhaps Connor has had a sharp blow to his head and it has shaken a few of his recollections loose."

Victoria pursed her lips. "You don't like him."

"He was a miserable ghost."

"He's mellowed."

Iolanthe smiled again. "Aye, for you he certainly has. I will give him another look." She got to her feet and swayed.

Victoria leaped to steady her, then found she was just as unsteady on her feet. She looked on in shock as Thomas and Connor climbed out of Thomas's rental. Thomas looked much as he ever did: good-looking and cheerful. But Connor . . .

Connor had had a makeover.

"Oh, my," Iolanthe said thickly.

Victoria frowned at her. "You're married."

"I have eyes."

"So do I," Victoria managed. "And in this case, I'm not sure that's a good thing."

But since she had eyes, there was no reason not to make use of them. She decided that it was her duty to take in every detail, no matter how slight, of Connor's changed appearance. Granny would want to know, assuming Connor headed back to medieval Scotland before Granny came back from modern-day London.

Connor's jeans fit. He was wearing work boots. He had somehow managed to stretch a T-shirt over his rather substantial chest.

"What does that say?" Iolanthe asked, holding her hand over her nose again.

"I'll tell you when he gets closer and I can see." To kill time, Victoria admired the shave and haircut he'd had. Nothing too drastic, just a trim. A little on the wild side, a little on the untamed side, a lot on the I'm-a-medieval-lord-dressing-up-like-a-modern-guy-to-humor-you side.

Then she managed to read his t-shirt.

"Does it truly say 'Kiss me, I'm Scottish'?" Iolanthe asked.

"I'm going to kill your husband."

"You may want to. I daresay there will be a line of wenches waiting to accept Connor's invitation." Iolanthe smiled. "And I can say as much, even though I spent several centuries wanting to rid myself of his irritating presence."

"Like I said," Victoria wheezed, "he's mellowed." But Thomas had not. He was fighting his smile as he walked up the path with Connor. Victoria glared at him. "You're a jerk."

"Why?" he asked innocently. "Oh, the shirt? It was all we could find in his size."

"The hell it was."

Connor looked at her, his brow furrowed. "That tongue you speak," he said in Gaelic. "It sounds familiar."

Iolanthe elbowed Victoria in the ribs and took hold of Thomas's hand. "I feel a little lie-down coming on, husband. Let us be away."

"But—whoa!"

Victoria wasn't sure if she was grateful or not for Iolanthe's sudden burst of strength. Thomas was dragged into the inn, apparently against his will, though he promised a quick return if he was needed. Victoria looked at Connor and was terribly tempted to ask him if he knew what his shirt said.

She didn't dare.

She might have been tempted to take him up on the offer.

And then she made the mistake of looking up at him. He was looking at her with what she could only assume was the same amount of, well, desire she was feeling.

She waited for him to take her into his arms. Indeed, she suspected she saw that very thought cross his mind. The intensity of his gaze intensified until Victoria was just certain he was going to haul her into his arms and profess something.

"Victoria," he said in a rough voice.

"Yes?" she said breathlessly.

"Um . . ." He flexed his fingers a time or two, started to reach for her another time or two, then cleared his throat. He looked horribly tempted by something.

She could only hope it was by the thought of kissing her.

"Um . . ." he said again, looking about him quite desperately. "Ah, your sword. Aye, your sword! Where is that thin sword of yours? I vow I should have looked at it more closely whilst you were in my hall."

She felt herself gaping at him and was powerless to assume any other more reasonable and attractive expression. "My *sword*?"

"Aye. Will you not show it to me now?"

Sure, before I wedge the hilt between two sturdy rocks and fall on it.

"You wouldn't have two, would you?" he asked, his eyes alight suddenly with barely restrained excitement.

"Do you want to fight me?" she asked incredulously.

"Well," he said, drawing himself up, "not *fight*, precisely. But it might be pleasing to have a go with one of those blades. I suppose you might be able to demonstrate its use."

There she stood, drooling over him and wanting nothing more than to go on drooling for the whole of the afternoon, and all he could think about was *swords*?

She knew she shouldn't have been surprised.

Amazing, that she still was.

She sighed. "Let's go get a couple of them out of the shed. We'll find somewhere to use them." *On you, if I'm lucky.*

"Not in Mrs. Pruitt's garden," he warned, tromping along behind her. "I've already run afoul of her ire by trampling her blooms."

"And considering that she's willing to feed you," Victoria said, "I imagine you're not going to irritate her unnecessarily."

"Your Gaelic improves with each day that passes. I should speak with you more. I daresay I'm aiding you greatly."

Victoria nodded, but didn't dare say anything. Spend more time with him? Lose her heart all over again each time she saw him, when she knew that he fully intended to skedaddle back home the first chance he had?

Hamlet.

Perfect.

She was going to kill her brother.

She went to the shed and rummaged around until she came up with two theatrical rapiers. The last thing she needed was to have Connor impale her by accident. Wouldn't that be the ultimate in ironies: Connor mortal and she a ghost.

It wasn't at all amusing, so she quickly turned her thoughts away from that and swished her blade a time or two. Connor did the same. He seemed to find the sound quite lovely because he continued to cut the air with his blade. Victoria was very happy she hadn't given him the rapier she'd taken back in time with her. The thought of the clean, lethal whistle *that* one made, multiplied exponentially in Connor's capable hands, gave her the willies.

"En guarde," she said, assuming her best fencing pose.

Connor looked at her, baffled, then lunged, as well.

Apparently, he didn't realize his arms were quite a bit longer than hers until after it was too late.

The sword did collapse as it poked her in the ribs, but still, it winded her. She gasped and dropped her sword.

"Ach, by the saints, nay!" Connor cried and tossed his sword aside in horror. He dropped to his knees in front of her. "Victoria! Victoria!"

"Stop bellowing," she wheezed.

He didn't seem to be paying any attention to her. He hauled her into his arms and clutched her to him, continuing to make noises of distress. And somehow, in spite of that distress or perhaps because of it, he managed to keep her clutched with one arm yet run his free hand over her hair, as if that very motion would restore her to good health.

What a dilemma.

Should she tell him she wasn't bleeding from a gaping wound, or should she just close her eyes and enjoy it for as long as it lasted? She was trapped in Connor MacDougal's arms. It was, she could say with all honesty, better than she'd dared imagine it could be.

There came a point, unfortunately, when she knew she would have to breathe again. She tried moving one of her arms, but Connor had that one pinned under his elbow. She tried moving the other arm, but it was mostly pinned as well, and all that happened was that she wound up patting the air. She tried to get Connor's attention by calling his name; his name came out as nothing more than a squeak. She looked around desperately for help.

Thomas stood at the kitchen door, regarding the little tableau with a smirk.

"Help," she mouthed.

Thomas put his hand to his ear. "What?"

"Help!" she squeaked. "Help, damn you!"

"Hey, MacDougal," Thomas called. "What's up?"

"I killed your sister!" Connor exclaimed in anguished tones.

"Nope," Thomas said. "It was a fake sword. But I think if you don't let go, you'll crush her to death."

Connor pulled back far enough to look down at Victoria with a frown. "Are you well?"

Her day of reckoning had come, and so soon . . .

She smiled weakly. "It hurt, but I'm not bleeding. Want to try again?"

He released her reluctantly, then looked her over. "What magic is this?" he asked. "A sword that does not pierce?"

Victoria found that she could reach her sword without having to really lean over too far. That was very handy; it left her with ample opportunity to practically recline in Connor's arms.

Damn, he even *smelled* good. Where had Thomas taken him?

She jammed the sword into the ground. It collapsed into itself. Connor gasped.

He set her aside without hesitation and reached for the sword. He poked it into the ground several times to the accompaniment of sounds of delight. He stood, tossed the sword up into the air, and watched as it fell, point down, into the dirt. He looked at Victoria.

"Well," he said finally, "this is something indeed." He caught sight of Thomas. "Have you seen this, Thomas? I daresay it removes some of the joy from a good brawl, but indeed, 'tis a very new and interesting contrivance." He went and fetched his rapier, then tossed it toward Thomas. "Shall we?"

Victoria stared, open-mouthed, as her brother and her erstwhile clutcher began to engage each other, commenting from time to time over the lack of sport there was in fighting with a sword that could not truly do damage.

"This will only hold my interest for a brief time," Connor warned. "Then I will need something more lethal."

"I understand completely."

Connor gestured toward Victoria. "You know, I think I have fond feelings for your sister."

"Do you?" Thomas asked.

"Damn me if I know why."

"I think I would feel the same way."

Victoria shot her brother a look he seemed to feel in spite of the fact that he refused to look at her.

"She is beautiful," Connor said. "And spirited. And rather handy with a blade." He looked over at her. "I never met a wench who could use a sword before. Is the Future so full of your kind of woman?"

"No," she said shortly, "it's not."

He grunted and turned back to her brother. "Did Mrs. Pruitt have something on the fire when you came out of the kitchen?"

"Yes," Victoria said loudly. "Probably a heavy frying pan."

Connor stopped and frowned at her. "A heavy frying pan? On the fire? Why?"

To clunk you over the head with. She pursed her lips.

"To fry tomatoes in the manner you find so pleasing, no doubt."

Connor looked at Thomas. "A right pleasing wench, your sister. Obviously she knows what is important to a man."

"Ha," Thomas said, apparently before he could stop himself.

Victoria rolled her eyes and turned to take refuge in the kitchen before the men got hungry beyond their ability to carry on. She was tempted to stand behind the door and bean both of them on the heads, but that would defeat her purpose. She would just bean her brother and hopefully render him unconscious and unable to speak. And then she might actually have a moment's peace with Connor, who thought her a right pleasing wench.

That was a step in the right direction.

A million more of those and there might be hope for them.

Chapter 34

Connor left his own chamber the next morning. It was his own chamber and not Victoria's floor, not because he thought she minded, but because he minded. Beyond all reason, but because he had two good eyes and a very fine sense of discernment, he was drawn to her. Very drawn to her. That did not bode well for his heart.

Witness the day before. After a most pleasant afternoon passed traveling at high speeds in Thomas's car, he had returned to the inn and found himself rendered quite speechless by the sight of Victoria McKinnon. It was difficult to imagine that he could have forgotten how lovely she was, but he supposed he could lay the blame for that on the car. Only his iron control had kept him from dropping to his knee and begging her to be his.

By the saints, he needed to go home.

Besides, as interesting a place as the Future was, the Past had its allures, as well. Never mind that he could not bring one to mind immediately. Who could blame him? Visions of automobiles, hot showers, and bangers and mash competed mightily, and quite successfully, with cold mutton, bathing in a cold stream once a year, and a lumpy mattress that crunched when he rolled over.

He caught his breath in consternation. Was he growing soft?

Nay, say it was not so . . .

He shook aside his foolish thoughts. He would depart for home the next day. But first, he would seek out Thomas McKinnon and thank him for his generosity. The clothing had to have come dear and though Thomas had magnanimously waved aside any of Connor's promises to repay him, it was right to thank him yet again.

Connor also wanted to express appreciation to Mrs. Pruitt for the many fine meals she had prepared for him. Indeed, the woman had spent a great amount of time each day tending the fire on his behalf. He would miss her fine victuals.

And before he departed, he would give the greater part of an entire day to what his heart desired: looking at, talking with, and, the saints pity him for a weak-spined fool, holding Victoria McKinnon.

By the saints, he found her bewitching.

He pushed away from the wall he'd been leaning against and made his way down the stairs and into the kitchen. Mrs. Pruitt was, thankfully, at the stove. Victoria was, the saints pity him, sitting at the table. He found that once he looked at her, he could not look away.

Her hair was cascading down her back in a riot of flame-colored curls. She was wearing jeans, as usual, and he now understood why she preferred them. He sat down with a plop in the chair next to hers, unable to look away.

Her skin was pale and her eyes bloodshot, as if she had spent the night weeping or being haunted by dozens of irritating ghosts.

"What is amiss with you?" he asked.

She shook her head with a wan smile. "I didn't sleep well."

Well, he supposed if she needed a nap, he could watch her sleep. He'd certainly done it enough times in the . . . past.

He blinked. Had he?

He looked at her again closely, then drew his hand over his eyes. Perhaps he should be grateful that he was going home the next morning. He was beginning to doubt his sanity.

Mrs. Pruitt set a plate down before him. He smiled gratefully at her, then he applied himself to eating it all before she handed him more. When that was finished, as well, he sat back and looked at Victoria.

Why, she hadn't even made her way through half of her meal!

He finished hers, as well.

Then he rose. "Mrs. Pruitt, my thanks for the tasty meal. Quite satisfactory. A pity I have no need for a cook in my hall at present."

Mrs. Pruitt turned and looked at him, her hand over her heart. "Indeed," she said, sounding pleased. "I appreciate the thought, Laird MacDougal. A high compliment, indeed."

"A cook of your skill deserves no less." He smiled once again, then took Victoria's hand and pulled her to her feet. "Come with me," he said, towing her from the kitchen like an unresisting horse who knew a pasture of high summer grass was over the next rise. Perhaps there was no grass, but there was a stage. Connor suspected it was Victoria's preferred place.

Actually, he knew as much. He had asked Thomas many questions the day before on their outing, and one of those questions had concerned what Victoria had been doing on the stage the day Connor had come to the Future and found her running about with her eyes closed. It had looked like madness to him, but Thomas had been certain it was something to do with plays and such.

Connor had little time and even less patience for frolics, but he supposed, since he was going to be loitering in the Future for the rest of the day with little to do, he might as well indulge in watching a little performance or two.

He found, as he walked up to the castle with Victoria

McKinnon's hand in his, that he had grown quite accustomed to touching her.

Today, he reminded himself. But not tomorrow. Tomorrow was for his future, which was firmly placed in the Past.

He rubbed his forehead with his free hand. It gave him pains in the head to think on, truth be told.

He stopped in the bailey of the castle. It was a derelict place, with walls crumbling and no roof for the great hall. But there was a stage there and that seemed to be well built. He supposed there were worse places to linger.

"Why are we here?" Victoria asked.

Connor released her hand and looked down at her. "I thought perhaps you would do something onstage for me. A bit of a play or some other such rot."

"Rot?" she echoed weakly.

"'Tis a manly term for a frolic. I can't appear too bloody eager to waste my time watching when I should be training, can I?"

She looked at him for a moment or two in complete silence, then she smiled faintly. "I suppose you can't. What would you like to see?"

"What can you do?"

"Lots of Shakespeare."

"Well, the Bard did have a lot to say." He paused and looked at her. "The Bard?"

"Another name for Shakespeare."

"Hmmm," Connor said uneasily.

It was tempting to sit down in the dirt and bawl like a bairn, but he did not weep. Well, not unless he was bleeding from a gaping wound, but under those circumstances, he always claimed any errant tear to be nothing more than a single drop of sweat. It was the only way to leave his ferocious reputation intact.

He gestured to the stage. "Up on the boards with you, woman," he said, anxious to move onto something less unsettling, "and entertain me."

He watched her climb up onto the stage. He supposed

he should have looked for a chair, but he suspected he was equal to the task of standing there and watching her perform. After all, how overwhelming could it be to watch a single wench be about her business?

"I'll do, well, there is a nice soliloquy Gertrude has."

"The queen?"

"Yes."

"After Ophelia dies?"

She stared at him for the space of several heartbeats, as if she had just seen a ghost. She nodded finally. "Yes. That one."

He waved her on. "One of my favorites."

Then he realized that he was either going to have to sit down or fall there. Gertrude? Ophelia? Who were they and why did he know them?

"Connor?"

"I am well," he said, planting his feet a manly distance apart and folding his arms over his chest.

"There's a chair behind the stage."

That would work, as well. He fetched it according to her directions, then placed himself in the middle of the bailey, where he could see Victoria best.

And then he wondered at his own foolishness.

She stood in the middle of the stage and began to weave a spell around him with her words, a spell he was certain he could not break and almost as certain he did not wish to.

There is a willow grows aslant a brook,
That shows his hoar leaves in the glassy stream;
There with fantastic garlands did she come
Of crow-flowers, nettles, daisies, and long purples,
That liberal shepherds give a grosser name,
But our cold maids do dead men's fingers call them:

She stopped. Connor could not speak, either. It was as if he had never heard words before. These sank into his soul and left him not so much bemused as silent and heartbroken. Dead men's fingers, indeed.

Connor knew she had begun speaking again, but he could no longer hear the words. The sadness of the tale made his eyes burn with tears. He continued to listen, open-mouthed, as Victoria painted a picture before his mind's eye that left him desperate to stop what he knew had already happened. Ophelia had drowned; Hamlet was soon to be lost as well.

Hamlet?

Connor blinked. Who in the bloody hell was Hamlet?

He dragged his sleeve across his eyes and glared at Victoria. "We'll have no more of that death and mayhem. Do something more cheering. Something that will make me feel anything but a desire to drawn my sword and fall upon it!"

She smiled.

It was as if the sun had shone for the very first time in his life. He caught his breath, then found himself laughing. He knew not what she quoted, but she was having a conversation with herself, playing two parts, blathering on about someone named Bottom and a wench named Titania, and fairies and other amusing creatures.

Fairies? He stroked his chin. He'd known they would have to make an appearance sooner or later.

He sat for the better part of the morning, by turns laughing, contemplating, and forcing himself not to weep. He could scarce believe Victoria preferred telling her players what to do, rather than capering about the stage herself. Well, there was no making sense of what a wench would do without a man to aid her.

And then she began something entirely new.

> *O thou, my lovely boy, who in thy power*
> *Dost hold Time's fickle glass his fickle hour . . .*
> *May time disgrace and wretched minutes kill . . .*
> *She may detain, but not still keep her treasure*

He listened as she leaped from thought to thought, now about time, now about love, now about the vagaries of life.

He wondered about the last. Was he in the Future merely as a matter of Time's caprice, or had there been a more solemn purpose? His grandmother's words came back to him and he wondered if this might have been the path she had foreseen him treading.

He wondered if he shouldn't make an immediate return to the Past, where he had obviously left his good sense.

"Anyone up for a drive?"

The masculine voice behind him giving vent to an invitation for one of his preferred Future activities was enough to have Connor on his feet. He looked behind him to find Thomas there.

"Where?" Connor asked, equally as happy for an outing as he was for the chance to escape his troubling thoughts.

"Edinburgh?" Thomas suggested.

"I'll come," Connor said immediately.

"I have tickets to a play." Thomas looked around Connor at his sister. "I thought you might be interested in this one."

"What's playing?" she asked.

"It's a surprise."

"I don't have anything to wear."

"The *Pretty Woman* shopping spree is on me," Thomas said with a smile.

Victoria hopped off the stage. "I'm there."

Connor smiled down at her. "You rob the world of your talent when you merely command the forces from below," he said frankly. "Why is that?"

"It's a very long story," she said. "I'll tell you on the way to Edinburgh."

Connor took her hand and pulled her from the keep. "I'm anxious to see how the city has changed since my day. Coming, Thomas?"

"I suppose, since I have to drive," Thomas said with a chuckle.

Connor started to offer his services, but before he could open his mouth, Victoria had sent him a warning look.

"Don't think it."

He drew himself up. "I could manage it."

"Not to Edinburgh. There are lots of cars. But I'll bet Thomas would let you another day."

"But I must return home tomorrow," he said, with sincere regret.

"Oh," she said quietly.

They walked along in silence for several minutes. Connor found, to his surprise, that she had pulled her hand from his at some point. She had her hands stuck into her pockets, as if she feared what they might do if she left them to themselves.

He supposed she might be tempted to cuff him. He couldn't blame her. He had powerfully fond feelings for her. Was it beyond the pale to suppose she might suffer the like for him?

"I do not *want* to go," he said defensively, before he thought better of it. He looked down at her. "But I must."

She met his eyes. Hers were very red. "I know."

"Allergies?"

She smiled. "The excuse is wearing thin, I suppose."

He wanted to ask her what she meant by that, but found that he did not have the will. She was, he dared hope, grieved that he would go. Would she be willing to come with him?

He considered that for a moment or two. To leave behind the Future and all its marvels? Cars, collapsible swords, fried tomatoes, pink garderobes . . . nay, he could see why she might not want to.

Yet, what was there for him in the Past? He would have been dead were it not for her. But given that he had survived that dodgy bit of business, what would it mean for him to remain in his own time? He would have spent the rest of his days wondering if he was doing something someone else should have been seeing to. He might have wed again, possibly stealing a woman from another who would have had her, had he been slain as he ought to have been.

His head began to pound.

He decided finally that perhaps there was reason to suppose that he might live out his life in a Past where he was destined *not* to be. But did that mean he was permitted to stay in the Future?

That he could not answer.

If he had some confirmation, some compelling reason, some sign beyond all doubt that he was meant to remain where he was . . .

But nay, the world did not work thusly. He belonged in his time and Victoria in hers. The specters he had seen were flights of fancy. Indeed, he began to wonder if his entire trip away from home had been one great, long dream.

He shrugged aside his doubts and his fears. It would all come clear to him when he was home.

For now, he had the remainder of the day to spend with Victoria.

That was enough.

It would have to be.

Chapter 35

V ictoria sat in the backseat of Thomas's rental car and listened to her brother and the man she loved discuss the gadgets that adorned the dashboard. Connor would have poked and prodded those gadgets with his knife, but Thomas told him not to. It was all so very normal, traveling in the backseat of a car with her sister-in-law, who threatened to toss her cookies every few minutes, while a medieval clansman sat in the front arguing with her brother over whether or not a knife thrust into the CD player would really bring results that he wouldn't care for.

Was she losing her mind?

She didn't dare speculate.

Iolanthe began to moan in a very unsettling manner. Victoria shoved a plastic bag at her. "Here," she said briskly, "puke in here. I checked; there aren't any holes in the bottom."

Iolanthe clutched the plastic sack like a lifesaver. Victoria looked out the window and watched the scenery rush by. It was beautiful country. She supposed that there wasn't a square foot of earth that hadn't been tromped on by some

Brit at one point or another. It would have been something to have been witness to that history over the centuries.

As Connor was.

She sighed deeply. Things were not going as she had planned, even given her new hands-off-the-destinies-of-those-around-her policy. All right, so when she'd come back to the present time, she'd despaired of ever seeing Connor again. Once he'd come to the Future, she'd hoped against hope that someday he would actually regain the memories he couldn't possibly have had unless Thomas's remember-the-future business was true.

But the time for that kind of thing was running out and for more than one reason. Connor said he was going home tomorrow, but he'd been saying that for almost a week. It was entirely possible that he could change his mind for another week.

Unfortunately, she was also feeling the pressure of time. It was the end of August already and her rehearsals were starting the middle of September for a November show that she hadn't even begun to advertise. She needed to find a venue and round up a few actors. Michael had probably taken with him half the cast of her first show and Mr. Yoga had definitely taken her rehearsal and performance place, yet still the show had to go on.

She rubbed her hands over her face and sighed deeply.

"Victoria?"

She looked at Iolanthe. "Yes?"

"You are unwell?"

She shook her head. "Stress."

"Speaking of stress," Thomas said, "have you thought about what you're going to do for the fall? You know, after you go back to Manhattan?"

"Why do I ever tell you anything?" Victoria asked, not really wanting an answer because she already knew the answer. She was a masochist.

"What is amiss?" Connor asked.

"Victoria has a group of players," Thomas began, "and unfortunately, they have lost the space where they've been accustomed to performing their shows. She will return to Manhattan with people lining up to want to see her shows and no place to perform."

"Manhattan? The Apple you told me about?"

"The very one."

"What will she do, do you think? Could she not use your castle for her productions?"

"She could," Thomas said, "but I think she wants to get back to the city. In fact, I imagine she just can't wait to get back to Manhattan. Isn't that true, Vic?"

Victoria wanted to hit her brother, but that might have been dangerous, given that he was driving. Could he make matters any worse? First, he'd broken the news to Connor about his ghostly status in that completely unfeeling manner and now he was making it sound as if she couldn't wait to get on the plane and leave Connor behind.

"Connor?" she said.

"Aye?"

"Kill him for me later."

Connor made a noise, something like a purr. "If I must. If it would please you."

"It would please me."

"Mayhap you would inherit his castle if he died," Connor offered.

Victoria smiled in spite of herself. "I knew there was a reason I liked you."

Thomas only laughed. "If I die by foul means, I'm giving the castle to Mom and Jennifer to use for a baby-clothes shop."

Victoria shivered. "You would, too, wouldn't you?"

He looked back over his shoulder at her. "Of course not. But seriously, Vic. What are you going to do? Don't you have season tickets already sold?"

She shook her head. "I never sent anything out. I had it all printed, but when I found out Moonbat was ripping the stage out from under me, I cancelled the company who does my tickets."

"People will wonder what happened to you."

"I'll send out notices when we find a new space." She sighed. "But I suppose I do need to get back and see if I can resurrect my company."

At least that's what she thought she needed to do. What she feared was that she would get back to Manhattan, find that her troupe was still intact, and not want to do a damned thing with them.

What she wanted to do was act.

Truly, she had lost her mind.

She sighed. "Some of it depends on what's left of my troupe once Michael Fellini's agent gets ahold of my actors."

"Fellini," Connor grumbled. "What a pompous, over-acting buffoon."

Everyone in the car went still. Victoria shared a startled glance with Iolanthe, then held her breath until Connor reached up and scratched his head.

"Too many chocolates after lunch," he said. "I have these dreams."

"I'll just bet you do," Thomas said easily. "All right, let me find a parking place, then we'll go shop and meet back here. Then I say we go have a nice dinner and see the show."

Victoria let her breath out slowly. So close, but yet so incredibly far from anything useful. Well, at least he was having dreams. That was something.

She was distracted suddenly by the sight of Connor leaping out of the car to study the traffic. At least he wasn't leaping out *into* the traffic, but she supposed that couldn't be far behind. Fortunately, Thomas managed to convince him to use the sidewalk for its intended purpose.

"Clothes, first," Thomas said. "Io, why don't you and Vic take the keys and meet us back here in an hour."

"An hour?" Victoria echoed. "I'm sure we'll be done long before then."

"I know. That's why I'm giving you the keys."

Victoria was pleased to find that Iolanthe had just as little patience as she did for lingering over clothes, but perhaps that came from being morning sick. She knew her own impatience came from dissatisfaction over how her vow not to control people anymore had panned out. She suspected that she might be happier telling everyone what to do.

She sighed as she and Iolanthe walked back down the street to the car to dump their casual clothes into the trunk. It would either all work out in the end or it wouldn't. Really, when it came to medieval Highlanders, there was not much to be done.

She had just shut the trunk when her sister-in-law caught her breath.

"Oh, my," Iolanthe said in surprise.

"What?"

"Look behind you."

Victoria hesitated. "Is it Connor and Thomas?"

"Aye. Dressed in their finery."

Victoria closed her eyes briefly. *Let him not be wearing Victorian ruffles mismatched with a tricorn hat.* She turned.

She caught her breath, as well.

All right, so the man looked fine in jeans. In a suit, he was absolutely breathtaking. Impressive and powerful and so put together that she wondered if she would ever take another money man in a suit seriously. He stopped in front of her and smiled.

"What do you think?"

"I think *wow*."

Connor made her a low bow. "Thanks must go to your brother."

"Thanks, Thomas," Victoria said weakly.

"Let's go," Thomas said with a laugh, "before my sister falls in a pool of drool of her own making. Dinner, anyone?"

"Always," Connor said promptly.

"Sure," Victoria said, looking forward to a place to sit.

"If we must," Iolanthe said, not sounding at all enthusiastic about the idea.

Dinner was as lengthy an affair as Iolanthe could stand, which wasn't all that long. Connor seemed rather sad to leave anything behind, but she managed to stop him before he finished off everyone's leavings. She watched him as they left the restaurant and made their way down the sidewalk. He wasn't saying anything; that might have come from being so busy gawking at everything around him.

"What do you think?" she asked.

He dragged his gaze back to hers. "I think you are very beautiful," he said frankly.

"I meant about Edinburgh."

"I think there are too many people here. Many more than the last time I was here, but I do not find it unpleasing." He smiled at her suddenly and took her hand. "I should hold on to you, lest you become lost."

Lost? She was already lost, lost so far in her feelings for him that she supposed she would never find her way out.

Good grief, how was she going to go on?

She was very grateful, half an hour later, to find herself in a theater with the lights about to go down. It allowed her to weep in peace.

Connor, meanwhile, was patting himself, then cursing, as if the lack of dagger was just too much to be borne.

"If we're attacked in the dark, I'll use my hands," he assured her.

She managed a nod. "I would expect nothing less."

She felt him turn in his seat and knew he was looking at her. "Ach, Victoria, why—"

"The play," she said, pointing to the stage. "Look, the lights are going down. And look, it's *Hamlet*." She managed to throw Thomas a glare. "What a surprise. This must be why Thomas made me close my eyes on the way into the theater and wouldn't let me have a program until now."

"Is it?" Connor said resettling himself. "One would hope that it would be worth watching. I daresay in a building this luxurious, the tickets come dear—"

And then he fell silent. Victoria snuck a look at him. He was staring at the stage, completely mesmerized. The curtain opened to allow them to see the men of the watch going about their business. Connor smiled in pleasure.

And then the ghost appeared.

And Connor went completely still.

Victoria nodded to herself. He was probably having some sympathy for the watchmen, given that he'd had his own brush with the paranormal up at the castle just recently. She abandoned him to his own devices and turned to watch the play.

She had to admit *Hamlet* was one of her favorites and the production was shaping up to be a good one. It was often very difficult for her to enjoy other productions, because she spent most of her time critiquing everything that went on up on the stage. Tonight it was different. Maybe it was because the accents were authentic. Maybe it was because the production was actually quite good. Or maybe it was something useful stemming from her new hands-off policy.

Yes, the actors onstage could do whatever they wanted; she didn't care. She found it quite freeing, actually, to let others go on about their business without feeling as if she were responsible for their actions. Still, there was something that got in the way of fully enjoying that freedom. She realized, with a start, that there was low murmuring going on nearby. She frowned. What idiot was playing Hamlet's part from the peanut gallery while the real acting was going on up on stage?

Then she realized that the idiot was sitting next to her. She looked at Connor and frowned a bit more. Didn't he know he was supposed to be quiet? She realized that she hadn't said anything and Thomas probably hadn't thought to. She leaned over to whisper to him that he really should button up, when she realized what he was doing.

He was whispering Hamlet's lines.

In English.

She found, quite suddenly, that she couldn't move. She did manage to catch Thomas's eye. He had leaned forward, as well, and was looking at Connor with satisfaction. Then he smiled at her.

"Bingo," he whispered.

Victoria sat back and kept her mouth shut. Connor groped for her hand and held it as if she were all that kept him from shattering into a million pieces. His fingers gripped hers in a way that was almost painful, but she couldn't bring herself to say anything. Heaven only knew what was going on inside his head, but she wasn't about to interrupt it on the off chance it was something good.

Hamlet.

It occurred to her that Thomas had chosen the play with great care. Maybe it would be the thing that would spark Connor's memories and bring him back to her.

One more thing to thank her brother for, damn it anyway. She closed her eyes and began to pray.

Chapter 36

Connor sat in the darkened theater with Shakespeare being blurted out on the stage in English and wondered if he could possibly sit still through the torrents of memories that were crashing down over him, wave after wave of centuries of recollections that left him gasping in their wake.

He was listening to *Hamlet*. In English. Just as he had performed it not two months earlier on the closing night of Victoria's run in Thorpewold Castle.

That wave receded and another came. There he was, raging over the injustice of his life ending unfairly, wreaking havoc on the Frenchman who had killed him for the sport of it, wanting desperately to leave the Highlands but being unwilling to go at the same time. Loving and hating until he could no longer recognize himself.

The centuries after he'd finally came south paraded themselves before him in glorious fashion, one after another, full to the brim with bad humors and dastardly deeds. He rubbed his neck uncomfortably, wondering how it was that he had popped his head off so often and with such impunity without suffering any kind of discomfort for the deed.

He saw himself arguing with Iolanthe MacLeod. He remembered doing his damndest to force Thomas McKinnon to leave the keep . . .

He paused. He frowned. He leaned over Iolanthe to glare at her husband.

"You promised me a roof for that bloody keep and you never built it."

"I got married instead."

"Damn you."

"Yeah," Thomas whispered with a grin. "Nice to have you back, Laird MacDougal."

Connor would have commented, but an entirely new collection of memories swept over him.

He saw Victoria coming into the hall for the first time, Victoria fawning over Michael Fellini, Victoria in the library of the Boar's Head Inn, sitting in her chair before a fire of his making, looking at him with growing affection in her eyes.

Victoria vowing to save him from death.

Then he viewed Victoria over the past week. He suspected she had spent most of that se'nnight wondering why it was he was so thick-headed. He looked at her as she sat next to him presently.

She had tears streaming down her face.

He couldn't help himself. He slipped his hand underneath her hair, leaned over, and kissed her.

And once he started, he just couldn't seem to stop himself.

"Och, and this is hardly the place for snogging, is it?" a very annoyed voice whispered crisply from behind him.

He lifted his head, looked behind him, and glared.

A finely dressed woman of at least eight decades lifted her purse and shook it at him threateningly.

Connor was not about to brawl with an old woman and her bag, so he graciously conceded the battle and contented himself with putting his arm around his lady and drawing her as close as their seats would allow.

"I remember," he whispered in awe.

"It's about time," she whispered back.

He smiled and continued to sit with Victoria, clutching her to him and fighting off the realization of how close he had come to losing her.

He thought a tear might have escaped his eye.

She looked up at him in surprise.

"Sweat," he bluffed.

"Right," she said, wearing the first tremulous smile he'd ever seen.

He took her hand in his own and stroked it. He closed his eyes briefly in thanks, then looked down at Victoria's hand in the dark. By the saints, how many times had he wished he could touch her in death, and there he was, in life, doing just that.

It was possible, he conceded, that another tear or two might have fallen to join the first.

The play went on without him. He couldn't watch it, didn't dare look at Victoria, and suspected another look behind him would earn him a lump on his head. So he kept his eyes on Victoria's hand as it grew increasingly damp.

The lights went up for intermission.

Connor dragged the sleeve of his suitcoat across his eyes and popped up to his feet, pulling Victoria up with him. He started for the doors.

"Wha—wait," Thomas said. "Where are you going?"

"I am going," Connor said distinctly, "somewhere where I might kiss my betrothed senseless in peace."

"But the show isn't over."

"It is for us." He looked at Victoria. "We'll go outside."

"Hey," Thomas said with a grin, "I think public displays of affection are against the law here. I guess you'll just have to wait for us to finish the rest of the play."

Connor looked at Iolanthe briefly, then back at Thomas. "Your bride is green. I believe the show is over for you, as well."

"She's fine—"

Connor stood aside as Iolanthe bolted past him. He smiled. "Keys?"

"Dream on," Thomas said with a sigh. "Let's go wait for Io in the lobby. Maybe this is for the best. I really don't think you should be alone with my sister."

"Thomas," Victoria warned.

"In fact, I think it's my brotherly duty to properly chaperone her. Don't you agree?"

Connor looked at Victoria. "I would like to kill him. Would that bother you?"

"I couldn't care less," she said tartly.

"Hey," Thomas said, "I'm directly responsible for bringing you two together. A little gratitude would not be unappreciated at this point. Besides, MacDougal, you're going to need a groomsman."

"I'll give that some thought," Connor said. He put his arm around Victoria's shoulders and pulled her toward the door. "Let's collect that poor MacLeod wench and be off."

"You're sure you don't want to finish the play?" Thomas asked from behind them.

"I can think of many things I want to do and not a one of them includes sitting through a play I have memorized. Indeed, I daresay I can do all the parts for you on the way home if you care to hear them."

"You have a good memory," Victoria said, sounding rather breathless.

"He has a *vast* memory," Thomas said with a laugh. "I'll bet it spans centuries."

Victoria looked at her brother, then burst into tears. Connor supposed they were tears of relief. He pulled her into his arms and found that even his eyes had begun to bother him.

"Allergies," he explained to anyone who was listening.

Thomas grasped his shoulder again in a friendly grip. "I understand completely, believe me. Congratulations and welcome to the twenty-first century."

Connor stroked Victoria's hair. "I can hardly believe it,"

he said reverently. " 'Tis a miracle. And listen. I can speak the King's English as well."

"Queen's," Victoria said, her words muffled.

Connor grunted. "I'll come to terms with that later. For now, I want to go back to the inn, take a very long walk to the castle, and have some privacy with you."

"I think," Thomas said slowly, "that you two really *will* need a chaperone. I have my sister's virtue to guard, you know."

"Thomas," she said, lifting her head to look at him with warning, "shut *up*!"

"And you'll have to convince my dad," Thomas continued. "You know, Connor, we just barely started to warm him up to the idea of you being a ghost after Vic's closing night. Now, we'll have to really dig deep and give him explanations he won't ever buy—"

"Thomas!" Victoria exclaimed.

Connor patted her back. "He must torment me a little. I am taking his sister away from him."

"I'm sure he's thrilled," Victoria said dryly.

"Actually," Thomas said with a smile, "I'm mixed about it. You won't be mine to drive crazy anymore without this big, hulking brute standing up for you. But I'll probably see you more because Connor will want to come and sit at a table where the native tongue is spoken so expertly. Maybe you can go one step further and buy a house nearby us in Maine."

Connor had a brief flash of unease come over him. How, by all the saints, would he support Victoria and whatever bairns they had? It wasn't as if he could raise cattle, grow crops, or raid his enemies' herds.

"Connor?"

He put the worry aside for later, when he would have the time to give it the proper attention. He looked down into his lady's beautiful face and smiled reflexively. "Aye, love?"

"What are you thinking?"

"That I am quite possibly the most fortunate man in eight hundred years; for I was the one to, beyond all reason, capture your heart."

"I'm fond of your grumbles."

"You'll have plenty of those," Thomas interrupted cheerfully.

Connor pursed his lips. "We will not live in the same hall with him."

"Heaven forbid," she said with feeling.

"Now, your granny is another matter entirely," Connor said, remembering how fond he was of her. "She could live with us. Think you she might knit me something with that Fair Isle technique she favors?"

"You'll never have to buy another sweater," Victoria said with a smile. "I imagine you'll be begging her to stop—"

"Oh, look," Thomas interrupted, "here comes Iolanthe." He looked at Connor. "If you're sure you want to go back to the inn."

"I am quite certain."

"Not much privacy there."

"More than here."

"You think?"

Connor realized he was patting himself for his sword and that it was not there. He settled for a glare that only earned him a laugh. He looked at Victoria. "We will not live anywhere near him."

"Whatever you say," she said with a smile.

"I love you," he said, finding that if he was going to say something, it behooved him to say what was in his heart.

"I love you, too," she said, her eyes bright with tears.

"Oh, good grief," Thomas said, pointing toward the entrance. "Let's get out of here before people start paying you two for the love scene, shall we?"

Connor did not want to let go of Victoria, but he found that he at least had to release part of her to be able to walk comfortably. They made their way to the car and he found himself unable to fit into the backseat. He frowned.

"You should have borrowed a larger car," he told Thomas.

"We're an hour away from the inn," Thomas said, getting in. "You'll survive."

Connor very much doubted it.

He clambered into the front seat and spent the entirety of the trip with his arm wrenched around the back of the seat so he could hold Victoria's hand whilst concurrently being bludgeoned by questions from her brother. He finally swore in exasperation.

"Aye, I remember it all!" he exclaimed. "Would you care for an exhaustive list of hauntings?"

"Ghosts Behaving Badly," Thomas said with a grin. "Now, there's a television show for you."

"I had reason," Connor said, through gritted teeth. "Though," he added, craning his neck around to look at Iolanthe, "I humbly beg pardon of you, Mistress MacLeod, for all the grief I caused you."

"She's a McKinnon," Thomas reminded him.

"Not when I was tormenting her."

"It's in the past," Iolanthe said, "but what's left of supper will be quite present if you do not make haste, husband."

Connor gave Victoria's hand a squeeze and quickly returned his own to the front seat. He was no coward, but he had no desire to have Iolanthe puke on him by mistake.

It seemed to take an eternity to get to the inn, but given that he had waited at least that long for Victoria, he could not complain. He helped her out of the car and pulled her into his arms.

What he wanted to do was crawl into her very soul and find himself completely surrounded by her. He thought the next best thing might be an extended bit of kissing, so he bid good night to Thomas and Iolanthe and started for the castle.

"Don't you want your sword?" Thomas asked. "You know, just in case."

Connor frowned. He couldn't exactly buckle it about him in a fancy, modern suit, so he supposed he would have to carry it in his hand. That left one less hand to hold Victoria with on the way to the castle, but who was he to complain? He looked at his love.

"Wait here."

He fetched his sword and found her where he had left her, looking so lovely in the moonlight that he could hardly bear the sight of her. He took a deep breath and strode forward—

"Wait," Thomas said. He returned from inside the inn with an umbrella. "It might rain."

"There isn't a bloody cloud in the sky."

"We're in England. It rains all the time."

"Bonk him over the head with it," Victoria suggested.

"I really think you two shouldn't be alone," Thomas said.

Connor frowned at Victoria's brother. "I will not ravish her."

"I'll come along to make sure."

Victoria elbowed Thomas aside. "Beat it. Get lost. Keep on truckin'. Do all those things before I find *my* sword, the one that does not collapse, and turn you into a sieve."

Connor found himself smiling. Aye, this was the woman for him, one who appreciated a good threat as much as he did and almost had the means to follow through on it. He took Victoria's hand and pulled her away.

"You'll be safe with me," he said. "I'll chaperone us myself."

"I'm sure you'll have help!" Thomas called helpfully from behind them.

Connor walked with Victoria to the castle, and could hardly believe he was where he was, with all his memories intact, as if he had lived two lifetimes to their fullest.

And now he would have yet another life with his love. It was more than he could ask for and certainly more than he deserved. He stood in the midst of the bailey and put his arms around Victoria, stunned that he could do the like, and smiled at her.

She smiled in return. "You're cheerful."

"Can you fault me for it? I have my heart's desire before me and I can actually hold her with mortal arms. My other choice is to weep, but I dare not lest I lose face with more than just you."

She looked around, then shrugged. "I don't see anyone."

He searched for observers himself, and realized she spoke the truth. It was quite a happy discovery. Connor smiled pleasantly, gathered Victoria closer, and began to be about the business of kissing her as thoroughly as he wanted to.

His knees grew a little weak. They might have buckled, had he not had such iron control over his form.

He buried one of his hands in Victoria's hair and drew her even closer, finding himself becoming caught up in truly expressing how much he loved her. He felt a little light-headed and supposed it might be time for them both to come up for a bit of air.

Briefly.

He lifted his head, then squawked. In a manly, gruff fashion, of course.

He was surrounded by the Boar's Head Trio, all staring at him with fierce frowns and folded arms. Even Roderick, that womanly fop, was there, looking displeased.

"Och," Hugh McKinnon said sternly, "and there'll be none of *that* much ado-ing afore the weddin'!"

"I was kissing her!" Connor exclaimed. "Can you fault me for it?"

"We cannot, 'tis true," Ambrose agreed, clasping his hands behind his back. "Well, carry on."

"Carry yourselves on—outside my gates," Connor suggested.

"Can't," Fulbert de Piaget said pleasantly.

"Can't," Connor repeated in disbelief. "Why the bloody hell not?"

" 'Tis our duty as progenitors to watch over her."

"Watch over her later."

"We'll watch now."

The ghosts resumed their folded arms and gruff expressions. Connor looked at them, then down at Victoria. He sighed.

"Let us return to the inn. We'll plan the wedding. I daresay 'twill be the only way we have any privacy."

"One could hope," she said with a laugh.

Connor bid the ghosts a curt good-night and walked with Victoria from the castle. He supposed perhaps 'twas for the best. There would be time enough, he hoped fervently, for a good deal of kissing and a good deal more later. For now, perhaps it would serve him well to sit and ponder the improbability and good fortune that was his.

A beautiful, spirited woman who loved him.

A time of luxuries and marvels.

And he himself, alive and able to enjoy them all.

"Do you realize you're running?" Victoria asked, running alongside him.

"I'm in a hurry," he said. "So much to do."

And so little time. And so little means. He would have to come to terms with that, and quickly, but for now, he would take his love back to the inn where they had passed so many pleasant evenings together, and rejoice in the fact that she was soon to be his.

He quickened his pace.

The Future was his and he didn't want it rushing away from him.

Chapter 37

L*ife* was, Victoria decided, indeed very strange.

It had been precisely five days since Connor had found his memories—or, rather, his memories had found him. Her wedding had been planned for the upcoming Saturday, with the Earl of Artane happily providing his local vicar to do the honors. Victoria had found herself measured and pinned and prodded several times already in preparation for the big event. Connor had been fitted once, but he'd managed to bellow his way out of any further indignities.

She should have borrowed his sword.

She leaned back in her chair and smiled at the sight around her. Her mother and father were there, as were her granny, Megan, and Gideon. Even Iolanthe was sitting upright and had the barest hint of color. Ghosts filled the room, as well, though out of respect for her father, they weren't doing much but nodding in appreciation of the talk going on.

Victoria looked at her father and smiled to herself. Now, that had been an interesting situation. When her father had arrived at the inn three days earlier, Connor had presented himself in his best light, sword in hand, and asked politely if he could speak with Lord McKinnon in private. Victoria wouldn't have been surprised to see her father grab for the phone and dial 911—or whatever it was they had in England. Actually, she wouldn't have been surprised to have had him dial for *American* emergency services—he had been that spooked.

But after an appropriately lengthy time in the library, Connor had emerged looking satisfied. Her father had emerged looking slightly green around the gills.

"He says," her father had said weakly, "that he will provide for you, even if it means using his sword in new and creative ways." He had paused. "I'm not sure what that means, but I know I'm not going to argue with him. Where in the *hell*, Victoria, did you find him?"

"Up in the castle, Dad," she'd said. "He did *Hamlet* closing night, remember?"

"Yes. He gave me the willies then. I suppose he'll be giving me the willies every Thanksgiving from now until the day I die."

"One could hope," she had said.

"He looks a little more substantial now than before," her father had said, eyeing the dining room as a possible refuge. "Has he gained weight?"

"We should probably talk about that later, Dad," she'd called after him as he departed for safer ground in the kitchen.

Unfortunately for her father, Connor had followed him shortly thereafter for precisely the same reason.

But now, her dad was calmer about, if not exactly clearer on, when Connor had first appeared in her life and where she'd met him. Her mother and her granny had listened with rapt attention to all the details.

While her dad was in the kitchen again, of course.

All of which left her sitting happily with her family and sundry around her, with her life completely changed for the better and, as usual, Thomas to thank for it. But those thanks might be mitigated if she ever discovered where he'd taken her groom. They'd gone off together that morning, thick as thieves, to be about some kind of mischief. If Thomas led him astray . . .

The door to the sitting room burst open and Victoria jumped. Jennifer stood there, her eyes wide.

Victoria was on her feet without any knowledge of how she'd gotten there. "What is it? An accident?"

"You have to come to the castle."

"What is it?" she said, dashing for the door and pulling her sister with her. "Is it Connor?"

"Not exactly."

Victoria slowed to a walk. "Not exactly?"

"Well, he's involved in it. So is Thomas." Jennifer paused. "I don't think you're going to like it."

Victoria looked behind her to see the rest of the sitting room inhabitants trailing after her. What was this, a surprise bridal shower? A bachelor party for Connor, to which she was invited?

"Is this a joke?" she asked her sister sternly.

"Just come and look."

Victoria sighed and walked quickly with Jennifer to the place where she'd first seen Connor as a ghost. She sincerely hoped she wouldn't find him in like condition this time.

She hurried up the path and through the barbican gate. Then she came to a teetering halt. In fact, it was so teetering that she tipped forward and stuck her foot into a hole.

It was one of many holes that were scattered all over the inner bailey.

"What in the world is going on here?" she said aloud. She looked at her sister. "What's going on? Giant moles? Small children running amok with shovels and pails?"

Jennifer pointed to the stage. "There are the perps."

"Are you in on this?"

"I was just taking an innocent walk," Jennifer said, holding up her hands. "The damage was done before I stumbled on the scene of the crime."

Victoria pulled her foot out of the hole and picked her way around a dozen or so more before she managed to get herself within spitting distance of the stage. She put her hands on her hips and prepared, all her former resolutions aside, to control the destinies of the two idiots in front of her.

Bellowing was unnecessary, apparently. Before she had the time to think up an appropriately dire threat or two, bums began to wiggle out from under the stage.

She kicked her brother's. She didn't dare kick Connor's.

"Hey," Thomas said, sitting up and cracking his head sharply against the edge of the wood, "who did that?"

"A ghost," Victoria said crisply. "What are you doing demolishing my venue? This may be the only venue I have, you know."

Connor heaved a small chest out from under the stage and dropped it at her feet. He smiled up at her.

All right, so his face was smudged with dirt and he had obviously been in on—if not the instigator of—all the digging. When he smiled, she just couldn't do anything but smile back.

"I like that," Thomas said crossly, rubbing his head. "I get the boot and you get the doe eyes."

"'Tis all those centuries of living well," Connor said in a superior tone. He beckoned to Victoria. "Come, lady, and look at what we've found."

She walked around to look over his shoulder. "It looks like a wooden box."

"It looks like a treasure chest," Jennifer offered, coming to stand next to her.

"It could be filled with gold," Connor said enthusiastically.

"It could be filled with petrified chamber-pot contents," Victoria countered.

"An Englishman buried it here," Connor said, tossing her a brief frown. "He dressed very well. It was with no small regret that I caused him to ruin his trousers."

"See?" Victoria said. "I told you so. Chamber pot."

Thomas looked around. "Crowbar anyone?"

"Boy Scout knife," John McKinnon said, coming to kneel down next to Connor. "Say, Connor, how did you know this was here? You saw someone bury this? Why would someone recently bury an antique?"

Victoria coughed to cover up a laugh. Connor was still trying to digest all her father's questions and Thomas was lying through his teeth as quickly as he could. By the time he had the chest open, her father looked thoroughly confused.

But Connor was chortling. He looked up at her triumphantly. "Shiny, aye?"

"Worth lots," Thomas added happily, wiggling his fingers purposefully. "I suppose you won't starve now."

"We wouldn't have starved, anyway," Victoria said absently, "but if it makes you happy . . ."

John looked at his son. "I still don't get it. Why would someone bury old coins in a derelict castle while a big guy like Connor was watching? I know the idyllic countryside can get to you over here, but—"

"John, love," Mary called, "I'm a little chilled. Will you walk me and your lovely wife back to the inn?"

Victoria looked over in time to catch her grandmother's very unsubtle wink.

"Well . . . ," Victoria's father said doubtfully.

"Brrr," Mary said, rubbing her arms vigorously.

John frowned, then reluctantly walked away. "Take good notes, Victoria. I want the whole story later."

"Sure, Dad," she said. She waited until the little party was gone before she turned back to the find. Connor and Thomas were almost giggling. Even Gideon had knelt down next to the box and was happily examining its contents. Victoria looked at her sisters.

"Who do you think will fill the holes back in?"

"You," Jennifer said promptly. "But do it today so you'll have time to get all the dirt out from under your fingernails before the wedding. Come on, Megan. You look a little flushed. You aren't going into labor, are you?"

"I'm due any minute," Megan said.

"Then let's get you back to the inn," Jennifer said. "You don't want to have your baby up here in the castle, do you? Wow, what an audience you'd have."

"Not funny, Jenner."

"Megan, I don't think you'd find anything funny right now. Gideon, don't dawdle!"

"I'm coming posthaste," he called after them.

Victoria watched her sisters leave the keep, followed by three grandfatherly ghosts, who seemed to have quite a lot to say to Jennifer. Victoria wondered if she was next on their hit list.

Victoria smiled to herself and supposed her sister would survive any matchmaking those three might do for her. It had certainly worked out well in her own case.

She turned back to the diggers and put her hand on Connor's shoulder. "Well, what do you think?"

"I think I now have a way to feed you," he said, smiling broadly. "What do you think, Lord Blythwood?"

"It's just Gideon," Gideon said, flashing him a brief smile, "and I think you have made out quite well here. Oddly enough, I just happen to have the name and telephone number of a coin dealer." He paused for a moment. "I have a friend who recently purchased a substantial amount of medieval coins from this particular dealer. The dealer would no doubt be pleased to replenish his supply, even though these don't look to be from the same era."

"Why would anyone want to buy a bunch of medieval coins?" Thomas asked.

Gideon smiled. "It's a very long story. I'll tell you later if you're really interested. For now, let me help you haul these down to the inn. I can't leave Megan for long."

Victoria stood back and waited while Connor, Gideon, and Thomas heaved the box up and carried it out of the inner bailey. She followed them back to the inn and watched with a smile as they muscled their burden into the library. She was still standing in the foyer when Jennifer came out of the sitting room.

"This is good," Jennifer said.

"This is fabulous," Victoria corrected. "His ego will be saved. Dozens of potential victims will be spared. Cattle will remain on grazing lands where they belong, instead of finding their way into Thorpewold Castle."

Jennifer laughed. "You know, you're the one who fell in love with him. He can't help being a medieval laird."

"I don't blame him. He is what he is and I wouldn't change him." She looked at her sister with a smile. "There's something to be said for fourteenth-century chivalry."

"I'm sure there is. Why can't we graduate these kinds of men from law school? Connor doesn't have a brother, does he?"

"He has a cousin, but I think he had to stay behind to lead the clan. I guess you're stuck with what Manhattan can produce."

Jennifer laughed. "Heaven help me." She smiled wistfully. "I envy you. He is quite a man."

Victoria had never been envied before, at least not to her knowledge and certainly not about her love life.

She had to admit that she envied herself.

She paused in the entryway and listened to the laughter coming from inside the library. There were Thomas and Gideon, of course, but rising above it all now and again was Connor's mirth, something she had never expected to hear.

Certainly not coming from him in a mortal way.

"The gift that keeps on giving," Jennifer whispered from beside her.

"The gold?"

"The man."

It was true and all the more wonderful for its being unexpected.

"The gift that keeps on giving," Victoria whispered to herself with a smile.

Another laugh from inside the library interrupted her musings. She smiled at Jennifer, then followed her over to the sitting room, leaving the men to their newfound treasure.

Life was good and cattle for miles were now safe.

It didn't get much better than that.

Chapter 38

C onnor leaned over the counter and peered into the glass jars. He lifted one, sniffed vigorously, then pulled back and sneezed heartily.

"What, by all the saints, is that?"

"Red raspberry leaf," Victoria said.

"What purpose does it serve?"

The girl behind the counter, the one with the silver ball coming out the side of her nose and the ring through her eyebrow, sighed wearily. "Female complaints."

Connor put the jar back with alacrity. "I think I'll leave all these things alone."

"That might be best."

Connor leaned against the counter and let Victoria be about her business. He looked about the Tempest in a Teapot and wondered how Victoria had managed to get her theatergoers out of this place with all its marvelous smells that seemed to make him want to go to sleep and up the stairs to the theater. Perhaps her patrons were made of sterner stuff than he.

And it had taken a bit of stern stuff to acclimate himself

so quickly to all that Manhattan had to offer. Indeed, the past fortnight had been a whirlwind of activity, starting with the selling of part of his buried treasure and finishing with trying to get to sleep in Victoria's small apartment that seemed to be in a place in the city where no one ever slept. And sandwiched between those two events had been a quite lovely wedding and a highly enjoyable honeymoon at Artane.

No wonder Thomas and Iolanthe went so often to visit. Connor had seen the sea before, of course, but there was something quite magical about visiting a keep that stood so close to the shore.

That might have had something to do with the company, though.

He looked at Victoria and couldn't help a smile. By the saints, she was magnificent, in looks and temperament both. He reached out and smoothed a hand down her hair before he could stop himself.

She smiled briefly at him, then turned back to her business.

"Look, Moonbat, I just want to talk to Mr. Chi."

"He's meditating."

Connor pursed his lips. He'd heard all about the forced takeover of Victoria's space by a man who apparently twisted himself into uncomfortable shapes and made his fortune teaching others to do the same. Victoria did not have fond feelings for the man. Connor could not blame her, given that the man had laid siege to her theater.

"Is he leasing his meditation space," Victoria pressed, "or has he bought it?"

Mistress Moonbat shifted uneasily. "He's leasing."

"Then I'll buy him out."

"But—"

"I'll offer you double what he's paying."

"Vic," Moonbat said, dragging her name out for a very long moment, "I can't."

"Why not?"

"It wouldn't be right."

"And jerking it out from under me was?"

Moonbat leaned forward. "Vic, it's a lot of money."

"I have more."

"I'll think about it. Until then, can I make you some tea?"

Victoria scowled fiercely. "No, thanks. We'll just go have a hot dog down the street."

Connor could have sworn Moonbat rushed off to the loo to puke, but what did he know? What he did know was that he had learned to appreciate the hot-dog vendors on the corners of the Big Apple and if Victoria was willing to indulge him again, he would not refuse. He followed her happily from the shop, leaving behind jars of things he was certain Patrick MacLeod would appreciate but that were not precisely to his taste.

"I don't get it," Victoria said, looking puzzled as they walked down the sidewalk. "If it's money, why won't she budge?"

"There must be more to it."

"I guess—" She gasped suddenly and dragged him into the alcove of a building. "Look!"

He looked. He saw Michael Fellini strolling into the Teapot as if he owned the place. "Ah," Connor said wisely, "there is your answer."

"I should go see what's really going on."

"Nay, allow me," Connor said. "Fellini won't recognize me."

"But Moonbat will."

"I'll be discreet."

She looked at him with one eyebrow raised, but didn't gainsay him. He patted her affectionately, thought better of it, and kissed her passionately, then trotted off whilst she was still distracted.

Being wed to Victoria McKinnon had been more delightful than he could have imagined—and he had imagined quite a bit.

He approached the store and scouted out any potential locations. He pulled his Yankees baseball cap out of his pocket and clapped it on top of his head, then slunk into the shop and pretended great interest in fruity soaps.

Er, herby soaps.

He decided right then that he much preferred the fruity sort.

He eavesdropped with enthusiasm, but wondered if his ears were beginning to fail him. He listened to Michael Fellini spew forth his drivel, listened to a very fond good-bye which, he saw by means of a casual glance over his shoulder, included much kissing, then waited until Fellini had left the shop before he followed him. He flashed Moonbat Murphy a glance of annoyance.

She grasped frantically for herbal comfort.

Connor quickly returned to Victoria's side. "You will not believe it."

"Tell me," she said. "Was there money exchanged?"

"More than that."

"Really? What?" she asked, wide-eyed.

He took her hand, then pulled her along with him. "It would seem that Fellini wants your wee Teapot for himself. I daresay he's enough of an actor to leave Mistress Moonbat believing that he loves her in truth."

"Really," Victoria said in surprise. "But the Bat isn't that gullible."

"Perhaps she's been sniffing too many of her wares and has dulled her senses."

"Did he kiss her?"

"Do you care?"

"Only in that I'm relieved I never succumbed," she said, giving his hand a squeeze.

"I might have had to do him damage, otherwise," Connor said pleasantly. He looked at her and knew she fretted. "There will be other theaters, Victoria. 'Tis not this one that holds the magic; it is you who brings magic to stage."

"I want to believe that."

"You should," he said firmly. "We will find another place."

She nodded and fell silent. Connor allowed her peace—

such as could be found in Manhattan. He looked about them as they walked, marveling that so much of humanity could dwell within such a small space, yet still manage to live their lives in relative contentment. Och, aye, there was the occasional bad apple, but that was to be expected. What manly man could go about his labors without the odd comment now and then? And what wench worth her salt could avoid a colorful pronouncement when vexed overmuch?

Connor had worried once or twice on the plane flight over if he would manage to live in Victoria's city without longing for the countryside. Of course, he'd wondered several things on that flight over, when he'd seen the earth below from a vantage point he never would have dreamed of during his lifetime. But Manhattan pleased him well for the time being. He supposed it was possible that they wouldn't be there forever.

They certainly wouldn't be there if Victoria could not find a site for her plays.

"We have to meet Fred in ten minutes," Victoria said. "You'll like the restaurant."

"I'll have a hot dog for dessert."

"Of course you will."

The interview with Fred was pleasant. Fred vowed to get to the bottom of the conundrum. Apparently, he knew a guy. What that meant, Connor couldn't have said, but Victoria seemed to be satisfied. All Connor knew was that Fred shared his dislike of Michael Fellini and his affection for Victoria McKinnon, and for that Connor approved of him heartily.

The afternoon was passed most satisfactorily, plotting Fellini's demise with Fred. Then he and Victoria retired to her small house. It was little more than a box with a window, but Connor found it to his liking. Then again, perhaps it was that he found the company to his liking.

In the end, what pleased him the most was the fact that Victoria was his and that she welcomed him into her arms and into her bed.

That took up a goodly part of the afternoon quite satisfactorily.

Connor considered over supper, then thought some more as they ventured out into the evening to take in a play on Broadway. It was a musical and Connor enjoyed it, though he was not overly impressed with the acting.

Victoria was better.

But he hesitated to tell her so. She would have to come to the conclusion on her own. Perhaps a return to Thorpewold now and again wouldn't be unthinkable. After all, Thomas had gifted it to Victoria as a wedding present—not that he'd needed to. Connor would have purchased it, but the damned stubborn man had refused. Connor had accepted it, more willingly than he normally would have, simply for Victoria's sake.

Aye, they could open their own theater there and likely make a goodly living doing so. Not that they needed the gold, but he suspected they would both go a little mad not doing something constructive. Bairns would hopefully come in time and then their lives would change again, but for the moment, he was content to watch Victoria tread the boards where she could.

"You're thinking," she said, tilting her head back to look at him from where she rested in his arms.

"I was thinking of your Ophelia," he said with a smile. "I would like to see you do something else."

"I've thought about it," she admitted, "but I don't know how. Then again, if Bernie the Bardmaker has made it so I have no actors left, maybe I will be happily without a choice."

"But until then," he said purposefully.

Aye, they would keep themselves busy somehow.

Chapter 39

Victoria could hardly believe she was engaging in her current activity, but all signs pointed to the fact that she was puttering. She never puttered, preferring to take on things that required the full use of all her mental faculties. It was amazing what losing her venue, losing her actors, and losing her reputation all in a single week had done to her.

She stopped in front of the window and stared outside. All in all, it had been a very good month. She'd gotten married, she'd had a wonderful honeymoon, and she was currently delighting in each day that brought her new hours to spend with Connor.

Of course, the fly in the ointment had been Bernie the Bardmaker, who had managed to make it so no one wanted to work for her. She hadn't been surprised.

She hadn't been happy, either.

Contemplating the potential for Michael's theatrical demise with Fred had taken up the better part of the past week, but now she was left with the tatters of her theater career and no needle and thread with which to mend it.

She looked down the street and found herself smiling in spite of it all. Connor was coming home from a brief trip to the local deli. She had frisked him for lethal weapons on his way out, so she hadn't really worried that he would get into trouble, but with Connor, you just never knew.

He bounded up the steps and into her apartment. "My lady," he said with a low bow. He straightened and presented her with his spoils. "Turkey and swiss on rye, hold the mayo and do some business with the mustard."

She laughed. "You're sounding very modern today, my laird."

"Och, nay," he said with a smile. " 'Tis just my line I practiced for the man at the deli. He glowered at me so the other day when I attempted to converse in a normal fashion that I felt I had to humor him. He makes bloody good sandwiches and I didn't want to anger—"

The phone rang. Victoria was so surprised she jumped. It had been days since the phone had rung in that businesslike, not-family-on-the-other-end kind of way. She looked at Connor briefly.

"I have a feeling about this," she said slowly.

"Fate?" he asked, unearthing his treasures from the deli sack.

"Indigestion, probably," she muttered as she walked over and picked it up. "Hello?"

"Victoria?"

She frowned. Not family, not Bernie, not Fred with news about a hemorrhoidal flare-up for Michael. "Yes," she said slowly. "This is Victoria."

"Stuart Goldberg here."

Victoria choked. She didn't mean to, but she was caught so off guard she couldn't stop herself. Stuart Goldberg was her arch-enemy, her nemesis, the man who had made a career of poaching her best actors for his productions, which were far closer to Broadway than hers were. It took her a moment or two to be able to speak. "Stuart," she wheezed. "How lovely to hear from you. What do you want?"

He laughed easily. "Always to the point, aren't you?"

"Really, is there any subtlety left between us?" she managed. "Unfortunately, I can't provide you with any sport today. My stable is quite empty."

"Sport?" he echoed. "What a quaint term."

"I've been in Scotland for the summer. It rubbed off on me."

"Yeah, that's what I heard."

Victoria waited. Stuart seemed to be taking an inordinate amount of time to gather his thoughts. "Well?" she prompted.

"Well," he said slowly, "this is the deal. I'm doing the Scottish play."

She pursed her lips. "How nice for you."

"Well, it was until three days ago when I lost my queen. I think you know her: Cressida Blankenship."

"She bailed on you?"

"Yes, damn her to hell. And get this: She's signed on to do *Twelfth Night* with Michael Fellini."

Victoria considered furiously. She didn't know anyone who was doing *Twelfth Night*. Well, she didn't know anyone doing it that Bernie would consider up to Michael's standards. "He's acting in it?" she said. "For whom?"

"He's not acting, he's directing."

"You're kidding."

"I'm not. I have no sense of humor."

"Well," Victoria said, somehow not very surprised by anything she was hearing. Michael had wanted to direct. Now he had his chance. "That's good for him, but it leaves you in sort of a bind, doesn't it?"

"Try not to enjoy it so much," Stuart said dryly.

"Can't help it."

"Try harder. And listen to this: The word is Fellini's going to be directing it at Tempest in a Teapot."

Victoria looked at Connor. "Michael's doing *Twelfth Night* at Tempest in a Teapot? How interesting."

Connor stopped in midmunch of his sandwich and looked at her with one raised eyebrow. "Ha," he said in a garbled tone.

"I never thought you'd let go of the reins of that stage," Stuart continued.

"I didn't. It was leased out from under me."

"Yes, I heard that, as well. I wonder how Fellini got ahold of it?"

"His ultracharming personality," Victoria said sourly. "How else?"

"Either that, or he's really brushed up on his yoga poses."

She laughed out loud in spite of herself. "I suppose so."

"Anyway, this is the thing," Stuart continued. "I need a queen for my show."

"Good luck."

He paused. "I heard you acted, once upon a time."

Victoria looked at Connor. "You heard I acted?"

He put his sandwich down and brought a chair over for her. She felt her way down into it.

"I also heard that Cressida walked out on your *Hamlet* in England and you filled in."

Victoria closed her eyes briefly. "That's true."

"I also heard you were terrific."

She looked around frantically for a paper bag. Damn. Not a one in sight. She forced herself to take three slow, even breaths. "Ah," she began, "you heard I was terrific."

"Victoria, stop repeating everything I say. You're driving me nuts."

Victoria took three more slow, even breaths. "Who'd you hear all that from, Stu?"

"Marv Jones."

She had to put her head between her knees. She took the phone with her, though. No sense in missing out on any of this conversation. "The *New York Pillar*'s theater critic?"

"Yeah. Apparently he went in disguise to your closing night. He talked the *Pillar* into footing his travel because he promised he would write something really nasty about you."

"Unsurprising," Victoria mumbled.

"I agree. He's been gunning for me for years. But didn't you read his column? It came out a couple of weeks later."

Victoria sat up slowly and waited until the stars swimming in front of her eyes dissipated. "Um," she said faintly, "I was a little busy after the run." Busy grinding herself into the ground at Jamie's boot camp, then subsequently popping in and out of medieval Scotland.

She was somewhat relieved she hadn't known the potential for career damage she was running afoul of.

"His column," she said weakly. "How bad was it?"

"Bad? Victoria, aren't you listening to me? The man said you were terrific. He gushed. He couldn't find enough positive adjectives to describe your performance. I think he even used *luminous* and you know he never uses that word unless it's describing his own prose."

"He said I was luminous," she repeated, stunned.

"Yeah, I couldn't believe it, either. So, are you interested?"

"Am I interested in what?"

He made a sound of impatience. "Aren't you over your jet lag yet? I need a queen!"

Victoria looked at Connor. "You need a queen? For the Scottish play?"

Connor began to smile.

"Victoria," Stu said sternly, "you're worrying me."

"I'll be better tomorrow," Victoria said promptly. "Sure, I'd love to play the queen."

"There's something else."

She could hardly wait. "What?"

"Marv said your Hamlet was, damn, what was his word . . ."

Victoria's hands felt very clammy. "I wouldn't presume to guess what he called my Hamlet."

"Perfect. He said he was perfect."

"Perfect?" Victoria echoed. "He said the actor playing Hamlet was perfect?"

"I told you, he was gushy."

Victoria looked at Connor. "He said Hamlet was perfect."

Connor, who had been sitting with his ankle propped up on his opposite knee and his hands casually clasped behind his head, dropped both feet to the ground, and leaned forward to gape at her.

She understood completely.

She cleared her throat. "That's interesting, Stu. And I have to admit, I thought the same thing."

"Well, I've been trying to find the guy, but there aren't any Connor MacDougals in Scotland. Well, there are, but they don't act."

Victoria looked at Connor. "You've been trying to find this Connor MacDougal."

"Desperately."

"Desperately?"

"Victoria, if you can't carry on a coherent conversation, I'm going to fire you. What's with you?"

Victoria felt a smile coming on. She could hardly stop herself from bursting into it. "Well, I know where to find that Connor MacDougal you're looking for, but first I want to know what you want with him."

"To do the role Fellini contracted for. The lead."

"Jus a sec, Stu."

"Just a sec? What does that mean?"

"Connor's right here. I'll ask him if he's interested."

"He's right *there*? How the hell did you manage that?"

"I married him a month ago, that's how."

"Do I get you both at a package price?"

"Forget that. Connor's *very* expensive."

"I'll pay it."

"You're very trusting of Marv Jones's opinion."

"Wouldn't you be?"

Victoria smiled. "I've seen Connor perform, so I'd have to say yes. Hold on." She put her hand over the phone. "Interested in a little theater?"

He looked a little green. "You're going to do Lady Mac—"

"Sshh!"

He rolled his eyes. "Very well, you've been offered the part of that hand-washing Scottish queen, aye?"

"Yep. And Stu would like you to do the part of that dastardly Scottish lord."

Connor swallowed with some difficulty.

"It's battle, my laird, only on a different stage."

"With mock swords."

"No, the swords will be real, just dull."

He smiled. "Well, I suppose if the part is offered me . . ."

Victoria laughed. "All right, Stu, we're in."

"Good."

"Ask him if he needs a witch," Connor said.

"Why?"

"Your granny made a fabulous one."

Victoria nodded. "Hey, Stu, need a witch?"

"Well, now that you mention it, I am looking for one. What are you, a full casting service now as well?"

"My family has suddenly developed stage fever," Victoria said.

"Yeah, well, don't let it take over."

Victoria blinked. "Why do you say that?"

"Because something's in the water. You wouldn't believe what Fellini's up to."

"Enlighten me," she said, feeling a little knot form in the pit of her stomach.

"Fellini's having delusions of grandeur. He claims that—and I can hardly believe I'm saying this—that he went back in time and saw the Globe for himself. That he met Shakespeare and the Bard told him to come back to the present and direct his plays as only Fellini can."

"He met Shakespeare," Victoria repeated, looking at Connor with wide eyes. "What do you think about that?"

"He's a nutcase," Stu said succinctly. "Rehearsals start Monday."

"We'll be there."

"Victoria, you are a dream."

"Why, Stu, I think I'll blush."

He laughed and hung up the phone. Victoria hung up

her end and looked at Connor. "Well, it looks like your New York debut looms large."

"The Scottish play?"

"It seems particularly appropriate, don't you think?"

"Am I allowed to use my own sword?"

Victoria laughed and went to throw herself into his arms. "No," she said, kissing him thoroughly, "you are most definitely *not* allowed to use your own sword. You do want this gig to last more than one night, don't you?"

"I want this gig to last forever," he murmured against her mouth. "We'll worry about the play later."

Victoria laughed and couldn't have agreed more.

It was quite a bit later that she paced about her small apartment, coming with every pass to stand at the foot of her very small bed and look down at the man who had changed everything; her life, her career, her heart.

Hamlet.

Perfect.

She smiled and paced yet another round. She would have quite a few things to say to her brother the next time she saw him.

Thank you would be the first thing out of her mouth.

"Victoria?"

She turned and smiled at her laird. "Aye?"

"I love you."

Yes, a very big thank you. Maybe even no complaints about Brussels sprouts.

She went back to bed with a smile on her face.

Epilogue

Ambrose MacLeod sat in front of the stove in the kitchen of the Boar's Head Inn and enjoyed a well-deserved mug of ale with a pleasant evening stretching out before him. Victoria was well settled and his work was done.

For the moment, at least.

The door behind him blew open and Fulbert stomped in, followed directly by Hugh. They grumbled about the weather—it was wet out—before they took up their own cups and settled themselves for their own well-deserved rests.

"That was a difficult case," Fulbert noted, after an appropriately long drink of ale. "I never thought he would come to his senses."

"But he did," Hugh allowed. "To my surprise, him being a MacDougal and all."

"Did you know him in life, Hugh?" Ambrose asked mildly.

"He was well after my time," Hugh said, "but I haunted his cousin, Cormac, for a bit. A sensible lad was that one, despite his propensity to attempt to steal McKinnon cattle." Hugh smiled pleasantly. "He didn't make off with many. I imagine Connor wouldn't be pleased to know that."

"Well, for pity's sake, don't tell him," Fulbert said with a snort. "For all we know, he'll attempt a return to the past to right the wrong."

"Nay," Ambrose said thoughtfully, "I daresay not. He and Victoria are perfectly suited. I cannot imagine anything with enough power over him to pull him away." He shook his head. "They will live out their lives in bliss, treading the boards where they can, raising their bairns, loving fiercely all the while." He smiled. "Their passion is enviable."

The door behind them squeaked open just the slightest bit. Fulbert leaned over to Ambrose.

"You could have that kind of passion," he said pointedly, with a nod toward the door. "There she is, bedecked in her finest wooing gear. I would take advantage of it, were I you."

"You aren't me," Ambrose said, tossing his cup into the open stove door and preparing to flee.

"Coward," Fulbert said with a glint in his eye.

Ambrose leaped to his feet. "You will pay for that remark!" He drew his sword with a flourish.

Mrs. Pruitt leaped into the kitchen. "Nay, Laird MacLeod, do not! Do not put yourself in danger!"

Ambrose wasn't the laird of a wily and ferocious clan without reason. He looked at Mrs. Pruitt, then made her a low bow.

"Dear lady," he said, straightening and putting his hand over his heart, "I must deal with this ruffian here. When I have put him to shame as he so richly deserves, I will return and we will have speech together."

Mrs. Pruitt's eyelids fluttered.

Hugh squeaked and fled.

"Oh," she said, fanning herself surreptitiously. "Oh, well, my laird, of course. Will ye be long at yer labors?"

Ambrose stroked his chin thoughtfully. "He is a particularly difficult case. It might take me quite some time. A se'nnight at least."

"I'll wait."

Fulbert snorted. "I daresay she will."

Ambrose pointed toward the door. "Outside with you," he thundered. "I'll teach you respect, if it is the last thing I do!"

Fulbert tromped out the back door. Ambrose made Mrs. Pruitt another low bow, then exited the kitchen with a flourish. He resheathed his sword with a great thrust.

Fulbert looked at him, open-mouthed. "Are we not going to do battle?"

"Are you daft, man? I'm for the Highlands!"

"But, you promised!"

"Aye, but I never said when! It will take me years to cow you properly. I daresay I should have a rest before that labor begins."

Fulbert folded his arms over his chest. "I'm disappointed in you. I thought you had more spine than this."

"I have an abundance of spine. I also have an abundance of aversion toward women who flutter their eyelashes in that manner."

"You gave your word."

Ambrose opened his mouth to protest again, but found that there was no defense for his actions. Aye, he had promised. 'Twas also true that he had never said exactly when he would parley with the woman.

And it was unfortunately too true that she might sit up for nights, waiting for him to have a simple mug of ale with her.

Ambrose sighed. "Very well. You have it aright. I will have my parley with her."

Fulbert smirked.

"Next week."

"Ambrose—"

"I said it would take me a bloody se'nnight and a bloody se'nnight it will take! Besides, I need rest from our recently accomplished labors before I think about anything else."

"Weenie," Fulbert said, with another smirk.

"What?" Ambrose thundered.

"Lily-livered, weak-kneed, white-knuckled woman." He snorted. "There. Now you have a se'nnight's worth of insults to repay me for and I have saved your honor."

Ambrose pursed his lips. "Perhaps you were not so unworthy of my dear sister as I suppose."

"Too much time making matches," Fulbert said, clucking his tongue. "You've gone altogether soft."

Ambrose thought he might have agreed, but he would think on that later, when he'd repaid Fulbert for his insults. He threw himself happily into the fray, but vowed he would visit the Highlands again before long. It was the home of his heart and he could not go long without being there, even after so many centuries.

Besides, he would need the rest. Mrs. Pruitt might be taxing, but she paled in comparison to his next match to be made.

Ah, but a shade's work was never done.

Fortunately.

He drew his sword and went about his current business, joyously throwing himself into the fray and leaving the happy contemplation of the future in the Future, where it belonged.

ROMANTIC ROOTS

MACLEOD

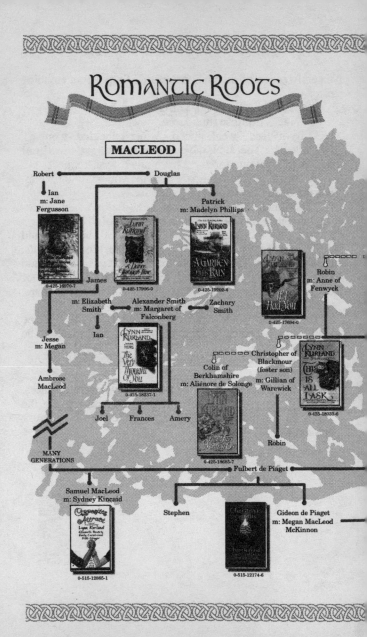

Robert ● ——————————————— ● Douglas

Ian
m: Jane
Fergusson

Patrick
m: Madelyn Phillips

0-425-16970-7

0-425-17906-0

0-425-19202-4

James

Robin
m: Anne of
Fenwyck

0-425-17694-0

m: Elizabeth
Smith

Alexander Smith
● m: Margaret of
Falconberg ●

Zachary
Smith

Jesse
m: Megan

Ian

0-425-18237-1

Colin of
Berkhamshire
m: Aliénore de Solonge

Christopher of
Blackmour
(foster son)
m: Gillian of
Warewick

THIS
IS
ALL
I ASK

0-425-18035-6

Ambrose
MacLeod

Joel   Frances   Amery

0-425-18665-7

Robin

MANY
GENERATIONS

Fulbert de Piaget ●

Samuel MacLeod
m: Sydney Kincaid

Stephen

Gideon de Piaget
m: Megan MacLeod
McKinnon

0-515-12865-1

0-515-12174-6

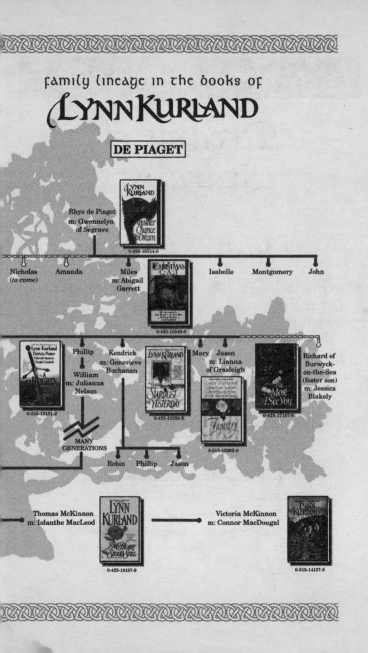

family lineage in the books of

LYNN KURLAND

DE PIAGET

Rhys de Piaget
m: Gwennelyn
of Segrave

0-425-16514-0

Nicholas   Amanda   Miles   Isabelle   Montgomery   John
(to come)   m: Abigail
                        Garrett

0-425-15542-0

Phillip   Kendrick   Mary   Jason   Richard of
             m: Genevieve   m: Lianna   Burwyck-
William   Buchanan   of Grasleigh   on-the-Sea
m: Julianna   (foster son)
Nelson   m: Jessica
                                                  Blakely

0-515-13151-2   0-425-18238-X   0-425-17107-8

                     0-515-13362-0

MANY
GENERATIONS

Robin   Phillip   Jason

Thomas McKinnon   Victoria McKinnon
m: Iolanthe MacLeod   m: Connor MacDougal

0-425-18197-9   0-515-14127-5